An Amish Christmas

DECEMBER IN LANCASTER COUNTY

Three Amish Christmas Novellas

BETH WISEMAN

KATHLEEN FULLER

BARBARA CAMERON

Steeple
Hill®

Published by Steeple Hill Books™

Beth: To my husband, Patrick…my forever love.

Kathy: To my family: my husband, James;
my son, Mathew; and my daughters,
Sydney and Zoie. I love you all very much.

Barbara: For Sarah and my family.

∽

STEEPLE HILL BOOKS

Steeple Hill®

PLEASE RECYCLE • THIS PRODUCT IS RECYCLABLE •

Recycling programs
for this product may
not exist in your area.

ISBN-13: 978-0-373-78670-1

AN AMISH CHRISTMAS: DECEMBER IN LANCASTER COUNTY

Steeple Hill Books/September 2010

First published by Thomas Nelson, Inc.

www.SteepleHill.com

Printed in U.S.A.

Glossary

ab im kopp – off in the head, crazy

aenti – aunt

baremlich – terrible

bauchduch – napkin

boppli – baby or babies

bruder – brother

daadi – grandfather

daed – dad

danki – thanks

demut – humility

dippy eggs – eggs cooked over easy

dochder – daughter

du bischt wilkumm – you're welcome

dummkopf – dummy

Englisch or *Englischer* – a non-Amish person

fraa or *frau* – wife

Frehlicher Grischtdaag – Merry Christmas

gebet – prayer

gern schöna – so willingly done

glay hotsli – little heart (endearment)

grossmammi – grandmother

guder mariye – good morning

guten nacht – good night

gut-n-owed – good evening

gutguckich – good-looking

gut – good

halt – stop

haus – house

hatt – hard

herr – mister

hochmut — pride

in lieb — in love

kaffi — coffee

kapp — prayer covering or cap

kind, kinder, kinner — children or grandchildren

liebschen — dearest

maedel or *maed* — girl or girls

mamm — mom

mammi — grandmother

mann — man

mei — my

mudder — mother

naerfich — nervous

narrisch — crazy

nee — no

onkel — uncle

ordnung — the written and unwritten rules of the Amish; the understood behavior by which the Amish are expected to live, passed down from generation to generation. Most Amish know the rules by heart.

Pennsylvania *Deitsch* — Pennsylvania German, the language most commonly used by the Amish

recht — right

redd-up — clean up

rumschpringe — running-around period when a teenager turns sixteen years old

sehr gut — very good

seltsam — weird

sohn — son

wunderbaar — wonderful

ya — yes

A MIRACLE
FOR MIRIAM

By Kathleen Fuller

Prologue

Miriam Fisher
  Mrs. Miriam Fisher
  Miriam and Seth Fisher
  Mrs. Seth Fi—

"What's this?" Caleb snatched the spiral notebook out of Miriam's hands.

She grappled for the book, but Caleb, who was three inches taller, held it out of her reach. "Give it back," she pleaded.

Caleb gave her a malicious grin. "Or what? You'll tell the teacher? Go ahead, she won't do nothing. Not when there's only a month left of school."

Panic flowed through her. "Caleb, please. Don't read it—"

"Miriam Fisher?" He glanced up from the page, looked at Miriam, then guffawed, his laugh bordering on a donkey bray. "Miriam *Fisher?*" He looked back down and kept reading, then turned another page and started laughing again.

Miriam wanted to die. Right there in the middle of the school yard, she prayed the earth would swallow her whole. It did not. Instead, she watched with horror as Caleb ran across the playground to the object of her affections, Seth Fisher, and interrupted the game of bare-handed baseball he was playing with his friends. Caleb thrust the notebook in front of him.

Miriam had harbored a secret crush on Seth since sixth grade but never dared tell anyone, not even her best friend, Hannah. Now they were both fourteen and near the end of their eighth-grade year. Soon she wouldn't get to see him every day, to watch him from across the classroom, pretending to be engrossed in her schoolwork when all she could think about was how good-looking he was. For two years she'd hoped he would notice her. For two years she had spent her recesses, not with her friends but sitting in the corner of the school yard, journaling her dreams in her notebook.

She couldn't breathe as she watched Seth take the notebook and thumb through it. His expression never changed while he glanced over page after page filled with crudely drawn hearts and their names written in various combinations. Her palms grew slick as he looked up from the notebook and caught her gaze. He tossed the baseball to one of his buddies and made his way toward her.

Her legs threatened to buckle. She had expected him to laugh like Caleb, but instead he strode across the playground, his dazzling blue-eyed gaze never leaving hers. Was it possible that he secretly liked her too? That he, like her, had been afraid to admit it? The thought of it brought a whole new wave of emotions flowing over her.

Could she really be Mrs. Seth Fisher someday?

Seth stopped in front of her, his friends straggling behind him. He was their leader and had been since they'd started school together. Tall, lean, he had filled out before most of the boys, and his voice had deepened last year. He wore his pale yellow straw hat tipped back on his head, giving her a full view of his handsome face. He looked much older than fourteen. More confident, without a trace of insecurity. Unlike Miriam, who was filled with it.

He held out the notebook. "This yours?"

Pushing up her glasses, she nodded, her tongue suddenly too thick to formulate a verbal answer.

"Here. Take it."

But when she reached for it, he jerked it out of her grasp, then dropped it on the ground. Stepping square in the middle of it, he said, "Four-eyed beanpole." Then he kicked the notebook at her and laughed.

Any flicker of hope she held inside died at that moment. Seth and his group walked away, some pointing and laughing, leaving her to pick up her journal. She lifted it from the ground, staring at the large heart filling the page, *Miriam + Seth* written in the middle. The dirty outline of a boot print was stamped on top.

Across the playground she could still hear the boys laughing. Seth looked at her and circled his fingers around his eyes.

Four-eyed beanpole…

Chapter One

Five years later

Seth lived with pain every day. At one time he'd tried to blame God for what had happened, but he knew that wasn't honest. He had no one to blame but himself.

He winced as he pulled on his trousers, his movements awkward. Still, just as he did each day, he silently gave thanks to Father God. If people had said to him even six months ago that he would be grateful to feel pain, that he would praise the Lord for each twinge and ache, he would have laughed in their faces. But today, the ever-present soreness reminded him that he was lucky to be alive.

He reached for his walking stick—plain, unadorned, but stained and lacquered to a smooth, shiny finish. His older brother, Noah, had made it for him shortly after the accident. The top of the stick was straight, so he couldn't call it a cane. Neither was it overly long, like a traditional walking stick. The knob at the top reached him at hip level, giving him the perfect amount of support without being unwieldy.

When he first saw the stick, he'd wanted to throw it at his brother. Now the gift had become indispensable.

Seth turned at a loud knock at his door. "What?"

"Caleb Esh is here." His father's gruff voice penetrated the wooden door. "You ready?"

Hearing his *daed*'s voice gave Seth pause. Considering their strained relationship, he was surprised his father had come upstairs to fetch him.

"Ya," Seth replied, reaching for his black felt hat, the one he usually wore in cold weather. He'd pick up his coat on the way out. "Tell Caleb I'll be right down." He heard the thudding of his father's work boots against the wood floorboards as Melvin Fisher left to deliver Seth's message.

Seth placed his hand on the knob of the door and started to turn it, then stopped. Before the accident he'd never been nervous about going out. But tonight was different. The Christmas sing at the Lapps' home was his first social outing in six months, a time span unheard-of for him. For the last three years, since he'd turned sixteen, going out had been a big part of his life. Not that he had wasted his time on the Amish social circuit. Frolics and singings and other gatherings had been too tame and too lame. Seth was too cool for that, choosing instead to hang with *Englisch* friends. When he was with them he drank. He smoked.

He learned to drive a car.

He ran his fingers over the thin ridge of scar tissue that started from his left temple and cut a straight line to the top of his jaw. The facial cut had healed faster than his leg, and far more quickly than his pride.

Shaking off the raw memories, he twisted the brass knob and opened the door. He'd learned some hard lessons that night six months ago, and they had shaped him into a new man. But he couldn't hide here forever, surrounded by his family. Not only had they accepted what had happened; they'd forgiven him too.

Perhaps not everyone would show him such mercy.

He ignored the sudden stab of low confidence and headed down the stairs, determined to renew the old acquaintances he had abandoned in favor of the outside world.

"I don't understand why you're helping me with this boring task when you could be at the Lapps', having a good time."

Miriam finished putting the plastic binding on a cookbook and looked into her older sister's weary face. The exhaustion she saw there explained why she chose to spend Sunday night helping her sister Lydia. But she would never say so aloud. Since the death of Lydia's husband two years ago, she'd had enough to fret over without worrying about how tired she looked.

"I like helping you," Miriam said, a little too brightly. "I can't think of a better way to spend my evening than with my sister and my niece and nephews."

"I'd believe you, except the *kinder* aren't even here right now." Lydia smirked. "The boys are spending the night with the Yoders, and Anna Marie is at the Christmas sing, where you should be."

Busted.

She had heard her niece use the term on occasion, and Miriam thought it fit her current situation. Pushing up her glasses, she glanced down at the cookbook, pretending to be engrossed in the artwork on the shiny cover.

"You can ignore me all you want, Miriam, but I know the real reason you're here." Lydia picked up her mug of lukewarm coffee, took a sip, then frowned. Rising from the table in the middle of her kitchen, she walked over to the stove, opened up the percolator, and started a fresh pot.

Lydia's bait was too tempting to ignore. Miriam's gaze shot up, and she watched her sister remove the lid from the metal coffeepot.

"I already told you why I'm here," she said.

"You told me what you wanted me to hear, not the real reason." Lydia added fragrant coffee grounds to the basket, then poured water over them and put the pot on the stove. Within minutes the kitchen filled with the coffee's comforting aroma.

"There's no other reason, Lydia." Miriam reached for an unbound cookbook. "Besides, if I weren't here, how would you get all this done?"

"I'd manage, God willing." She sat back down at the table. "Not that I don't appreciate all the help you've given me. But you're spending too much time either here or at the quilt shop. You're nineteen years old, Miriam. You should be enjoying life."

"I enjoy life. I like my job, and I have my quilting." She started inserting the binder into the square holes on the left margin of the loose pages.

"But what about your friends?"

"I have plenty of friends. A lot of them are just as busy as I am."

"What about a *boyfriend?*" Lydia leaned forward, her gaze steady and serious.

"What about Daniel?" Miriam said, eager to switch their conversation to something else. She suspected that Daniel Smucker was the main reason for Lydia's singular focus tonight. Since her late husband's brother had returned to Paradise, her normally steadfast sister had been out of sorts.

Lydia averted her gaze, but only for a moment. "I'm not talking about me and Daniel."

"You and Daniel?" Miriam lifted a brow. "What about you and Daniel?"

"There is no 'me and Daniel'."

"But you just said–"

"Stop changing the subject." Lydia sat up straight in her chair and folded her hands on the table. "Miriam, it's time you started thinking about your future. There are several available young men in the community. Isn't there at least one you're interested in?"

At her sister's last question, Miriam's thumb slipped and slid against the sharp edge of the binder, hard enough to draw blood. She put her thumb to her mouth.

Concern suddenly etched Lydia's features. "Do you need a bandage?"

Miriam looked at her hand. The cut was tiny, negligible actually. She shook her head and rose from her chair. "I'm fine. I'll just give it a quick wash."

As she stood over the sink and lathered her hands with Lydia's homemade lavender soap, Miriam stared out of the window into the darkness of the night. A chill suddenly flowed through her, as if the cold outside air had somehow seeped through the clear glass pane and entered her body. Lydia didn't want to talk about Daniel, and Miriam certainly didn't want to talk about men, so she wished her sister would drop the topic altogether.

At nineteen Miriam was old enough to marry. Several of her schoolmates had already married or had steady beaus. But she remained single. She'd learned her lesson a long time ago. She wasn't about to open herself to ridicule again. Although she was expected to get married and raise a family, she wasn't in any hurry to do so. At least she tried to tell herself that.

Trouble was, her heart refused to cooperate. At times she had to admit she was lonely, especially when she saw other young couples together, enjoying each other's company. So she made sure not to put herself in situations where she would be reminded of what she didn't have.

"Miriam? Are you all right?"

Lydia's voice broke into her thoughts. Quickly Miriam rinsed and dried her hands, then went back to the table and delved into her work.

A few moments later Lydia placed her hand on Miriam's forearm. "That's enough. I can get the rest. You go on and have a good time."

"Lydia, I already said I'm not going."

"And I said you are. This is the last singing before Christmas, and you don't want to miss that. Go home and put on a fresh dress. I'm sure Pop won't mind dropping you off at the Lapps', and Anna Marie can bring you back home." As if to make sure Miriam would follow orders, Lydia gathered the cookbooks and binders and carried them into the next room.

Miriam frowned. The last thing she wanted to see were boys and girls flirting with each other as they played the awkward and thrilling game of courtship. Or worse, she'd be subjected to all the young people who had already found someone to love, or at least to like well enough to date.

She planted herself in the chair. She was nineteen years old, not a little girl. Her sister couldn't force her. Could she?

Lydia came back into the room, glanced at Miriam, and grimaced. "I can see this is going to be harder than I thought." She left abruptly, and returned a moment later with her black winter cloak slung over one arm. She adjusted the black bonnet on her head with the opposite hand.

"Where are you going?" Miriam asked.

"Drastic times call for drastic measures." She stood in front of Miriam, hands firmly planted on her hips. "I'll take you to the singing tonight."

"You can't. Your *kind* has your buggy, remember?"

"*Ya,* but that doesn't mean I can't drive yours. I'll drop you off, then pick you up in a couple of hours. Then you can go home to *Daed* and *Mamm,* or you can spend the night here. You know we always love having you."

A scowl tugged at Miriam's mouth. She was being coerced. "You say you love having me, but you want me to leave."

Lydia nodded, her expression resolute. "*Ya,* I do. Just know that I'm doing this for your own good. Now, are you coming, or do I have to physically force you?"

Miriam didn't doubt her for a minute. Although Lydia was a couple inches shorter than Miriam, when she set her mind on a goal, nothing would keep her from achieving it. Even if it meant making her younger sister do something she didn't want to do.

Trapped, Miriam slowly stood. "You said I needed a fresh dress."

"You look fine."

Miriam doubted that. "Let me at least freshen up in the bathroom before we go."

"*Ya,* but don't dally. The singing has already started. You're missing all the fun!"

Miriam headed for the bathroom, more than a little irritated. Why couldn't Lydia mind her own business? Entering the small room, she closed the door and turned on the battery-operated lamp on the vanity. As with all the rooms in Lydia's house, this one had also been adorned with Christmas decorations. An evergreen-scented candle burned next to the lamp, filling the small space with its fresh fragrance. A pine bough sporting a bright red bow perched above the small mirror over the sink. Nothing fancy, but a festive touch.

The light was a bit on the dim side, but she could see her reflection clearly enough. Plain, plain, plain. A stab of insecurity hit her. While she lived among a people who valued simplicity and plainness, there was such a thing as being too nondescript. She knew that firsthand.

There was nothing pretty, nothing extraordinary, nothing striking about her appearance. Her hair and eyes were the shade of brown mud while her complexion was fair, even stark. Small, wire-framed glasses with round lenses did little to enhance her features, while her chin angled to a point. Unlike her sisters, Miriam had no curves, and her dress hung loosely on her boyish frame. A sharp chin, lean hips, and a tiny bosom. No wonder men weren't falling at her feet.

She knew that inner beauty was more important than a pretty face or appealing figure. She also knew that the Lord valued the heart, not the shell that protected it. Still, that didn't keep her from secretly longing for at least one attractive physical quality. Seth Fisher's words were still true: she was a four-eyed beanpole.

Closing her eyes against the insult ricocheting in her brain, she fought the humiliation and resentment pooling in her stomach, unabated by time. Her path hadn't crossed Seth's since they left school, and that had helped—at least she hadn't been constantly reminded of how ugly he thought she was. He had turned into a wild boy and run around with a bunch of *Englisch* people, constantly getting into trouble. A few months ago he fell into more trouble than anyone would have thought, and that was the last she'd heard of him. While she had never wished him any harm, it would suit her just fine if she never saw him again.

Opening her eyes, she leaned over the sink and splashed some cold water on her cheeks. She mentally pushed the past away as she stood up, adjusting the hairpins affixed to her *kapp*. Staring into the mirror, she forced a smile. She could do this. She could do anything for a couple of hours.

Opening the door, she thought of the one good thing about attending the singing, and that put a genuine smile on her face. At least *he* wouldn't be there. She wouldn't have to worry about Seth Fisher ruining her night.

Chapter Two

"*Ach*, what's with that buggy moving so slow?" Caleb tapped his foot in a rapid staccato rhythm against the floor of his buggy as he pulled on the reins. His horse slowed almost to a standstill as they pulled up to the modest white house at the end of the street.

"You sound like an *Englisch* driver," Seth remarked, shifting in his seat. Sitting in one position for very long still made his leg ache. The physical therapist who had helped him regain his motion said that the pain would subside, but it would take time.

Patience—another hard lesson learned.

"*Ya,* and they got a right to complain if they get behind someone like this," Caleb said. "We're running late as it is."

"Sorry."

"*Nee,* it's not your fault. Well, it is, but I don't blame you. I blame this!" Caleb pointed as the buggy made a left turn into a driveway. "Great. He's also going to the Lapps'. It'll probably take him forever to find a place to park."

But instead of parking, the buggy pulled to a stop just as Caleb's horse drew up behind it. In addition to their large circular driveway, the Lapps had another driveway that split off from the main one, which led to the barn in the back. There was ample parking there, so Seth wasn't sure why Caleb was concerned.

The passenger door opened, and a woman stepped out wearing a black cloak, her face obscured by a bonnet. She walked around the back of the buggy and headed toward the Lapp house.

"Finally." Caleb tapped the reins on the flanks of his horse as the buggy in front of them moved, then turned around in the driveway.

In the dim light of dusk Seth could see the driver was another woman.

"Would have been easier if she had dropped her off at the road." Caleb maneuvered his buggy into an empty space by the barn. "And faster."

Seth regarded his friend. "Why are you in such a hurry?" As soon as he asked the question, he knew the answer. "That's right. Mary Lapp."

Caleb shrugged. "Maybe."

Seth knew that was all he would get out of his friend, and he was fine with that. He was glad his first outing would be here. The Lapps were a good family, Mary included. She had always been a nice girl, friendly to all and a stranger to none. If anyone would help him not feel out of place, it would be Mary. Besides Caleb, of course. He was the one Amish friend Seth had kept in touch with during his wild years, and one of the few to visit him when he came home from the hospital.

Caleb jumped out of the buggy, and envy stabbed at Seth. He swiveled in the seat as he opened the door, then slid to the edge and grabbed his walking stick. By the time Caleb had tethered his horse, Seth had just gotten out of the buggy.

"Need some help?" Caleb asked.

"*Nee.* I've got it." Leaning on his stick, Seth shut the door behind him and turned around. "Go ahead and go inside. Don't want to slow you down."

"I'll wait."

Seth shook his head. "I know how eager you are to see Mary—"

"I never said that."

"You didn't have to. Now, go."

Caleb hesitated again, then nodded and walked to the house, taking long strides. Again jealousy came to the fore, but Seth ignored it. He was determined to walk one day unassisted, no matter how long it took. He would accomplish that by continuing the exercises his therapist had given him, even though they were painful.

Seth hobbled along until he reached the front door. He knocked out of politeness, though he had been to the Lapps' many times as a child.

Mary's mother, Katherine, opened the door. She stood still for a moment as she looked at Seth's face, then at his walking stick, then back up until her gaze focused on his scar.

"*Gut-n-Owed,*" Seth said, breaking the silence.

She blinked a couple times, then grinned. "Seth Fisher! I'm so glad to see you."

His earlier nervousness dimmed a little at the warm welcome. "*Danki, Frau* Lapp."

"Come in, come in. Everyone's downstairs. I'm sure they'll be happy you came." She stepped aside, and Seth entered through the doorway, then turned and faced her, inhaling the sweet scent of cinnamon that wafted through the room.

He knew the brighter light in the Lapps' front room made his scar more pronounced, and that was evident by the way *Frau* Lapp was looking at him. A mixture of pity and curiosity filled her eyes, but for only a moment.

"Do you need some help getting down the stairs?"

"*Nee.* I can manage on my own. But *danki* just the same."

Katherine glanced at his walking stick. "All right, but if you need anything, just let me know. Jeb and I will be right upstairs."

Seth nodded and headed for the basement. The murmur of conversation, peppered with a few laughs, drifted up the stairwell. He couldn't help but smile. He sorely missed the company of people his age, especially after spending weeks in the hospital, then months at home trying to heal. He hadn't realized how isolated he'd been until now. But his eagerness to join the others was tempered by a hike in his anxiousness. How would they react? Would they ask a million questions? If they did, he wouldn't hold back. He'd tell them everything they wanted to know.

Realizing he was wasting time, he made his way down the stairs, using both the handrail and his stick for support. When he reached the bottom he turned left, which led to a large, open room that held about twenty-five young people. The scent of pine wafted from the boughs decorating the walls, reminding him that Christmas was only a couple weeks away.

At first no one noticed his arrival, as they were all

involved in their own conversations. Then Mary Lapp, with Caleb at her side, spotted him. "Seth?"

The conversation died down to nearly nothing. It seemed that everyone in the room had turned their focus completely on him.

"Goodness, it's *gut* to see you, Seth." Mary gave him a huge smile, the dimple in her right cheek deepening. She wore a white *kapp,* and her dark hair was neatly parted and pulled back, exposing her pretty brown eyes.

He hadn't seen Mary in a couple of years, and while she had been sort of a cute girl when they were younger, she had grown into a pretty woman. No wonder Caleb was smitten.

As if to remind Seth that Mary was his, Caleb stepped closer to her. Seth didn't miss the slight spark of warning reflected in his friend's blue eyes. He didn't blame Caleb for being concerned. In the past when Seth Fisher saw what he wanted, he took it, without any regrets.

Seth would have to earn his friend's trust. And not only Caleb's, but everyone else's as well.

"Don't just stand there; come on in." Mary, the consummate hostess, led Seth into the room. "Look who's here, everyone. Seth Fisher!"

Reactions varied, from outright gaping at the scar on his cheek to polite smiles and nods. The ages of the group ranged from sixteen to twenty-four, so it was no surprise that the younger kids were the ones staring. He didn't mind; he'd expected both surprise and curiosity.

"Are you hungry? There's plenty of food. *Mudder* prepared a feast." Mary gestured to a long table situated against the wall on the other side of the room.

Seth took in the bowls of chips, potato salad, ham slices, three different kinds of cheeses, an abundance of bread, Christmas shortbread cookies frosted in red and green, and several varieties of soda. Everything looked delicious, and normally he would have dived right in. But tonight he wasn't interested in eating, not when everyone was still scrutinizing him. "Maybe later," he said.

"That's fine. Just fill up a plate whenever you want." Mary smiled again, reassuring him that he had made the right decision in coming.

The three of them chatted. While Mary described her job waitressing at a local restaurant, Seth surveyed the room. Instantly something caught his eye. Not something. *Someone.* A young woman. Angling to get a better look, he turned his head as far as he could while still appearing to listen.

The *maedel* had caught his attention because she was standing apart from the group, leaning with her entire body pressed against the wall, as if it would fall down around her if she walked away. Her black bonnet obscured part of her face, and she took small sips from the plastic cup in her hand. He guessed she was the woman he'd seen being dropped off earlier.

"Seth?" Caleb tapped him on the arm.

"What? Oh, sorry." He tore his gaze away from her and looked at his friend. "What were you saying?"

"Mary and I are going to get a drink. Do you need anything?"

"*Nee.*" He lowered his voice. "Don't worry about me. I'm fine. Enjoy your time with Mary."

"*Danki.* I intend to." Caleb tilted his head to the side.

"What?"

"You wishing me a good time. You really have changed, haven't you?"

"I hope so, Caleb. I really hope so."

Miriam wanted to throw up.

Lydia had given her a few last words of encouragement before dropping her off, and Miriam had held on to those words and entered the party with feigned confidence. While her niece Anna Marie and some of her friends had greeted her, a quick scan of the room told her that not very many of her own friends were in attendance. Before long, several young men and women started pairing off, while others huddled into small groups of three or four, forming small cliques that Miriam had no desire to try to penetrate. How she wished her best friend, Hannah Beiler, was there. Then at least Miriam would have someone to talk to. But Hannah and her family were visiting her mother's cousin in Lititz and wouldn't be back until after Christmas.

She watched with a little bit of envy as Mary Lapp confidently greeted her guests, making everyone feel equally welcome in her home. Miriam wished she had the self-assurance to walk right up to anyone and just start a conversation. But the thought of doing that made her stomach spin, so she stayed on the sidelines.

Knowing she had to endure only an hour or so of the singing, she filled a cup with lemon-lime soda pop and leaned against the cold basement wall, a true wall-flower. But being invisible to everyone else had one advantage: it allowed her to people-watch, something she did enjoy. She noticed right off that Caleb Esh and Mary Lapp were sweet on each other. They made a striking couple, with her dark hair and his lighter features. Anna Marie had captured the attention of Amos Zook, but Miriam would keep that tidbit to herself, not wanting to insinuate herself in her niece's business. She observed several others, making mental notes as she did. She was almost enjoying herself.

Then Seth Fisher walked in.

Even before Mary spoke, Miriam had seen him.

Which made her stomach turn inside out.

What was he doing here? He'd made pretty clear his disdain for Amish social activities when he was fifteen. Why show up to one tonight?

Maybe he wanted to be the center of attention, as usual. She noticed he walked with a limp and used a wooden walking stick. The stick was quite beautiful, actually, probably one of his father's or brother's designs. Both had sterling reputations as carpenters. Already she could see several people crowding around Seth, more than likely entranced as he regaled them with tales of his accident. She didn't know the exact details, but she'd heard it had been pretty severe.

Well, she really didn't care. It was callous of her, but why should she? While she would never have wished for anything bad to happen to him, she didn't have much pity for him either.

Well…maybe a little. *Very* little.

"Hi."

She jumped, splashing some of her drink onto her dress. Annoyed not only with the speaker but with herself for being on edge, she grimaced and tried to dry the soda off the bodice of her dress with little success.

"Sorry, didn't mean to startle you. I can get you a *bauchduch*—"

"*Nee,* I don't need it. I'm fine," she said, unable to hide her irritation. "It'll—" At that moment she made the mistake of looking up—directly into the eyes of Seth Fisher.

Chapter Three

How had she not heard him approach? She should have at least heard the thump of his walking stick. Now there was no chance for escape. She was trapped between Seth and the wall, forced to be polite to the one and only man she'd ever dared to have romantic feelings for, the one and only man who had crushed them to dust.

"Are you sure you don't want me to get something to wipe that up?" Seth bent down slightly to look at the darkened splotches on the upper part of her dress. Then, realizing what he was doing, he jerked up and looked her in the eye. "You're right," he said, clearing his throat slightly. "It's not too bad."

"*Ya*. The stain will come out." What was she doing even talking to him? She should just stride right past him and head to the refreshment table. It wouldn't take much for her to pretend to be interested in the plentiful food the Lapps had provided. But it would only be pretense. If she thought her stomach was in a knot when Seth had walked into the room, it was a pretzel right now.

Tall for an Amishman, he had broad shoulders, slim

hips, and long legs. All in perfect proportion, of course. But that wasn't his most arresting feature. Seth Fisher had the most incredible eyes she had ever seen. They were an odd shade of transparent blue, aquamarine almost, and the irises were rimmed with gray. Long, black lashes surrounded those amazing eyes, and she remembered in school how she would sit and stare at him in class, hoping he would turn around and look at her, maybe even give her a smile....

She bit the inside of her cheek, hard. She should leave. Maybe she could convince Anna Marie to take her home. Searching the room, she found her niece talking to Amos. Miriam recognized that moony look on Anna Marie's face and couldn't bring herself to interrupt.

If she couldn't leave, she should at least walk away. She could go hold up the wall on the other side of the room, even. Why weren't her feet *moving?*

She knew why. Even after all this time, even after she tried to forget him and prayed for God to take him out of her mind and heart, Seth still had an effect on her. She could still be mesmerized by his unreal eyes, the perfect shape of his lips, his—

Scar?

For a moment she couldn't take her eyes off the raised ridge that traveled the length of his cheek. Crooked in some places, with a faint outline where stitches had been. Though noticeable, it did very little to detract from his attractiveness. It figured—Seth Fisher could even make a scar look good.

"I see you noticed my souvenir." Seth reached up and touched the scar with the tip of his index finger.

Embarrassed at being caught staring, Miriam looked away.

"It's not as if I can hide it. People are going to stare anyway, so why worry about it?"

She looked at him, surprised to see his lopsided grin. How could he be so nonchalant about such a disfigurement? If her face had been marred even slightly, she would have been devastated. Not that she liked her face, but she didn't want it to look worse than it already did. Yet here he was, speaking about his scar as if he had picked it up from a store and was trying it on for size.

He looked at her for a moment, his head tilted slightly, a small frown tugging at his mouth.

She shifted from one foot to the other, wishing he would just leave. Why was he looking at her like that?

"Miriam," he finally said, then smiled again. "Your name is Miriam Herschberger."

Well, he remembered her name, at least. That was something. *"Ya."*

"I thought I recognized you, but I just couldn't figure out where I'd seen you before. We went to school together, right?"

"Ya." Wow. She was a witty conversationalist tonight.

"It's all coming back to me now. In eighth grade you sat in the same row, but on the other side of the room."

Heat started to creep up her neck. She was not enjoying this walk down memory lane.

Seth grinned, oblivious to her discomfort. "I'm telling you, I couldn't wait to get out of school. Those last two months seemed to last forever."

"I know," she said quietly.

"Ya, I…" Seth looked at her for a moment, not saying anything. Then he shut his eyes. "Miriam," he said,

almost to himself. When his eyes opened, his expression changed. "Now I remember you."

Miriam squeezed her plastic cup. The only thing that kept her from crushing it in her hand was the possibility of staining her dress again.

"I wasn't very nice to you," he admitted.

That was putting it mildly. She thought about just brushing it off, acting as if being insulted to her very core hadn't bothered her a bit. But she couldn't bring herself to do that. She couldn't lie, not about this. "*Nee.* You weren't."

He scrubbed a hand over his face. "I was a big *dummkopf* back then."

Seth Fisher, admitting he had a flaw? That didn't jibe with the boy she went to school with, or the young man who had sowed some extremely wild oats these past few years. Then again, the fact that she was having this conversation with him showed he was different. The fact that they were having this conversation at all was some sort of miracle.

"I'm so sorry for what I said to you. I was an idiot."

"And a *dummkopf.*" The words were out before she could stop them.

"Thought I said that already." The corner of his mouth lifted. "I've done a lot of things I regret. I hope someday you can forgive me for the way I treated you."

Miriam honestly didn't know what to say. Over the years, when she thought about Seth Fisher, it was never in the context of his apologizing or asking forgiveness.

He limped over to stand next to her against the wall. "Hope you don't mind." Uncertainty crept into his eyes. "Unless you wanted to be alone?"

It was on the tip of her tongue to say that was exactly what she wanted, but for some irritating reason she couldn't form the words.

"I can see why you picked this spot," he said, apparently taking her silence as affirmation that she wanted company. "You can see everyone in the room."

She nodded slowly, still trying to take in the knowledge that not only had he apologized to her, but he was now standing next to her. Without much space between them. If she moved her hand over a few inches, she could touch his index finger; they were that close. Not that she would ever do something like that.

"So fill me in on what's going on," Seth said.

"What?"

"I've been gone awhile, so I've missed out on a lot." He looked down at her and grinned.

Her insides turned to mush.

This wasn't right. It wasn't fair, either. She'd spent so much time chasing him out of her mind and heart, and now with an apology and a grin he had snuck his way back in again. Would she never learn?

No, she wasn't going through this again. Steeling herself, she decided to tell him what he wanted to know, then leave. Simple as that.

"You probably know about Mary and Caleb. Eli Bontrager—he's over there by the food; he never strays far from anything he can eat—is still working for his father's cabinetry company. My niece Anna Marie is helping with her *mamm*'s business, and Marlene's sister Sarah Anne just had a baby. Now, if you'll excuse me, I need to be going."

He looked surprised. "You're leaving already? You just got here."

Prickles stood out on her arms. How did he know that?

As if he sensed her discomfort, he quickly added, "Caleb and I pulled up behind you when you were dropped off."

Miriam relaxed. A little. "He must have been irritated, then, because Lydia drove so slow. Our horse has a sore foot, so she tries not to hurry him along too much. Tomorrow the shoer is coming out to take a look at it."

Seth grinned again, then turned and faced her, leaning on his stick. "That's the most you've said to me all night."

"You find it funny that my horse has a sore foot?"

"*Nee, nee.* Of course not. I'm just glad you're talking to me, that's all."

She thought about asking why, but she stayed silent. Maybe if she didn't speak at all he would take the hint and leave.

But he must have been slow on the uptake because he leaned in closer and said in a low voice, "So what have you been up to all these years?"

Seriously? He wanted to know about her? If she didn't know it was December 10, she would have thought it was April Fool's Day, because this had to be a joke.

When she didn't respond right away, he said, "Okay, I'll go first. After I finished school I moved away from Paradise to live with my *Englisch* friends. I bought a car, and six months ago I wrapped it around a tree. Nearly killed myself. I'm lucky I only have the scar and a limp."

His initial good humor faded as he relayed his story, and melancholy seeped into his tone. By the angst shadowing his expression, Miriam could see how deeply the consequences of leaving the Amish and the accident affected him. Beyond the outward injuries, she suspected there were wounds inside that hadn't healed yet. She knew from experience that those were the toughest to mend.

"So," he said. "Your turn. Tell me something about yourself."

She still didn't understand why he was so interested. And it didn't matter, because she wasn't going to tell him anything. In a few minutes he would walk away and forget about her, so why bother?

"There you are, Seth." Mary walked up to them and smiled. "Hi, Miriam. How are you?"

"I'm well, *danki*."

"Have you heard from Hannah since she left?"

Miriam shook her head. The three young women had gone to school together, but Miriam wasn't as close to Mary as she was to Hannah. *"Nee.* I only know she'll be back before January 1."

"I hope she has a *wunderbaar* Christmas." Mary smiled and glanced over her shoulder. "Oh, look. John Hostetler just came in. Late as always." She turned to Seth. "I'm sure he'll want to catch up with you. You guys were good friends at one time." She looked at Miriam. "You don't mind, do you?"

"Nee," Miriam said, a little relieved that Seth was finally leaving. And, to her great dismay, a little disappointed.

"Danki," Mary said. "Make sure you try the oatmeal cookies, Miriam. They're delicious."

Seth looked at Miriam. "Talk to you later?"

Tingles traveled through her body as his striking eyes locked with hers. Seth Fisher was looking at her. *Really* looking at her. For the briefest of moments, her young teenage fantasy had come true. She opened her mouth to speak.

Nothing came out. Not a single word.

Her cheeks flaming, she turned and fled the room.

"Well, that wasn't very nice of her. She could have at least answered you."

Seth glanced at Mary, who seemed genuinely upset by the way Miriam departed. Not wanting her to be mad at Miriam, he said, "She's fine. Probably needs some air. Don't worry about it."

"Is there something wrong?"

Yes, there was something wrong, but it wasn't Miriam. It was him. *"Nee,"* he said, swallowing the lie. It tasted like the bitter pill it was. He didn't blame her for not wanting to talk to him again. Not after what he'd done to her when they were young.

For the rest of the night, Seth visited with old friends, who accepted him back into the fold as if he'd never left. He was thankful to them, and thankful to God for softening their hearts. After the way he'd behaved, as if he had been too good for them, too high and mighty to be Amish, they had every right not to want to talk to him.

Like Miriam Herschberger.

He hadn't even realized the identity of the young woman standing against the wall until after he'd started talking to her. When he did, he wanted to kick himself. When he remembered what he'd said to her, and how he and his friends had laughed in her face, his spirit withered.

She could have thrown that back at him, but to her credit she didn't, and he found that a bit intriguing. Her voice was unique, soft but with a slight hoarseness to it. He didn't remember her sounding like that in school. Then again, until that day when he found out she liked him, he hadn't paid much attention to her at all.

"Seth?"

He turned and looked at Caleb.

"This is the second time you've blanked out on me. What's going on?"

Seth shook his head, giving his shoulders a slight shrug. Again, another lie. "I guess I'm just tired."

"You ready to go home?"

"I don't want to cut your night short," Seth said.

"I'm ready to go. Gotta get up early, ya know." Caleb did odd construction jobs that often took him many miles beyond Paradise.

"All right, then, let's go."

By the time Seth had made it up the stairs, thanked *Frau* Lapp, and walked out the door, Caleb had already brought the buggy around to pick him up. His leg ached from standing on it so long, even though he'd sat when he could throughout the night. The cold temperatures also added to his discomfort. No doubt the pain had slowed his pace to turtle speed.

When they were on their way, Seth stifled a yawn. He was glad he could sleep in a bit tomorrow morning. He wouldn't start officially working at his father's woodshop until after Christmas. His *daed* and brother, Noah, specialized in beautifully crafted items—carved hope chests, shelves, and smaller decorative pieces that sold well to the *Englisch* tourists visiting Paradise. Every once in a while his father would take on a larger project, like a porch swing or a pergola, but he preferred to work on smaller objects that allowed him to use his skills as an artist. Noah had also inherited his father's artistic bent and had been his apprentice since he was a young boy.

Seth didn't have that gift. He had worked in the shop for a year after he finished school, but fights with his father drove him to find work elsewhere, and soon after that he left Paradise altogether. He was determined not to let that happen again. He may not have the talent his brother and father had, but he would show them that he was a hard worker. After everything they had done for him since the accident, he owed them that much. And although his relationship with his *daed* was still strained, he was determined to mend the fences his own foolishness had destroyed.

"Ho, Seth." Caleb broke into his thoughts. "Do you see that?"

Seth squinted at the barely visible shadow on the side of the road. As the buggy neared the dark shape, he could see that it was a woman walking. Even though she wore a cloak, her arms were folded together in an effort to ward off the cold. As they pulled closer, he recognized her and grabbed Caleb's arm. *"Halt!"*

Caleb yanked up on the reins. "What are you doing?" he asked, his tone bewildered.

"That's Miriam."

"Who?"

"Miriam Herschberger. She was at the singing; didn't you see her?"

"Ya. What does it matter?"

"We need to pick her up."

Caleb groaned. "Have you looked in the backseat of my buggy? It's filled with junk."

"Maybe you should clean it out once in a while."

"Where is she gonna sit?"

Seth looked at the bench seat. There wasn't much

room between him and Caleb, but Miriam was on the small side. It would be a tight squeeze, but better than letting her get chilled to the bone. "She'll sit between us."

"*Not* a good idea."

"Caleb, it's freezing out here." Although there was no snow on the ground, the temperatures were frigid. He didn't know where Miriam lived, but he didn't like the idea of her walking two feet out here in the cold, much less a couple miles.

"She's probably almost home anyway," Caleb said.

"What if she isn't?"

Caleb paused for a moment. "*Ach,*" he said as he set the buggy in motion again. Miriam, with her quick stride, had passed them moments earlier, barely giving them a glance. "I knew you'd changed since the accident, but I didn't realize you had such a bleedin' heart."

"You should try a little compassion sometime." Seth moved his walking stick and put it on top of the pile of stuff in the back of the buggy. In the dim light he couldn't tell what was back there, and he really didn't care. All he wanted was for Miriam to be warm and safe. *Bear ye one another's burdens...* The verse popped into his head. Although he hadn't officially joined the church yet, he'd attended every service once he'd healed enough from his accident to leave the house. This past Sunday's sermon had been on compassion, and the bishop had singled out that particular passage from 2 Corinthians. He couldn't think of a better situation to apply it.

"*Halt,*" he said as they pulled up alongside her.

"Again with the *halt,*" Caleb mumbled. "Next time you're driving."

Seth ignored him, seeing Miriam glance over her shoulder, then rush her steps until she was almost jogging. Why was she running away from them? He opened the door and called out her name. "Miriam!"

She slowed, but didn't stop.

He hollered at her again, this time hanging halfway out of the buggy. "Miriam!"

"Obviously she doesn't want to be picked up," Caleb said. "Get back in here and let's go."

But he couldn't let it go. He couldn't let *her* go. Despite his weariness and the intensifying ache in his leg, Seth hurtled out of the buggy and landed on both feet, ignoring the pain. Surprised and grateful that he was still in a standing position, he started to yell again when his leg suddenly buckled, and he crashed shoulder first into the sharp gravel on the side of the road.

"Yeesh!"

This utterance came from inside the buggy. Now Seth was going to hear it from Caleb, probably all the way home. Maybe he deserved it. He shouldn't have bothered, since Miriam clearly wanted nothing to do with—

"Seth! Are you all right?"

He pushed up on one elbow and lifted his head. She had not only come back; she was crouched down in front of him, concern filling her husky voice. He was all right, despite the stinging in both his shoulder and leg. But the pain was worth it when she reached out and touched his arm.

Caleb had reached them by this time, hot with anger. "Are you *ab im kopp?*"

"I'm fine," Seth muttered, moving himself to an upright position. "You're overreacting."

"You're fine? Then get up and walk."

Seth looked up at him, his jaw tightening. "You know I can't." He paused, ashamed to admit in front of Miriam what Caleb already knew. "Not without help."

"Then let's help you." Miriam put her hands under his arm, prepared to either push or pull, he wasn't sure which. The idea of her slender arms lifting him off the ground would have been amusing, if he weren't so embarrassed.

"For crying out loud. I should have never stopped." Caleb, on the opposite side, did the same as Miriam, and together they lifted Seth to a standing position. A lopsided position, but Seth wasn't about to complain. Caleb was doing enough griping for the both of them.

When they led him to the buggy and started to help him in, Seth resisted. "Miriam, you get in first."

There was very little light outside to guide them, only the exterior lamps on the buggy. He couldn't see her face, but by the way her hands tensed on his arm, he could tell she was surprised. Okay, more than surprised, probably stunned, with a little bit of shock thrown in there.

"T-that's okay," she said, her eyes cast slightly downward. "I can walk home."

"*Nee*. It's freezing out here." His breath hung in the air, punctuating his statement.

"I only have a couple more miles to go. I'll be fine."

Walking a couple of miles was easy, if it was daylight and the weather was decent. But that wasn't the case tonight, and he wasn't going to let it drop. "Miriam, we can stand out here and argue about this, which will make Caleb even more ticked off than he already is—"

"You got that right," Caleb grumbled.

Seth shot him an annoyed look. "Or you can get in the buggy and let us take you home."

She hesitated again, and he thought she would pull away from him and flee down the road. He didn't think he could convince Caleb to stop again. Just as he was about to prod her one more time, she let go of his arm and climbed in.

"Finally," Caleb said.

"What's your problem?" Seth hissed.

"My problem?" Caleb countered, thankfully keeping his voice down. "I told you, I gotta get home. And since when did you care about Miriam Herschberger, anyway?"

"When did you become such a jerk?" *Like I used to be.*

Caleb grimaced but went ahead and assisted Seth into the buggy before shutting the door and dashing around to the other side. In a few seconds he hopped in, and they were on their way.

The three of them were crammed next to each other like little fish in a can. Caleb needed the use of his arms to steer the horse, so Miriam scooted over a bit until she was sitting as close to Seth as she possibly could without climbing into his lap.

For some bizarre reason, he didn't think he'd mind very much if she did.

Tossing the illicit and surprising thought out of his head, he glanced at her. Her head was cast down, her hands clasped together so tightly he thought she might snap her fingers in two.

Due to the cramped conditions, his arms were pressed tight against his sides. Way too tight to be comfortable. The position increased the pain in his shoulder, and as they rolled along the road, he knew he wouldn't be able to sit like this for very long. He needed more room. She needed more room. Caleb would definitely like more room. Maybe his friend had been right.

Maybe this was a bad idea.

Chapter Four

What had she done wrong?

She had to have done *something* for God to punish her like this. Okay, maybe sitting so close to Seth Fisher that she could inhale the clean scent of his clothes and skin wasn't exactly punishment.

More like torture. Sheer torture.

She should have never stopped and turned around when Seth fell out of the buggy. Better yet, she should have waited for Anna Marie to take her home instead of leaving the Lapps' early on her own. Above all, she should have never left Lydia's in the first place. If she hadn't, then she wouldn't be wedged in between one man who was sizzling mad and another who was just plain…sizzling.

The thought popped into her head, unbidden and unwanted. Her cheeks heated, and she dipped her head lower, despite knowing that it was impossible to see much in the almost nonexistent light in the buggy. Yet she wouldn't risk Seth seeing her blush.

"Where do you live?" Caleb ground out, after a long, uncomfortable stretch of silence.

Ach, he was mad. In a way she didn't blame him.

They had never been very good friends, ever since the incident with Seth years ago. In fact, for a long time she had resented Caleb almost as much as she had Seth, but she had found a way to forgive him. While his teasing had hurt her feelings, it hadn't come close to Seth's outright meanness.

"I'm going to my sister's," she said. "Lydia Smucker." She gave him the address.

Caleb nodded curtly and sped up the horses.

"That's not a couple miles away."

She turned toward Seth slightly—very slightly because they were so close to each other—and looked at him.

"More like five," he added.

She pushed up her glasses, which were always slipping. "I'm quite capable of walking five miles."

"In the dark? In the cold?"

"Ya." And she could too. But she wouldn't like it, and her hands and feet would have been near-frozen by the time she got to Lydia's. Not warm and cozy like she was right now.

They sat in silence for a few moments, the *clip-clopping* of the horse's hooves the only sound she could hear through the black curtain that covered the front and sides of the buggy, protecting them from the winter cold and wind. Tonight wasn't windy, but it was cold. Downright cold.

She felt Seth move farther away from her. Or at least he tried. There really wasn't any room to move at all. She tried to dismiss the prickle of hurt that he didn't want to sit so close to her. All she wanted was for the ride to be over.

Then suddenly Seth pried his left arm loose from in between them and swung it over the back of the seat.

A gasp of surprise nearly escaped her lips. This was the closest she'd ever been to having a man's arm around her.

"Hope you don't mind," he said. "'It's a little tight in here."

Unable to say anything, barely able to breathe, she simply shook her head.

"Gut."

"I could use a little more room." Caleb's elbow lightly touched her arm. Then he glanced at her. "If you can scoot over a bit, I'd appreciate it."

His tone wasn't as harsh as before, and for that she was glad. She looked to see if there was any way she could move to the right and not be up against Seth, but she didn't see how.

"Here." Seth made the decision for her as he pressed his hand on her shoulder and guided her to close the minuscule gap between them. He leaned down and whispered, "Don't worry about Caleb. His bark is worse than his bite."

But she wasn't worried about Caleb. Not at all. In fact, she forgot Caleb altogether. She kept reminding herself that Seth was only being polite, which was nothing short of amazing. She had never known Seth Fisher to be nice. Confident, yes. Cocky, even. But never nice.

He moved his hand from her shoulder and laid his arm against the backseat again. "So you're staying with your sister?" he asked in a low, smooth voice that reminded her of molasses pouring out of a jar.

"Ya," she said, irked by her disappointment that he'd moved his hand. "She was widowed a couple years ago, and I help her out when I can."

"What does she do?"

"Lots of things, but her most recent project is her new cookbook. It's a collection of recipes handed down through our family."

"How original," Caleb remarked.

Miriam winced. Sure, there were a lot of Amish cookbooks filled with family recipes for sale in Lancaster County, but Caleb didn't have to be so sarcastic.

"Lydia's is special," she said, feeling the need to defend her sister. "Not because it's from our family. There are recipes, *ya,* but there are also photographs of the quilts my grandmother and I have made. The cover shows a very special quilt."

The photograph was of her grandmother Emma's favorite quilt, a beautiful masterpiece Miriam cherished beyond description.

"I'm sure it's a great cookbook," Seth said.

His kind comment set off a tiny spark of warmth, and again she marveled at the change in him. She found it hard to reconcile the kind man sitting next to her with the cruel boy from her childhood. "*Ya.* It is. I know she's going to sell a lot of copies. I'm taking a box with me to sell at work tomorrow."

"Oh? Where do you work?"

"Stitches and More," she said, stating the name of the fabric and sewing supply store in Paradise.

Seth didn't say anything, and the conversation came to a discomfiting conclusion. The silence filling the buggy grew awkward, as none of them seemed to have anything else to say. Caleb had set his horse on a brisk pace, and they soon came upon Lydia's house, causing Miriam to let out an inward sigh of relief. He turned in the drive and brought the buggy to a halt.

Before she could say anything, Caleb slipped out the door and motioned for her to follow him out the driver's side. "I don't want him taking another spill," he explained.

She understood that and agreed. But before moving away, she needed one more look at Seth. She'd never be this close to him again, which was a good thing. She didn't like the tumult of conflicting emotions churning inside her. Against her will, her body started to shake.

"You better get inside and warm up," Seth said.

One thing she didn't need to do was warm up. She was already warm. Warmer than she had a right to be.

She nodded, pulling herself away from his magical gaze before Caleb started grousing again. *"Danki,"* she said over her shoulder to Seth, then quickly exited the buggy. *"Danki,* Caleb."

"No problem. Sorry for being a grouch. Patience is a virtue I'm still trying to master."

His apology surprised her. He'd seemed so put out with her before, and now he was saying he was sorry. First Seth, and now Caleb. She had spent years distrusting and thinking the worst of most men, save her *daed* and her brothers. Now two men were being kind to her in one night. That had to be some kind of record.

"So what was that all about?" Caleb asked as he climbed back into the buggy.

Seth looked at his friend. Now they had plenty of room and he could stretch out his leg a bit. He welcomed the movement, while at the same time he kind of missed having Miriam next to him. Why, he had no idea.

"You know. You and Miriam. First you're hanging out together at the party; then you practically kill yourself making sure she'd let us take her home. What's going on?"

"Nothing." Which was the truth. Nothing was going on, and he doubted anything would. Not when he'd been such a jerk to her back in school. Some girls might have put that behind them, but he could tell Miriam hadn't. Distrust radiated from her like heat off a woodstove. And for some reason he couldn't fathom, that really, *really* bothered him.

"I'm just surprised, you know. You and a girl like Miriam. Doesn't add up exactly."

Obviously Caleb had forgotten about the playground incident, and Seth wasn't about to remind him. "First of all, there is no 'me and Miriam.' I haven't seen her since we left grade school. Second, I talked to everyone at the Lapps' tonight, not just her. Third, I would have wanted to stop for anyone walking on the road on a night like tonight. It's the right thing to do."

But Caleb wasn't buying his protests any more than was Seth himself. "Uh-huh. Well, that all may be true, but I think there's more than that."

"There isn't."

"I should hope not. I can't see you with a snob like her."

Seth turned and looked at Caleb, surprised. "You think she's a snob?"

Caleb nodded. "You've been gone a long time, Seth, and you don't know her like we do. The way she was at the singing tonight, separate from everyone? She always does that, like she's too *gut* to be with us. I'm surprised she was even there. Usually she doesn't show up at all."

"Maybe she's just shy."

"Maybe." Caleb cast Seth a sideways glance. "You gotta admit, she's kinda hard to look at."

"No, I don't."

"Oh, c'mon, Seth. Wait, don't tell me…you actually think she's pretty?"

He didn't respond right away. He couldn't, because in all honesty, he didn't find Miriam physically attractive. "She's not…that bad."

"Wow, you *really* have changed. Sure that accident didn't affect your eyesight?"

"It didn't. Just drop it, all right?"

Caleb moved on to another topic of conversation before Seth could say anything in Miriam's defense. A short while later they arrived at Seth's house.

"Need a hand?"

"I'm *gut*," he said, waving off Caleb's help. "*Danki* for the ride."

"Du bischt wilkumm," Caleb said in response. "But I mean it next time, Seth."

"Mean what?"

"You're gonna be the one driving."

Seth chuckled. "Fair enough."

As Caleb left, Seth made his way to the house. He entered the front room, surprised to see his parents still up.

"Did you have a *gut* time?" Rachel, his mother, gazed up at him, and he could see the worry sneaking into her light-gray eyes.

"*Ya*. I had a great time."

She let out a breath and set down the knitting she was working on. "Any problems?"

He knew she meant with his leg. Since the accident, she had been hovering, only stepping back these past couple weeks when it became obvious that he would eventually heal and be all right. If he even hinted at the fact that he'd hit the ground, bruising his arm and his dignity, she'd never let him out of the house again. "*Nee*. Everything was fine."

"*Wunderbaar*. We're glad you had a chance to go out and have some fun. It's not *gut* for you to be stuck in the *haus* all the time." She stood and cleared her throat as she looked down at his father, who was sitting in his well-worn chair.

Daed set aside his paper on the end table and followed her lead. "Bedtime," he said in his usual gruff manner, not looking at Seth. He rose from his chair. "See you in the morning."

"*Guten nacht.*"

His parents made their way to their room on the main floor, while Seth climbed the stairs to his bedroom. He passed by his brothers' old room, then his sisters', which was also empty. At the end of the hall was the smallest bedroom. As the youngest of the family, he had his own room, but it was tiny. Still, he didn't mind and appreciated the privacy. Limping into his room, he went to the bed and plopped down on the soft mattress with gratitude. The fatigue he'd kept at bay during the latter part of the evening had caught up to him.

But sleep wasn't all that easy to find. And as he lay there in bed, hands clasped behind his head while he tried to ignore the throb in his leg and the ache in his shoulder, he thought about Miriam. Guilt seeped into him once again over how he had hurt her. But as her image remained in his mind, his conscience tempered a bit.

She had certainly changed since the last time he had seen her in school five years ago. He thought about Caleb calling her a snob and saying she was hard to look at. Seth thought his friend was wrong on both counts.

She wasn't pretty by most men's standards—his standards too. Yet there was something unique about her, not only physically, but beneath the surface. He had enjoyed their brief conversation at the Lapps', along with their ride to her sister's. She hadn't tried to get his attention or flirt with him the way most girls usually did. That in itself was different and fascinating.

As his eyes drooped, he also realized something else about her. Behind the wire frames of her glasses, her eyes held a glint of sadness. He couldn't help but wonder what that was about. Maybe someday he would find out.

"This is a lovely pattern, Miriam," Sarah Fisher said the morning after the singing. "One of your own designs?"

Miriam smoothed out the wrinkles on the quilt square with her palm. When business was slow in the fabric shop, she worked on her own quilting. Tammy, the *Englisch* owner of Stitches and More, didn't mind, as long as Miriam's work was done. That included not only handling the sales but also putting out new stock, rotating old, and making sure the myriad of fabrics, patterns, and notions were neatly arranged on the shelves and displays.

"*Ya*, this is my work, but it's not really a formal design," Miriam said, pleased by Sarah's compliment. Sarah was an excellent quilter, and she didn't give out praise lightly. "More like an experiment."

"The colors are striking." With delicate fingers, Sarah touched the intersecting rectangles. "So many different hues of red and green, and so many different textile patterns. I would have never thought to put some of these fabrics together." She glanced up and smiled.

"I've seen your grandmother's quilts at Lydia's. You have your *grossmammi*'s gift, you do."

Miriam blushed. She had to be careful not to let the compliments bloat her ego—to maintain *demut* at all times. Humility was an important part of Amish life. The Scriptures said that pride goeth before destruction, and they were words to live by.

"*Danki,* Sarah. I cherish the quilts *grossmammi* gave me."

"She knew you would appreciate them like no one else." Sarah stepped to the side and looked at the quilt block from another angle, her gray eyes filled with curiosity. "I think you should continue with this experiment. It will make a wonderful Christmas quilt. Will you bring it when you come to visit David and me on First Christmas?"

Sarah and Lydia had been friends for years, and Sarah and her husband had invited all the Herschbergers to their house for First Christmas. Miriam knew it would be a bittersweet occasion for the young couple, who had lost their baby the previous Christmas.

"I'd be happy to." Miriam smiled as she folded up the quilt block and tucked it into her bag, which she had made from scraps and bits of discarded fabric.

Like the block Sarah admired so much, the bag was made with vibrant colors and vivid patterns, no one fabric the same as the other. Somehow it worked, and more than one *Englisch* tourist had spotted the bag and asked where she purchased it. A couple of them even offered to buy it from her, when they found out it was one of a kind. Miriam had thanked them, but turned down the offer. She had used some of her grandmother's old fabric, and she could never part with the bag for that reason.

"I'm surprised to see you here today," Miriam said. "Is school out of session?"

Sarah nodded. "Vacation started a couple days ago. I have to admit, even though I love my job, I'm glad for the break." She looked around the store. "Is Tammy here today?"

"*Ya.* She stepped out for a moment, but she should be back soon. Maybe I can help?"

Sarah frowned slightly. "When I was here last week, she was out of green thread. She was ordering more, and she said it should be in by today, but I don't see any."

"I haven't seen any spools up front here, either," Miriam said, "but I can check in the back."

"*Danki.* I'll just keep looking around while I wait."

Leaving Sarah to browse through the wide variety of colorful fabrics in the store, Miriam went to the back. The space was small, with Tammy's desk in the corner, a diminutive round table in the middle where they could sit and eat their lunches, and a tiny bathroom off to the side. Tammy's desk, as usual, was a mess, covered with papers, order forms, and catalogs.

As Miriam searched for the thread, she said a silent prayer of thanks for her job. She only worked three days a week, but spending the day in the fabric shop helped keep her mind off what happened last night. It had been hard enough for her to fall asleep, thinking about Seth and the buggy ride home. She didn't need to spend the entire day focusing on him. Instead she would set her attention on her work, like finding the thread for Sarah.

Amid the disarray on Tammy's desk, Miriam spotted a brown box. She opened it, finding standard spools of green thread inside, and smiled, knowing Sarah would be pleased.

Miriam took a couple of the spools back up front.

"Here they are, Sarah. What are you making with—"

The rest of the words disappeared in her mouth when she saw who was standing in front of the counter.

Chapter Five

"What are you doing here?"

Seth lifted a brow, not at Miriam's question, but at her tone of voice. While he certainly hadn't expected her to welcome him with open arms, he hadn't thought she would react with horror. Well, not exactly horror, but close to it.

"I came to pick up *mei mudder*'s order." When he'd found out this morning that she needed to pick up some things from Stitches and More, he didn't hesitate to offer to run the errand for her. Maybe it hadn't been such a good idea.

"Why here?" Miriam said.

"This is where she placed her order."

Miriam's cheeks flushed, and she cast her gaze downward. "Oh. *Ya*. That makes sense."

He liked her white *kapp* better. The black bonnet she'd worn last night hid too much of her face. Now he could get a good look at her, and he liked what he saw. Maybe Caleb was the one who needed an eye exam. Her skin was so smooth, not marred by a single blemish except for a small, light-brown freckle above her lip on the right side. Her eyes were a deep brown color, rimmed with long, black lashes.

She had high cheekbones, lips that were a bit on the thin side but still appealing, and a prominent chin. Why had he thought she was ugly back in eighth grade?

Because he was an idiot, that's why.

"You found the thread, Miriam?"

He turned around at the sound of a woman's voice, making sure he didn't knock anything over with his walking stick, then stepped to the side. He recognized his cousin David's wife and smiled. "Hello, Sarah."

A grin crossed her face. "Seth!" She came toward him and put her hand on his forearm. "You're looking well."

"*Danki,* Sarah. How is David?"

"Just fine. Busy this time of year."

"Sarah? Your thread?"

Both he and Sarah looked at Miriam, who held out the spools in front of her. She kept her gaze on Sarah as she asked, "Did you prepay for these?"

"I did," Sarah said. "If you could just put them in a bag for me, I'll be on my way."

Miriam reached underneath the counter and retrieved a small plastic bag. Seth watched as she carefully placed two spools of dark-green thread inside. She had such small hands. But her fingers weren't short and stubby; they were slender and proportionate. Delicate. He glanced at his free hand. Large, rough. Her hand would probably get lost in his.

He groaned inwardly at the erratic and unexpected thought. What possessed him to think about holding Miriam's hand? Like that would ever happen.

Pulling his gaze away from her hands, he glanced around the shop as Miriam finished up the transaction.

He'd never been in here before—he doubted many men had. The store was crammed to the brim with fabric and sewing supplies. On the walls hung colorful hand-made quilts—his mother was a quilter, and he recognized the high quality and intricate, yet artistically simple patterns that were typical Amish. There were also various gift-type items scattered around the small space. Taking a deep breath, he inhaled the mingling aromas of scented candles and potpourri, stuff women seemed to love.

"*Danki,* Miriam. Say hello to your *mamm* for me." Sarah moved toward the front door, then turned around. "I just thought of something. I remember Lydia had one of your *grossmammi*'s quilts displayed in her living room. It was absolutely stunning. But I didn't see it the last time I visited."

"Was it a star pattern?"

"*Ya,* cream and navy blue."

"*Mei mamm* and I are repairing some of the stitching. We're doing that for all twenty of her quilts."

"Do you display them on a rack?"

"*Nee.* I have one at the end of my bed, and the others are packed away in the closet. I'd like to buy a hope chest to put them in, so they can be stored correctly. Right now that's out of my reach."

Seth saw a flush of color bloom on her cheeks as she finished the sentence. She shouldn't feel bad about not being able to afford the chest. He had very little money himself, and almost all of his future earnings would be applied to his doctor and hospital bills. Since he and the rest of the community didn't have insurance, they often pooled their resources when one of their brethren had a medical crisis. Seth's bills had been paid off, but he was determined to pay the community back.

"I'm sure you're taking very good care of them," Sarah said. "And someday after you're married, hopefully you can buy one."

Seth didn't think Miriam's cheeks could get any redder.

"Regards to Tammy." Sarah turned to Seth. "Tell your *mamm* I'll stop and see her before Christmas. 'Bye!"

Sarah went out the door, leaving Miriam and Seth in the store. Alone, as far as he could tell. Just them and the awkward silence that filled the shop.

"You needed to pick up an order?" Miriam finally asked.

Seth nodded and reached into the pocket of his trousers. He retrieved the slip of paper his mother had written her order on and handed it to Miriam.

She glanced over it. "I think I saw her fabric behind the counter this morning." Miriam ducked down and disappeared for a moment, then popped up with two different, short bolts of fabric, one a dark green with tiny, white flowers, another a plain Christmas red. Consulting the note again, Miriam tucked the bolts under her arm. "I'll just take these to the cutting table," she said, leaving him standing at the counter.

She crossed the short distance to the other side of the shop. Her steps were too quick and the store too packed with stuff for him to follow.

Spinning around, she frowned when she didn't see him. "Seth?"

"Still at the counter." He clenched his jaw.

"Oh." He heard her hesitation. "I'll just be a minute, then."

As he waited, he tried to stem his frustration at not being able to do something as easy as crossing a room.

Before his accident he had been nimble and a pretty decent athlete. Now he couldn't go five feet without worrying about knocking something over or taking twice as much time as an able-bodied person. But as he always did when he came perilously close to self-pity, he reminded himself that he was lucky to be alive. God, for some reason, had spared him, and he was sure it wasn't so he could spend the rest of his life feeling sorry for himself.

Miriam appeared behind the counter again, holding two neatly folded piles of fabric. "Four yards of green and two yards of red, correct?"

Seth shrugged. "That's what she had on her list. I think she's finishing up a quilt."

"Your *mudder* quilts?"

"*Ya.* I take it you do too."

She nodded. "*Mei grossmammi* taught me."

He watched as she put the fabric in a bright-yellow plastic bag, the name Stitches and More emblazoned on the side in black letters. As she rang up his purchase, he made a last-minute decision. "Candles," he said, mostly to himself, as he spied a small, snow-white candle next to the register. "What kind of candles do you sell?"

"All kinds," Miriam replied. "We usually keep more in stock over the holidays. Why?"

"I'd like to purchase some. Christmas presents," he added. Since he'd left Paradise, he hadn't really paid much attention to Christmas and hadn't purchased any gifts in the past five years. Today he could rectify that and buy something for his mother and his sisters. He would also get something for Sarah. This Christmas marked the anniversary of her miscarriage, which had devastated her and his cousin David. In the past Seth probably wouldn't have thought twice about their loss, but this year was different. Like Caleb said, he was different, and he wanted to show everyone just how much.

"What kind of candles were you looking for?" Miriam looked up at him with her chocolate-brown eyes.

"Um…not sure. Something that smells good."

A smile quirked on her lips, and he realized he'd never seen her smile. It softened her features, making her seem almost…pretty.

The hint of a smile instantly disappeared, and her expression became all business. "First of all, who are the candles for?"

"My *mudder,* two sisters, and a cousin."

"All right. Do you know their favorite scents?"

Now it was his turn to go red. "Ah, not really. I never paid much attention."

She tapped her finger against her chin, obviously deep in thought. She seemed to be more relaxed than when he first entered the store. "I have just the thing."

Walking around the counter, she met him on the other side and led him to a tiered display of candles only a few steps away. She picked up a small, round candle that had been dyed a light purple. "This is a lavender tea light. It looks tiny, but the scent is strong. Lavender is soothing and calming. We sell a lot of these, not just at Christmas. We try to keep them in stock year-round."

Seth looked at the candle. It covered almost her entire palm. He plucked it from her, again noting the contrast in size of their hands.

"You can smell it if you want."

He brought it closer to his nose and took a big sniff. Too big. He turned away and sneezed.

"I told you it was strong."

There was that hint of a grin again. He really liked her smile. "Smells pretty good." He handed the candle back to her. "How much?"

"We sell them individually or by the box. The boxes are in the back."

"All right, how much is a box?"

When she told him the amount, he inwardly breathed a sigh of relief. He could afford that and still have a bit left over, thankfully. He would have felt stupid buying only four tiny tea lights.

"I'll get the box for you."

He watched her as she turned around and walked away. She had an air of confidence about her, one that she didn't have when he first came into the shop, and it was definitely missing last night at the Lapps'. Clearly she was in her element here.

Moments later she brought the box and laid it on the counter. "Now, what do you think your *mamm* would like?"

Uh-oh. "Actually…I think I'll give her the lavender tea lights too."

"Okay. I'll go get three more boxes." She started to go when he reached out and touched her arm.

"I'll just take the one."

Their gazes met for a moment, and he knew she understood his meaning.

"No problem. I'll ring this up for you."

"Make sure the fabric is separate."

"I will."

"Danki." He leaned his hip against the counter, relieving some of the pressure off his leg. He appreciated her not making him feel like a fool over not having enough money to buy more than one box of

candles. As she punched a few buttons on the cash register, a chiming sound echoed through the store. He glanced over his shoulder to see a petite woman with dark-red hair walk through the door. A blast of cold air followed her in.

Miriam told him the amount, and he fished in his pocket for his wallet.

"Good morning," the woman said, giving him a big smile as she strode toward him. "I hope you found everything you needed."

"I did, thanks to Miriam." He glanced at her, but she had her head down, counting his change. He could only see the top of her *kapp*.

"It was my lucky day when Miriam walked into my shop," the woman said. "She could run the whole thing herself if she had to."

"I'm sure she could."

Miriam handed Seth a few coins without making eye contact. She retrieved a plastic bag from underneath the counter and started to pack up his box as if he and the woman were comparing the price of horse feed instead of singing her praises.

Demut. Miriam understood it and exemplified it.

It was a lesson he still had to learn.

Most of his life he'd been filled with *hochmut*. He'd had an ego the size of Pennsylvania and didn't care who knew it. He'd been told so many times he was handsome that he believed it. He'd been popular, not only with girls but with the guys as well. Athletic, strong, he'd done well in school without even trying. By the time he was sixteen, he knew he was the golden boy. Untouchable. Unbreakable.

He'd been broken all right. Not only his body, but his pride as well.

The shop owner stood at the opposite end of the counter. "I'm back for the rest of the day, Miriam. Why don't you go ahead and take your lunch break?"

"It's not quite noon yet. I can wait twenty more minutes."

"Don't worry about it. Go."

"All right." She handed Seth his bag of candles. *"Danki,"* she said in her usual soft, slightly raspy voice. "Have a *gut* day." Without waiting for him to respond, she picked up a multicolored quilted bag, then turned away and headed for the back of the store.

Seth limped out of the store and searched for his father. They had ridden into town together. He didn't see him right away, and even though his leg was sore, he decided to take a short walk down Lincoln Avenue. Next door to the sewing store was a bakery, and he stopped in front of the window, staring at the mouthwatering treats on display. Then he glanced back at Stitches and More…and had an idea.

Miriam's stomach growled. Relief had washed through her when Tammy gave her the go-ahead for lunch. She'd overslept this morning, which made her late for work and caused her to skip breakfast. The reason for her bad morning had fortunately just left the fabric store.

She'd stayed up half the night thinking about Seth— and fighting with herself. But it wasn't just that she thought of him. Hope jabbed at her defenses, weakening them with each punch. He had apologized to her, talked to her, even made sure she had a ride home on a freezing cold night. That was more attention than anyone had ever given to her before. How was she supposed to resist that?

To make things worse, he had to show up here. To-day. When she hadn't yet fortified the buttress around her heart. At first when she was helping him with his *mamm*'s order, she tried not to stare at the scar, remembering how rude she'd been at the Lapps' last night. Yet after a few moments she didn't even notice it. All she could see was the beauty of his eyes, which never seemed to stray from her face. Why had he looked at her so intently?

His reasons didn't matter, and she didn't need to ponder them. He completed his purchase and went on his way. Now things could go back to normal. Like her heart rate, for example. And her life.

Tammy breezed into the back room and leaned against the doorjamb, crossing her arms over her chest. "Pardon me for saying this, but that guy you were talking to a minute ago? He is way *cuh-ute*."

Miriam looked at her, shocked. Her boss had never referred to any male, Amish or *Englisch*, as *cuh-ute*.

Then again, she'd never seen Seth Fisher before.

"I know we don't get that many men in here, at least not by themselves. But still, he's the best-looking young man I've seen in a long time. He seems nice too. Like he'd be a sweetheart once you got to know him."

Miriam clamped her teeth down on her lower lip. *Oh, if only Tammy knew...*

"So what's with the scar? And the limp?"

Miriam hesitated. Although she considered Tammy a friend—easy to do since she was only ten years older than Miriam—she rarely spoke with her about life in her community. Tammy, who transplanted herself to Paradise from Philadelphia three years ago after her divorce, had asked Miriam the usual questions—did she use electricity (no), did she have a phone (no, but some of her friends' families did, for business use only), did she use an outhouse (she didn't), did she wish she could drive a car (not at all), and several others. Miriam didn't mind answering those, but she made sure not to reveal too much about her family or things that happened in the community. Not that there was anything to hide; she just didn't feel it was Tammy's, or anyone else's, business.

"He was in an accident," she finally said, but offered no further explanation.

"That must have been some accident."

"It was." From what she'd heard and Seth confirmed last night, he was lucky to have survived it.

"Okay, enough chitchat. Go ahead and have lunch." Tammy hooked a lock of her chin-length, auburn hair behind an ear that held five piercings. "Take a full hour, Miriam. You deserve it." She turned around and went back out to the front of the store.

Miriam picked up her quilted bag. Besides the experimental quilting square and a few quilting supplies, it also held her lunch and her wallet. She spread her meal on the table in front of her—a ham sandwich and a banana. Bowing her head, she whispered a prayer of grace.

"Dear Father God, bless this food I am about to partake of. And please have mercy on me, Lord. Help me not to think of Seth Fisher anymore."

She ended her prayer and slipped her sandwich out of its small plastic bag. She was just about to take a bite when Tammy barged in.

"Your friend's back." Tammy's plum-tinted lips formed a wide grin.

"Friend?"

"The one that was just here? The cute one? What's his name?"

"Seth." Miriam's mouth had suddenly gone dry, and she set her sandwich down. Her appetite instantly disappeared.

Tammy nodded. "I heard him say he would see you soon, but I didn't think it would be this soon."

"Neither did I."

"Don't keep him waiting." Tammy walked toward her, making shooing gestures with both hands.

Miriam slowly rose from her chair, wiping her hands on the paper towel she'd taken from the roll in the bathroom. In her haste at home, she had forgotten a napkin. Maybe Seth had forgotten something too, and that's why he was here. Or he'd discovered she'd given him incorrect change. That was possible, especially when his mere presence made her brain go haywire. Unable to resist touching her *kapp* to make sure she didn't have a hair out of place, she left the room and walked behind the counter, the long stretch of pale-green formica-topped wood making a good barrier between them. Be professional. Professional. Professional...

He's so cuh-ute.

So much for professional.

"Did you forget something?" she asked, pleased that her voice sounded businesslike even though most of her mind was thinking about anything *but* business.

"Nee." He leaned against the counter, and she thought she saw him flinch. Was he in pain?

"Are you all right?"

He nodded. "As fine as I can be with a bum leg. Here." He plopped a small white bag on the counter. The top was folded down and stapled together.

"What is this?"

"A little something to go with your lunch. To thank you for helping me."

She eyed it skeptically.

"Open it up. I promise nothing's going to jump out at you."

Tentatively she unfastened the bag, less suspicious of the contents than she was of his motives. Peeking inside, her eyes grew wide as she saw what the bag contained.

A nice big chunk of raspberry fudge. Her favorite.

"The lady at the bakery said you come in every so often, and you always get the raspberry fudge."

"*Ya.* She's right, I do." Miriam looked up from the bag, still inhaling the sweet aroma of sugar and raspberry. "Why?"

"Why what?"

"Why did you give me this?"

"Because I wanted to." Without saying another word, he straightened; then he limped to the door and left.

Tammy instantly appeared, as if she'd been watching them from the back room, which she probably was. "I saw him holding that bag, and I just knew it was for you." She grinned, as if she were the one getting an unexpected gift from a man. "What's inside?"

Miriam tilted the bag in her direction and showed her.

With a sly grin Tammy said, "That's your favorite."

"I know."

"You get that every time you go to Weaver's."

"I *know.*"

"But he's not your boyfriend."

She looked at Tammy and hid her irritation. "*Nee,* he's not."

"Are you sure? Because a guy doesn't just surprise a girl with her favorite dessert and not have some intentions."

Miriam looked at the exit, where Seth had just been. "I know," she whispered, taking a deep breath and steadying her nerves. Part of her wanted to know what kind of game he was playing with her. The other part was scared to find out.

Chapter Six

"I appreciate you letting me come with you to town," Seth said to his father as they headed home from Paradise.

Melvin Fisher gave his son a curt nod.

Not that Seth expected anything more. Even when the man felt like talking, his father had a staccato form of communication that used to grind on Seth's nerves. But now he appreciated the older man's measured phrases. Melvin usually spoke only when spoken to and made his points quick and concise. He did his work, took care of his family, worshipped his Lord. As far as Seth knew, his *daed* had always lived a solid Amish life. The kind of life Seth tried to run away from, with disastrous results.

When he was a kid, he never thought much about being Amish. He'd grown up in a tightknit community and never had a complaint about it. And even though his relationship with his father had become rocky early on, Seth hadn't considered leaving. It wasn't until his *daed* fired him from the shop and he got a job working in a warehouse in Lancaster that the *Englisch* world grabbed hold of him. Before long he'd moved to the city and shared an apartment with another *Englisch* friend and fully left his Amish life behind. He cut his hair to a length much shorter than the Amish wear, wore *Englisch* clothes, dated *Englisch* women.

Yet during those four years away from his family and his community, there was an empty space in his soul, one that kept growing larger with each passing day. He truly believed that God had used his accident to bring him back to Paradise and to the Amish. Despite having his work cut out for him where his relationship with his father was concerned, Seth felt a measure of peace, something he'd never experienced living in Lancaster. As soon as he was able and had convinced his family and the church leaders of his sincerity, he wanted to be baptized into the Amish faith.

Melvin steered his horse, Gravy, onto the road. The horse's full name was Biscuits 'n' Gravy, as christened by Seth's niece, Ruth, when she was four years old. Biscuits 'n' Gravy had been too much of a mouthful even for the adults, and especially for his father, who wanted to please his granddaughter but couldn't bring himself to call the horse by its full name. Gravy was a good compromise.

"Got your *mamm*'s order?" he asked Seth.

"Ya." Forgetting about the fabric he'd purchased, he thought about Miriam's reaction when he had given her the fudge. A combination of surprise and wariness. He had to admit he had surprised himself with his impulsiveness. He hadn't planned on buying her anything, but when he saw the bakery next door, the idea just came to him. That fancy treat had been quite dear and cost him the last of his money, but he didn't mind.

He frowned. He'd never had such a confusing reaction to any *maedel* before. He'd had lots of girlfriends, especially when he had been out whooping it up with his *Englisch* friends. They'd all been pretty. Actually, *hot* was a better word, one he'd learned from those same buddies. According to them there was *cute*. Then there was *pretty*. And finally, what every man wanted and what Seth had all the time, there was *hot*.

And then there was Miriam. Plain Miriam, who had liked him at one time—he vaguely remembered the notebook with his name surrounded by crooked hearts—but now seemed to barely tolerate his presence. He'd never met a girl he couldn't charm within five minutes. Yet she seemed anything but charmed.

"You're thinking deep thoughts," his father remarked as they continued down the road toward home.

Seth waited for his *daed* to ask what those thoughts were, but he didn't. They'd never shared much in the past, unless he counted the numerous heated arguments they'd had when Seth was a teenager.

But that didn't mean his father didn't love him. That had been made clear the night of the accident, when his parents showed up in the emergency room. Seth had been in and out of consciousness, partly because of the pain medication they'd given him and partly because the pain medication didn't help too much, so passing out at least gave him some relief. But before he'd gone to surgery, he remembered his father's voice as they wheeled him down the hallway. *Heal my boy. Whatever it takes, whatever it costs–heal my boy.*

No, he didn't doubt his father's love. Not anymore.

What he did doubt was that his father would ever trust him again. He had betrayed that trust, first when he had slacked off and caused trouble in his *daed*'s shop, then when he had left for Lancaster without saying good-bye. His mother had forgiven him completely, but his father, in his customary way, had said little. Seth knew it would take time for him to earn back his *daed*'s confidence. He just had to figure out a way to do it.

"Gotta make a stop at Matthew Herschberger's," Melvin said, breaking into Seth's musings.

Seth lifted his brow at the sound of Miriam's last name. He wondered if she and Matthew were related. There were several Herschberger families in Lancaster, but it was a possibility.

Twenty minutes later they turned onto a dirt drive, which led to a huge spread about half a mile from the main road. As they neared the large, pristine white house, Seth saw a white rectangular sign that read "Herschberger Lumber." When they pulled onto the asphalted driveway, he could hear the whirring of a gas-powered bandsaw.

"You don't have to get out," Melvin said, yanking on the horse's reins.

"I'd like to." Seth grabbed his walking stick.

Matthew must have seen them approaching, because he met them at their buggy. After exchanging greetings, Melvin got to the point.

"I'll need that delivery tomorrow instead of Friday. Just got a big order from Philadelphia for some fancy bookshelves."

Matthew tilted his hat back and scratched his head. He didn't look much older than Seth, but Seth didn't recognize him.

"I promised to pick up *mei* cousin Miriam tomorrow and take her to work in the morning." Matthew paused for a moment. "I think she has to be there at eight. She works in Paradise. Once I drop her off and come back, I can probably deliver the wood. I can get it to your house by ten."

"No earlier?" Melvin stroked his salt-and-pepper beard.

"*Nee. Daed* and *mei bruders* are leaving first thing in the morning for Lancaster. They have a big delivery to make. We hadn't planned on getting you your wood until Friday."

"Guess that'll have to do. *Danki,* Matthew. I'll see you tomorrow."

On their way home, Seth stared out the window. The winter sky cast a pall over the barren landscape. The fields, normally lush with grass and towering cornstalks in the spring and summer, were now empty and brown.

So Matthew was related to Miriam. An idea suddenly occurred to Seth. Maybe there was a way to get in his dad's good graces.

"*Daed?*"

Melvin nodded.

"I'm ready to start driving again."

His father didn't answer for a long time. Seth could tell he was stewing it over. Big decision or small, it didn't matter. Melvin Fisher always thought everything through. Finally he spoke. "We talking car or buggy?"

"Buggy. I'm done with cars, *Daed.* Done with all those worldly things."

Melvin paused and gave him a hard look.

"I'd like to prove it to you," Seth said. "I know I've let you down in the past, but I promise, not this time."

Gravy's hooves clip-clopped against the asphalt road as cars whooshed by them.

"How's the leg?" Melvin asked.

"Feeling better." While it still ached constantly, at least he wasn't in massive pain anymore.

Tugging on his beard, Melvin said, "Church is at the Yoders' this Sunday. You can drive there."

Sunday? He didn't want to wait that long. "I was kinda thinking I could drive tomorrow."

His *daed* looked at him. "You got somewhere you gotta be?"

"I thought I might help you out. I could pick up Miriam so Matthew could deliver the wood to you before ten."

"Sure this ain't more about seeing that girl than about helping me?"

Seth frowned. He should have known better than to offer to help. "Never mind."

"Wait." Melvin paused. "Is Miriam the *maedel* at the fabric store?"

"How did you know?"

"I was across the street. Saw you go to the bakery. Then you went back to her shop. Put two and two together." He switched the reins from his right hand to his left. "Been in the shop with your *mudder* before. Seen the *maedel* who works there. She got glasses?"

"*Ya.*"

Glancing at Seth, he said, "She's nice."

"*Ya.* She is. We went to school together, and I hadn't seen her in a long time. I'd kind of like to renew our... friendship."

"So that's what you're calling it."

"I'm not calling it anything right now." He leaned back against the seat and tilted down his hat slightly. He doubted he could make his father understand, and based on his past behavior, his *daed* had every right to be suspicious of his motives. But he was willing to try.

"There's something about her, *Daed.* She's not like the other girls."

"Not like the *Englisch maed?*"

"She's not like *any* other girl."

Their modest house appeared in view, and Seth spied the line of plain Amish dresses, blue shirts, and gray trousers stretched across the front porch, drying. They would take longer to dry in the cold temperature, but the slight breeze in the air that lifted up the clothing would help.

After Seth's confession, his father remained silent for a long time. So long, that Seth began to regret revealing so much. By the time they turned into the driveway, he wondered if Melvin would acknowledge his words at all.

Melvin pulled on Gravy's reins and stopped the buggy. Seth turned to climb out, but his father stopped him, laying his big, beefy hand on his son's arm.

"Pick her up in the morning." He dropped his hand, opened the door, and got out.

Seth sighed with relief and said a small prayer of thanks. He knew that was the closest to approval he would get from his *daed,* at least right now. He gladly took it.

The next morning a knock sounded on the front door, surprising Miriam. She glanced at the clock on the fireplace mantel. Seven o'clock. Who would be calling at this time in the morning?

"Miriam? Can you get that?" her mother called from the kitchen. "Breakfast is almost ready."

"All right." Miriam shoved a bobby pin in her *kapp,* her bare feet padding against the hardwood floor.

When she opened the door, she let out a gasp, and not just from the gust of cold air that greeted her.

"I'm sorry," Seth said, looking contrite. "I didn't mean to startle you."

She opened her mouth to say something, but couldn't. Once again he had rendered her speechless. Then again, who could blame her? As usual, he looked gorgeous with his black felt hat tipped back from his forehead, giving her full view of his stunning eyes. His black coat fit his broad shoulders perfectly. She knew that with an *Englisch* haircut and clothes, he could pass for a model, like those she saw in some of those magazines at the library.

He glanced down at her bare legs and feet. "Sorry. Guess I came too early." He winked.

Something inside her crumbled. Just a bit, but that's all it would take, a small fissure in her defenses, and he would be back in her heart. She couldn't let that happen. She *wouldn't* let it happen.

"Who's at the door?" Mary Herschberger appeared behind her. "Hello. Can we help you?"

Seth extended his hand to Mary. "Seth Fisher," he said, giving her a brilliant smile. "Melvin Fisher's *sohn.*"

Recognition dawned on Mary's face as she shook his hand. "*Ya,* I remember now. Nice to see you. How are your parents?"

"Doing well, *danki* for asking."

"Well, don't just stand there." She looked at Miriam. "Why didn't you invite him in?"

Miriam stepped back, allowing Seth room to walk inside. The worn end of his walking stick made a thumping sound against the floor as he entered the living room.

"I just finished cooking breakfast," Mary said. "Eggs and sausage. Would you like some?"

"*Mamm,* maybe we should find out why he's here first." Miriam glanced at her mother and nearly groaned. Even her *mamm* wasn't immune to Seth's charms.

"Oh, *ya.* Of course." Mary smiled. "What brings you by, Seth?"

"I came to give Miriam a ride to work, if that's all right with you."

Miriam sucked in a breath. "My cousin is picking me up."

He shook his head. "Matthew had to make a delivery for my *daed* this morning. So I thought I'd help them both out by offering you a ride to work."

"What a nice thing to do." Mary grinned. "We appreciate the offer, don't we, Miriam?"

"*Ya,*" Miriam said slowly with little enthusiasm.

"Seth, why don't you come in the kitchen and have a bite to eat while Miriam finishes getting ready." Mary's gaze landed on Miriam's bare legs, her brow raised in disapproval.

"*Danki,*" Seth said. "It smells *gut.*"

As Mary led Seth to the kitchen in the back of the house, Miriam ran upstairs to her bedroom to get her socks and shoes on. As she slid her feet into the black woolen socks, she tried to stem the panic rising within her at the thought of Seth driving her to work. The trip would take at least thirty minutes. Alone with him. In close quarters.

She didn't think her heart could take it.

But she also knew she couldn't refuse him. Her *daed* had already left to help a friend across town repair the fence around his pasture, and he had driven their one and only buggy. Now, with Matthew otherwise occupied, she had no choice but to accept Seth's offer. But only this time. She would make that clear to him as soon as possible.

Slipping her feet into her black shoes, she quickly laced them and dashed downstairs. As she walked into the kitchen, she saw Seth at the table, already diving into a plate piled high with fluffy yellow eggs and perfectly browned sausage patties. Her stomach coiled into a knot. She didn't think she could eat a single bite.

Mary set another plate on the table, in front of the chair next to Seth. "Here, Miriam. Have a seat."

"*Danki.* You go ahead, *Mamm,*" she said, fighting to keep a normal tone to her voice. So what if Seth Fisher was sitting in her kitchen, eating breakfast with gusto? That was no reason to have an attack of nerves. She glanced at her hands, which shook slightly. Unfortunately her body refused to be reasoned with.

"I already ate. I need to get started on the laundry. It always takes so long to dry in the winter." Mary glanced at Seth. "*Danki* again, for taking Miriam."

"You're welcome."

When Mary left, Miriam stood for a moment, watching Seth as he scooped a forkful of eggs. As if he sensed her gaze on him, he looked up. "Aren't you going to eat?"

"I'm not hungry."

Seth held up the bite of eggs. "I don't know how you can resist this." He paused for a moment. "At least sit down. I feel *seltsam* eating your *mamm*'s cooking while you're just standing there."

Pressing her lips together, Miriam slowly lowered herself into the seat next to Seth. "You don't have to do this."

"Eat breakfast?" Seth grinned. "I think I do. I'm starving, and your *mamm* is a great cook."

"I mean take me to work."

"I have to do that too. Matthew is probably already loading his wagon to take the wood over to *daed*'s. Unless you have someone else to take you?"

"*Nee.*"

He flashed her one of his trademark smiles, the kind that could melt ice in winter. "Then it's settled." Pushing his empty plate a few inches away from him, he added, "Are you ready to go?"

"*Ya.*" Apparently only capable of one-syllable answers, she stood from the table and crossed the kitchen to get her coat, which was hanging on a hook near the back door. Moments later they were outside and walking toward the buggy.

Seth took a few quick but awkward steps as he passed her and went to the passenger side. His movement confused her until she realized he wanted to open the door for her.

"You didn't have to do that." She meant it, and not because he'd done it for her, but because he had to limp the extra steps. Now she could add guilt to the mixing pot of emotions simmering inside her.

"I know." He untethered the horse, then climbed in the driver's side of the buggy. Soon they were off.

She crossed her arms over her chest and kept her gaze directed straight ahead. Miriam felt more awkward than she had the other night when he and Caleb had brought her home from the Lapps'. He didn't even try to draw her into conversation, and she thought his father must have desperately needed Seth's help for him to agree to take her to work. Finally the excruciating ride was over as he pulled into a parking lot behind the store.

"Danki," she said, throwing open the door, eager to get out. She had one foot on the ground when she heard him say her name.

"What time do you get off work?"

Her eyes widened. "Why?"

"So I can take you home."

She searched his face, but didn't see a trace of humor in his expression. "You don't have to do that. Matthew usually picks me up."

"Not anymore."

She gaped. "Why?"

"Because I told him you already had a ride home. With me."

He was flashing that grin again, obviously trying to pour on the charm. And it was working. Her heart kept jolting out of rhythm. But despite her body's traitorous response, she had to keep her distance. Physical distance would be a start. She stepped completely out of the buggy and held the door partway between them.

"Miriam, did you hear me?"

"I heard you." She was just trying to process the words. "Won't Matthew be finished with his delivery to your *daed* by then?"

"Ya."

"Then why would you tell Matthew you're taking me home?"

He leaned toward her, lowering his voice. "Because I want to."

This wasn't going to work at all. How was she supposed to remain unaffected if everything about him dazzled her? The husky way he answered her question made her mouth go dry. She knew the way he said those words was calculated, but for one tiny moment she didn't care.

Then she snapped to her senses. "That was presumptuous of you."

His facade faded a bit, as if her statement caught him off guard. Then instantly he was back in full form, grinning, gazing at her with those heavenly eyes in a way that threatened to buckle her knees. "Maybe it was," he said. "But it doesn't matter, because I still want to take you home. Just tell me what time you're done, and I'll be here."

She weighed her options. Should she tell him no and risk the chance of not having a ride home at all? Tammy would be glad to take her home, but Miriam didn't want to count on it. Or should she just take him up on his offer so he would leave her alone?

With a sigh she said, "I get off at five."

"Then I'll be here at five." Leaning back, he gripped the reins and gave her another mesmerizing smile.

Over the past five years he had obviously honed his skills. She had a feeling that whatever Seth wanted, especially from a woman, Seth got. Every time.

Her hands went cold. Suddenly she wished she hadn't said yes.

Chapter Seven

Ttrue to his word, Seth showed up at five o'clock. Technically 4:55…not that she was watching the clock.

"I'll see you tomorrow," Tammy said, walking Miriam to the door. Then she saw Seth standing outside, far enough to the right of the entrance so as not to block customers who might want to dash in at the last minute.

Miriam briefly wondered why he chose not to come inside.

"Hold on there." Tammy grabbed Miriam's arm. "Is that who I think it is? The cutie?"

"His name is Seth."

"Oh. Nice name." She smiled wryly at Miriam. "Seems like there are a lot of nice things about him. Is he here to pick you up?"

"Ya." Unfortunately.

"Then I'd say you were a lucky girl. So go on." Tammy opened the door and practically shoved Miriam outside. "Hi, Seth," she said in greeting.

"Hello." He turned to her and extended his hand. "And your name is?"

"Tammy. Just call me Tammy." She winked at Miriam in such a blatant way that Seth couldn't have possibly missed it, and told them good-bye.

Miriam groaned. Why had she agreed to this?

They walked to the end of the block, where Seth had tethered the horse and parked the buggy. *Awkward* didn't even begin to describe how she felt as the silence grew between them. He hobbled over to the passenger side of the buggy and opened it for her.

She didn't know if she was up for another silent drive, but she would have to endure it. At the very least she could close her eyes and feign sleep.

They drove along in silence for a few moments, and Miriam stared straight ahead, listening to the horse's hooves click on the asphalt road. Darkness had descended, and she watched as the taillights of the cars whizzing past them disappeared into the distance. The clear winter curtain protected them against most of the cold, but she couldn't help crossing her arms over her chest anyway. She was just about to close her eyes when Seth spoke.

"So, Miriam. Tell me about your day."

His interest surprised her. Everything about him pretty much shocked her lately.

"Fine," she said, not eager to go into details, especially when she doubted his interest was sincere. It was more like a desperate attempt to break the deepening silence.

"C'mon, now. I'm sure there's more to it than that. Were you busy? Are sales good?" He took his eyes off the road for just a moment and gave her a sly look. "Did anyone buy any more green and red fabric?"

She turned away from him. He was funning her, and she didn't appreciate it one bit. But she wasn't without recourse. If he wanted to know how her day went, she would tell him. In minute detail. She'd bore him to death the rest of the ride home, and then she'd be done with him for good. And that was all she wanted.

Wasn't it?

"Well, first Tammy came in the door. She was supposed to be there at 8:30, but she was late and came in at 8:31. She had on a red sweater and blue jeans—"

"*Ya,*" he said, his brows furrowing a bit. "I saw her, remember?"

"Oh, that's right. Anyway, she had brought some new fabric catalog of summer fabrics, and we looked at those. On page 1 were the pastels, on page 17 the jewel tones…"

She continued talking until her mouth started to ache. She hadn't said so many words in a very long time, if ever. And she could see her banal conversation was having an effect. First he stopped grinning at her. Then he wouldn't even look at her. She took great pleasure in seeing him trying to stifle a yawn not once, but twice. By the time they turned in her driveway, she was confident Seth Fisher wouldn't be taking her anywhere again.

He pulled his buggy to a stop in front of her house. "What time do you have to be at work in the morning?"

"What?" It was the only word that would come out of her mouth. She'd used all the other ones up.

"I asked you what time you needed to be at work." He was looking at her, and despite the dimness of the interior of the buggy, she could see the expectation on his face. Instead of his charm-filled grin, his lips twitched in a half smile, making his mouth lopsided.

And adorable.

She pushed up her glasses. "Let me guess. You want to take me to work tomorrow."

"You got it."

Without warning, her bravado disappeared, and she suddenly couldn't fight him—and her feelings—anymore. Every emotion she'd been suppressing since that night at the Lapps' simmered inside her. All the anxiety, resentment, and confusion came to a boil, and she fought the tears that came to her eyes. "Why are you doing this to me?"

Having Miriam get teary eyed wasn't the reaction he was expecting. Or looking for. Alarm dashed through him. "Miriam?"

"Wasn't it enough for you?" Her voice was thick, like something was clogging her throat.

"What?" he asked, bewildered.

"Didn't you have your fun at my expense years ago? Or do you have some unfinished business?"

"Miriam, I don't know what you're talking about."

"I'm talking about me, Seth. Plain, ugly Miriam. I have feelings, you know."

He moved a little closer to her, his chest aching from the pain he saw in her eyes. "*Ya,* I—"

"Don't *do* that!"

"Do *what?*" His voice raised in volume to match hers.

"Don't get close to me." She leaned back against the door of the buggy.

He froze for a moment, then understood what she meant. Gentling his voice, he said, "Miriam, I just want to get to know you, that's all."

"Why? Why would anyone, especially someone like you, want to have anything to do with me?"

"Someone like me?" he scoffed. "The question should be this—why would you want to be around me?"

"I—I don't."

All of his charm, energy, and confidence dwindled away. He stared straight ahead. "I don't blame you."

"What did you say?"

Realizing he'd been whispering, he raised his voice slightly. "I said I don't blame you. I haven't been a good person to be around for a long time. I'm trying to change that…but maybe it's not working."

He waited for her to open up the buggy door and rush out, as if she had flames licking at her heels. He waited…and waited.

But she didn't move. Instead, she sat there and stared at her hands for a long time. Finally she took a deep breath and said, "Eight o'clock."

"What?"

"I have to be at work at eight, but I'm off tomorrow. Pick me up at seven-thirty on Thursday…if you still want to." With that she exited the buggy and ran inside, her cloak billowing around her thin body.

Seth remained still. Her words confused him. He had been sure she was going to refuse him, but then at the last minute she changed her mind. But why?

Even more important, why did he offer? He had only intended to take her to work and pick her up to-day, but then he found himself offering to pick her up again. But he knew the answer to that question. When he'd told Miriam he wanted to get to know her better, he meant it. He'd spent the entire afternoon thinking about her. She had been so quiet on the ride to work, deepening that mysterious quality he found so fasci-nating. Most girls he'd known gabbed nonstop or tried to impress him. Instead, he found himself wanting to impress her. However, that seemed to be the last thing she was interested in.

He turned Gravy around, then headed for the road. During the ride home he tried to sort things out, but it was useless. All he knew for sure was that she didn't hate him so much that she wouldn't let him take her to work. At this point, that was all that mattered.

Lately, it seemed, Miriam collected regrets. She added one more to her growing cache by wishing she'd just told Seth to leave her alone Tuesday night when he dropped her off from work. If she had, she wouldn't be standing on her front porch this morning, waiting for him to pick her up.

Maybe he wouldn't show. The thought filled her with relief. And, of course, disappointment. She wondered how long she could handle her contradictory emotions.

She looked out into the near-barren fields surrounding her house. Across the road she could see her neighbor's herd of beef cattle nibbling at the short, frosty grass in the shadow of the huge white barn.

The days were shorter now, and dawn had just broken a little while ago, swathing the heavens in transparent washes of pale yellow and dark gold. There were only a few clouds in the sky, and she predicted it would be a sunny day, but cold. Folding her arms across her chest underneath her cloak and seeing her breath take the form of wispy puffs in the air, she wished she could feel some of the sun's warmth now.

Miriam checked the small clock fob pinned to the inside of her coat. Seven-fifteen. She'd left the house early to escape her mother's probing questions about

Seth picking her up. Explaining the situation would be pointless, since she didn't understand what was going on herself. She wondered if Seth even knew.

What did he mean about wanting to get to know her? She'd pondered that the last two nights, but didn't come up with any answers. She still couldn't get past the thought that his attentions were one big joke. Or maybe he was involved in some kind of community service program as part of his reparations for the accident, where he had to be nice to a lonely girl for a couple of days.

She rolled her eyes. Even her thoughts didn't make sense.

The *clip-clop* of the horse's hooves alerted her to Seth's approach. Just like Tuesday, he was a little early. She walked to the end of her driveway so he wouldn't have to pull in. When she saw he was going to scramble out to open the door for her, she held up her hand and opened it herself.

"Got it," she said. Warmth enveloped her as she sat down.

"Cold morning." He blew on his hands and rubbed them together. "Should have worn my gloves." Picking up the reins, he glanced at her. "Ready to go?"

"Ya." She was still focused on his hands. They were huge. Strong looking, but not weathered like most Amishmen's hands were.

She pulled away her gaze. What was she doing, staring at his hands? They were just hands, for goodness' sake. And she had no business wondering what they would feel like, clasping her own.

"Did you sleep well last night?" Seth tapped the reins on the horse's flanks, and the buggy lurched forward.

As with every question he asked, she wondered why he cared. "Well enough." Then, before she could stop herself, she asked, "You?"

"Pretty good."

Silence engulfed the buggy once again. Not the comfortable kind. The self-conscious kind, where she wished she could just disappear and escape the awkwardness of it all.

Seth lifted the brim of his hat with two of those long fingers of his, pushing it a little farther back on his head. "Nice bag you have there."

"My quilt bag?"

"*Ya. Mei mudder* and sisters make quilts." He grinned. "But I decided it wasn't for me."

A chuckle escaped her lips before she could prevent it. "I can't picture you holding a needle and thread."

"You'd be surprised what I learned at my *mudder*'s knee."

"Then you know how to sew?"

He shook his head. "Hardly. But when I was a kid, she let me help her in the kitchen sometimes. I learned to cook a few meals. Nothing complicated."

"Like what?" Despite her vow to be uninterested, she found herself intrigued.

"Meat loaf, lasagna, tuna salad, and of course, whoopee pies."

"Whoopee pies aren't that easy to make."

"Sure they are. They're just a little time-consuming. I haven't made any in a long time, not since I was a little kid." He looked at her. "Do you like them?"

"They're okay."

"But not as *gut* as raspberry fudge?"

"Nothing is as *gut* as raspberry fudge."

They both laughed, and Seth gave her a grin. But it

was a different smile this time, more genuine, not so calculated and forced. She put her hand on her stomach to calm the swirl of butterflies.

Resist!

"So what kind of quilts do you make?" he asked, nudging the horse to turn right onto the main street.

"Just your average quilt. Nothing special."

"I think Sarah would disagree. She was pretty complimentary about your work."

"It's nothing compared to my grandmother's. She made the most beautiful quilts. Every stitch was perfect, and her eye for color was amazing." Her gaze dropped back to her hands. "Sorry. I'm sure hearing about quilts is *really* exciting."

He shrugged. "Maybe not exciting, but interesting. I never understood how a woman could sit in a chair for hours making tiny stitches on small squares of fabric. That would drive me crazy."

"I could say the same for what your father does. It must take a lot of patience to cut and carve all those intricate designs he makes."

"It does. But he loves to do it."

"Just like I love quilting."

He smiled again. "Exactly."

By the time they reached the fabric shop, all the tension that had been building in Miriam was nearly gone. Their conversation hadn't been of much import, but it had been nice. Friendly. Comfortable. She'd never thought she could be comfortable around Seth Fisher.

He pulled the buggy into the small parking lot at the end of the block.

She turned and looked at him. "*Danki*. For the ride. I appreciate it."

"You're welcome. So I'll see you at five, then."

"What?"

His brows furrowed. "Do you get off at a different time on Thursdays?"

"*Nee,* but…Seth, you don't have to do this. There are lots of people who can give me a ride."

"I'm sure there are."

"And I'm also sure you have other things more important to do than pick me up and take me home."

He turned in his seat and looked at her straight on. "Now, that's where you're wrong, Miriam."

Her guard shot up again, but not as quickly this time. Warmth enveloped her as he held her gaze.

"You'll be late for work," he said softly. "We'll finish the conversation when I pick you up."

"But—"

He held up his hand. "No buts. See you at five." He reached for the reins and dipped his head toward the buggy door.

She complied, because he was right—she would be late if she dallied any longer. Giving him one last look and seeing the resolute expression on his face, she knew he would be there at five to take her home.

But this would be the last time.

Seth pulled out of the parking lot, fairly pleased with himself.

Carrying Miriam to work this morning had been pleasant. Far more pleasant than the trip on Tuesday, when she'd done everything in her power to be as bland and uninteresting as possible, but he'd seen right through her. She wasn't the type of girl to run at the mouth over nothing. This morning proved that.

It had taken him a while, but he had finally realized his mistake. He'd overdone it. He'd been too charming, too earnest. He could only imagine how he'd appeared to her. While that tactic had worked with girls in the past, he should have known it wouldn't with her. He didn't have to be an extra-strength version of himself to pique her interest. With other girls he'd always felt the need to be "on." To be the center of their universe, at least until he was tired of them. But maybe it hadn't been the girls he'd been weary of. Maybe he'd just been sick of the false version of himself.

With Miriam, he didn't have to worry about that. She responded to the real Seth. From now on he intended to be as real with her as he possibly could.

Chapter Eight

"Is everything all *recht,* Miriam?"

Miriam looked at her mother. "*Ya.* Why do you ask?"

"Because you just sewed the tie of your *kapp* to the quilt."

Glancing down, she saw her mother was right. She hadn't even noticed that the ribbons of her *kapp* had been dangling on the quilt laid out on the kitchen table in front of her. Carefully she removed the needle and pulled out the three tiny stitches, then took the flat, white ribbons and tucked them into the front of her dress.

"You seem preoccupied tonight." Mary continued with her own stitching.

They were repairing one of *Grossmammi* Emma's quilts, a navy blue and cream–colored Amish star design. It was one of the first quilts her grandmother had made as a young girl, and after almost ninety years some of the stitches had loosened.

Miriam rethreaded her needle with navy blue thread. "*Nee.* Well, maybe just a little."

"Anything you'd like to talk about?"

She looked at her mother, who had her head bowed as she formed small, perfectly even stitches. Perfectly parted gray hair peeked out from her *kapp*, and she paused to adjust her eyeglasses before she resumed her stitching. There was a considerable age gap between her parents and Miriam, their youngest child—over forty years. Still, while she had a close relationship with both of them, she had never confided in her mother about Seth. She wasn't sure she ever wanted to.

The back door to the kitchen opened, and Lydia stepped inside, saving Miriam from having to answer *Mamm*'s question.

"Hello," her sister said, holding a large wicker basket by its handle. She set it down on the kitchen counter. "Here are the soaps you asked for."

Mary put down her needle and rose from her seat. *"Danki,"* she said, peering into the basket and examining the contents. "These will make lovely Christmas presents for the family."

Lydia gave her a satisfied smile, then glanced down at the quilt. "Making repairs?"

"Ya," Miriam replied. "We're starting with this one, since it's the oldest. I'd like to reinforce as much stitching as I can on all her quilts."

"They certainly are beautiful," Lydia said, nodding. "You really are taking *gut* care of them, Miriam."

"Can you stay for some coffee?" Mary asked. "I've got a few cookies and half a pumpkin pie left over from Sunday's potluck."

Lydia shook her head. *"Nee.* I'm sorry, *Mamm,* but I can't. I just came by to drop these off. I know you want to get them wrapped to take on First Christmas." She looked at Miriam. "I have to go into Paradise tomorrow morning. I can give you a ride to work, if you need one."

Miriam hesitated. Seth had offered to pick her up again in the morning, and again her resolve melted and she'd said yes. They'd had another pleasant ride home, and she found she really enjoyed his company. Yet she knew this had to end. Soon Seth would find something—or someone—else to pay attention to, and he'd forget about her. But a tiny part of her desperately wanted to enjoy his interest as long as it lasted.

"*Danki* for offering, but Seth's picking me up in the morning."

"Seth?" Lydia's brow lifted with interest.

"A friend," she responded, wishing she hadn't said his name.

"He's been nice enough to pick her up and take her to work the past couple of days," Mary added. "He's also been bringing her home. It's been a big help."

Lydia gave Miriam a pointed look, but Miriam purposely blanked her expression. She didn't need her sister's well-intentioned interference.

Lydia just shot her a knowing smile, then gave their mother a hug and turned to leave. "I probably won't see you until we go to Sarah and David's. Tell Pop I said hello."

"I will. He's at a church meeting, but when he gets home I'll tell him."

After Lydia left, Miriam tried to focus on the quilt again. All night she'd been chasing away thoughts of Seth—romantic thoughts, to her dismay—with little success. Actually saying his name aloud made his image in her mind more real and harder to dispel.

Mary sat down at the table, but she didn't pick up her needle. "Is Seth the reason you're so pensive tonight?"

Miriam looked up, ready to deny it, but unable to do so. She nodded.

"Do you like him, Miriam?"

"He's a...friend."

"Are you sure that's all?"

Miriam glanced up. "Of course. Why would there be anything else?"

Mary smiled. "He's going to a lot of trouble to carry you to and from work."

"I know. I told him not to, but he keeps insisting."

"Seems to me like he wants to be more than friends."

Miriam shook her head. "That's impossible."

"Why?"

Miriam suddenly felt transported back to eighth grade. She closed her eyes, wishing away the past. "Because it just is."

"Oh, honey." Mary placed her hand over Miriam's. "I don't know why you find it so hard to believe Seth is interested in you."

"You don't understand."

"Then help me to."

Miriam hesitated. She'd never told anyone what happened on the playground long ago. But her mother's genuine concern tugged at her, untying her pain until she couldn't hold it in any longer.

Saying it out loud made her feel slightly foolish, but also a bit relieved. When she finished, she looked down at the table as she smoothed a wrinkle in her *gross-mammi*'s beautiful quilt.

"Miriam," her mother said softly. "I'm so sorry. You're right, Seth was cruel. But he was fourteen. Everyone knows fourteen-year-old boys do stupid things."

"Except for fourteen-year-old girls."

"True, but they eventually figure it out. And the best thing is that no one stays fourteen forever. We make mistakes. We grow up; we learn from those mistakes; we mature." She dipped her head to look at Miriam. "Do you really think Seth is still that thoughtless teenager?"

"*Nee*...well, maybe?"

Mary laughed. "As long as you're sure."

Miriam couldn't help but smile.

"Seth's not the same boy he was back then. A lot has happened to him, especially the accident. Trauma has a way of changing people. Some for worse, and some for better."

Miriam thought about that for a moment. Seth had told her he was different, and she'd seen glimpses of that. But had he really changed? Even if he had, that didn't explain his sudden interest in her.

Mary looked at Miriam for a moment, her blue eyes softening. "I'm thinking your problem with Seth has more to do with you than it does with him."

Miriam frowned. "What do you mean?"

"You're letting a comment made by a young boy several years ago dictate your behavior today. You've kept most people, especially young men, at arm's length."

"Can you blame me? What he said is true." Miriam sighed. "I am a four-eyed beanpole. Still."

Mary lifted Miriam's chin. "Let me tell you what I see. I see a young woman who is intelligent and good with people. I see a fantastic quilter who has skills and artistry I could only dream of. I see someone who cares for her family and who takes her job seriously. I see someone with a big heart she's just waiting to share with someone."

Tears came to Miriam's eyes. She should deflect her mother's compliments, reflect the humility she knew was expected of her. But at that moment, she really needed to hear those words.

"Those are the qualities you need to focus on, Miriam. Not what's on the surface. Look at Seth. He has the body of a young man, but he can't walk without his stick. He has a beautiful face, but it's forever scarred. Yet he carries himself with confidence. He's not letting his physical imperfections keep him from being himself, or from getting what he wants. And though you deny it, you might have to accept that it's you he's wanting."

Wiping her eyes with her fingers, Miriam said, "But I don't understand why. He could have his pick of any girl. Any *pretty* girl. Why would he choose me?"

A small smile formed on Mary's face. "Because he sees what I see. He sees you for the wonderful woman you are. If you ask me, I think he's a smart *mann*."

Miriam chuckled through her tears. "*Danki*. I really needed to hear that."

Taking her daughter's hand, Mary said, "Maybe I've been neglectful in telling you."

"*Nee,* I've just been prideful."

"Listen to me, Miriam. We're all prideful; it's something we fight every day. It's a battle we can't win without God's help. Remember—God doesn't care what you look like on the outside. What he cares about is your heart. And you have a beautiful heart, *dochder*." Tears glistened in her eyes. "Don't ever forget that."

Miriam smiled and wiped a tear from underneath her glasses. Both women resumed working on the quilt. While Miriam concentrated more carefully on repairing the stitches, her mother's words remained in her mind.

Was it possible? Had the boy who thought she was a four-eyed beanpole grown into a man who truly liked her? Her mind couldn't grasp the concept.

But her heart was willing to try.

Something was different about her.

Seth couldn't put his finger on it, but Miriam seemed more lighthearted the next morning when he picked her up. When he opened the buggy door, she *almost* smiled at him. He wanted to ask her what was making her happy, but they hadn't gotten to that point in their relationship yet, where he felt he could pry.

Relationship. When had he started thinking about Miriam in terms of a relationship? He couldn't pinpoint the exact moment, but he took her agreement to let him take her to work as a sign that he was making some headway. Right now he would be happy to move past acquaintance to friendship.

And maybe something more.

She didn't say anything until they were well on their way to Paradise. They had just passed a large field of grazing black-and-white dairy cows when she said, "Tell me about your accident."

Seth's hands tightened on the reins. It was an inevitable question; he just hadn't expected her to ask it so soon. Or so bluntly.

"Not much to tell. I got drunk, got in my car, and hit a tree."

"Why?"

He turned and looked at her. "What do you mean, why?"

"Why would you do something like that?"

"I didn't do it on purpose," he said, flustered.

"Somebody forced you to drink and then made you drive?"

"Nee!" He pulled on Gravy's reins, slowing the horse down. The road was clear of cars, so he took the opportunity to face Miriam.

She glanced down at her hands, her glasses slipping down her nose a bit. "I didn't mean to make you mad. You said yesterday that you were different. I just wanted to know how that happened."

He blinked. She'd never expressed an interest in knowing anything about him before. But why did she have to ask about that? Because he knew that he couldn't sidestep the truth. Not with her.

Seth swiveled around and faced the road, but he kept Gravy moving at a slow pace. Let the *Englisch* drivers honk their horns. He didn't care. They hogged the road anyway.

"After I finished school, I went to work with my *daed*. That didn't last very long. We fought all the time, mostly about stupid stuff. I see now that I wasn't doing my share, but at the time I thought he was being too critical, too harsh. At the same time I'd made a few *Englisch* friends from the local high school. They invited me to their parties, and I brought them to some of ours." He glanced at her. "I'm not talking about the frolics and singings. I'm talking about the drinking parties."

"I know. I never went to those parties, but I knew a few girls that did."

"I'm glad you didn't go. Because if you had been there, you would have likely seen me. And it would be hard to look you in the eye right now if you had. I'm not proud of the way I was back then. But at the time I thought I was living the life. Finally my *daed* got fed up with me and fired me, with *gut* reason. That's when I left for Lancaster, got a job in a factory, and bought the car. I honestly thought they had given up on me, especially my *daed*. So if they didn't care, I didn't. One thing I knew for sure, I couldn't stay in Paradise. I couldn't join the church and be Amish."

"But you did," Miriam said. "You came back."

"It's only by the grace of God that I'm here. And I found out after my accident that my parents had prayed for me every day while I was gone. They hadn't given up on me. They had given me to the Lord."

A chill ran down Miriam's back as she thought about how difficult that must have been for Seth's parents.

"I really screwed up, Miriam. I didn't even have a driver's license at the time. I bought the car used off a friend of one of my *Englisch* buddies. I paid cash and drove it illegally. I got my hair cut; I wore *Englisch* clothes. I tried to strip away everything about me that was Amish."

The loud blast of a horn blared in their ears, making Miriam jump. The car whizzed by, but Seth didn't look at the driver. "Sorry," he said to her. "I'll go faster."

She shook her head. "We're fine."

"Okay." It pleased him that she wanted to lengthen their time together. But he hadn't told her all the details. What would she think of him then?

Chapter Nine

Miriam found herself drawn in to Seth's explanation. She had never felt the pull of the world, and she didn't have a *rumschpringe* the way some kids did. She joined the church when she was eighteen and had never had any doubts about her faith. Listening to Seth's story only reaffirmed that she had made the right decision. The outside world held nothing but trouble.

"As I said before, my parents were praying for me," he continued. "And not only them. My brothers and sisters, they were all praying. And God must have heard them, because the night of the accident, I was so down on myself I didn't know what to do. I was tired of the partying, tired of my so-called friends who were only interested in what they could score—booze, women, drugs."

As he spoke, he mixed in more English with his Pennsylvania *Deitsch,* as if he were being transported back to relive his time with the outlanders. "I felt like I was divided in two—the wild part of me that longed for worldly things, and the Amish part that longed for my family. I missed them so much, more than I ever thought I would. I wanted to come back, but I didn't want to admit that they were right and I was wrong.

"That night I was staying at some guy's apartment—I didn't even really know who he was, but I needed a place to crash—and I drank more than I ever had before. I knew I couldn't stay, not just in that apartment, but in that world. I didn't belong there. But I couldn't go home either. I didn't know where I belonged, and that scared me more than anything."

They had reached Lincoln Avenue, and Seth steered Gravy to the left, toward the fabric shop. People, both *Englischers* and Amish, were already walking up and down the sidewalks, looking into the candle, quilt, and handicraft stores, waiting for them to open. The contrast between the two peoples was striking—the *Englischers* with coats and jackets of bright colors and modern styles alongside the Amish in their dark cloaks, coats, bonnets, and hats.

When Seth completed the turn, he continued talking. "One thing I did know is that I couldn't stand to be in that apartment another minute. So I got my keys, somehow made it to my car, and got in. I hadn't gone very far when I swerved off the road and hit the tree. I don't remember much after that, until I woke up in the hospital after I'd had surgery on my leg."

He paused, casting a glance at Miriam. She stared at his profile, the scar on his face so prominent when they were this close to each other. She could only imagine the pain he'd gone through, not only physical, but inside too.

"They had given me a lot of painkillers, so everything was pretty fuzzy for a couple of days. But once the haze had cleared and I could think straight, I realized what a gift God had given me. The gift of life, along with a second chance. I wasn't about to disappoint him."

"But what about your *Englisch* friends? Didn't they want you to come back with them?"

"That's just the thing, Miriam. There was no bond between us, other than hanging out and having fun. I think the accident probably scared a few of them, too, because it could have easily been one of them that smashed into a tree. Whatever the reason, they didn't visit. But you know who was there? My family. My *mudder* came every day and stayed as long as she could. You know how far away the hospital is. She had to hire a taxi to take her there. My *daed* would come when he could, as well as my brothers and sisters. They never gave up on me. Not when I strayed, and not when I got hurt because of my own dumb choices. That's when it became clear. I belonged with my family. I belonged in the church. I was Amish, and for the first time in my life, I was glad to be."

Miriam sat there for a moment, taking in everything he'd said. Then she spoke. "I don't understand."

His head whipped toward her, surprise etched on his features. "You don't? What part confuses you?"

"I understood what you said. What happened to you. I guess what confuses me is why you felt so divided. I've never experienced that myself. I always knew where I belonged."

"I can sum it up in one word. *Hochmut.*"

"Pride?"

He nodded. "I was overflowing with it. I don't know how people stood me back then. From the time I was small I'd been able to manipulate a situation to get what I wanted. I thought I was too *gut* for the Amish. I wanted to be cool, like the *Englisch* I hung around with. With them I had no rules. I could wear anything, say anything, do anything.

"I had a lot of time to think in the hospital, and then when I came home to finish my recovery. I also had a lot of time to pray. God showed me some things about myself over those five months. How I had put my family through so much pain because of my selfishness. That I had treated so many people so badly. I wasn't going to do that again. I had a lot to make up for, and as soon as I was able to walk without crutches, I got started."

As he spoke his last words, a sinking feeling came over Miriam. "I see."

He pulled into the parking lot and stopped the buggy. Turning to her, he smiled. "Well, we're here, and I talked your ear off. I'll be by to pick you up this afternoon, *ya?*"

She shook her head. "I have a ride already." She didn't, but she would find one. He had finally given her the strength she needed to turn him down. For good.

His smile dimmed. "Okay. Then I'll pick you up tomorrow morning."

"I don't think so." She opened the door and hurried out, keeping her head down so he couldn't see her face. Because if he looked at her one more time, the tears she was holding on to so tightly would fall. She scurried to the fabric shop, yanking her key out of her patchwork bag as she did, blinking back the tears stinging her eyes. She wouldn't cry. Not now, when they would have customers in a few minutes.

It took her more than three tries to unlock the door. When she finally did, she ran into the store and headed straight for the back room, not turning on the lights.

She went into the bathroom and slammed the door, taking a deep breath as she leaned over the sink.

Now she knew why Seth had talked to her at the singing. Why he had bought her raspberry fudge. Why he was taking her to and from work.

Guilt.

He was paying penance for his sins. How could she have been so stupid as to believe her mother's words? Or to let herself entertain romantic feelings for him? Seth didn't see anything special in her. All he saw was a way to assuage his guilt. If only she had discovered it sooner. Before she had let him back in her heart.

Seth sat in the buggy, stunned. He couldn't move. He couldn't do anything, not when his mind and emotions had been knocked so far out of whack. He had worried about what Miriam's reaction might be to his confession, but he hadn't thought she would be so cold. So harsh. So unfeeling.

But that wasn't exactly true. When she got out of the buggy, she tried to hide her face from him, but he caught a quick glimpse of her expression before she ran inside.

She was upset. Deeply upset. That wasn't his intent at all.

It hadn't been easy, laying himself open like that. But it had been cathartic, and until she had shot out of his buggy like a bullet out of a rifle, he had felt better. He hadn't told anyone the things he told her. He had trusted her. If anyone would understand what he'd gone through and what he had learned, he thought she would. She was smart and compassionate. But he'd also thought she was nonjudgmental, and clearly he'd been mistaken.

He had half a mind to go into the shop and see her. Ask what she was so upset about.

But why should he? She had told him yesterday she had feelings. Well, he had them too, and right now they'd taken a beating. Grabbing the reins, he steered the buggy around and left.

His mind whirled as he drove back to his house. The sun was glowing bright in the morning sky, but he barely noticed. Why was he bothering with her anyway? She had been nothing but trouble since he'd had the stupid idea of getting to know her better. He'd spent the rest of his Christmas money on her. He'd gone out of his way to take her to and from work—it wasn't as if he lived down the street from her; his house was a good four miles away. And what did he get for his trouble?

The buggy door slammed in his face.

Fine. He was done. He had better things to do than chase her around. There were a dozen other girls who would welcome his attention with open arms.

But none of them were like Miriam.

He sighed, all his internal bluster gone. One word kept piercing through the mixed-up scramble of emotions consuming him.

Demut.

Humility. He'd rejected the trait years ago, preferring to embrace his pride instead. Taking that road had led to near destruction.

He had told himself that he was through with being proud, done with making sure his ego was intact. He wanted to be clothed in *demut,* to be humble, to follow Jesus' perfect example. Today had been his first true test of that new resolve, and he had failed miserably.

The path was before him, divided in two. He could leave her alone while he pursued someone who didn't make him feel like the bug on the bottom of a boot. Or he could scrape off all remnants of his pride and find out why she got upset so suddenly. He had no idea which road to choose.

"You sure you don't want anything to eat before you go to work?"

Miriam nodded. "I'm sure."

"But you didn't eat much last night." Mary set the plate of pancakes on the table. "Are you ill?"

"*Nee.*" Only heartsick.

All through the night and this morning she tried to leave Seth in the dust of her memories. A small part of her hoped he might ignore what she said and pick her up after work anyway, but he didn't. Not that she was surprised. Guilt stabbed at her, but she pushed it away. Seth wasn't the hurt party here; she was.

But as much as she tried not to think of him, he kept stubbornly popping back up, like a jack-in-the-box with a broken lid. She should never have gone to the singing Sunday night. If she hadn't, she wouldn't be trying to fit the shattered pieces of her heart back together. The next time Lydia tried to force her to do something she didn't want to do, she would stand her ground.

"I wish you'd eat something, Miriam. You're thin enough as it is."

She'd heard that comment all her life, from various family members and friends who had good intentions when shoving food in her face. She couldn't help being thin. Just like she couldn't help being unattractive. That was how she was.

That was who she *really* was. A four-eyed beanpole. Despite what her mother said.

"All right," Mary said. "If you're not eating, then go

ahead and tell Pop you're ready to go. He's on a tight schedule today." Normally a very placid woman, Mary gave her a stern look. "Next time don't wait until the last minute to ask for a ride."

"I won't. I promise."

"Too bad Seth couldn't pick you up today. He's freed up your *daed* to finish up some projects around here. Ah, well." Mary scooted away to finish cleaning up the rest of the dishes.

Miriam stared at the short stack of pancakes before her. Her stomach turned at the sight of them. She rose from the table and smoothed the skirt of her sky blue dress, adjusting the apron she wore over it. Checking to make sure the pins were secure in her *kapp,* she donned her cloak and put on her gloves. After slipping on her black shoes, she went out the back to find her father, who was hitching up the horse in the barn.

"*Danki,* Pop," she said, the cold morning air seeping through her black cloak. She shivered. "I appreciate the ride."

He gave her a curt nod, his gray beard bobbing against the collar of his black coat. She could see that both her parents were put out with her, and for good reason. But she was willing to deal with her guilt and her father's gruff demeanor if it meant she wouldn't have to see Seth Fisher again.

"*Herr* Herschberger?"

Both Miriam and her father turned around at the sound of his name. She drew in a sharp breath. Seth was standing there, leaning on his walking stick, looking her straight in the eye. His expression was inscrutable.

"May I take Miriam to work?" he asked.

It was as if her feet had been nailed to the ground.

She couldn't move; she couldn't say anything. Only silently pray her father would say no.

"*Ya,* Seth," he said, sounding relieved. He let go of the horse's reins and adjusted his glasses. "And *danki.* I have a generator to repair, and I promised the woman I'd have it done by noon."

Miriam closed her eyes. Was it too much to ask God to answer her prayers just once?

"Miriam, go with Seth," her father said, hanging up the horse's reins on a peg on the barn's wooden wall. He walked past them toward the house. "Oh, and can you bring her home too? I can pay you for your time and trouble."

"That won't be necessary. I'll bring her home, but I'll accept no payment."

After her father left, the two of them stood in the barn, neither of them moving. Seth's expression seemed set in stone. It dawned on her that she'd never seen him angry before. But if he was mad at her, then why was he picking her up? As long as she lived she would never understand this man.

"Ready?" His tone wasn't the least bit friendly.

"You don't have to do this," she said. "I don't want to bother you."

His blue eyes softened a bit, and he tilted his head to the side. "It's not a bother."

Her heartbeat doubled. With a tiny shake of her head she steeled her resolve. "I don't *want* you to pick me up."

His expression hardened once more. "And why is that?"

"Because…because…" She couldn't bring herself to say the words.

He scrubbed his hand over his face, then pulled on

his clean-shaven chin. "Miriam, are you trying to drive me *narrisch?*"

"I'm trying to drive you away!"

"Fine, but you at least owe me a reason. And an explanation as to why the minute after I poured my heart out to you, you shut the door in my face."

"You want to know why?" She could feel her mouth trembling with ire, but she was powerless to stem the emotion. "I don't like being used."

"Used? How have I used you?"

"You think I don't realize what you're doing?"

"Miriam, stop answering questions with questions. Would you just tell me what you mean?"

She licked her dry lips. "I'm not a balm for your guilt."

Seth couldn't believe this. Here he was, standing in her parents' barn in the freezing cold, trying to be a nice guy and give her a ride. Instead, he found himself on the receiving end of her accusation. He shoved his hat off his forehead and stared at her. "Unbelievable. You think I'm doing this because I feel guilty?"

She nodded. "Why else?"

His hand fisted tightly around his walking stick. Again he asked himself why he was here. He'd gone home last night, determined not to see her again, choosing pride over humility. Then he had prayed and asked God for direction, only to discover the Lord's ideas were the opposite of his own. When he woke up, he headed straight for the barn and hitched up the horse. Now he was here, trying to figure out how everything got so complicated. Relationships weren't supposed to be this hard.

There was that word again. *Relationship.* Right now

they could barely look at each other. This was as far from a relationship as two people could get.

The air between them was as frigid as the temperature in the barn. In one of the stalls he could hear the rustle of the Herschbergers' horse. Seth's hand relaxed, but only because it couldn't stay in that stiff position.

"Miriam, it's true; I do feel bad for a lot of the things I did back then, including what I said to you. But I thought when I told you I was sorry I had paid for that transgression."

She didn't say anything, merely pressed her lips together in a thin line.

Why wasn't she responding?

Moisture suddenly collected in her eyes.

Then he knew. He'd hurt her more than he realized. Had she been carrying around that pain for five long years?

"Miriam," he said again, softening his voice. "I was so young back then. So stupid and full of myself. It was a throwaway comment from a dumb kid trying to make his friends laugh. I didn't mean it."

"*Ya,* you did." She looked at him, and his heart shattered. "Because it's true. Now, if you'll please take me to work. I'm going to be late."

Chapter Ten

Seth was tempted to curse. Salty language had filled his mouth during his *rumschpringe,* but he had put that, and so many other things, behind him. Yet old habits died hard, and he had to bite his bottom lip to keep from swearing.

Miriam didn't say a word on the ride into Paradise. More than once he thought about drawing her into conversation but decided against it. He needed more time. They needed more time. Pat answers weren't going to solve this problem or convince Miriam that her words were so, so wrong. That she thought that way about herself broke his heart. Knowing he was the source of it just about killed him.

Seth pulled up to the parking lot. Miriam grabbed her bag, that quirky bag made of so many colors and patterns it should hurt his eyes, but somehow looked like a work of art.

"Miriam." At first he thought she would ignore him, and he was grateful when she paused. "We'll talk more when I pick you up this evening."

She hesitated one more moment, then left.

He wanted to go after her, but he held back. Not

only did he know it wouldn't do any good; he wouldn't have been able to catch up to her with his bum leg. He hung his head, trying to stem his frustration at being so physically limited. If it weren't for his injury, he could have tracked her down and at least made another attempt at settling things.

He stared at his leg. It was thinner than the other one, but the difference wasn't noticeable through his trousers. Still, he knew, and it would be a long time before he would gain his full strength. Some days he handled that knowledge better than others. And sometimes, like right now, he hated his crippled body.

He took a deep breath. If it weren't for his injury, he wouldn't be here, dealing with the past and trying to forge a new future. The somber thought yanked him out of his brooding.

He looked up and slapped the reins against Gravy's flanks, guiding him toward the road. He couldn't go after Miriam, and he didn't think he should. The only thing he could do was go home. And wait. For what, he didn't know.

On the ride home he thought about what she'd said. How she felt about herself. Granted, there were women out there with curvier figures and prettier faces, but now that didn't matter to him. At one time it had; he couldn't deny that. There was only one woman he was interested in, one woman who could drive him crazy one minute then sneak into his heart the next.

Miriam Herschberger.

He had thought he had his work cut out for him before when he just wanted to be friends with her, but now that he admitted his feelings, the challenge seemed insurmountable. Not only did he have to battle his own demons; he had to help Miriam fight hers.

* * *

"Aww, honey. You should have stayed home today." Tammy ushered Miriam to the back office soon after Seth had dropped her off.

Miriam fought to gain her composure. "I'm so stupid," she said. "I'm stupid for thinking he had changed, stupid for hoping he liked me."

"You're not stupid. You're human. And unfortunately we were created to love and be loved. It's just hard to find the right person. Trust me, I know. I had to learn the hard way."

"I'm not in love with Seth." Miriam sniffed and reached for a tissue.

"You can say that, but a girl doesn't melt into tears over a guy unless she feels something for him."

"I'm not crying."

"Not *yet*." Tammy gave her a sympathetic smile.

Miriam sighed. If he had said something, just one word of denial after she admitted she was ugly, things would have been different. Instead he just looked at her. The silence spoke volumes.

"He's supposed to come back for me after work," she said.

"Do you want him to?"

She shook her head vehemently. *"Nee."*

"All right. We'll close up a little early today—"

"But—"

"And I'll take you home."

When Miriam tried to protest again, Tammy waved her off. "We've both been working hard enough lately. We deserve a little reward, okay?"

Miriam nodded. Tammy was resolute, and when she set her mind on something, she couldn't be persuaded off course. Besides, if the shop closed up early, she would surely miss Seth. And that was all she cared about.

The day went by quickly, as they had a steady stream of customers. Christmas was a little over a week away, and people were buying last-minute gifts such as sewing supplies, stitchery kits, and skeins of yarn. After Miriam had checked out the last customer, Tammy went to the door and turned the sign to Closed.

"Are you ready to go home?" she said.

"But the store's a mess."

"It will wait until morning. Who's the boss here?"

Miriam allowed a little smile. "You are."

"So I make the rules, and I say when we can bend them. And we're bending them backward today. Let's go."

Closed?

Seth tilted his hat back a little. The shop was closed? He checked his timepiece. No, he was on time. Even a few minutes early. He looked at the sign again and grimaced.

He'd missed her.

He'd spent the entire day thinking about what he would say to her. How he could reassure her that what she thought of herself wasn't true, and it wasn't what he saw when he looked at her. He even practiced some of his points out loud as he drove to town to pick her up. Now he couldn't say anything to her, because she was gone.

Turning around, he walked back to the buggy, trying to figure out what to do. The businesses lining Lincoln Avenue were adorned on the outside and inside with beautiful gold, green, and red ribbons and ornaments, holly boughs, and wreaths, and other silver sparkly things, but he barely noticed the frippery. Instead he focused on what had happened to Miriam. Her boss probably took her home, since they'd closed up early. The thought of driving back to her house popped into his mind, but there was no guarantee she would be there. It probably would be a wasted trip.

It seemed like he was spinning his wheels in a mud pit, and not for the first time.

He untied Gravy, then threw his walking stick inside the buggy, hurled himself in, and set off. He scratched an itch on his cheek, feeling the scar. Then he looked at his walking stick. What a pair they were. *He* was the damaged goods, not her, no matter what she thought of herself. But maybe they were both too broken—him on the outside, her on the inside.

Thirty minutes later he was back home and heading for his *daed*'s shop. Officially he was supposed to start work next week, but he had been filling his time in between chauffeuring Miriam with a special project. He didn't want to work on it today, but if he didn't it wouldn't be finished by Christmas.

Entering the shop, he saw his father hunched over a table, a chisel in his leathery hands. With speed and precision gained over years of carving, *Daed* made wide, shallow cuts in the dense wood. Usually he worked with oak, but Seth saw that today he was using cherry. Melvin pushed on the chisel a couple of times, then brushed away the thin strips of excess wood.

Not wanting to interrupt him, Seth limped over to another table where his project lay. He ran his hand over the wood he had sanded smooth yesterday. If only he could sand away the rough edges of his life so easily.

"Didn't hear you come in."

Seth turned to see his father rising from his chair. He arched his back a bit, then shook out his arms, stiff from being in one position for so long.

"I didn't want to disturb you," said Seth.

"You're not." Melvin strolled over to Seth's workstation. He picked up the sanded wood and examined it. "Looks good." He put it back down.

"*Danki*. Where's Noah?"

"Making a delivery. He'll be back in a bit."

Seth nodded, then turned to stare at the wood. He looked at it for a long time, not really seeing it, as he tried to figure out what to do about Miriam, if he should do anything at all.

"Something on your mind?"

He started, not only at the sound of his father's voice, but at the interest in his tone. His first reaction was to tell him nothing, to say everything was fine. He'd never revealed his personal problems to his father before.

But maybe this time he should. Maybe that had been one of their problems all along—he and his *daed* had never really talked *to* each other. Sure, they'd talked *at* each other, and had done a lot of yelling along the way. But now, for the first time ever, Seth wanted his father's counsel.

"*Ya*," he said. "There is something on my mind."

"Anything to do with that gal at the fabric shop?"

"*Ya*," he repeated.

Melvin shook his head. "Womenfolk."

With a small smile Seth said, "They never used to be this complicated."

"I reckon you never cared as much before."

Seth nodded, unable to deny the truth and surprised by his father's flawless assessment. "Exactly. I do care, more than I realized."

"I take it you're courting her."

"*Ya, Daed.* I am. At least I'm trying to. But I'm not sure I want to bother with her anymore. I've tried everything I can think of to get her to just like me. I charmed her, bought her a gift, gave her rides to and from work, but she doesn't want to have anything to do with me. I don't understand it."

His father tugged on his nearly completely gray beard, which hung past his throat. Then he ran his fingers through it, something he always did when he was deep in thought. He peered at Seth, tilting his head, as if he were sizing up his son. "Sounds like a problem."

"It is."

"Leave her alone."

Seth's eyebrows shot up. "What?"

"Leave her be."

"I—" He looked at the pieces of wood on the table, suddenly regretting being so open with his *daed*. His father didn't understand at all. "I can't do that."

"Why not? You just said you didn't want to be bothered."

"*Ya,* but…I didn't mean it to come out that way… I…I don't know." He sighed. "I don't know anything anymore."

"*Ach.* That's a first for you."

"*Ya,* it is." His leg was aching, so he pulled up a stool and sat down.

"You've always gotten what you wanted, Seth." Melvin put his hand on his son's shoulder as he walked past him. "Things have come easily to you. Too easily, I'm thinkin'. Maybe now you've finally found something you can't have. That's where your real trouble is. Accepting that something you want real bad is out of reach."

"So I'm just supposed to forget about her?"

"Maybe." He cocked his head to the side. "Or maybe you just have to work harder, harder than you ever had to in your life. Guess you need to figure out if she's worth it." Melvin paused. "What did God tell you to do?"

His cheeks heating, Seth said, "I don't know. I didn't ask."

"Then ask him." Removing his hand, he turned, walked back to his table, and went back to work.

Seth pondered his words. Was *Daed* right? Was his dogged pursuit of Miriam fueled by the need to attain, instead of a true attraction? He wasn't sure. One thing was clear, however. His father said to leave her be, and that was a wise recommendation. He also said to talk to God, something Seth should have done in the first place.

He glanced across the room at his *daed,* who was once again engrossed in his carving. Rising from his stool, he went over to him, swallowing the lump that had suddenly appeared in his throat. So many times he had dismissed his father as a fool, a stubborn old man who didn't understand anything. How wrong he had been.

"Danki," Seth said quietly when he reached him. "I appreciate the advice."

Melvin looked up, his face remaining as placid as it always did. But his eyes reflected something else. *Respect.* Seth had never seen it before, at least not directed toward him. The two men didn't say anything else, and after a moment Seth turned away and went back to working on his project, silently praising God that at least one of his strained relationships was moving in a positive direction.

* * *

Miriam was relieved when Seth didn't pick her up for work on Saturday morning. Her father hadn't needed the buggy, so she drove herself to work, picking up extra hours because of the Christmas holiday. Near closing time her stomach twisted in knots as she expected Seth to show up and ask to take her home. He didn't. She didn't see him at church on Sunday, and he never made an appearance at the shop on Monday. Apparently, she had gotten through to him. She wouldn't have to deal with Seth Fisher anymore. She should be pleased.

Instead, she felt more miserable than before.

On Wednesday morning Tammy came into the shop, clad in jeans and a green and red–striped sweater. Red metallic jingle bells hung from her ears, and a strand of tiny, blinking Christmas lights were around her neck. She rivaled some of the Christmas trees in the shop windows. Miriam looked at her, not knowing what to think.

"Time to get into the Christmas spirit!" Tammy set down her large tote bag on the counter and pulled out another strand of gaudy lights. "Here's one for you."

"*Danki,* but I can't take them."

"Oh." Her cheeks flushed. "Can't believe I forgot that."

"It's all right."

"What do you all do for Christmas? Do you have a tree? Presents?"

"A tree, *nee*. We do exchange presents, usually the second day after Christmas. The day of Christmas we gather with friends and family and celebrate Christ's birth."

"Sounds nice." Tammy smiled.

"It is." Miriam put the cash drawer in the register and went to the front door. They had a few minutes before the store opened for business. She paused and stared out the glass door, watching as cars, buggies, and people, both Amish and *Englisch,* passed by.

"Looking for someone?" Tammy came up from behind.

Miriam stepped back. *"Nee."* Casting her gaze to the ground, she slid by Tammy and went to straighten a shelf that didn't need straightening.

"Is he coming today?"

"Who?" Miriam adjusted several bolts of flannel.

"You know who I'm talking about. Seth."

Miriam shook her head, hoping she appeared more nonchalant than she felt. "Matthew is picking me up."

"So you're back to having your cousin provide your transportation."

"Ya. It's easier that way."

"You mean it's safer that way." Although Tammy was dressed comically, her expression was serious.

Miriam turned around and looked at her, dumbfounded. "Matthew is a *gut* driver, *ya.*"

Tammy shrugged. "Suit yourself."

Frowning, Miriam turned away, not appreciating the disapproval in her boss's voice. She said very little for the rest of the day, and nothing on the ride home. Fortunately Matthew wasn't much of a conversationalist, and Miriam didn't feel the need to make small talk. She was free to focus on her last encounter with Seth. He had said he poured his heart out to her. And all she had cared about was whether he thought she was pretty or not.

No wonder he didn't come back.

For the first time she realized how self-centered she

had been. She'd always thought of Seth Fisher as being so full of himself, but he was nothing compared to her. He talked about how his pride had led him on a path of destruction. Where was her self-absorption leading her?

To loneliness. Resentment. Even envy when she saw other couples together.

"I'll pick you up tomorrow, *ya?*" Matthew slowed the buggy in front of their driveway. He didn't drive to the house like Seth always did.

"Ya," she said, almost as an afterthought. In a haze, she walked up the driveway and entered the house, heading straight to her bedroom. Dropping her bag on a nearby chair, she sat down at the edge of her bed.

A soft knock sounded at the door. "Miriam?" her mother asked. "Is everything okay?"

"Ya," Miriam said.

"Can I come in?"

Miriam hesitated. She really didn't want to talk to her mother right now, but she knew *Mamm* wouldn't relent until they spoke. "Okay."

Her mother walked in and sat down next to her. "I noticed Seth hasn't been around lately."

Looking away, Miriam shrugged. "I guess he's busy."

"That might be so, but I'm guessing there's another reason why Matthew is driving you to work again."

When Miriam didn't respond, her mother continued. "I don't understand, Miriam. You fret that no one is interested in you, and when a young man shows interest, you push him away."

Miriam blanched. "It's not that simple."

Mary put two fingers above her gray eyebrow and frowned. "I thought when we had that talk the other day you two were going to work things out. Instead your cousin is dropping you off, and you've been sulking around here for two days. I can see this is tearing you up inside, and I'm sure he's going through the same thing."

"I doubt it."

"Honey, don't slam the door without looking at what's on the other side." She took Miriam's hand in hers. "What do we value above everything else, except of course the Lord?"

Miriam frowned at the unexpected question. "Faith, family—"

"Let me stop you there. Do you want a family?"

"I have a family," Miriam said, confused.

"I mean one of your own. A husband. Children."

Miriam paused, tempted to shake her head. But that would be a lie, one her mother would see right through. *"Ya,"* she said quietly. "I do."

"How will that happen if you don't let anyone get close to you?"

"But I'm—"

"What? Unattractive?" Mary ran her hand over Miriam's cheek. "Miriam, self-pity is unattractive. Low confidence is unattractive. Pushing people away is unattractive." She softened her tone. "Your attitude is standing in the way of what you want. That and your fear of getting hurt. But can't you see, you're already hurting? You will be for the rest of your life if you don't change how you feel about yourself." She leaned forward and kissed her cheek. "I could sit here all day and tell you what a beautiful *maedel* you truly are. Yet it won't mean anything if you don't believe it yourself." She rose from the bed and left the room.

Miriam sat for a moment, frozen. Were her *mamm*'s

words true? Was she pushing Seth away not because of him, but because of herself?

Her grandmother's beloved quilt hung over the back of the chair. She stared at it, wishing her grandmother were here. Miriam knew what she would say. She could even hear her gentle voice speaking the words.

Take it to the Lord, mei kind. *Take your problems to the Lord.*

Her grandmother was right. She should have been praying all along.

Rising from the bed, Miriam turned around and knelt on the floor, folding her hands and closing her eyes. She prayed for forgiveness for her pride and her self-centeredness, she prayed for wisdom about Seth, and she prayed for healing—not just for her own hurt, but also for Seth's. She poured out her heart to the Lord and admitted to him all of her fears and insecurities. There were so many of them, and it took a long time before she felt the healing spirit of God flow through her. But when it did, when God's peace descended upon her, she realized what she had to do.

Chapter Eleven

Seth continued to rub his thigh as he glanced across the room at his father. After supper they had both retired to the living room—his father to read, and Seth to think more about his situation with Miriam. His mother had remained in the kitchen, peeling apples to make filling for the shoestring apple pies she would be taking to Sarah and David Fisher on First Christmas. Seth looked forward to spending some time with his cousin and his wife, along with other friends and family. He used to find First Christmas boring, as it involved Bible reading and hymn singing instead of opening presents. But this year the holiday held special meaning for him. For the first time he recognized its holiness, and he wanted to show his reverence for the birth of the Savior.

Melvin turned the page of the newspaper he was reading, the newsprint crackling with the movement. "Leg bothering you?"

"A little."

"Got some of that salve left from when you came home."

Pinching his face at the thought of using the smelly

goop his mother and father swore took care of all their aches and pains, Seth said, "It's fine, *Daed*. Just a twinge." Actually it was more than a twinge, but he could live with it. Still, he appreciated his father's concern. "Think I'll help *Mamm* with the apples."

Melvin nodded, but kept his nose buried in the paper.

Seth looked at his walking stick. Lately he hadn't been using it as much in the house, although he did rely on it when he went out and while he was in the woodshop.

He limped to the kitchen without it, inhaling the mild, fruity scent of fresh apples. He looked at his mother, who was seated at the square table, slicing an apple in half. "Need some help?"

Rachel smiled. "*Ya*. That would be nice. You can peel while I cut."

After retrieving another paring knife from the utensil drawer, he went and sat down next to his mother. A tall gas lamp stood in the corner of the room, flooding the room with plenty of light. They peeled apples in silence for a short while.

Rachel dropped several pieces of cut apple into a large bowl. "You used to help me a lot when you were younger." She glanced at him. "I missed that."

"You know, I do, too." Looking at her, he smiled. "I didn't realize how much until right now." Applying the blade to the top of the apple, he broke the green skin, then slid the sharp blade beneath the peel until he had removed it from the apple in one strip. Setting the peel aside, he grabbed another Granny Smith.

"When you were little, you used to eat the peels," his mother said, working her knife with her plump hands through the middle of an apple, this time a Jonathan. "They're yours if you want them."

He grabbed a short piece of green peel and put it in his mouth, letting the tart sweetness coat his tongue. "Don't think I can eat all these, though."

"We'll give the leftovers to the pigs."

"I'll take them out there when we're through."

His mother put down her knife, worry instantly appearing on her round face. "I don't think that's a good idea."

"I have to start doing my share around here."

"But you're still healing."

"I'm healed enough to feed the pigs. Don't worry, I'll be careful, and I won't go inside the pen."

She picked up her knife and started slicing again. "A mother never stops worrying about, or loving, her children."

He glanced down at the pile of peelings in front of him. "I haven't always deserved it."

"Seth," she said, stilling the knife and looking at him again. "A mother's love isn't earned. It's freely given. Don't ever forget that."

Swallowing the lump that suddenly appeared in his throat, he said, *"Danki."*

"Seth."

At the sound of his father's voice, he turned around. Melvin was standing in the kitchen doorway.

"Ya?"

"Someone's here to see you." His *daed* stepped to the side. A slender woman walked into the room, an unsure expression on her sweet face.

"Miriam?"

She gazed down at the floor, as she so often did

when she was around him. "I hope I'm not interrupting anything."

"*Nee,* you're not." Seth stood from his chair and gestured toward his mother. "*Mamm,* this is Miriam Herschberger."

Rachel smiled, dimples forming on her plump cheeks. "Hello, Miriam. I've known your *mudder* for a long time. How is she faring?"

"She's well. *Danki* for asking." She looked at Seth for a fleeting moment, then back at Rachel. "If this is a bad time, I can talk to Seth later."

"*Nee.* I won't hear of it. Seth and I have just finished our conversation."

He caught his mother's knowing look and gave her a small smile of appreciation.

Rachel put down her knife and stood. "If you don't mind, Miriam, I could use some help with these apples. If you and Seth could peel and cut them, then I can finish the present I'm working on for Sarah and David."

"Sarah and David Fisher?" Miriam asked.

She nodded. "David is my nephew, my youngest brother's *sohn.* We're going to their house for First Christmas."

Seth thought he saw something flicker across Miriam's face, but he wasn't sure, as she still wore her uncertain expression.

"I'm putting the last few touches on a lap quilt for them," Rachel explained. "I've made one for all my nieces and nephews and their families. It's taken a while, but David and Sarah are the youngest, so they had to wait to get theirs." She smiled. "I hope they'll be pleased with it."

"I'm sure they will," Miriam said. "I'd love to see it when you're finished."

"Of course. Seth says you like to quilt."

Miriam looked at him, surprise in her eyes, as if she couldn't believe he would talk about her to his mother. *"Ya,"* she said quietly, still keeping her gaze on him. "I do. Very much so."

"Hopefully I can see some of your work one day. He told me you're very talented."

A flush heated her cheeks, and she cast her eyes to the ground. *"Danki,"* she said in a nearly transparent voice. "I would be happy to show you some of the projects I've been working on."

"Gut. Before you leave, we'll figure out when we can do that." She looked at Seth, a small smile teasing her lips before she addressed Miriam again. "Would you mind helping him with the apples?"

"Nee."

"You can use that knife right there. *Danki,* Miriam. I appreciate it."

At some point during the conversation, his father had disappeared, and after thanking Miriam, his mother beat an equally hasty exit.

Cautiously, Miriam pulled out the chair and sat down. She reached for a peeled apple and picked up the knife. He noticed the slight shake of her hands, but she still handled the knife with expertise as she cut the fruit into medium-sized chunks.

Seth peeled an apple and handed it to her, waiting for her to say something. What was she doing here? It was on the tip of his tongue to ask her, but he remained silent, letting her take the lead this time. Obviously she wouldn't be here unless she had a specific reason, and he would bide his time until she decided to talk.

But instead of speaking, she kept cutting. So he kept peeling, his patience wearing thin. After they went through four apples, he couldn't take it anymore. When she reached for another apple, without thinking he took her hand in his. "Miriam, what are you doing here?"

She glanced at his hand, which had covered hers completely. Quickly she slid it out from beneath his grasp. "I—I…" Taking a deep breath, she started again, this time looking at him while she pushed up her glasses. "I came to apologize."

"Apologize?"

"For being so selfish."

"Selfish?"

"You were right. You were open and honest with me, and I didn't appreciate that. I was too caught up in my own problems that I wasn't there for you. I'm sorry for that." Her gaze shot down again, as if her nerve had suddenly drained from her. She grabbed another apple and started chopping.

"Miriam," he said, watching her slice the apple with even more zeal than before. *"Miriam."*

Finally she stopped and looked at him, as if exasperated that he would interrupt such an important task. "What?"

He pointed to the apple pieces. "I was supposed to peel it first."

She looked down at the apple she'd been cutting, the peel still completely on the fruit. Her shoulders slumped, and suddenly she laughed.

The sound both surprised and delighted him. "You have a great laugh."

Looking up at him, she smiled.

"And a great smile." He grinned. "You need to smile more."

Her face flushed, almost matching the color of one of the Jonathans he'd been peeling.

He picked up another piece of apple peel and put it into his mouth. Then he offered her some. "You don't have to take it," he said. "Most people don't care for the peel on its own."

"Not me. I like the peels." She accepted a piece and took a small bite. "*Gut* apples," she said.

"*Ya.* They'll make *gut* pie, although my *mudder* could probably make bad apples into something delicious." Seth watched as she took another bite, savoring the taste, the light brown freckle above her lip moving up and down as she chewed. He could watch her eat for the next lifetime or so, but they needed to finish or his mother would have his head. "We better get this done or there won't be any pies."

They went back to cutting and peeling. "I accept your apology," he said after a short stretch of silence.

"*Danki.*"

"Do you accept mine?"

"Yours?"

"About what I did in school. I'm really sorry, and I'm not just saying that out of guilt."

She looked at him. "*Ya.* I see that now." Once again, her lips curled in a smile.

His heart slammed against his rib cage. How could he have ever thought she wasn't pretty? Her smile made all the difference, bringing a light to her chocolate-brown eyes. Somehow he'd find a way to make her smile as much as possible.

"Do you think we could start over?" Her smile faded, replaced by insecurity again.

He quickly reassured her. "I'd like that, Miriam. But I have one condition."

Alarm lit her delicate features. "What?"

"No games. Don't make me guess what you're thinking. What you're feeling."

She expelled a deep breath. "I'll try. It's just that…"

"What? Miriam, you can tell me."

"I'm scared."

Her admission touched a chord in his heart. "Scared of what?"

"Of everything." She wiped her damp hands on the light blue kitchen towel lying near the cutting board.

"You mean like spiders and the dark?" he teased. When she chuckled, he knew he'd struck the right tone.

"*Nee.* Although I used to be afraid of the dark when I was little."

"Me, too."

"Really? I didn't think you had ever been afraid of anything."

"Well, I got over it pretty quickly. That's the thing with fear: you can't let it rule your life. You have to put it behind you as fast as you can."

"I wish I could."

"I'd like to help you try. If you'll let me." He knew it was a risk, but he held out his hand to her anyway. His heart soared when she tentatively slipped her small hand in his.

Her skin was soft, just as he'd imagined it would be. And just as he'd expected, his hand dwarfed hers. Yet holding it was so natural and seemed so right. He squeezed her hand, and even though he didn't want to, he let her go.

Without speaking they resumed their task of peeling and cutting, but this time the silence between them wasn't as awkward. Her coming here had taken a lot of courage; he could see that now. She had finally let down her defenses a little bit. He would take anything she offered.

"Do you mind if I ask you something?"

He popped another piece of peel into his mouth and chewed. "Sure. Go ahead."

She hesitated, glancing down at the table again. He hoped she eventually wouldn't be so shy around him.

Finally she looked up. "Your scar...it doesn't seem to bother you."

"Not anymore. The cut healed really well, considering I had forty stitches." He touched the upper part of his cheek. "A few more inches and that glass would have pierced me in the eye." When he saw her blanch, he said, "Sorry. Didn't mean to be so graphic."

"That's okay. I just feel bad you had to go through something like that. It must have been very painful."

"It was, but my leg was worse, so it kind of took my mind off my face."

"But aren't you worried about what other people might say? That they might..."

"Make fun of me?"

She nodded.

He shrugged. "Once that would have bothered me. A lot. But what I am on the outside is insignificant. I realize that now. What counts is what's in here." His hand went to his heart. He paused. "Now let me ask you something."

"What?"

An unexpected attack of nerves assaulted him as he realized how much her answer meant to him. "Does my scar bother you?"

She put her elbow on the table and rested her chin

on her hand. After studying his face for a few torturous moments, she said with a smile, "What scar?"

At that moment he knew he could never let her go. If he had to fight to win her heart until he took his last breath, he would, just for the privilege of seeing her gaze at him with stars in her eyes the way she was looking at him now.

After she sliced the last apple, she spoke again. "I should be going." She stood. "I told *Mamm* I wouldn't be long."

"Do you need a ride home?" He scooted his chair from the table and rose.

"*Nee.* I brought our buggy."

"How's your horse's foot?"

"Getting better. That's nice of you to remember."

While he was still in her good graces he asked, "May I take you to work in the morning?"

"Matthew is giving me a ride."

"Oh." He kept the disappointment out of his voice. Maybe he'd misread her. Perhaps she wanted to take things slower than he thought.

"Seth?"

"Ya?"

"I will need a ride home tomorrow, if you're able."

He grinned, feeling like he'd just struck gold. "I'll be there."

After she left, he picked up his walking stick and went out to his father's woodshop next to the house. He turned on the gas lamp, and the hissing sound coming from the lamp filled the large room. The shop was cold, but Seth didn't care. He limped over to the table and sat down. The block of wood he'd been working on was starting to take shape, and he tackled the project with new enthusiasm.

"Need some help?"

He turned around and saw his *daed* standing in the doorway. Grinning, Seth said, "You bet."

Chapter Twelve

Wow, you're in a much better mood today." Tammy lifted up the small lid on top of the cash register and replaced the receipt tape with a fresh roll. First Christmas was two days away, and again they had been very busy. She looked at Miriam and smirked. "But I noticed you haven't taken your eyes off the front door for the past hour. Expecting someone? Someone who might be the reason for your jolly mood?"

Had she been that obvious? All day long she tried to suppress a smile but found it difficult to do. After talking to Seth last night, it seemed that not only had her heart changed, but so had everything else in her life. The shimmer and sparkle of the Christmas decorations were more beautiful than she'd ever noticed before. The tinkling of the bell over the front door was sharper; the colors of the fabrics more vibrant than ever. It was as if the moment she opened her heart to Seth, the world had opened up to her in return.

Miriam would have never had the courage to go see him if God hadn't prodded her. He had given her the strength to bring down her defenses, to take a chance that Seth would accept her apology and not send her away. He would have been within his rights to do just that, but instead he, and his parents, had been welcoming. Her stomach did a tiny flip as she remembered holding his hand. Even though the moment had been brief, their hands seemed to fit perfectly together, her small one in the protective cocoon of his large grasp.

But she tempered her excitement. Holding her hand had been a gesture of friendship, not of any romantic interest. He had never indicated that he was interested in her that way. She had to be content with that. To wish for anything more would be foolish.

Yet she couldn't completely extinguish the flicker of hope in her heart that someday, somehow, he might see her as more than a friend.

She checked the digital clock Tammy kept near the register and tried to keep her mind off impossible things. Nearly five o'clock. Her gaze kept straying to the front door, expecting to see Seth standing there, waiting for her. He'd always arrived a few minutes early, but when she came back from retrieving her cloak and bag, he still wasn't there. She stood by the door and peered outside.

Tammy dimmed the lights and put on her heavy winter coat. "Have you got a ride, Miriam?"

"Ya," she said. Where was he?

"If you need me to, I can run you home." Tammy swirled a red and white–checked scarf around her neck.

"Nee. He'll be here."

"Matthew?"

"Seth." Miriam tried to hide her smile, but couldn't.

Tammy's mouth broadened in a wide grin. "Good

for you guys! I'm glad you were able to work things out. I always thought you made a cute couple."

"We're just friends. Friends," she repeated, needing the verbal reminder.

With a wink Tammy said, "Whatever you say, Miriam. See you tomorrow. Just make sure to lock up before you go."

"I will."

Tammy left, and after waiting a few minutes more, Miriam stepped outside. The temperature had dropped considerably since the sun had set, and an intermittent breeze cut right through her cloak and dress, chilling her skin. She'd overheard some customers talking about the weather forecast. There was a possibility of snow over the next few days, and they might just have a white Christmas after all.

Another breeze whipped her cloak about her calves and shot through her black kneesocks, chilling her legs. She thought about going back inside to wait. But she was positive Seth would be there any minute. Locking the door behind her, she then turned around, hugging her arms around her body underneath her cloak.

Lincoln Avenue, the main road in Paradise, was still pretty busy, with several people strolling up and down the sidewalks that lined the street. But most of the shops were closing for the night. As more and more and more lights went out inside the stores, her confidence that Seth would arrive started to wane. He should have been there by now.

Darkness descended, and she couldn't wait any longer. Her hands and feet were freezing, and the longer she lingered, the colder she would be. She didn't want to walk home, but she had no choice.

"Miriam!"

Seth! Following the sound of his voice, she turned and looked up Lincoln Avenue. He stood by the parking lot, waving his hands at her. Relieved, she hurried to meet him halfway.

"I'm so sorry," he said, his breath exhaling in big, white puffs. A mix of panic and remorse filled his eyes. "How long were you standing out here?"

"Long enough." She hugged her arms around her frigid body.

"I didn't mean to be late." He moved closer to her. "I'm really, really sorry."

"Seth," she said, her teeth close to chattering. "It's okay. I'm just glad you're here now."

His brows lifted with surprise. Then he took in her shivering frame. "You're freezing. Let's get you inside the buggy."

They walked to where he had tethered the horse. He went to the passenger side, opened the door, and reached into the backseat. "Here," he said, putting a quilt around her shoulders.

Warmth immediately seeped into her. Then he did something completely unexpected. Her heart stopped as his hands slowly rubbed her arms through the quilt.

"Better?" he asked, his voice close to her ear.

"Ya." She could barely hear herself speak. His large hands covered almost all of her upper arms. He'd never been this close to her, and they were almost in an embrace. If she turned around she would be only inches from his chest. She fought a strong desire to lean against him, to take advantage of his kindness and indulge her own dream. But she stopped herself. They were just friends. But oh, how she wished they could be more.

* * *

Seth inwardly groaned as he continued to rub Miriam's arms. He told himself he was just helping her get warmed up. But being this close to her, where all he had to do was bend down a couple inches and he could easily nuzzle her neck...

He cleared his throat, then stepped away. Those were definitely thoughts he had no business entertaining. In the past when he had made a move like that on a girl, she had happily accepted it, and usually wanted to do more. But he fought those feelings, not only for Miriam's sake, but also because it was the right thing to do.

She climbed into the buggy, seemingly unaffected by his attempt to warm her. He hobbled around the front and settled in his seat, trying to calm his emotions. Once they were on their way, he said, "Are you warm enough?"

"I am now." Turning, she gave him a small smile before pushing up her glasses.

"*Gut.* I feel really bad about you standing out in the cold. I want to make it up to you."

"You've been kind enough to give me so many rides, Seth. You don't have to make anything up to me."

"But I want to. Are you hungry?" When she didn't respond right away, he said, "Miriam, be honest. I know I'm starving."

"*Ya.* I am a bit hungry."

"Then it's settled. Let's go get something to eat. My treat." His father had given him a few dollars earlier in the week. He hadn't wanted to accept the money, but his *daed* insisted, saying that Seth would more than make up for it when he returned to work after Christmas. "Dienner's is just ahead. That sound okay?"

"Sure."

* * *

Over and over Miriam reminded herself that she was *not* on a date with Seth Fisher. They were both hungry, and it was suppertime. It made perfect sense for them to stop and get a bite to eat. Sure, he had offered to pay, but she wouldn't let him. They would go Dutch, just like friends do.

But when he held the door of the restaurant open for her, and then walked behind her, putting his hand on the small of her back for just a split second, she was finding it harder and harder not to wish they were on a real date.

Dienner's Country Restaurant specialized in Amish and German food. Miriam scanned the small dining room while they waited for a hostess to seat them. She didn't see any empty seats, even though it was forty-five minutes until closing time.

"Table for two?" A diminutive woman with platinum blonde hair and purple-framed glasses picked up two menus from the stack near the front door.

"Ya," Seth said, over Miriam's shoulder.

"Would a booth be all right? We don't have any empty tables right now."

"That will be fine," he told her.

"Right this way."

Miriam followed the hostess to the back of the dining room, noticing that Seth was right behind her. He had stood near her since they walked into the restaurant. They passed by a table where two Amish girls were eating dinner. One looked up and caught Miriam's gaze.

"Hello, Miriam," Martha Yoder said.

"Hello, Martha." She didn't know Martha very well, as the girl was a few years younger than she was.

Martha's other companion smiled in greeting, but Miriam didn't recognize her.

When they reached the table, the hostess set down the menus. "Your waitress will be here shortly."

"Thanks," Seth said as they both sat down. He slid his walking stick underneath the table, then took off his black coat and set it down next to him. Removing his hat, he slid his long fingers through the thick locks of his dark-brown hair. He'd always worn a hat, and Miriam never noticed how rich the color was until now.

She tried not to gape, but she couldn't help it. A quick glance around the dining room showed that she wasn't the only one who noticed him. Martha and her friend kept looking at Seth, then whispered between themselves. They didn't do much to hide their appreciation for his looks.

Oblivious to their attentions, he grabbed a menu and opened it. "Everything looks great. Have you been here before?"

"*Ya,* a couple times." She removed her cloak and folded it neatly, placing it beside her on the bench seat. Then she picked up her menu and tried to focus on the variety of food listed inside. How could she focus on food with him sitting right across from her?

"All right, I know what I want." He put the menu down on the table. "I'm warning you, I've got a big appetite."

"Uh-huh." She didn't know why her cheeks suddenly flushed, but she didn't want him to see her blushing.

"Have you decided?"

"Uh, not yet."

He reached across and pulled the menu down so

they were face-to-face. "Order what you want. I've got it covered."

She shook her head. "I can't let you do that, Seth. I'll pay for my own meal."

"Miriam, relax and don't worry about it. Let's just enjoy ourselves, okay?"

His words were spoken in a gentle tone that had an immediate calming effect on her nerves. He was right; she was too uptight. Lifting up her menu, she perused it for another minute, then settled on her order. "Chicken noodle soup and a side salad." She folded the menu and laid it to the side.

"That's all you want?"

"It's enough for me. My appetite isn't as big as yours."

He chuckled. "Not many are. *Mudder* always made sure she had made enough food for me to have seconds *and* thirds. I always out-ate my *bruders*."

"The woman you marry will have to be a great cook." Her eyes grew wide, and she nearly clapped her hand over her mouth.

"She'll have to like to cook, at the very least." He leaned forward, a teasing spark dancing in his gorgeous blue eyes. "What about you, Miriam? Do you enjoy cooking?"

She licked her lips. "*Ya.* I do."

A grin spread across his face as he leaned back, his gaze holding hers, causing a pleasant jolt to flow through her.

Their waitress suddenly appeared at the table. Miriam placed her order, hiding her disappointment at being interrupted. Once she scribbled down what they wanted, the waitress left, returning shortly after with glasses of water.

Seth picked up his water and took a big drink. As he set down the glass, he said, "You haven't asked me why I was late."

She shrugged. "I figured you had a good reason."

"I do." His lips twitched in a semi-smile.

Tilting her head to the side, she asked, "What is it?"

"Can't tell you."

"What?"

"Can't tell you. At least not now." He was full-blown grinning now.

She couldn't help but smile in return. "Now you're keeping secrets from me?"

"Just one." He lowered his voice. "But something tells me you've been keeping a few from me."

Her face flushed, and she glanced at her water glass. "What makes you say that?"

"You have an air of mystery about you, Miriam Herschberger. I knew that the first time I saw you at the Lapps'."

She scoffed. "There's nothing mysterious about me, Seth. You know everything about me."

He leaned forward, putting his elbows on the table and folding his arms. "I disagree. Sure, I know where you live. Where you work. That you like to quilt. What you do on Sundays. But I don't know your hopes. Your dreams. Your plans for the future."

The lightness of his tone had disappeared, replaced by absolute seriousness. The intensity in his eyes threatened to take her breath away. Suddenly she no longer heard the voices of the other restaurant patrons, or the bustling of the waitresses and bussers. In this crowded restaurant, they were the only two people there.

"Miriam, I want to know everything about you."

Forcing herself to look at him, she said, "There's not much to know."

"I don't believe that."

"Then you'll be disappointed."

"Miriam." His voice was nearly a whisper. "I hate when you put yourself down like that."

Her *mamm*'s voice suddenly entered her head. *Self-pity is unattractive. Low confidence is unattractive. Pushing people away is unattractive.* Here she was with the man of her dreams expressing an interest in getting to know her, and she was putting him off. She wasn't being fair to him, or to herself.

The waitress appeared with their food, saving her from having to answer him. After a short prayer of thanks, they both started on their suppers. Seth had half of his wolfed down before she had finished her small salad. He was right; his appetite was voracious.

They made small talk during the meal. Seth expressed his satisfaction with his chicken dinner, and she said the soup was delicious. But in the back of her mind, she kept thinking about what he had said before their food arrived. Seth wanted to know her hopes and plans for the future. How did she tell him that she only hoped for one thing—marriage and a family? And how did she admit that out loud, especially to him, when she could barely acknowledge it herself?

She had finished the last sip of her soup when the waitress returned, asking if they cared for dessert. To her surprise, Seth declined, and Miriam was full.

"Then I'll just take this when you're ready." The waitress tore the check off her pad and put it on the table, then left to tend to other customers.

Miriam reached for the slip of paper, but Seth was

too fast for her. "You're stubborn, you know that? I told you that this is my treat."

He folded the bill and tucked it into his hand. "Now, if you still insist on paying your share, you'll have to fight me to do it."

She looked at his huge hand, knowing she was no match. Still, she couldn't resist a little teasing in return. "I may just do that. But I feel it's my duty to let you know that I don't always fight fair."

"Oh, I'm counting on it."

Unable to resist, she moved to touch his fist when he suddenly grasped her hand with his free one. "Gotta be faster than that."

They both laughed, and she loved the way he put her at ease. She also loved how he held on to her hand. Really, there was so much to love about him.

Love? She shoved the thought out of her head. She couldn't afford to think about Seth and love in the same context. Loving Seth would be easy, but pointless. He would never return it.

But then again…what if he did? Was it even possible? His smile, his touch, his interest in her thoughts and feelings, gave her a glimmer of hope. And as her mother, Lydia, and even Tammy had been telling her, she deserved happiness. She deserved love. Was it so impossible to believe she could have both with Seth?

He let go of her hand, a little reluctantly, she thought. "You ready to go?"

She nodded. "I just need to stop by the ladies' room."

"No problem. I'll meet you up front."

Excusing herself, she passed by Martha's table, but she paid the girls no notice. Her thoughts, and heart, were consumed with Seth. Unable to stop smiling, she went into the bathroom and went inside a stall. When she finished, she was moving to open the stall door when she heard someone enter.

"I feel so sorry for Seth Fisher." Martha's voice echoed against the walls.

Miriam paused, listening. Why would Martha feel sorry for him?

"I heard he almost died in that accident," the other girl said.

"*Ya,*" Martha said. "He's lucky he only has a limp."

"And the scar."

"But even with the scar he's still *gutguckich*. Those eyes are to die for."

Miriam smiled. Martha and her friend had echoed her own thoughts. She opened the stall door a crack. The two young women were checking their reflections in the mirror, making sure their *kapps* were well secured. Martha tucked the ribbons of her *kapp* into the front fold of her dress. "What I don't understand," she said to her reflection, "is what is he doing with Miriam?"

"That's your friend's name?"

"She's not really my friend. I just know her in passing." She lowered her voice. "Talk about homely."

Miriam sucked in her breath.

"I mean, they surely weren't *together* together. Like, courting together," Martha said.

"But he was holding her hand," her friend pointed out, slipping on her black cloak.

"*Ya,* but probably because he felt sorry for her."

Miriam slumped against the stall, her confidence slashed to ribbons. Is that how they looked to other people? Beauty and the beast, like the fairy tale she had read as a child—only in her story the woman was the beast? Thoughts assaulted her like hailstones hitting the pavement. What would his friends say if she and Seth did start dating? Would they point out how ill suited they were for each other? Probably. Would she have to compete with other girls for his attention? Absolutely.

Tears burned in her eyes; pain clogged her throat as she heard the girls finally leave. She stood there for a few more moments, unable to move, wishing she had never agreed to go to supper with him. He was waiting for her, and she couldn't hide in the bathroom forever.

Lord, help me!

Drying her eyes, she went and washed her hands, unable to bear looking in the mirror. But it was as if it had a magnetic pull, and she couldn't help herself.

Her eyes were red-rimmed behind the lenses of her glasses. Her skin was pasty white, and her lips were trembling. She couldn't go out there looking like this. Seth would notice and want to know what was wrong.

Taking a deep breath, Miriam sucked in all her negative emotions. She tried to force a smile, realized she couldn't do it. She couldn't fake how she felt, and she couldn't hide her emotions anymore. Seth said he wanted to know her, and now he would. The real her. The insecure her. And if he couldn't handle it…then she would have to accept that. Somehow.

Chapter Thirteen

Something was wrong with Miriam. Seth couldn't pinpoint what it was, but she wasn't the same woman that he'd just shared a wonderful meal with. During supper she had been more relaxed than he'd ever seen her, open to his teasing, even kidding him in return. He hadn't enjoyed himself so much in a very long time.

But now, as she approached him from the restroom, he could see something was wrong. Her shoulders were slumped, and when she neared him he could see her eyes were a bit bloodshot. Had she been crying? What in the world could have upset her so much in such a short period of time?

He was determined to find out.

"You forgot these," he said. He held out her quilted bag and her cloak.

"Danki."

Not missing the melancholy tone in her voice, he handed her the bag, then moved to help her with her cloak. But she shook her head and took the garment from him. "I've got it," she said.

"All right." Puzzled, he watched her as she put on

the cloak, but she refused to look at him. Without a word she headed for the front door and walked briskly in front of him. He couldn't limp fast enough to keep up with her. Annoyed, he said, "Hey, Miriam. Could you slow down a bit?"

"Sorry." She did slow her steps, but she didn't turn around and look at him.

When they reached the buggy, he was truly concerned. He slid between her and the buggy's passenger door. He wasn't graceful to say the least, but he didn't care. He had her attention and that was all that mattered. "Miriam, tell me what's wrong. We were having such a good time a little while ago—at least I was, and I thought you were too." When she tried to look away from him, he reached out and touched her chin, gently forcing her to face him. "Don't shut me out. Talk to me."

"I—I can't." Tears sprang to her eyes.

At the sight of her sorrow, he wanted to grab her in his arms. But he resisted the urge. Embracing her now would either scare her or put her off, and he didn't want either. What he wanted was for her to share her burden, whatever it was, with him. "Miriam, please."

She slid her finger underneath the right lens of her glasses and wiped her damp eye. "Just take me home, Seth."

"*Nee.* I'm not taking you anywhere until you explain yourself. You promised me you'd be honest. Now's the time to honor that promise."

Rivulets of moisture flowed down her cheeks, each drop piercing his heart like a shard of glass. "Please," she said. "Just take me home."

He grasped her shoulders, thankful for her sake they had parked at the far end of the lot and were secluded from any passersby. "Miriam," he said softly, trying to reassure her. "You can tell me anything. I just want to help you." Unable to resist, he took her face in his hands, wiping her tears with his thumbs. "Trust me. That's all I ask. Just trust me."

Seth's hands were so warm, his touch so gentle that she thought she might melt in a puddle right there in front of him. The lights illuminating the parking lot were strong enough that she could see his face clearly. She read the sincerity in his eyes. But something still held her back.

"Don't be afraid, Miriam," he said, his thumbs grazing her cheeks again. "I said I wanted to help you fight whatever you're scared of. I meant those words."

She put her hands over his and removed them from her face. "Seth, why are you pushing so hard?" Turning from his embrace, she put her back to him. "Why are you even bothering with me?"

She felt the heavy weight of his hands on her shoulders. "You want to know why?" He let out a heavy sigh as he guided her to face him. "I've been lying to you, Miriam. I should have been honest with you from the beginning."

Fresh tears sprouted from her eyes. This was an awful, confusing mess, and she didn't understand any of it. "You want me to trust you, but now you're telling me you lied?"

"I'm telling you I lied so you *can* trust me. Miriam, we can't be friends. That's the absolute truth."

Closing her eyes against the words, she swallowed. "I see."

"*Nee,* you don't." He dropped his hands from her shoulders, then rubbed his hand over his face. "I care for you, Miriam. A lot. And *not* as a friend." He leaned down until he was looking her straight in the eye. "Do you understand what I'm saying? When I'm not with you, I'm thinking about you, and wishing we were together."

Her eyes widened. "You are?"

"*Ya,* I am."

This still seemed beyond her ken. "But why? There are so many other *maed* you would be better…" She bit her bottom lip.

"Better what?"

"Better suited for." There, she said it out loud.

"Better suited?" He scoffed. "I can't think of a single *maedel* I'd rather be with than you."

"You say that now, but what about next week? Or the week after that?" She pushed up her glasses. A chill entered her bones, but she wasn't convinced it was totally due to the frigid weather. "Seth, you've been through a lot. You say you've changed, and I see that you have. But just because you want to have *demut* doesn't mean you have to be with an ugly duck like me."

"Is that what you think? Miriam, you are so wrong."

He moved closer to her, but she stepped away. She couldn't handle being near him. It made what she had to say next that much harder. "Think about what your friends will say when they see us together. You don't think they'll ask you why you settled for something less than you deserved?"

He grabbed her shoulders again. "*Stop* this! I don't care one whit about what anyone else thinks about me, or about us. Miriam, here's another bit of honesty. I've dated a lot of girls. A *lot.*"

"That's supposed to make me feel better?"

"Just let me finish. I'll admit those girls were beautiful on the outside. But inside, they left much to be desired. Then I met you. Again." He stepped toward her, his eyes glistening. "You showed me what true beauty is. It's what's in here." His hand covered his heart. "You're so full of beauty inside it overflows. You might not be able to see it, but I can." He touched her face, then cradled her cheek in his hand before drawing her into a kiss.

Shock coursed through her as his lips caressed hers, at first insistently, then with such gentleness it made her cry. Her arms automatically went around his waist as the tears flowed down, wetting both their cheeks. He pulled away for a moment, only to press his lips to hers once again.

Finally, he broke the contact. "It's me who doesn't deserve you," he said, sounding breathless.

She fought to catch her own breath. His kiss had washed away every doubt she had.

He slowly slid off her tearstained glasses. "Do you understand now?"

She nodded, unable to speak.

"Miriam, you are so beautiful to me. And I will always think that, no matter what anyone else says." He wiped her cheek with the back of his hand. "Do you believe me?"

"I—I want to."

"Well, that's a start." He grinned and replaced her glasses. "I'll spend every day showing you how much you mean to me, Miriam Herschberger, until you do believe it."

"But Seth," she whispered. "What if I can't? I've never been as self-confident as you."

He took her hand in his. "Then we'll find our way together."

Her heart soared. "Are you saying you want to date?"

He looked up to the sky. "Finally, she gets it." Looking back at her, he said, "*Ya,* I want to court you. As soon as possible. What are you doing on First Christmas?"

She smiled. "The same thing you are. I'm going to the Fishers' house."

"*Sehr gut.* Can I offer you a ride, then? I think I know where you live." He chuckled. Leaning in close to her, so close she thought he might kiss her again, he said, "Just remember that I won't take *nee* for an answer."

Miriam hesitated, looking into Seth's handsome face. His tender words and gentle kiss were almost too good to believe. But she had to believe. Not only in him, but in herself. She suspected the journey wouldn't be easy, but with Seth by her side, and with lots of help from the Lord, it was one she was willing to take.

Chapter Fourteen

Miriam pulled back the curtain and peered outside in the darkness. It was First Christmas, and she was at home, waiting for Seth to pick her up. Just thinking about him brought a smile to her face. Touching her lips, she remembered his kiss. They had seen each other one time since, but he had been a perfect gentleman, not even kissing her on the cheek when he brought her home from work last night. But she saw in his eyes that he wanted to kiss her, just as badly as she wanted him to. Knowing that was enough.

Her hand went to her stomach, trying to calm the butterflies that were steadily growing there. The news that she and Seth Fisher had started dating had run quickly through her family, who had all given their approval—especially Lydia.

"See, I was right about you going to that singin'," she had said. "You should listen to me more often."

When she saw Seth's buggy pull into her driveway, Miriam dropped the curtain and retrieved her cloak. Her parents were already at the Fishers', so she turned off the gas lamp and stepped out on the front porch, using a small battery-powered flashlight to illuminate her steps. Feather-light drops of moisture landed on her skin, and she realized it had just started snowing.

Seth came out of the buggy and walked toward her. She noticed there was something different about him right off. Then she realized what it was as he neared the house. "Where's your walking stick?"

"Don't need it. Are you ready to go?"

She nodded and walked in step with him. He opened the door to the buggy and helped her in, then entered on the other side. But instead of grasping Gravy's reins, he just sat there.

"Is something wrong?" she asked, a tiny thread of alarm winding through her.

"*Nee.* Nothing's wrong."

Then she realized the buggy had an extra light inside, making it easier to see the interior, along with being able to see him. Curious, she said, "It's brighter in here tonight."

"*Ya.* There's a reason for that." He pulled a small rectangular package out of his pocket. "I wanted to see your face when I gave you this." It was wrapped in brown paper, with a silver bow on top. He held it out to her. *"Frehlicher Grischtdaag."*

Slowly she took the gift from him. "Merry Christmas to you." She flushed. "I'm sorry, but I didn't get you anything."

"You're present enough for me."

She rolled her eyes. "That's laying it on a bit thick, don't you think?"

He laughed. "Sorry, it's a habit. Go ahead, open it."

She removed the silver bow, then carefully unwrapped the paper. Inside the package was a tiny wooden chest, a small replica of a large one. The letter *M* had been burned into the lid, along with dainty ivy leaves. The entire thing had been stained and lacquered to a smooth sheen.

"It's beautiful," she said, running her finger over the grooves in the *M*. "Did you make it?"

"*Ya*. That's why I was late the other night picking you up. I was working on it in *Daed*'s shop, and time got away from me. It isn't much. Most of my money from now on is going toward paying back the community for taking care of my medical bills." He took her hand and looked at her. "But I want you to know that someday, as soon as I'm able, I'm going to make you the real thing. You'll have a beautiful hope chest fit to hold your grandmother's quilts."

"Oh, Seth." She squeezed his hand, barely able to believe she could be this happy.

He grinned. "Ready to go?"

"*Ya*," she said. "I'm ready." And she wasn't just referring to going to the Fishers' to celebrate the birth of the one true King. Instead of hiding in the past, she was ready to face her future, with Seth, God willing.

She had always thought having Seth Fisher in her life would take a miracle. As she glanced at his profile, she realized that the Lord, in his merciful grace, had given her just that.

* * * * *

A CHOICE
TO FORGIVE

By Beth Wiseman

Chapter One

Lydia opened the front door, expecting her friend Sarah or one of the children's friends. Instead, a ghost stood in her doorway, a vision from her past—*Englisch* in appearance, Amish in her recollection of him. A man long buried in her heart and in her mind, he couldn't possibly be real. But his chest heaved in and out, and his breath clouded the air in front of him, proof that he was no apparition. He was real. *He* was Daniel Smucker.

Up till this moment, Lydia was having a routine day, busying herself with baking and household chores. On this Thursday afternoon she was enjoying some solitude while her children visited her sister Miriam for a couple of hours. Chilly November winds whipped around the farmhouse, hinting of a hard winter to come, but a cozy fire warmed the inside of the hundred-year-old structure. Aromas of freshly baked pies and cookies wafted through the house—shoofly pie and oatmeal raisin cookies—just like her mother used to bake when Lydia was a child.

Lydia smoothed the wrinkles in her black apron, tucked strands of dark-brown hair beneath her white prayer covering, and headed to the front door, thankful to God for all that she'd been blessed with. Three beautiful children, a lovely home, and a church community that encouraged her to be the best Amish woman she could be, especially since the death of her husband two years ago.

Elam's fatal heart attack shocked everyone, especially since there was no family history of heart problems. After he died, Lydia had struggled to get out of bed each morning, but with the help of the Old Order district, she and the children were doing much better.

Today she was trying to keep her thoughts in a happy place, one filled with hope for the future, the promise of good times with friends and family during the upcoming holiday season, and a blessed Christmas to celebrate the birth of their Savior.

Then she opened the door, and this man's presence threatened to steal all that she'd been working toward.

"Hello, Lydia."

He stood tall before her in black breeches and a black coat buttoned to his neck. His half smile was enough to produce the boyish dimples she remembered from their youth. His sandy-brown hair, now tinged with gray at the temples, reminded her how much time had passed since she had seen him—eighteen years.

His voice was deeper than she remembered. But his slate blue eyes were unmistakably the eyes of her first true love, tender and kind, gentle and protective, reflective of a man she'd known as a nineteen-year-old girl. And now he stood shivering on her doorstep, clearly waiting for an invitation to come in out of the cold.

But Lydia couldn't speak. She couldn't move. And she didn't want to ask this man into her home—this man who had once promised to marry her, then disappeared from her community and her life in the middle of the night. And on Christmas Eve, no less.

But that was a long time ago, and she'd gone on to marry his brother. Thank goodness Elam had been there to comfort her after Daniel's desertion. Elam, the man she was meant to be with, whom she'd married and shared fifteen wonderful years with.

"Do you think I could come in for a minute?" Daniel finally asked, teeth chattering. "My ears are frozen." His smile broadened.

Lydia swallowed hard and took a deep breath. She was trembling, but not from the frigid air blowing in from behind him. Had he come to ask for forgiveness after all these years? Curiosity compelled her to motion him through the threshold.

As he brushed past her, he began to unbutton his coat and then hung it from a peg on the coatrack near the door—the coatrack *Elam* built. She scowled as she reached for the garment to move it, but stopped herself when she realized there was nowhere else to hang it up. Her arm fell slowly back to her side, and she watched Daniel walk toward the fireplace as he scanned the room—a room filled with memories of the life she'd lived with Elam.

Daniel warmed his palms above the flames for a moment and then focused on her husband's collection of books on the mantel. He gingerly ran his finger along each one, studying the titles. Lydia cringed. *Those are Elam's things.*

"You've made a fine home, Lydia." He pulled his attention from the books and turned to face her.

His striped *Englisch* shirt reminded her that his Amish roots were long gone.

"You are more beautiful than I remember."

Lydia couldn't recall the last time she'd thought about Daniel, but suddenly old wounds were gaping open. "What are you doing here, Daniel?"

He walked toward her as if he might extend his arms for a hug. She backed away and walked to the other side of the room.

He raked his hand through his shaggy hair, hair not fit for an Amish man. He wasn't Amish, she reminded herself, and hadn't been for many years. What length he chose to wear his hair was of no concern to her.

"I just thought you should know that I have talked to my family, and also to Bishop Ebersol. I'll be baptized back into the community two Sundays from now."

Lydia's heart was thudding against her chest. Had she heard him correctly?

"I'm back for good," he went on. "I'll be making my home at the old Kauffman farm up the road, eventually. Right now, I'm staying with my parents." He smiled again.

"*Ach,* I see." She nodded, then turned away from him and took a few steps. She folded her arms across her chest and tried to steady the quiver that ran from her toes to the tip of her head. "What made you decide to come back?"

She heard his footsteps close the space between them, and as he hovered behind her, she recognized his scent. Oddly, it was as though he still used the same body soap, toothpaste, and whatever else made him smell the way he did. She breathed him in, closed her eyes, and imagined his arms wrapped snugly around her waist, his lips nuzzling her neck, the way he'd done so many times back behind the barn following the Sunday singings.

Lydia silently chastised herself for having such

thoughts. She blinked away any signs of distress and turned to face him.

Daniel shrugged. "It's time. My family is here. My roots. I want to live out the rest of my life here."

He sounded like an old man on a course with death, not a man of a mere thirty-eight years.

"But you can't just go be *Englisch* for eighteen years, come back, and expect to just—to just be welcomed back into the community. You've been shunned, for goodness' sake." She shook her head. "I don't understand."

"You know as well as I do that if I seek forgiveness from the bishop—which I have—and commit myself to the *Ordnung,* then I can be rebaptized into the community. And that is what I choose to do."

This can't be happening, Lydia thought, as she soaked in what he was telling her.

"I'm hoping you'll forgive me too," he said softly, with pleading eyes.

Lydia knew that forgiveness freed the soul of an unwelcome burden, and she'd forgiven Daniel many years ago. So what were these resentful feelings spewing to the surface now?

"If God can forgive me, if the bishop can forgive me…maybe you can, too."

"I forgave you a long time ago, Daniel." *Even though you left me one night without a word.*

Daniel breathed a sigh of relief. "I'm so glad to hear that. I know that leaving a note wasn't the best way to handle things."

It was a terrible way to handle things. Lydia recalled Daniel's hand-scribbled missive. He'd left a similar letter for his parents, telling them all that he could no longer adhere to the strict guidelines of the

Old Order district and that he would be heading out into the *Englisch* world.

She quickly reminded herself what a wonderful life she'd had with Elam for fifteen years, a life she wouldn't have known if she had married Daniel. Nor would she have Anna Marie, now sixteen; Jacob, who'd just turned twelve; or nine-year-old John. "I suppose everything turned out as it should."

Daniel's brows drew together in an agonized expression, but he didn't say anything.

Lydia studied him for a moment, wondering exactly how much his being here would affect her and her family. Quite a bit, she decided. And she knew that to harbor any bad will toward Daniel was not only wrong in the eyes of God, but it would also hurt her more than anyone else. She would need to pray hard to keep any bitterness away.

"I just thought you would want to hear the news from me," Daniel finally said.

Lydia nodded, then walked toward the door, hoping he would follow.

Daniel reached for his coat on the rack. He looked like he had more to say, but Lydia didn't want to hear any more. His presence was enough of an upset for now. As she reached toward the doorknob, the door bolted open, almost hitting her in the head. She jumped back and bumped right into Daniel, whose hands landed on her hips. She slid sideways and out of his grasp instantly.

"*Aenti* Miriam sent this lemon pie," Anna Marie said. She handed Lydia a pie as Jacob and John bounced in behind her.

John closed the door behind him, and all three of her children stood barely inside the doorway, waiting for an introduction. And Lydia realized that Daniel's return was going to complicate her life in more ways than one. Her children had a right to know their uncle, but did Daniel really deserve to know her children? He hadn't even shown up for Elam's funeral. His only brother. But her children were waiting, and so was Daniel.

"Children, this is Daniel, your *daed*'s *bruder.*"

Lydia watched as Anna Marie, Jacob, and John in turn extended a hand to Daniel, who smiled with each introduction. Lydia wondered if maybe she was dreaming all of this. A disturbing dream, one she hoped to wake up from any minute.

"Very nice to meet you all," Daniel said.

"Your *Onkel* Daniel will be making his home here in Paradise, at the old Kauffman place," Lydia said. Not even a half mile down the road. "Right now, he is staying with your *mammi* and *daadi.*" Lydia steadied her voice and tried to appear casual in the presence of her children. "He is being rebaptized into the faith."

Lydia's sons nodded, then excused themselves. But Anna Marie eyed Daniel with suspicion. "You are dressed *Englisch*," she said.

Daniel shifted his weight. "Uh, yes, I am. I haven't been in town long, but I'll be stocking up on the traditional clothes."

Anna Marie narrowed her eyes into a scrutinizing gaze. "Where've you been?" She paused, but before Daniel could answer, she added, "Why weren't you at *mei daed*'s funeral?"

Good question, Lydia thought, as she waited to hear Daniel's answer. Elam had told the children that their uncle chose a life with the *Englisch,* and that he was shunned for doing so after baptism. But he never told them that their mother almost married his older brother before she married him.

Daniel rubbed his forehead, and Lydia could see the regret in his expression. "It's a long story," he said.

Anna Marie, a spirited girl in the midst of her *rumschpringe,* questioned everything around her. Daniel's return was no exception. "I have time," she said. She edged one brow upward and lifted her chin a tad.

Lydia cupped her hand over her own mouth to hide the grin on her face. Anna Marie reminded her so much of herself at that age. She glanced at Daniel, who seemed rattled by the inquisition.

"I'm sure I'll be seeing lots of you. We can talk later," he said to Anna Marie. His eyes shifted to Lydia.

Lydia pulled from his gaze, and his words echoed in her mind. *I'll be seeing lots of you.*

She and the children had remained close to Elam's parents and his two sisters and their families. Of course, his family would be including Daniel in all of their activities from now on, which would indeed mean that Lydia and her children would see him often. It wouldn't be fair to the rest of the family to keep away just because Daniel was in the picture now. Lena and Gideon had been wonderful to their grandchildren, and to Lydia, since Elam's death. So had the rest of the family. But they all had to realize how strange this was going to be for her.

"Fine." Anna Marie responded flatly to Daniel's offer to talk later. "*Mamm,* I'm going to go finish sewing Jacob's shirt upstairs." She studied Daniel hard for a moment. "Nice to meet you." And she headed up the stairs.

"They're beautiful children," Daniel said when

Anna Marie was out of earshot. His tone was laced with regret.

"*Ya,* they are." Lydia pulled on the doorknob and swung the door wide, allowing the chilling wind to coast inward. She had no parting words.

Daniel pulled his coat from the rack and slipped it on. When the last button was secure, he looked down at her, towering over her five-foot-five frame. "I know this is a shock for you," he said.

"It's fine." She tried to sound convincing, unaffected. There was a time when Daniel knew her better than anyone. She wondered if he could see past her words now and into her heart, where everything was anything but fine.

He walked out the door, then turned to face her.

Lydia started to close the door, but Daniel put his hand out, blocking her effort. "Lydia…"

Her cheeks stung from the wind, but she waited for him to speak.

"I've come home to start a new life." He paused, fused his eyes with hers. "Thank you for forgiving me."

Lydia forced a smile, then pushed the door closed. She stood still and faced the door, not moving, as an angry tear rolled down her cheek.

Had she really forgiven him?

Chapter Two

Nothing about Daniel's life had felt right since the day he left Lydia. But leaving Lancaster County was the right thing to do all those years ago, no matter how much the separation had pained him and hurt those he loved. If Elam were still alive, Daniel would have never returned home, despite his longing for family. His love for both his brother and Lydia had overshadowed his own desires.

He regretted not receiving his mother's letter in time to make it to Elam's funeral, but he'd moved too many times for his forwarded mail to catch up with him. By the time he'd gotten word, the funeral had long since passed. He recalled his sobs of regret, his feelings of despair at the news, and his confusion as to what Elam would want him to do. But it took another two years before he was ready to come home. Hopefully, he could be a friend to Lydia and a good uncle to the children. To speculate about more after so many years seemed far-fetched and out of reach at the moment.

Daniel parked the rental car in the designated parking area at Avis. It was strange to think this was the last time he would drive an automobile for the rest of his life. Change was on the horizon, and he continued to hope and pray that he was making decisions that were right in the eyes of God.

His parents openly wept when Daniel told them the truth about the night he left the community—that Christmas Eve so long ago. Their forgiveness partially plugged the hole that had been in Daniel's heart since then. But if things were going to be right for all of them, Lydia would need to know the whole story too—a secret that Daniel had carried for eighteen years, and one that Elam took to his grave. Daniel worried whether his confession was a betrayal of his brother. He could only pray that now Elam would want him to step forward with the truth.

Lydia's olive skin still glowed, just as he remembered. The dusty rose of her cheeks and full pink lips lent a natural beauty to her delicate face, a face that reflected the perfect combination of strength and femininity. Her dark-brown hair, barely visible from beneath her *kapp,* hadn't speckled with gray over the years like his own, and her deep brown eyes still reflected her every emotion. She still moved with grace and poise. And she still rubbed her first finger and thumb together when she was nervous, something she'd done more than once today.

But did Lydia have enough forgiveness in her heart, not only to forgive him, but also to forgive her own husband—a man no longer in a position to explain his choices? Could she forgive two brothers who had betrayed her one Christmas Eve so long ago?

Daniel climbed out of the car and closed the door.

I hope so.

* * *

Lydia heard a knock at the door shortly after Daniel left.

Please don't be Daniel again.

She was relieved to see Sarah Fisher, but one glance at her friend's face told her that Sarah had heard the news of Daniel's return. Sarah scooted past Lydia into the den. Lydia followed her in and closed the door behind them.

"Have you heard?" Sarah asked, breathless.

Lydia gulped and fought the tears welling on her eyelids. "*Ya*. He was here."

Sarah put both hands to her mouth. "Oh no. Are you all right?"

"*Ya*. It was a shock though." Lydia shook her head, then stared hard into her friend's eyes. "It was so long ago, Sarah. But after seeing him, it feels like just yesterday that he left. How can the pain bubble up after all these years?" She swiped at her eyes and hung her head.

Sarah walked to one of the wooden rockers near the fireplace and sat down. Although fifteen years Lydia's junior, she and Lydia were close friends, and Lydia knew Sarah would sympathize with her distress. Lydia took a seat in the other chair.

"You were *in lieb* with him once," Sarah said soothingly. "It's only natural to have these feelings."

Lydia yielded to the tears as heaviness settled in her chest. "I will have to see him all the time. His parents are the children's grandparents. He'll be at church services, family gatherings, social get-togethers—" She searched Sarah's eyes for answers. "It will be awkward."

Sarah seemed to be choosing her words carefully.

She reached over and touched Lydia's arm. "*Mei* friend, is there any chance that you and Daniel—"

"No! I could never have a life with Daniel. I don't even know him anymore. He lived his life in the *Englisch* world, the world he chose." Tears ran down her face, and her voice choked in her throat. "Besides, I loved Elam with all my heart. We had three beautiful children together. We had a *gut* life. I would never, never…" She shook her head, determined to stay true to her words.

Sarah patted her arm. "But you did love Daniel very much once."

"*Ya,* I did. But he left me, Sarah. We had so many plans, and to this day I can't understand his choice." She paused. "I don't want to have any bad feelings toward him. I forgave him a long time ago." *I did. I know I did.* Lydia looked up and stared into her friend's hazel eyes, sympathetic and kind. "I loved *Elam,* Sarah."

"Of course you did."

Sarah understood about love and loss, and Lydia suddenly regretted dumping all this on her young friend. She attempted to pull herself together. "What about you, Sarah? How are you doing?"

Lydia knew that the approaching holidays would be a hard time for Sarah. Her friend had lost a baby last Christmas Eve, and Lydia knew the miscarriage still lingered painfully in Sarah's heart.

"I'm all right," Sarah said. She tried to smile.

Lydia knew Sarah better than that, but before she could say more, she heard footsteps coming down the stairs. She quickly gathered the edge of her apron and blotted her tear-streaked face. "I don't want the children to know of this."

Sarah nodded.

"What's wrong?" Anna Marie asked when she entered the den.

"Nothing." Lydia tried to sound casual. "Just chatting with Sarah."

Anna Marie narrowed her eyes in her mother's direction. "You've been crying. What is it, *Mamm?*"

"I'm fine, Anna Marie. Did you finish your sewing?" She held her head high, looked at her daughter.

"*Ya,* I finished." Anna Marie cupped her hands on her hips and blew out a sigh of exasperation. "Why? Do you need me to do something else?"

Lydia cringed at the sound of Anna Marie's tone—and she needn't show such disrespect in front of Sarah. She sent her daughter a warning with her eyes and said, "We need to put labels on the jams and jellies later, and bind more cookbooks. I also have some soaps packaged to sell. Pauline Sampler said she has sold everything we've brought to her store."

"That's *wunderbaar,*" Sarah chimed in.

"A true blessing." Lydia walked across the room to a small table, where her loosely bound cookbooks were piled. She picked one up. "We've sold enough of these to pay for all of our winter supplies this year. The *Englischers* seem to love them."

Anna Marie stomped across the den toward the kitchen. "I'll go put the labels on, but I don't know why Jacob and John can't help more. Plus I'm tired of putting cookbooks together." She twisted her head around. "And I know you are not telling me something. You treat me like a child."

"We do not talk that way in this *haus,* Anna Marie," Lydia said as her daughter rounded the corner.

Sarah stood up. "I should probably go," she said. "I

still need to stop by the market. I just wanted to check on you."

Lydia walked alongside her. "Ever since Anna Marie began her *rumschpringe,* she is testy with me."

Her friend smiled. "It's her age."

"I reckon," Lydia conceded.

She hoped and prayed that Anna Marie wouldn't do half of the things she'd done during her own running-around period. The thought instantly brought her back to Daniel, and recollections of the time they spent together in their teenage years. Then the reality of his return punched at her gut, and she grabbed her side.

Sarah leaned in for a hug. "Everything will be fine, Lydia. You will see."

Lydia returned the embrace, unsure how her friend could possibly think things would ever be fine again.

Later that same afternoon, Daniel's father was in the front yard when Daniel pulled up in his new buggy, led by Sugar, a fine horse he'd purchased from Levi Lapp. It was surprising how quickly it all came back to him—gentle flicks of the reins and the subtle gestures necessary to guide the animal.

"He's a fine horse," Gideon Smucker said. He looped his thumbs through his suspenders and pushed his straw hat back to have a better look. "How does he handle?"

"*Gut.* I had no troubles." Another surprise—how easily his Pennsylvania *Deitsch* was coming back to him as well. Daniel could tell that it pleased his father to hear him speak the dialect.

"And I see you are back in plain clothing and got yourself a proper haircut," his father added. He eyed

Daniel's black pants, dark blue shirt, and straw hat, then nodded his approval. But his face quickly grew serious, and he stroked his gray beard. "Did you talk to Lydia?"

"Just briefly." Daniel paused, secured his new horse, and then walked alongside his father toward the house. "She was surprised to see me, to say the least."

"*Ya*. I reckon she was."

He pulled the door open for his father. As Gideon Smucker shuffled across the wooden floor in the den and headed toward the kitchen, Daniel breathed in the smells of his childhood home, flooding his mind with precious memories—and awful pangs of regret.

He continued through the den behind his father. The years that had passed were evident in the older man's stance. His shoulders curled forward, forcing him to bend over slightly at the waist as he walked.

The house was almost exactly as it had been when Daniel left—two rocking chairs to the right side of the fireplace, a dark green couch against the far wall, and the rug in the middle of the floor, now much more weathered and lacking the vibrant colors Daniel remembered. He'd played a lot of card games on that rug with his sisters. When he first saw Bethany and Eve upon his return three days ago, he'd been so proud of the fine women they'd become. They were just kids when he left—Bethany ten and Eve twelve. Now each woman had two children of her own. More regret plagued Daniel's heart for all that he had missed.

He pressed his lips closed and breathed in the familiar smell of fresh bread baking, then headed to the kitchen.

"Smells mighty *gut*," his father said to his mother as he took a seat in one of the wooden chairs surrounding the table—a long, wooden structure that could seat ten comfortably.

Daniel stood in the kitchen. A stranger in what used to be his home. But when his mother turned around and smiled in his direction, it calmed Daniel, just the way her smile had when he was a child.

"Sit down, Daniel," she said warmly. "I'll serve you up some butter bread. Got plenty of jams there on the table too. Supper won't be ready for a bit. Havin' meat loaf." She paused, fused her green eyes with Daniel's. "Is it still your favorite, no?"

Daniel recognized the same regret in her voice that he himself felt. "It is still my favorite," he assured her. He sat down in a chair across from his father, but he couldn't seem to pull his eyes from his mother. Her warm smile was exactly the same, but most everything else about her face was different. Deep lines webbed from the corners of her eyes, and similar creases stretched across her forehead. Daniel wondered how many of those wrinkles had his name on them. Like his father, Lena Smucker was much thinner than he remembered, and frail.

Daniel was lost in regret for what he'd done to his parents. The event itself. And then the lie. But he reassured himself that his choice at the time had been best for all of them.

As if reading his mind, his father said, "You said you spoke with Lydia. Did you tell her the truth about why you left?"

"No. Not yet." It had been hard enough to tell his parents and the bishop.

"The sooner you do that, the better. You owe her an explanation." His father shook his head. "It was so wrong what you boys did—the both of ya. I'll never understand—"

"Gideon, please…" *Mamm* spun around and faced the two men, a wooden spoon dangling from her hand, dripping brown sauce onto the floor. "Let's please don't do this now. Please." Her voice begged Pop to let the conversation drop.

Gideon's mouth thinned with displeasure, but he stayed silent.

Daniel knew that his father's response to his confession could have been much worse. His anger seemed padded with gratitude that Daniel was home now.

Bishop Ebersol, too, had accepted the news much better than Daniel expected. But Daniel knew who his harshest critic would be. Lydia. Daniel and Elam made decisions one Christmas Eve that changed the way all three of them would live their lives, with no consideration of Lydia's thoughts on the matter. And for that, she might never be able to forgive either of them.

Three days later, Lydia went to bed early after spending a quiet Sunday with her children. Thankfully, she hadn't seen Daniel since Thursday, but she couldn't shake the memories that continued to flood her mind, which kept her tossing and turning until much too late. She'd barely been asleep an hour when she bolted from her bed at eleven o'clock. Mother's instinct. Something was wrong. She scurried into her robe, pushed back tangled tresses, and blinked her eyes into focus as best she could in the dark.

She grabbed the flashlight she kept on her nightstand and made her way down the hall. She quietly pushed open the door to John and Jacob's room and pointed the light toward them, enough to see that they were both sleeping soundly. After breathing a sigh of relief, she closed the door and took a few steps to Anna Marie's door on the opposite side of the hallway. She stood still for a moment and recalled all the times she'd sneaked out of the house during her *rumschpringe*— most of those times to meet Daniel.

She rubbed her left temple and tried to push away the visions of him, but Daniel's presence in her home— in her and Elam's home—kept replaying like a bad dream, the kind you can't wake up from. She squeezed her eyes closed and took a deep breath, blowing it out slowly.

Please, God, let her be in there. Times were much different now than during her running-around period. The *Englisch* world was a far more dangerous place.

Lydia's heart pounded. She hesitated for a moment, then pushed the wooden door wide and shined the flashlight.

Anna Marie wasn't there.

After searching the entire house, and even outside, she finally went back into John and Jacob's room. She knelt down beside her older son.

"Jacob. Jacob, wake up." She shined the light on his quilt, away from his eyes, but illuminating his blond locks.

"*Mamm?* What is it?" He rubbed his eyes with one hand and pushed the flashlight away with the other. "It's too bright."

"Jacob, I can't find your sister. She's not in her room."

Jacob sighed. "*Ya,* she does that sometimes." He attempted to roll onto his side.

Lydia poked him on the shoulder. "She does what? Tell me, Jacob."

"She sneaks down the stairs and leaves," John said from across the room.

Lydia bolted up and turned the light toward John, who immediately shielded his eyes. His own blond hair spiked upward. Only Anna Marie had inherited her mother's dark hair.

"What?" Lydia looked back and forth between the boys. "What do you mean?"

Was it possible that both her sons were aware of this treason going on right under her own roof? Why didn't they tell on their sister? Lydia could recall a time not too long ago when both younger boys wouldn't miss an opportunity to snitch on their older sister—most recently, when Anna Marie had purchased a portable phone at the store in town. Her daughter had prepaid minutes and spent hours on the device before Lydia found out. The boys told on their sister when she wouldn't let them use the phone.

"Why haven't you told me about this?" she demanded. She flashed the light from one boy to the other.

Young John shrugged, but Jacob spoke up. "She said we'd be havin' our *rumschpringe* some day, and if we told on her, she'd tell on us."

Lydia stomped her foot. "Neither of you made a *gut* bargain, since Anna Marie will likely be gone and married before either of you have your *rumschpringe!* Shame on you both for keeping this from me. Anna Marie could be in danger, or—"

"I reckon she's with Amos Zook." Jacob sat up and rubbed his eyes again. "She done took a fancy to him months ago."

Amos had driven Anna Marie home from Sunday singings on several occasions, but Lydia didn't think they were officially courting. They seemed like an unlikely couple to Lydia. Her daughter was very outspoken and social, always right in the middle of any youth activities, especially volleyball after the Sunday singings. Amos stayed more to himself and could often be found on the sidelines. He seemed a very nice boy, but a bit timid.

Again her mind raced back eighteen years—to how unmatched everyone thought she and Daniel were. Lydia had been spirited, like Anna Marie, but mostly followed the rules. Daniel was softspoken until he felt an injustice had occurred, and then he reacted in a way that often got him into trouble.

She recalled a time in the eighth grade, when Daniel thought the teacher had treated a student unfairly in class, reprimanding the boy unnecessarily in front of the other students. Daniel voiced his feelings to the teacher—in front of the entire class. He told Lydia later that his behavior earned him a paddling from his father when he got home, but he said he had no regrets.

When they were a little older, Daniel even approached the bishop when a member of the community was shunned for installing a small amount of electricity in his barn, claiming it was necessary for his business. The man was a carpenter, but because of arthritis in one hand, he could no longer operate some of his non-powered tools—devices not available in gas-powered or battery-operated versions. He refused to disconnect the power, and the bishop had been unsympathetic and upheld the shunning. Daniel voiced his opinion about that too.

Lydia shook her head, trying to clear the images from her mind.

She sat down on the side of Jacob's bed and looked

hard at her son. "You best tell me where your sister is, if you know."

Jacob avoided her threatening stare and scratched his chin.

"Jacob!" Lydia snapped.

Her son rolled his eyes. "She's going to be real mad at me."

When did her children start being so disrespectful? Jacob would have never rolled his eyes if Elam were in the room.

"You best stop rolling those eyes at me," she demanded. "*I* will be mad at you if you don't tell me where Anna Marie is."

Jacob twisted his mouth from side to side, then said, "The old oak tree."

"How do you know this?"

Jacob shrugged.

"I will deal with you later, more than likely out by the woodshed!"

Elam had spanked all the children from time to time, out by the woodshed, but Lydia could never bring herself to discipline them in that way. Maybe she should. Maybe if she had, Anna Marie wouldn't be at the old oak tree—with Amos Zook.

A muscle quivered in Jacob's jaw, and his hurt shone in his sleepy eyes. Lydia knew her comment was fueled by fear. She reminded herself that Jacob was barely twelve, a long way from being a man, but too old for her to make idle threats. She pushed back his hair, then leaned down and kissed him on the cheek.

"I'm sorry I snapped at you, Jacob. I'm just worried about Anna Marie."

Jacob responded with a lazy half smile. "I know, *Mamm.*"

Lydia patted his knee and then stood up. She pointed her finger back and forth between her boys. "Don't you boys ever do this." She blew them both a kiss. "Watch your brother," she said, and walked out the bedroom door.

Lydia went to change out of her nightclothes. She couldn't believe that the teenagers were still going to the old oak tree off Leaman Road. So many times she'd met Daniel there.…

She hoped that the innocent encounters at the old oak tree hadn't escalated into something else over the years.

But times were different. And Lydia's heart was heavy with worry.

Chapter Three

Daniel couldn't sleep, and it was no wonder. Ever since he'd seen Lydia again, his mind twisted with longing, regret, and feelings that he'd suppressed for almost two decades. And yet, when he'd laid eyes on his first love a few days ago, it was as if no time had passed at all.

But the years *had* passed, and they weren't the same people anymore. Lydia wouldn't approve of the life he'd led in the outside world. Daniel himself didn't approve of the choices he'd made.

He turned onto his side and buried his face in the white pillowcase, appreciating the fresh smell of line-dried linens. A small gas heater warmed his childhood bedroom, and the aroma of meat loaf and baked bread hung in the room like a reminder of all he'd missed. How different his life would have been had he not left this idyllic place.

Instead, he'd moved in with Lonnie, an *Englisch* buddy he'd met during his *rumschpringe*. Lonnie gave Daniel a place to stay until he could get his own apartment, but Lonnie also introduced him to a world he hadn't known anything about prior to him leaving the

Old Order district—a world filled with alcohol, drugs, parties, and women. Even though he'd never felt comfortable there, Daniel had allowed himself to live that life for much too long. Almost six years. He took odd jobs to get by, mostly carpentry work since that was all he really knew. But with each step he took further into the *Englisch* world, he felt more and more detached from all he'd ever known. Most important, from God.

Then he'd met Jenny, a beautiful woman who'd been raised Catholic. Jenny had a strong faith, and his friendship with her was a turning point for Daniel. He said good-bye to a way of life in which he'd merely been existing. He dated Jenny and ultimately reestablished a relationship with God. He thought about Lydia often during that time, comparing the two women. Perhaps that's why he'd never asked Jenny to marry him. For almost two years he found a sampling of what he remembered from his youth, a certain calm that settles over a man when he is living the way the Lord wants him to live. He went to work every day, spent time with Jenny in the evenings and on weekends, and even attended church with her.

But when Jenny was killed by a drunk driver, Daniel in his grief wasted no time returning to his old ways. His relationship with God suffered, and accepting anything as his will became a challenge. How could his Father have put him on this path of self-destruction, when all Daniel had ever wanted was to do the right thing by God and by others? For the next seven years he moved from place to place, working at jobs that barely afforded him enough to live on. With each year that had passed, it was harder and harder to remember the peace he'd known when he was young.

But then Daniel met Margaret. When he was as down

on his luck as a man could be, seventy-year-old Margaret took him in and showed him another way to live. Daniel felt a connection to this wise woman that he could only explain as divine intervention.

He started out doing handyman work in exchange for room and board, but eventually he became to Margaret like the son she'd never had. They'd often drink hot tea late in the evening, and Daniel would tell her all about his childhood. Margaret listened intently, never pushing Daniel to confide more than he was ready to share. But eventually he told her everything, even what had happened that fateful Christmas Eve. When Margaret passed peacefully in her sleep four years later, Daniel was in a new spiritual place, and it was time. Time to go home.

He tossed and turned again. He closed his eyes to pray, but his communication was interrupted when he heard horse hooves, faint at first, then louder.

He glanced at the clock on his bedside table. A quarter to midnight. He threw the covers back, stepped onto the cool wooden planks, and then crept across the floor, purposely stretching his legs wide to avoid two slats in the floor that creaked loudly enough to wake his parents—something he'd found out in his youth.

His pants were thrown across the bed instead of hung on the rack or stowed in the dirty clothes bin. His mother would be appalled by his sloppy housekeeping. He pulled on the dark trousers, then grabbed a crisp white shirt from the rack and buttoned it on his way down the stairs.

By the time he reached the door, the visitor was already on the porch. Lydia. And she was frantic.

"What's wrong?" he asked, opening the screen for her.

She just stood there.

"I need your *daed*. He's the only person Anna Marie listens to these days." Lydia cupped her cheeks with both hands. "I hate to wake him and Lena. I should just go myself." She turned to leave, then swung back around. "But I'm so afraid…and if anyone can get through to her, it's Gideon."

Daniel wasn't sure what to do. Lydia couldn't even stand still, twisting about, shaking her head. He felt guilty for thinking how beautiful she was even in her desperate state and with her daughter in some sort of trouble.

"What are you afraid of? Do you know where she went?" Daniel glanced down and realized his appearance. Shirttail hanging, barefoot, slept-on hair.

Lydia finally brushed past him and into the den, shivering. Her black cape and bonnet were not enough protection from the night air. "I'm going to go wake him," she said, stepping around Daniel.

"Wait." He gently grabbed her arm. "Don't wake Pop. I'll go with you to look for Anna Marie."

Lydia pulled out of his hold. Anger swept across her face, and her hands landed on her hips. "I don't need to *look* for her. I know where she is." Then her face softened a tad. "I—I just don't know what to do when I get there. It will be awkward, and I—"

"Where is she?"

Lydia looked down for a moment. When her eyes finally lifted to meet his, a blush engulfed her cheeks, and she gazed into Daniel's eyes. "She's at the old oak tree—with a boy."

Daniel stifled a grin. "Kids still go there?"

"Ya." She pried her eyes from his. "And you know what they do there."

Daniel didn't know Lydia as a mother, only as a young woman with dreams—dreams she had fulfilled with someone else. He didn't recognize this maternal Lydia, whose eyes shone with worry. "They kiss," he said softly as his eyes homed in on Lydia's lips.

Then her eyes met with his in such a way that Daniel knew Lydia, too, was recalling the tenderness they'd shared, innocent kisses beneath moonlit nights, stars twinkling overhead. It was no surprise that young love still flourished underneath the protective limbs of the old oak tree.

"Times are different now," she whispered. "Elam and I…"

She paused, and now it was Daniel who couldn't look her in the eye. They'd had a life together, Elam and Lydia. Three children. To hear her refer to them as a couple was difficult.

"Elam and I," she went on, "tried our best to protect the children from outside influences, but with Anna Marie in her *rumschpringe* and all—I'm just worried. Times aren't the same as when we were…"

"Under the old oak tree?"

"Ya," she said softly.

Daniel stepped forward and reached for the words. "Lydia, I'm sure that you and Elam raised Anna Marie properly, and given that, I'm sure you have nothing to worry about. Why don't you let me go with you to get her?"

"No," she said, straightening to attention.

"Pop sure looked tired when he went to bed. Sure you want to wake him?" It was a stretch. His father hadn't looked all that tired, but suddenly Daniel was desperate to go with her, to be a part of her life.

Lydia took a deep breath. "No, I really don't want

to wake him, but he has been so *gut* with Anna Marie since Elam died. She listens to her grandfather, and mostly she just gets angry with me. Besides, what would I say to her and Amos?" She scrunched her face into a scowl, then rapidly shook her head back and forth. "Anna Marie shouldn't be in such a place."

"The old oak is a beautiful place." But Daniel could see in Lydia's face that somehow what seemed fine for her so many years ago did not seem okay for her daughter. "I'm sure Anna Marie is using good judgment, Lydia. Let me put my shoes on and grab a jacket. I'll go with you."

Her forehead creased, and she pressed her lips firmly together. "All right," she finally said.

Daniel hurried up the stairs, quietly as he could. In his room, he fished around in the dark for his shoes and then remembered the flashlight on his nightstand. He shined the light around the room until he located his black tennis shoes in the far corner, then pulled a pair of black socks from the chest of drawers. He sat down on the bed, stretched the socks over his cold feet, and slipped his shoes on, his stomach rolling with anticipation.

He tiptoed to the bathroom, swooshed mouthwash, and spit, wishing he had more time to groom himself properly. But she was waiting.

Daniel walked briskly down the stairs, shining the light as he walked. When he hit the floor in the den, he stopped abruptly, his heart thudding against his chest. *Where is she?*

Her scent tarried in the room, but he knew before he even reached the window that she was gone. He gazed out into the night just in time to hear a faint whistle, the pounding of hooves against the dirt, and to see her buggy begin its descent down the dirt driveway.

Daniel flung open the door and hurried onto the porch. He opened his mouth to yell out to her, but remembered his parents asleep upstairs.

"Lydia," he whispered instead, as he watched her disappear into the darkness.

Chapter Four

Lydia maneuvered her buggy across Lincoln Highway, propelled by the kind of determination that only a fearful mother could understand. Her glove-clad hands trembled as she neared Leaman Road, and she fought to keep a steady hold on the reins. As the lights from the highway grew dim behind her, Lydia pushed forward into the darkness of the cold night, wondering why her daughter and Amos would be so silly as to choose the old oak tree in this frigid weather.

But, of course, she knew why.

Lydia recalled the massive trunk and the sprawling branches that stretched upward, then draped to the ground. She remembered the way the moonlight charmed its way between the forked offshoots, gently illuminating those seeking to bask in the magic of the moment. Lydia could almost feel the misty dew dusting her cheeks, clouding the air around her—around her and Daniel—and the tenderness of his lips against hers. She should never have gone to get Gideon, knowing there was a chance she'd run into Daniel.

She pulled back on the reins, slowed the buggy, and

pulled to the side of the road, trying to remember what it was like to be sixteen and in love, and how she would have felt if one of her parents had ever approached her when she was under the old oak tree with Daniel. Lydia leaned out the window, making sure she was completely off the road, and clicked off the lights on the buggy.

She had shared tender moments of first love with Daniel underneath that tree. Did she really want to ruin that for Anna Marie by charging in there like a hysterical shrew, demanding Anna Marie hightail it home, and destroy what Lydia knew deep in her heart was an innocent encounter between a boy and a girl enjoying the thrill of sneaking out during their *rumschpringe?*

She'd raised Anna Marie well, and despite the recent distance between them, she knew her daughter would make wise choices. Perhaps she should trust her, let her enjoy this special moment, and then make it clear to her tomorrow that sneaking out was unacceptable. Even more improper on a Sunday.

Lydia smiled, thinking how her parents would have never taken that approach. Her mother would have sent her father to drag her home, and she would have been humiliated beyond recovery. *Thank goodness we never got caught.*

She wrapped the thick, brown blanket tightly around her, hoping Amos had been smart enough to at least bring a blanket, the way Daniel always had. Lydia sat in the buggy and recalled the events of the day, still not confident enough to ride away and leave the two teenagers. In the distance she could see the spanning might of the old oak against blue-gray skies.

Part of her still wanted to storm forward and drag Anna Marie home—the motherly part of her. But the woman inside of Lydia beckoned her to let the girl be, just for tonight. Recollections invaded Lydia's mind, sending her back to a place and time with Daniel. For a few moments she lost herself in the past, a place she seldom chose to visit.

Then pangs of guilt stabbed at her insides, and she reminded herself that she'd married another, and that such memories should be squelched in honor of Elam. Daniel had betrayed her, and she had married his brother—a wonderful man who had picked up the pieces of her broken life and patched her back together. Over time, Elam's patchwork grew stronger and became a thick barrier of resistance against the memories she harbored of Daniel. And she'd fallen in love with Elam.

Why did Daniel have to come back? After all these years, she'd never considered the possibility that he might return. The way he looked at her today, the sound of his voice, his touch—it rattled her. She could feel her heart starting to spider with tiny cracks, threatening to tear down the protective armor where memories of Daniel had lain dormant for all these years.

Her thoughts were interrupted by a faraway rustling, and Lydia watched as Amos's buggy began the trek from the tree to Leaman Road. She considered trying to turn around and get back on the road ahead of them, get home, crawl into bed, and talk with Anna Marie in the morning, but instead she stayed where she was.

It was several minutes later when the headlights from Amos's buggy drew closer, and she shielded her eyes from the light in front of her. As they passed by her, Amos did not look her way, nor did Anna Marie.

But they knew she was there, and that's all that mattered.

Lydia doubted Anna Marie would be sneaking out again, at least for a while. And no one had been embarrassed or humiliated, and her daughter would be home soon enough. She knew the Zooks well. Amos was a good boy, and he would be a fine choice for courting Anna Marie. Although tomorrow Lydia would need to sit down and establish some boundaries for her daughter.

Lydia twisted her neck around and waited until Anna Marie and Amos had safely crossed Lincoln Highway, then she motioned her horse into action. But she didn't turn the buggy around. Instead, she headed toward the old oak tree.

Daniel made his way down Leaman Road, unsure what he'd walk into but determined to be there for Lydia if she needed him. Maybe in some tiny way he could start to make up for his own past by helping her with her children in the absence of Elam.

But as he neared the old oak tree, wondrous recollections of his time there with Lydia paraded through his mind, mixing with a sense of anguish over the life he'd missed out on. He reminded himself, the choices were his to make.

He turned onto the worn path created by generations who had sought privacy beneath the tree, where he had first told Lydia that he loved her. As he traveled down the winding trail, it felt like he was entering a time warp, a magical place where the past stayed the past and you never had to leave.

Daniel pulled up beside the only buggy parked near

the tree. Since all the buggies looked almost exactly the same, he wasn't sure who he would find. Maybe Lydia had changed her mind about coming out here, and Daniel was about to intrude on Anna Marie and her beau, which certainly was not his place. He stepped out of the buggy, closed the door, and knew that whoever was beneath the branches was certainly aware of his presence.

With slow, intentional steps he moved forward, tucked his head to pass under a low branch, then straightened within the magical dome. He filled his nostrils with the familiarity of the air around him, a sweet, dewy fragrance that he'd never smelled anywhere else. Lydia used to say that no one left the old oak without falling in love.

He blinked his eyes several times, adjusted to the darkness, and briefly wondered if he was dreaming. But there she was—his Lydia—standing alone, delicate rays of moonlight brushing her cheeks, her eyes twinkling mysteriously, and Daniel wondered if there was enough magic in the night to re-create what they'd shared so long ago.

"Is everything all right?" he asked. She had the strangest look on her face, and he couldn't help but wonder if her thoughts mirrored his. "When I came downstairs, you'd left, and I just wanted to make sure you were okay."

She didn't respond, but took two steps toward him.

"Lydia?" he said after a few moments. She took another step toward him, her eyes hazy with emotion.

"Do you remember the first time we came here?" she asked.

Of course he did. He remembered every single time

he'd been with her anywhere. "As if it happened yesterday," he said, hoping his eyes would convey the importance of his statement.

"You promised to love me forever," she said as her lips curved slightly upward.

But her brown eyes narrowed, confusing him. She leaned close to him and looked up, putting her lips within a few inches of his chin. He could feel her breath, and she smiled again. But something about the smile caused Daniel to feel uneasy.

"You lied," she added simply. Then she backed away from him, but she never took her eyes from his.

You lied. You lied. You lied. The words echoed in Daniel's head, reverberating against the part of his brain that was trying to decipher whether or not he really had lied. He'd always planned to love her forever.

"I didn't lie," he said with boyish defensiveness. "I wanted to love you forever, but..."

She shook her head feverishly. "It really doesn't matter," she said, and then shot him the same confusing smile. "I found my true love. If you hadn't left, Elam and I would never have married and had three wonderful children." She arched her brows proudly.

Daniel hung his head for a moment, then raised his eyes to hers. "I guess you're right." He couldn't deny the truth in what she said. Maybe his leaving was meant to be.

He filled his lungs with the atmosphere around them, losing hope that there was enough magic to let them pick up where they'd left off so many years ago. *Please, God, let me do right by her,* he silently prayed.

"Of course I'm right!" she finally said.

Then why was she raising her voice in such a way? Daniel took a couple of steps toward her. "Lydia," he whispered. As he grew closer, he could see tears in her eyes. He took a chance and stretched his arms forward. "Lydia," he said again.

But she backed away.

"Leave me alone, Daniel." She swiped at one eye and held her chin high. "It's true that you are my children's uncle. I will respect that. For the children, and for Lena and Gideon. But I would prefer to keep company with you only when—when it's necessary."

All he could muster was "I'm sorry." Then he realized that the whole purpose of the mission had gotten lost somewhere. "What about Anna Marie? Is she all right?"

"Ya." Lydia didn't elaborate, and her eyes were still fused with his.

Did she have more to say? Was she waiting on him to say something else?

"That's *gut*," he said finally.

Maybe now was the time. Maybe he should tell her the truth now, tell her why he'd left Lancaster County that Christmas Eve. But would it even matter? She said she'd forgiven him, but it sure didn't sound like it right now.

As he considered his options, Lydia walked toward him once again, and this time she cut him off at the knees.

"I never loved you the way I loved Elam," she said coolly and with the same smile on her face as before. Then she turned away, bent low, and slid beneath the branches.

Daniel listened to her rush across the grass and

climb into her buggy. His feet stayed planted with the roots of the tree beneath him.

Hooves met with dirt, and with each *clippity-clop*, Lydia grew farther and farther away. Until it was quiet, eerily quiet, beneath the old oak tree.

Chapter Five

Lydia spooned dippy eggs onto Jacob's and John's plates the next morning, so the boys could eat and get started on their morning chores. Evidently, Anna Marie had overslept. She knew breakfast was served promptly at five, and Lydia assumed her daughter was exhausted from her little trip last night. No excuse. There's a household to run and much to do in preparation for Thanksgiving in less than two weeks.

Lydia had hosted Thanksgiving since the first year she and Elam were married. Both her side of the family and Elam's would gather at her home again this year. She pulled the biscuits from the oven, put them on the table, and realized that there was no way to exclude Daniel from the festivities.

"Where's Anna Marie?" Jacob asked with a mouthful of eggs, trying to stifle a grin.

"I'm sure your sister is tired this morning." Lydia shot Jacob a look signifying that no more discussion was needed.

"Anna Marie's in trouble," John added with a twinkle in his bright blue eyes.

Lydia put her hands on her hips. "No one said anything about trouble. You mind your manners and eat your breakfast." She glanced toward Jacob. "Both of you. Those cows are ready for milking, and I have a very long list of things we need to do to get ready for Thanksgiving."

Lydia refilled John's glass with milk, then turned when she heard footsteps descending the stairs.

"Sorry I'm late." Anna Marie slid onto the wooden bench across from her brothers and bowed her head in silent prayer.

"*Ya,* and we know why." Jacob chuckled.

Anna Marie raised her head and cut her eyes in Jacob's direction. "You better be quiet."

"Stop it," Lydia said sternly. She served Anna Marie some eggs and then turned to Jacob and John. "Finish your breakfast. Quietly. You both have chores to tend to."

All the children ate silently, and Lydia contemplated the conversation she would have with Anna Marie after the boys left for school. There was a fine line between parenting Anna Marie and pushing her away, but Lydia knew she couldn't tolerate sneaking out of the house, no matter how sympathetic she was about her daughter's budding romance.

It was hard for Lydia to believe that Jacob would be sixteen in four years and also entering his *rumschpringe.* Thankfully, nine-year-old John had even longer to go before Lydia would have to watch her baby boy venture out to learn about the *Englisch* world.

She walked to the kitchen counter, placed her palms on the edge, and took a deep breath, wishing Daniel's face would stop creeping into her thoughts. It was a distraction that caused her a variety of emotions, none of which she wanted to feel. This morning, it was mostly guilt. It was as if her heart had been dipped in truth serum and was sending confessions to her brain about a love that had never died.

But I loved Elam.

"I'm done. I'll go start the washing." Anna Marie pushed her plate away. "Hopefully we have enough gasoline left to power the wringer."

Lydia nodded, but was mentally calculating. Today was Monday, wash day. No worship service yesterday, which meant they would attend church this coming Sunday, as was always the case—every other Sunday. Lydia cringed, realizing that Lena and Gideon were scheduled to host worship in their home this next weekend. She was sure Daniel would be attending, no matter who hosted, but it would seem even more intimate being at his childhood home.

The first time Lydia ever ate supper at Lena and Gideon's house, she was Daniel's guest, with no way to know that she would end up spending fifteen years alongside his brother at that very same table.

She recalled the first time Daniel asked her to a Sunday singing, when she was sixteen and just entering her *rumschpringe*. They were both working at the annual mud sale at the fire station in Penryn. The event was mostly run by Amish men and women. Plows, farm equipment, and large items were auctioned in the field next to the firehouse. Inside, the women auctioned quilts and household wares.

On that particular day, the auction had held up to its name. Heavy rain had doused the ground, and everyone's shoes were covered in mud. Lydia left the indoor auction to go find her father. Instead, she'd bumped into Daniel and Gideon. Her father-in-law to-be was bidding on a plow out in the open field. When Daniel saw her, he sloshed toward her in mud up to his ankles, smiling as he maneuvered his way through the crowd.

He'd already been in his running-around period for a year, and Lydia recalled the smoothness of his voice on that day. "Wanna get out of here?" he'd asked.

She'd nodded. No words were really necessary. She'd seen the way Daniel stared at her during worship service. They sneaked away from the mud sale, walked down the paved street that ran in front of the fire station, and then cut down a gravel street that wound through the meadows, speckled with mostly *Englisch* farms. Lydia was sure they walked five miles that day. She had blisters when they returned to the auction site. They'd talked and talked, about anything and everything. She knew on that day that she would marry Daniel Smucker.

She sighed. Thanksgiving, then Daniel's baptism, worship every other Sunday, family visits, social gatherings… There was no way around it, Daniel was sure to become a permanent part of their lives. She'd need to harness any feelings that attempted to creep to the surface and focus on the things she had been tending to prior to his arrival—raising her children and running her household in a way that would make Elam proud.

And with that thought, she finished packing Jacob's and John's lunches.

"*Mamm,* we're out of gasoline for the washer." Anna Marie walked back into the kitchen, toting the red gasoline container they kept in the shed. "I'm going to take the buggy to *Mammi* and *Daadi*'s house to get some."

Lydia nodded. Her father-in-law always had plenty

of gasoline on hand, and he always enjoyed a visit from one of the children.

Daniel. He would be there, of course. Lydia clamped her eyes tight, again fighting the visions of him.

"Anna Marie," she said before her daughter reached the front door.

"Ya?"

"We need to have a talk when you get back."

"I know, *Mamm,*" Anna Marie said. "Thanks to my brothers, no doubt." She smiled slightly and then turned to leave.

Maybe it was Anna Marie's tone—calm, understanding, all-knowing—but Lydia had a sudden realization. Her baby was growing up.

Daniel had just finished helping his father milk the cows when he heard a buggy pulling up.

"That'd be Anna Marie," Gideon said to his son. "It's Monday. I reckon she's out of gas for the washing machine." He chuckled. "I think she does that on purpose as an excuse to come visit and avoid some of her chores. She's become such a regular on Mondays, your *mamm* usually bakes somethin' special for the girl to snack on when she gets here."

Daniel watched Anna Marie step out of the buggy. She looked a lot like her mother. Similar in height and frame, dark hair, deep brown eyes with a brightness and wonder all their own.

"I'm out of gas," Anna Marie called to her grandfather in such a way that Daniel knew immediately his father had been right—she ran out on purpose.

"Ain't that a surprise." Gideon grinned. He tipped his straw hat with his finger, walked toward the girl, and retrieved the empty can. "Get on into the house now and see what your *mammi*'s got cooked for ya."

Daniel started to follow his father across the yard, but Gideon turned and said, "Go spend some time with your niece. Get to know the girl." He pointed toward the farmhouse.

Daniel complied, but to himself he said, *I'm not so sure Anna Marie wants to get to know me.*

"I'm headed to town," his mother said when Daniel walked into the kitchen. "Daniel, sit down and have yourself a muffin with Anna Marie." She pointed to a chair across the table.

If Daniel didn't know better, he'd think that his parents had set up this whole scenario. He pulled out the chair and sat down.

When his mother left the room, Anna Marie eyed him with the same skepticism as before.

"Great muffins," he mumbled after he took a large bite and swallowed.

Anna Marie finished chewing and narrowed her eyes. "Why don't you have a *fraa* and *kinner?*"

Daniel shrugged. This was not a conversation he wanted to have with Lydia's daughter. "Just don't."

"Haven't you ever been *in lieb?*" Anna Marie's eyes began to sparkle, reflective of someone who was in love herself.

"*Ya,* I have been in love," he said.

"With who? Why didn't you marry her? Was she *Englisch?*"

Daniel cocked his head to one side. "You sure ask a lot of questions."

"I'm *in lieb,*" she said breezily.

Daniel stifled a grin. "Really?" He reached for another muffin.

"*Ya.* We're going to be married next November." Anna Marie propped her elbows on the table and rested her chin in her hands.

Daniel wondered if Lydia had heard this exciting news. "And what does your *mamm* think about this?"

Anna Marie's expression soured. "She doesn't know yet." Her brows furrowed. "And please don't tell her."

Daniel shook his head. "No, I won't. That's your place." He paused. "Why the secrecy?"

"*Ach,* it's no secret. Amos just proposed last night, and I haven't had a chance to tell yet."

Her face lit up, much like Lydia's did when she was really happy—from what he remembered.

Daniel couldn't help but smile, knowing Amos had proposed under the old oak tree. He recalled his proposal to Lydia. While it wasn't under the oak tree, like their first kiss, it had been equally as romantic—a picnic on a spring day, wildflowers in full bloom, and enough love to sustain the two of them forever. At least, that had been the plan.

He and Lydia sat on the paisley quilt with the picnic lunch his mother had prepared, the bubbling creek only a few feet away. Blue skies and a gentle breeze, the best chicken salad he could remember eating, and Lydia—her eyes gazing into his.

Daniel returned to the present to find Anna Marie scoffing at him. "Are you listening?" she asked.

"Uh, sure." Daniel left the creek and the past and tried to focus on what his niece was saying, wondering how much he'd missed.

"Why, then?" Anna Marie leaned slightly forward and widened her questioning eyes.

"Why what?"

Anna Marie sighed. "I didn't think you were listening. I asked you if you knew why *mei mamm* was crying after you left. Did you say something to upset her?"

Daniel pulled his eyes from hers and hung his head. "I certainly didn't mean to." He looked up to see Anna Marie growing less fond of him with each passing second, her eyes clawing at him like talons. Lydia's daughter was not going to be easy to win over. He wondered why the girl had already formed such a harsh opinion of him.

"I'm sorry I missed your *daed*'s funeral," he said. "I used to move around a lot, and my forwarded mail didn't make it to me in time." Daniel sighed, his heart filled with anguish. "I regret that more than you know."

But Anna Marie's expression didn't soften. She narrowed her eyes and pressed her lips together. Daniel reached for another muffin and tried to avoid her icy glare.

"What are you *really* doing here?" she finally asked.

Daniel took a bite of muffin, swallowed, and chose his words carefully. "I've spent enough time in the *Englisch* world to know that this is where I want to be. I miss my family."

"It took you eighteen years to realize that?"

Daniel leaned his head to one side and glared at her, wondering if the girl was always this disrespectful. *"Ya,"* he said sternly. "It did."

Anna Marie rose from her chair, and it was then that Daniel noticed her right hand curled into a fist. She slowly opened her hand, and Daniel hoped she wasn't holding what he thought she was. *Couldn't be.*

She showed him her open hand. "Is this why you're back?"

Daniel took a deep breath and reached for the worn piece of blue paper crumpled atop her flattened palm. His heart raced as he unfolded the note. There hadn't been much time, and he recalled how he had hurriedly scribbled the words. Seeing it again ripped open wounds that had never fully healed.

Dear Lydia,

I will love you until the day I die, but I can't stay here. The Englisch world is calling to me, and I can't live within the confines of our Old Order district. I hope that someday you can forgive me.

Forever yours,
Daniel

"Where did you get this?" Daniel asked. *And why does Lydia still have it after all these years?* He wondered if he should be hopeful about this.

Anna Marie leaned down on both palms and looked Daniel in the eyes. "I hope that you have truly come back for the reasons you stated, that you miss your family and realize that you belong in the Amish community. Because if you have any hopes of rekindling a romance with *mei mamm,* you will be greatly disappointed. She loved my *daed* with all her heart and soul. He was her forever love. Not you."

And then she left without looking back.

Daniel stared at the note and wished that there was some way to change history, go back in time. He thought about how a split-second decision had changed the course of his life, and how he would forever live with its consequences.

Chapter Six

Lydia walked across the yard to join Anna Marie at the clothesline.

"This is the last load," her daughter said as she pinned up a pair of black socks.

Lydia scooped up a brown towel, grabbed two pins, and shivered. "Mighty cold out here."

"Not as cold as this morning when I took the buggy to *Daadi*'s *haus*. I plumb near froze."

Lydia twisted her mouth from side to side and debated how to approach the subject of Anna Marie's late-night outing. "I reckon it was even colder under the old oak tree last night," she said.

Anna Marie finished hanging another pair of black socks, then turned to face her mother. "Please don't be mad, *Mamm*. Not today. I promise I won't sneak out again." She grabbed both of Lydia's hands in hers and squeezed. "Amos asked me to marry him last night!"

"What? But I didn't even know the two of you were officially courting. Don't you think that's a bit quick?" But Lydia couldn't help but smile. Anna Marie was glowing, and she recognized the look.

"But I love him so much, *Mamm*. You know we've

been going to the Sunday singings, and we spend all of our free time together. We want to get married next November!"

Relief washed over Lydia. They weren't going to have to plan a wedding within the next month or two, and both Anna Marie and Amos would benefit from a year of courting, giving their relationship more time to mature. They would still only be seventeen when they married.

Lydia hugged Anna Marie and kissed her on the cheek. "It's *gut* to see you so happy." She pulled back and pointed a finger at her daughter. "But no more sneaking out of the house at night, Anna Marie. It worries me so. If your *daed* was here—"

"I won't, *Mamm*."

They were silent for a few moments as they pinned clothes to the line. Chilling winds blew through Lydia's black cape, and she could see Anna Marie shivering.

"One more towel," Lydia said. She clipped it to the line, then grabbed Anna Marie's hand. "Let's go sit by the fire."

"I talked with *Onkel* Daniel when I was at *Mammi* and *Daadi*'s," Anna Marie said when they walked inside.

Lydia closed the front door behind them and headed toward the fireplace. "I see." She tried to sound casual, but just the mention of Daniel's name caused her stomach to knot.

Anna Marie joined her mother in front of the hearth and warmed her palms. "I don't like him," she said as she scrunched her face in a most unbecoming way.

Lydia quickly turned toward her. "It's not proper to say such things." She wasn't sure what upset her more—the fact that Anna Marie would make such a comment, or the fact that it was directed at Daniel.

"Yes, ma'am."

"Let's get to putting these cookbooks together." Lydia walked to the table by the window where stacks of crisscrossed recipes were waiting to be organized and bound.

Anna Marie sat down at the table across from her. "Do you like him?" she asked. She lined the piles up in front of her and began to slip one page behind the other.

"Who?"

"*Onkel* Daniel."

Lydia took a deep breath and blew it out slowly. "He is your *daed*'s *bruder*. Of course I like him." She paused and then said, "Although, I don't really know him." The words stung with truth.

Anna Marie stopped working and twisted a strand of loose hair that slipped from the confines of her prayer covering. "Did you know him when you were young?" Her daughter's bottom lip quivered, and Lydia wondered what exactly Anna Marie and Daniel had talked about. Lydia clicked the pages on the table, smoothed the edges, and started inserting the binder into the square holes on the left margin.

"Of course I knew him. We all grew up together." Lydia sat up a little taller. Anna Marie was working again and handed her another stack ready to bind. "Why do you ask?"

Anna Marie shrugged. "He just seems very different from *Daed*."

"He spent many years in the *Englisch* world. I'm sure he'll come back around to our ways, since he's planning to be rebaptized the Sunday after Thanksgiving." Lydia knew that Daniel's shunning would be cast aside following his baptism, but she also knew that in *her* heart the shunning would continue.

"I bet he hurt a lot of people when he just up and left," Anna Marie said. "Especially—especially *Mammi* and *Daadi*."

"*Ya*. It was hard for them." Lydia didn't want to talk about this anymore. "What do you think about this cover your *aenti* Miriam came up with? I like the wood-burning stove she drew and all the little details. Look at the smoke swirling up from the pot." She held the book up and faced it toward Anna Marie.

"I like it." Anna Marie looked up and smiled briefly.

"You finish up here," Lydia said. "I reckon I'll go brew us some hot cocoa. Your brothers will be home from school soon, and I'm sure they'd enjoy something warm in their tummies after a cold walk home."

Anna Marie nodded, but Lydia could tell her thoughts were somewhere else.

Daniel helped his father ready the house for Sunday worship. The sun was barely over the horizon when they carried the last of the benches from the barn into the house. His mother had been busy preparing food since before Daniel woke up, and the smell of freshly baked bread permeated the farmhouse.

"This should do it," Gideon said when the last bench was in place. "What else, Lena?" he hollered into the kitchen.

"That's all. I think we're ready." His mother walked into the den and touched Daniel's arm. "*Wunderbaar gut* to have you home for worship service."

Daniel smiled. His mother's joy warmed his soul,

but regret still plagued his heart. Margaret had helped him learn to forgive himself through prayer, but true peace would come when he knew that Lydia's words of forgiveness were sincere. He hadn't seen any of her family all week, not since Anna Marie had sprung the note on him. He wondered if his niece said anything to Lydia about the letter. He suspected not.

Daniel felt the sting of the girl's words. *She loved my father with all her heart and soul. He was her forever love. Not you.*

As it should be, Daniel thought. But it didn't lessen the pain. He suddenly wondered if coming back here had been a mistake. Would it be simply a constant reminder of all he'd missed?

He could hear buggies pulling up outside and faint voices. He walked onto the front porch to greet visitors, many of whom he hadn't seen since he left the district. But when Lydia stepped from her buggy, smiled, and hugged his mother, Daniel closed his eyes and sighed.

"Hello, Daniel," she said politely when she walked up the porch steps. Then she turned to her sons. "Remember your *onkel* Daniel, boys?" She seemed intentionally formal.

Each son shook Daniel's hand. Anna Marie walked in behind the rest of them and crinkled her nose.

"Hello, Anna Marie." He tipped his straw hat in her direction.

She raised her chin a bit. "Hello." Then she scooted past him and into the kitchen.

Daniel's back started to ache about an hour into the service. It was going to take some time to adjust to the backless benches again, particularly during the three-hour church services.

As was customary, the men and boys sat on one side of the room, the women and girls on the other. From where Daniel was sitting, he couldn't see Lydia, but he could see Anna Marie, who took every opportunity to fire him a look that screamed, *You stay away from my mother.*

Sunday worship hadn't changed one bit in eighteen years, and Daniel was glad he could still understand the service, spoken mostly in German. The temperature had dipped into the thirties, leaving it much too cold to eat outside. The men and boys sought seats throughout the downstairs, where tables had been placed. Women and young girls bustled around, serving meadow tea and placing applesauce, jams, and jellies on the tables. Daniel had missed the sweet tea leaves that grew wild in the meadows along the creeks in the area.

Lydia brushed past him, carrying two loaves of homemade bread. Their eyes locked, but she quickly looked away. Daniel joined his father at a table on the far side of the den.

He wasn't sure how or when, but he knew he needed to somehow find a quiet moment to speak with Lydia, to let her know that Anna Marie had found the note. It wasn't going to earn him any points, but Daniel felt Lydia needed to know.

It was almost two hours later before the large crowd disassembled. Daniel saw Lydia gathering up casserole dishes, and it looked like she was preparing to leave. She had avoided him all afternoon, refusing to even make eye contact again.

"Can I talk to you for a minute?" he whispered to her in the kitchen when no one was around.

She didn't look up, but continued gathering up miscellaneous kitchen items and placing them in a brown paper bag. "Talk," she said.

Daniel was hoping to talk somewhere quiet, away from everyone, but this might be his only chance. He touched her arm, and he could feel her body go stiff.

He found his way to her hand and slipped the note into her palm. "Anna Marie gave this to me."

Lydia kept her head down, unfolded the note, and appeared to be reading it over and over again. For several moments, he watched her trembling hand.

"I didn't tell her anything," he finally said. "I felt like it was your place to explain in your own way."

Her head twisted in his direction, her eyes blazing with anger and tears. "Explain to her? How do I do that, Daniel? What do I tell my daughter? That I loved you but ended up marrying her father when you abandoned me? Is that what I tell her?"

"Lydia—" Daniel touched her arm, but she pulled away.

"Haven't you caused me enough pain for one lifetime? Why did you come back here?"

Her eyes pleaded with him for some sort of relief from the pain she was feeling, and Daniel wanted nothing more in the world than to love her and take care of her for the rest of their lives. But seeing her like this, so distraught, hurting…

He knew he had made a mistake by coming back.

Lydia swiped at her eyes and waited for an answer.

"I missed this place, my family." He looked at the floor for a moment, and then back at her. "And I missed you. It was never my intention to hurt you a second time, Lydia."

She didn't bother to brush away the tear as it rolled down her cheek and dripped onto the wooden floor.

Daniel took a slow, deep breath, never taking his eyes from hers, and he spoke the words he thought she wanted to hear. "I won't stay, Lydia. I'll leave in the morning."

Chapter Seven

Lydia stuffed the note down in the bag with her casserole dishes, wooden spoons, and other items she had brought for dinner. Such an important piece of paper among such mundane items, she thought, as she dabbed at her eyes and turned toward Daniel.

"No. Don't go," she told him firmly. His expression lifted, and Lydia knew she needed to clarify her response. "It would be *baremlich* for your parents." She paused and, for the first time all day, gazed into his eyes.

"I'll be fine, Daniel. You and I were a long time ago, but I have to explain this to my daughter now. And I'm not looking forward to that." She shook her head. "I don't know how she found this. It was in my trinket box, in a drawer, underneath a bunch of other things, and—"

"The cedar trinket box I made for you?" He raised his brows.

Lydia let out a heavy sigh. *"Ya."*

"I remember when I gave that to you."

"Let's don't do this. No traveling down memory lane. You are a part of this family, and as such, we will be together for a number of activities. It is taking me some time to get used to you being back, but we simply must accept what *was* and what *is*."

He leaned forward, a bit too close for her. "Any chance that we can be friends?"

"I already told you, Daniel. I think it's best if we only keep company when necessary." She paused, but kept her eyes fused with his. "I married Elam, and I lived with him for fifteen years. We have three children. I am not the same young girl you—you proposed to so long ago."

"I think you are exactly the same, Lydia."

She chuckled. "Look closer, Daniel." She pointed to her face. "Do you see nineteen in this thirty-seven-year-old face? I think not." She was suddenly embarrassed, and she pulled her eyes from his and looked down.

"No, I don't see nineteen," he said as his face drew closer to hers. "But what I see is more beautiful than I even remember."

His tone was so tender, Lydia feared she might cry again.

"I'm just asking for a chance, Lydia," he said. "I'm the children's uncle, and I'd like to get to know them. And I'd like to get to know you again."

Lydia opened her mouth, but quickly clamped it shut.

"You were happy with Elam, weren't you?"

"Very happy. His death was devastating. I wasn't sure how I would go on without him..." She paused. "It's been hard for me and the children."

Pounding footsteps entered the kitchen. "Let's go, *Mamm*. Jacob and John are already in the buggy."

Anna Marie stood poised like a snake, with fangs ready to puncture the air from Daniel's lungs.

Lydia picked up her bag and ignored her daughter's attitude. "We will see you on Thursday, Daniel. For Thanksgiving."

She didn't look back, and barely saw him nod as she followed Anna Marie out the back door of the kitchen. Anna Marie did enough head spinning for both of them, glancing over her shoulder several times, cutting her eyes in Daniel's direction.

"I'm going to go take these cookies I made to Amos," Anna Marie said later that afternoon.

"Not before you and I have a little talk." Lydia pointed to the stairway. "In my room, away from the boys."

"But I told Amos I would—"

"Now. March." Lydia gently tapped her foot and waited for Anna Marie to move toward the stairs.

"I know what this is about," she huffed.

Lydia didn't answer. She was busy trying to plan out some sort of explanation about the note. Ironically, she was hoping to soften Anna Marie's heart toward Daniel.

Anna Marie sat down on her mother's bed, and Lydia stood in front of her. She opened her hand and offered her daughter the note.

Anna Marie shook her head. "I've already read it."

"Anna Marie, I have had just about enough of your attitude. That tone of yours is about to get your mouth washed out with soap. I don't care how old you are." Lydia paced the room as she spoke. "Daniel and I had a courtship before I married your father. The relationship ended, and then I married your father. And that's all there is to that." She stopped and faced Anna Marie, and put her hands on her hips. "And another thing, young lady. What were you doing snooping through my things?"

"I wasn't snooping. I was looking for my black sweater, and I thought it might have been put in your drawer by mistake." She hung her head. "But then I saw the pretty box. I know I shouldn't have opened it, but…"

Lydia sat down on the bed next to Anna Marie and patted her on the leg. "All right."

After a few quiet moments, Anna Marie said, "He wants to court you now, doesn't he?"

"What makes you ask that?"

"I can tell by the way he looks at you."

Lydia twisted the ties on her apron and avoided the girl's inquisitive eyes. "That's nonsense," Lydia said after a few moments.

Anna Marie sighed. "*Mamm,* I am *in lieb,*" she said smugly. "I recognize that look he gives you."

"*Ach,* Anna Marie, you're not old enough to recognize anything." Lydia shook her head, but then turned to Anna Marie, whose eyes shone with unshed tears. "I'm sorry," she added. "I keep forgetting that you are growing up."

"And getting married next year." Anna Marie held her chin high and folded her hands in her lap.

Lydia thought for a moment. "Anna Marie, I loved your father very much. But before him, it's true that I loved Daniel." She reached over and squeezed one of Anna Marie's hands. "But that was a long time ago. I'm sure you mistook any looks between us."

"*Gut!*" she said. "Because I don't like him!" And she bolted off the bed.

"Anna Marie!" Lydia hollered before her daughter reached the door. "Daniel is your *onkel,* and I will not have such talk from you. I expect you to treat him with the courtesy and respect that you would anyone else. Do you hear me, young lady?"

Anna Marie slowly turned around and faced Lydia. "Yes, ma'am."

"Now go check on your brothers and see if they've tended to the cows yet this afternoon."

When Anna Marie was out the door, Lydia unfolded the note in her hand and slowly read it again.

By Thanksgiving Day Lydia was a bundle of nerves, worrying about way more than the Good Lord would approve of.

Was the meal going to come together and would the turkey be juicy enough? Did she forget anything? Would Anna Marie mind her manners with Daniel? And—how was Daniel going to act?

"Jacob, more wood for the fire," Lydia instructed from the kitchen. "And John, I think your *Daadi* John and *Mammi* Mary are pulling in with *Aenti* Miriam. Go see if you can help them carry things into the house."

Jacob and John moved toward the door, and Lydia realized that she'd been barking a lot of orders at them the past couple of days. She'd been so preoccupied with Daniel's return and Thanksgiving preparations, she hadn't spent much time with her sons.

"John. Jacob."

The boys turned around.

"When you get done, I have one more chore for you."

John sighed, and Jacob twisted his mouth to one side.

Lydia smiled. "I need testers for my desserts. Is that something you boys might be interested in?"

"Before our meal?" John's eyes grew wide, and a grin stretched across his small face.

"*Ya,* I think so," Lydia said with a nod and wink.

Both boys scampered out the door.

Lydia's mother always brought more than was on her list. Lydia peeked out the window and wasn't surprised to see them coming up the walkway with their arms full. Her two brothers, John Jr. and Melvin, were pulling up with their families. Daniel and Elam's two sisters were also arriving with their spouses and children.

Mary Herschberger entered the kitchen, carrying two casserole dishes covered in foil. "Yams and a fruit salad." She placed the food on the kitchen cabinet, then walked to where Lydia was standing by the stove. "Lydia?"

"*Ya.*"

Her mother wiped her hands on her black apron and pushed her eyeglasses up on her nose, ignoring the strands of gray hair that hung loose from beneath her prayer covering. She glanced around the room, then whispered, "Are you all right, dear?"

"I'm *gut, Mamm.*"

Her mother's forehead creased with concern as she pressed her lips together.

"Really, *Mamm,*" Lydia assured her. "I'm fine." Now if she could only convince herself she was all right.

"I know this must be *hatt* for you, having Daniel return."

Lydia loved Thanksgiving Day, and if nothing else, she was going to pretend things were all right. "That was a long time ago, *Mamm.*"

Mary frowned a bit. "I know, dear. But I remember the way it was with you and Daniel."

So did Lydia. And those images kept assaulting her thoughts. She kissed her mother on the cheek. "No worries today, *Mamm*. It's Thanksgiving."

Her father was less subtle when he entered the room. "So, I hear Daniel is back." John Herschberger looped his thumbs beneath his suspenders. Lydia quickly glanced around the room to see if anyone else had heard her father's remark. Only Miriam. Her sister scooted past her father, carrying two large bags. She smiled sympathetically in Lydia's direction.

"Shush, John. We all know he's back," Mary whispered as she rolled her eyes at her husband.

"Hi, *Daed*." Lydia hugged her father, then made her way to where Anna Marie was hovering over the sink.

Her daughter was peeling potatoes cheerfully, since Amos was coming for dinner. Lydia had always served the Thanksgiving meal at noon, and the Zook family planned to eat much later in the day.

Lydia glanced at the clock on the wall. Eleven-fifteen. Everything was running smoothly.

Next to arrive was Lydia's sister Hannah, with her family, followed by her other sister, Rachel, and her group. Lydia poured the brewed tea from the pot into a pitcher and looked up to see Gideon, Lena, and Daniel standing nearby in the kitchen.

"*Ach*, hello. I didn't see you come in," she said to the three of them. She tried to avoid looking toward Daniel, but her eyes seemed to have a mind of their own.

"Gideon pulled up 'round the back of the house," Lena said. "Which is making it a mite hard to carry in all of my dishes."

"Anna Marie, I'll finish the potatoes," Lydia said.

"You go help *Daadi* and *Mammi* bring things in." Lydia took the knife from her hand.

"Let me," Daniel said when Anna Marie was out the door. "I seem to recall that you dislike peeling potatoes." He reached for the knife, but Lydia pulled away and slid the blade down one side of the potato.

"You've been in the *Englisch* world too long. You know that the men folk don't help with meal preparation," she said. "You best go busy yourself in the den."

"Suit yourself," he said. Then he picked up a peeled potato, inspected it, and placed it back in the colander. "You missed a spot."

Lydia looked up to see him wink before he turned and walked toward the den. That type of flirtatious behavior would get him nowhere. Even so, she felt herself blushing. Several men in the community had shown an interest in her over the past couple of years, but she couldn't recall any of them invoking a blush with such a simple gesture. And none of those potential suitors caused her heart rate to speed up the way it did when Daniel was in the room.

She picked up the potato and sliced off the leftover piece of skin. She recalled fussing to her mother every time she was asked to peel potatoes. *Hmm. Daniel remembered that.*

At straight up noon, everyone began to find a seat. Two tables were set up in the den, plus a small table for the young ones. Once everyone was settled, Lydia took a seat at the table in the kitchen. She was glad that Daniel had chosen to sit at a table in the den—but not so glad that he'd selected a seat near her father. Pop thought Lydia should have remarried by now, and she worried what thoughts her dad might be having concerning Daniel's return. Then she noticed Anna Marie by the window, and she realized that Amos hadn't shown up yet.

"I'm sure he'll be here, Anna Marie," Lydia said. "Come sit down so we can offer our blessings."

Anna Marie pried herself from the window and joined her mother at the kitchen table, along with Lena and Gideon and other family members. One seat was left for Amos.

But two hours later—after everyone had stuffed themselves with rhubarb pie, shoofly pie, banana pudding, and a variety of other desserts—Amos still hadn't arrived. Anna Marie had barely touched her food. Lydia knew how much she'd been looking forward to spending her first holiday with a boy, the one she intended to marry...

That was a concept still hard for Lydia to believe. Anna Marie seemed so young to her. Lydia knew that seventeen was an acceptable age for marriage, but it was still considered young by community standards. It saddened her to know that she would only have her daughter under her roof for one more year. Since weddings were always held in November or December, after the fall harvest, there'd be plenty of time to pick a date and prepare.

"Maybe his kin changed the time of their Thanksgiving meal," Lydia whispered to Anna Marie after everyone was gone. Everyone except for Daniel and his parents.

And Daniel didn't seem in a hurry to go anywhere. She scowled in his direction.

But what she saw next softened her mood. Jacob, John, and Daniel were huddled together, laughing and carrying on. Anna Marie might not have taken a fancy to Daniel, but clearly her sons had. Lydia had done her best to be both parents since Elam's death, but boys needed a male role model. They had her father and Gideon, but for the first time, she began to see something positive in Daniel's return to the community. Perhaps he would play catch with the boys or teach them things their father hadn't been able to before he passed.

"Come on with us, Anna Marie," Lena said. She retrieved her cape and bonnet from the rack by the door. "We'll run by the Zooks' place and make sure everything is all right over there."

Anna Marie's face lit up, and she rushed to her grandmother's side.

"You fellas come on too," Gideon said, much to Lydia's horror. "We'll dig out your Pop's old box of games."

Lydia knew how much the boys loved it when Gideon offered to play games with them, games that had belonged to their father when he was a boy.

"Gideon, they best stay home," Lydia blurted out, "with school and all tomorrow."

Jacob and John were already at the door. "Ain't no school the day after Thanksgiving, *Mamm*," John said. He scooted past his grandfather and out the door.

No, no, no. They can't all leave me here alone with Daniel.

But that's exactly what they did. Even Anna Marie didn't come protectively to her defense. She was too anxious to see Amòs to worry herself about her mother's crisis.

Daniel was once again warming his hands by the fire. Everyone else was outside and loading into the buggy, except for Lena. It had taken her a little longer than the others to bundle for the weather. After she tied her black bonnet, she leaned over and hugged Lydia.

Then she whispered in her ear, "I love you, Lydia, like my own daughter. Please hear him out. It might make a difference to you." Then she pulled away, smiled, and walked out to the buggy.

It appeared Lydia didn't have a choice in the matter. She closed the door and turned to face Daniel.

He just shrugged, as if to say, *I had nothing to do with it.*

Lydia knew better.

Chapter Eight

Daniel watched as Lydia lit two lanterns and placed them on opposite sides of the den. After the door closed behind his parents, he was prepared for her to ask him to leave. But to his surprise, she didn't.

"It will be dark soon." She turned to face him. Her blank expression didn't offer any hints as to her thoughts about being coerced into this meeting. But one thing he remembered about her—the woman had an independent way of thinking and doing things. Daniel knew she was not happy at being set up.

He smiled slightly in her direction, afraid to say too much too soon, and waited—waited for her to tell him to get out.

She didn't return the smile, and her voice was monotone when she spoke. "Would you like some *kaffi?*"

"That sounds great. I mean *wunderbaar gut.*" Again he smiled, but she just turned and walked toward the kitchen. Daniel followed her. "I'm surprised how much Pennsylvania *Deitsch* I remember."

Lydia poured two cups of coffee into white mugs, and Daniel noticed how she'd retained her youthful figure. Her black apron, tied snug atop her dark green dress, defined the smallness of her waist.

He sat down at one of the wooden chairs at her kitchen table and glanced around the room. Lydia owned more gadgets than his parents, who still did everything the old way. His mother still mashed potatoes with a hand masher and refused to buy a modern gas stove, but Daniel noticed a battery-operated mixer on the counter and a shiny white gas range next to the propane refrigerator in Lydia's kitchen. There was also a weather-alert radio at the end of the counter, also charged by battery.

"I was surprised to see that *mei mamm* still uses a woodstove to cook," he said. Lydia handed him the coffee and took a seat across from him at the kitchen table. He noticed a shift in her expression, from blank to fearful. Her coffee cup was in one hand, but she was grinding her thumb and forefinger fiercely with the other hand. "I would have thought that *Mamm* and *Daed* would have upgraded to something more modern. Something like what you have." He nodded toward Lydia's stove.

"They have talked about purchasing a gas range, but—" She stopped, locked her eyes with his. "But they haven't yet." Her eyes stayed fused with his, and her fingers were on overdrive.

She was so nervous and upset, Daniel wasn't sure this was the right time to tell her what he wanted to say. Perhaps he should just use this time to reconnect with her, hear about her life, her children—and Elam—see how all that went first.

"I told Anna Marie about us, about the note," Lydia finally said after a few moments of silence between them. She pulled her eyes from his and clutched her cup with both hands. She took a long sip, then kept a tight hold on the mug and lifted her eyes back to his. "She doesn't like you very much." She eased into a grin.

"It's nice to see you smile," he said. "And no, I don't seem to be Anna Marie's favorite person at the moment."

"That's understandable, I reckon. Now she knows her father wasn't my first true—" Her cheeks flushed, and she looked away. "She'll come around."

"But will you?" Daniel 's pulse grew rapid as he waited for her to respond. She wasn't kneading her fingers together anymore, but her cheeks were still a rosy shade of pink, and her eyes reflected her unease.

Lydia sat taller and released her firm grip on the coffee cup. She folded her hands in front of her on the table, took a deep breath, and fused her eyes intently with his.

He waited for what seemed like an eternity.

"We will be friends," she said matter-of-factly. "You are the children's *onkel,* and I love Lena and Gideon as if they were my own parents. But…" She sat taller and lifted her chin a bit. "There can be no courtship between us."

"I never said anything about *courtship.*" He couldn't help but smile at her presumption. Not that he didn't want exactly that.

"Well, I'm just—just making that clear." She paused, but held her head high and went on. "I was thinking earlier, when I saw you with Jacob and John, that perhaps it would be *gut* for you to be in the boys' lives."

"I'd like that," he said.

She was softening a little. During their first encounter, she'd made it quite clear that there would be no unnecessary socializing.

And he would settle for being her friend, although he didn't think it would ever be enough—for either of them. But one thing loomed over him, something equally as important to him as having her in his life.

"Lydia…" he began slowly. "I need to know if you have truly forgiven me in your heart. You said the words, but…"

She gazed at him with a faraway look in her eyes. Lydia had always been transparent, and he could tell she was about to tell a lie. An unintentional lie that she might not even recognize as such, but a fib just the same. "Yes, I forgive you."

He considered her response for a moment. "You said that awfully fast." Then added, "And I don't believe you."

"You think I would lie?"

"Not intentionally." Daniel looked her in the eye. "I think you *want* to forgive me, because you know it's what God wants you to do. But I think you are struggling to do so."

"Well, you're wrong," she huffed. "I do forgive you. I reckon you might give yourself a bit too much credit."

"Maybe," he said. Then he leaned his elbows on the table and leaned forward. "But I don't think so. We were in love, Lydia. It was real, and I've never gotten over it. I have missed you every single day, dreamed about you—and I know you felt it too. I think you still do."

She stood from the table. "Get out!"

He stood up and faced her from across the table. "Lydia, wait. I'm sorry. We don't have to talk about that, but there is something I need to tell you. Some-thing about that night, Christmas Eve. Maybe you will understand—"

She rounded the corner of the kitchen into the den, and Daniel followed in time to see her yank the front door open. Flames flickered in the fireplace as a cold rush of wind swept into the room. "Please leave," she said.

"Lydia, just let me explain."

She refused to look in his direction and kept her chin held high. Daniel walked toward her and stood in the doorway as she reached for his coat on the rack by the door. She handed it to him without glancing his way. "Good-bye, Daniel."

"Lydia, please…let me tell you about the night I left."

Lydia closed her eyes and remembered what Lena had said. *Please hear him out. Listen to what Daniel has to say. It might make a difference to you.* She took a moment to silence the voices in her head and con-centrated on the only voice that was important. She lowered her head and asked God for his guidance. Then she slowly opened her eyes and faced Daniel to see his eyes brimming with tenderness, begging her to reconsider. She pushed the door closed and motioned him to the couch in the den.

"Danki," he said.

Lydia flung his coat on the sofa and sat down in one of the rocking chairs facing it. She wasn't sure if she wanted to hear what Daniel had to say, or if it would make any difference. He'd given up on their love and left her. What more did she need to know? Besides, it was such a long time ago. Although, even all these years later, despite her marriage, the children, and her own belief that she had led the life she was meant to live, the raw hurt had resurfaced.

She wanted to forgive him. To understand. But those untapped emotions were bouncing around in a tight box of fear that gripped her, and she worried the lid might pop off any minute and expose what her heart screamed to her—that she'd always loved Daniel, and still did. And that thought made her feel like she was betraying Elam.

Lydia knew she needed to live righteously in the eyes of God, to forgive those who trespassed against her. *All this worry and guilt is a sin,* she thought. Daniel opened his mouth to talk, and Lydia made up her mind to forgive him and mean it, no matter what he had to say.

His expression seemed full of the life he'd led, in a world she knew nothing about. His brow furrowed, and the pain in his eyes was unmistakable. Whatever he was about to tell her, it was of great importance and discomfort to him.

"Go on, Daniel. I'm listening."

"Lydia, that night, on Christmas Eve—" He shook his head.

What in the world is he going to tell me? She realized she was literally holding her breath, and she forced herself to exhale. "It's all right," she said soothingly, as she would to anyone so tormented. And she hoped it would be—all right.

The sound of footsteps coming up the porch steps diverted their attention. No sooner did they both look in that direction than they heard a loud knock on the door.

Lydia rushed across the den and pulled the door open. "Amos! What are you doing here?"

He struggled to catch his breath. "Hello. I, uh— could I please talk to Anna Marie?"

Lydia scrutinized him for a moment, and then gently touched his elbow and pulled him over the threshold. She closed the door and glanced at her clock on the mantel. "Amos, Anna Marie was expecting you for dinner at noon. When you didn't show up, she left to spend the night with her *mammi* and *daadi*. They said they were going to stop by your house on the way. Is everything all right?"

Amos's eyes jetted toward Daniel.

"This is Elam's brother, Daniel." Lydia nodded in Daniel's direction, but then quickly turned back to Amos, who was still struggling to catch his breath. "I didn't hear a buggy," she said. "Did you run over here? And where is your coat?"

Daniel stood up and approached Amos with an extended hand. "Nice to meet you, Amos."

"Everything is *gut,* no?" Lydia asked again.

"*Ya*. Everything is *gut*."

Lydia eyed him suspiciously and noticed Daniel wearing a similar expression.

"I just need to talk to Anna Marie." Amos sounded desperate. "It's important, and I need to find her, and—" The boy leaned over, put his hands on his knees, and seemed to be gasping for air. When he lifted his head up, his eyes were clouded with tears. "I have to find her," he repeated.

"Amos, what is wrong?" Lydia brought her hand to her chest. "Is someone hurt? Did something happen?"

Amos stood straight again. He glanced back and

forth between Lydia and Daniel and seemed unsure whether to talk.

Lydia put her hands on her hips. "Amos Zook, you tell me right now what's the matter."

"I'm in trouble," he finally said. He looked down toward his shoes and shook his head. "I'm in a lot of trouble."

Chapter Nine

Daniel heard the anguish in Amos's voice. "What kind of trouble?" he asked.

"Yes, Amos, what kind of trouble?" Lydia echoed.

"I—I..." Amos shook his head, and his eyes darted back and forth between Daniel and Lydia. "I have to go." He turned to face the door, pulled on the knob, and bolted down the porch stairs into the yard.

Lydia was instantly behind him. "Amos! Amos, wait!"

Daniel joined her on the front porch and watched the boy sprint across the yard.

"What could possibly be so bad?" Lydia asked. "Amos!"

Then something inside of Daniel ignited. "I'll go after him."

He hurried down the steps, into the yard, and then broke into a run. When he reached the street, he stopped to listen. In the darkness he could hear something moving down the road to his right. Daniel ran, thankful for his time at the gym the past few months. He slowly began to close the gap between them. "Amos, stop!" he yelled.

But the boy didn't slow down, and Daniel wasn't sure how long he could keep up this pace. He pushed himself to run faster, stretching each stride to its fullest length.

Now he was within a few feet of Amos. "Stop!" *Please.*

Thankfully, the boy slowed his run to a light jog. Daniel tried to catch his breath as he drew near Amos, who finally stopped in the middle of the road.

The boy turned to face him. "There's no need to come after me," he said, breathless himself. "I will handle *mei* troubles."

Daniel held his palm forward, signaling that he couldn't quite choke out any words yet.

"Please tell Anna Marie that I love her. I'll always love her," Amos announced with the authority of someone much older than himself. He took a step backward.

"Please don't take off again," Daniel mumbled. He stood up straight and drew in a breath, releasing it slowly.

"Why are you following me? You don't even know me."

"But I know Anna Marie," Daniel said, hoping to entice the boy to talk to him. "And if you love her as much as you say you do, you won't run away from whatever trouble you're in."

"I don't have a choice." Amos pulled off his straw hat and wiped sweat from his brow.

Daniel wondered how the boy had kept it on. He'd lost his own hat early into the chase.

"We always have a choice." A cool trickle of sweat ran down Daniel's spine, beneath his long-sleeved blue shirt. "It's freezing out here. Can we talk back at the house? Just give me a few minutes to talk to you."

Amos instantly shook his head. "I don't want to talk in front of Anna Marie's *mamm*," he said firmly.

"I understand. Maybe we can talk man-to-man on the walk back—*walk,* no running." He smiled, trying to lighten Amos's mood. "What do you have to lose? If you don't like what I have to say, you can take off again." Daniel chuckled. "Believe me, I don't have the energy to chase you."

Amos stewed a moment, then agreed. Slowly the story unfolded.

He and two other boys—*Englisch* boys—had walked into a convenience store to get a soda. One of the boys, Tommy, noticed that the store attendant had gone into the back storage room. Tommy opened the cooler, and instead of a soda, he grabbed two beers and stuffed them inside his coat. The other boy, Greg, also snatched two beers and hid them in his jacket. Amos didn't want to do it, but the others kept nagging at him, so Amos finally hid two beers in his coat too. None of them counted on the camera in the store feeding to the back room, where the man watched them steal the beers.

To make things worse, when the man confronted them, Tommy took off at a run. Greg followed, then Amos—who ran right into the police officer that the attendant had called. The other boys were caught shortly thereafter.

"I've never stolen anything in my life." Amos shook his head. "I broke one of the Ten Commandments."

Tommy's father was the first one to show up and post bond for his son. It took about an hour for Greg's father to arrive. With no way to get in touch with

Amos's family, the judge had allowed Greg's dad to post the bond for Amos as well. And since all three boys were underage, they didn't have to spend the night behind bars.

But Amos was standing right next to the police officer when he left a message on the phone in the Zook barn: "Mr. Zook, I have your son Amos at the jail. He has been charged with theft."

"I can just picture the look on Pop's face when he hears that message. I have shamed my family." Amos hung his head. "And Anna Marie."

Daniel looked at Amos. The boy was three years younger than Daniel had been when he left on Christmas Eve. Even though Amos's problems didn't compare to Daniel's, it was still a heavy burden for an Amish boy. There might be a trip to the woodshed and a harsh reprimand, but in the end, the boy's father would forgive him for his poor choice. It wasn't like Amos had assaulted anyone.

Daniel stopped in the road and pulled on the boy's arm, and they stood facing each other. "Amos, you have to keep this in perspective. You made a mistake. Your father will be disappointed in you, and Anna Marie might be too, but if she loves you as much as she seems to, then she will stick by you. If you run away, sometimes it's too hard to come back."

"But I went to jail on Thanksgiving Day!" Amos blasted. "It's a day for family and fellowship, and I spent it eating a peanut butter and jelly sandwich in a room that had a toilet in the corner." He shook his head. "It was *baremlich*."

Daniel started to say something, but Amos went on.

"And the police officer—he said I have to go to

court! I reckon I'm going to have to pay money and—"
He paused and shook his head. "I can't talk to *mei
daed* about this."

"It takes a real man to face what he did. Amos, don't
make a decision right now that could affect the rest of
your life." Daniel took a deep breath and pushed the
past out of his head. "What is news in the community
today will be forgotten in no time. Are you really willing to lose Anna Marie over this? Where would you
go?"

"I don't know," Amos said. "I just wanted to see
Anna Marie one last time before I left."

They took a few steps. Daniel's teeth were chattering, and he was anxious to get into Lydia's house
where there was a fire going, but not too anxious to
take the time to help this young boy see things in the
right light.

"Before we get back to the house, I have a story to
tell you. A story that might help you decide whether
leaving is the right thing to do."

Lydia heard footsteps and faint voices outside. She
opened the front door and was relieved to see Amos
with Daniel.

"Thank goodness you are all right." Lydia touched
Amos's arm and then glanced at Daniel. "Both of you."
She quickly looked away when his eyes met hers.

As she pushed the door closed, Daniel and Amos
walked to the fireplace.

"I'm going to give Amos a ride home," Daniel said.
He continued to warm his hands in front of the fire.

"Gut," Lydia said. "It's too cold out there for walking." She eyed Amos with curiosity.

"I need to go home and talk to *mei daed*," he humbly said to Lydia. Then he turned to Daniel, and appreciation swept across his face. "*Danki,* Daniel."

Daniel smiled affectionately at him. "You're welcome, Amos."

Lydia wanted to ask Amos why he was thanking Daniel, what the two had talked about. A little earlier she'd been afraid to hear what Daniel was going to tell her; now disappointment nipped at the fear. While they were gone, she'd tried to prepare herself for anything, dreaming up every possible scenario that could have happened on that long-ago Christmas Eve. *Did he leave because he found another love? Maybe an* Englischer? *Did he have some grand opportunity for success in the* Englisch *world that he couldn't pass up? Did he decide he didn't love me after all?*

Lydia said good-bye and hugged Amos at the front door. After the boy walked outside, Daniel turned back to her.

"I'd still like to have our talk," he said. "Could I come back over after I take Amos home?"

It was still early in the evening, and Lydia didn't think she'd sleep a wink without hearing what he had to say. "*Ya.* I'll brew a fresh pot of *kaffi.*"

Daniel slowly lifted his hand to her face and brushed away a strand of hair that had fallen from beneath her prayer covering. His finger lingered on her cheek. "I'll see you soon," he said softly.

"*Ya.*"

She watched him walk to the buggy, mechanically closed the door, and didn't move for a moment. All the fear she'd fought to harness suddenly returned with a vengeance. If his touch invoked this type of reaction, how in the world was she going to be around him on a regular basis without facing her true feelings? That she had always loved Daniel. And still did.

Chapter Ten

It was almost eight o'clock when Lydia heard horse hooves coming up the driveway. She stood from her chair at the kitchen table where she'd been putting cookbooks together to use up her nervous energy, wiped sweaty palms down the sides of her black apron, and headed to the front door. Her stomach churned as she turned the knob, then waited for Daniel to come across the grass and up the steps. Lydia swung the door wide, stepped aside, and motioned him in.

She usually went to bed at eight-thirty. She considered mentioning that in case things didn't go well, but she didn't have to.

"I know it's getting close to your bedtime—and mine too," he said. "I'm getting back on *Mamm* and *Daed*'s schedule, so I promise not to keep you up too late."

"I made fresh *kaffi*," she said. "Warm yourself by the fire, and I'll bring us each a cup."

When Lydia walked back into the den, Daniel was sitting on the couch. She handed him one of the mugs she was carrying and wondered where to sit—at the far end of the sofa, or in one of the rocking chairs.

She backed away from him, eased into the rocker, and pushed the chair into motion with her foot while clutching tightly to her coffee cup with both hands.

"Lydia—" Daniel locked eyes with her. "As much as I want you to forgive me for leaving you that Christmas Eve, by telling you what really happened, I run the risk of losing you yet again."

"You don't *have* me," she said.

Lydia could see pain in Daniel's eyes.

"You might be angry with me after I tell you this story, but it's only fair that you know the truth." He paused. "I just hope that Elam would agree with me."

"Elam?" Lydia's eyes widened, and her pulse picked up. "What does Elam have to do with anything that happened that night?"

"Do you remember when Elam came to your house on Christmas Eve and gave you the note I wrote?"

She shot him a look that nearly knocked him over.

"I guess you do." He diverted his eyes and rubbed his hands together. "Anyway. That morning, Elam and I went to pick up your Christmas present, something I'd made for you. I was having it professionally engraved at a shop in town, and—"

"What was it?" The words flew from her lips. She recalled the present she bought for Daniel that year—a fine set of woodworking tools that she had eventually given to Elam.

Daniel's eyes met with hers again. "A cedar chest."

Lydia gasped. "You made me a cedar chest?" A gift like that was certainly allowable in their community, but considered somewhat extravagant in comparison to the small presents that are routinely exchanged at Christmas.

"*Ya,* I did," Daniel said in a low voice.

Lydia remembered telling Daniel on their way home from one of the many Sunday singings how she longed to have a cedar chest to store heirlooms for their future. She'd told him, but she'd never expected him to make her one for Christmas.

But wait a minute. Daniel was picking up her Christmas present that very day…?

"Daniel…"

His eyes reconnected with hers. *"Ya?"*

"If you were picking up my Christmas present on Christmas Eve morning, what changed by that afternoon to—" Her voice broke. "To make you decide you didn't love me enough to stay?"

"What? Is that what you think?" He scooted toward the edge of the couch and leaned forward. "I loved you enough," he said with a quiet but desperate firmness. "Enough to leave."

"That makes no sense." She set her cup on the table next to her, crossed her arms, and waited.

"Something happened before Elam and I were able to pick up the cedar chest." Daniel leaned back against the couch. "We decided to get a glass of homemade root beer and a whoopee pie from the Stoltzfus Bakery."

He seemed to be struggling with every word he spoke, which only added to Lydia's apprehension.

"After that we were strolling past the shops on Lincoln Avenue, and then we cut through a back alley to go pick up the chest." Daniel clamped his eyes shut. "We heard sounds of a struggle," he finally said. "An *Englisch* boy had a girl pinned down on the ground, and—and he was doing unthinkable things to her. The girl looked about our age, maybe younger. An *Englisch* girl."

He shook his head, and anger swept across his face. "At first Elam and I kept walking. It wasn't our place to get involved, nor was it our way. But then the girl saw us, and she cried out to us for help. I can see her face as though it happened yesterday. She had blonde hair and a pink shirt. I can still remember the fear in her eyes, begging us to help her, as the boy held her down on the gravel."

Lydia cupped her hand to her mouth.

"There were shops that backed up to the alley, and a few houses farther down the way. I kept waiting for someone to come help her, but there was no one around but Elam and me. She kicked at the boy and tried to scream, but he slapped her across the face and told her to shut up." Daniel paused. "And then something in me just snapped."

Lydia had stopped rocking in the chair and sat immobilized with visions of that poor girl, but she didn't understand Daniel's comment. "Snapped?"

"*Ya,* I snapped—I just couldn't take it anymore. I told Elam to stay back. The boy—his name was Chad—swore at me and told me to be on my Amish way, that it was none of my concern. But I kept walking toward him. He was big too. Muscular. And about my height. I told him to let the girl up.

"Finally, I was standing right beside them." Daniel took a deep breath. "I could hear Elam calling my name. I took a step backward, but then that girl's eyes met with mine again, and I moved forward and told the boy to let her go—or else."

Lydia held her breath and tried to imagine Daniel, or anyone from their community, speaking in such a way.

"He let her go, jumped up, and within seconds my

face went numb, and I could taste blood. I knew my nose was broken, but I wasn't sure if the blood was coming from my nose or my lip, which was on fire. I landed on my back, and when I was able to stand up and focus, I saw the girl running and screaming, but he went after her, grabbing the back of her collar and throwing her back on the ground.

"I couldn't imagine him hurting that girl any more than he already had. Elam was yelling for us to go home, but instead I marched over to Chad, grabbed him by the shirt, and returned an equally sound blow to his face. Then I hit him again and again, until he went down and stayed down. When I looked up, the girl was gone, and two men were running toward us."

Lydia's mouth hung open. She knew that violence was wrong, but she still admired his chivalry. And in the back of her mind, she wondered, *What did this have to do with his leaving on Christmas Eve?*

"As it turns out," Daniel went on, "Chad told everyone I'd assaulted him while my brother stood and watched, egging me on. It would have been a pretty unbelievable story—two Amish boys involved in such a mess—but Chad looked much worse than I did, and he knew the policeman who showed up. Officer Turner. I remember the way the cop looked at me with such shock, but he handcuffed me just the same and hauled me to jail."

Lydia gasped as more fearful images swirled in her head. "What about the boy, Chad? He went to jail too, no?"

Daniel shook his head. "Not only did Chad know Officer Turner, but his father knew him too. He didn't spend even one minute behind bars. Only me."

"Where was the girl? Couldn't she explain what happened? And what about Elam? He saw everything."

Lydia was wondering why Elam never told her this story.

"The girl was long gone, and Chad refused to admit that there was even a girl there. He stuck to his story that two Amish boys approached him in the alley, and that I beat him up." Daniel cringed. "I wasn't proud of my actions, by any means. Chad had a broken nose, like mine, but also two broken ribs. And always in the back of my mind was Pop. I'd shamed my family."

Lydia searched anxiously for the meaning behind his words. What was he trying to say?

"I just couldn't come back, Lydia. I was being charged with assault of another human being, something unheard-of in our community. I spent the night in a cell with four big, burly-looking men, and the jailer that night asked me repeatedly if I wanted to make a phone call. It wasn't until morning when I decided to call someone, an *Englisch* man I'd met a couple of months earlier; he was someone I trusted not to tell anyone. But it was Christmas Day. I had to wait until the day after Christmas for him to post bail and get me out. It was a *baremlich* two days."

Lydia finally understood. "You left our way of life—and me—because you couldn't face your father?"

"I know it sounds cowardly, Lydia, but I didn't want to shame my family like that. It seemed like I was always getting a lecture from Pop about not being able to hold my tongue, and this was much worse. But not a day went by that I didn't think about you and miss you."

She fought the tremble in her voice. "Did you not think to pen me a letter to explain all of this after you left?" Lydia brought her hand to her mouth as another realization hit her, one equally as bad, if not worse.

"Elam knew all this." She rose from the chair and began to pace the room.

"Lydia, let me explain." Daniel stood up and walked toward her.

She held both arms straight out in front of her.

"He befriended me. I cried on Elam's shoulder." A tear rolled down her cheek. "And all the while, he knew! He knew what happened. Elam let me wonder why you would leave me, repeatedly telling me that you just wanted to live in the *Englisch* world. How could he do that to me when he knew how much I was hurting?" Her eyes blazed. "Did the two of you keep in touch?"

Daniel stood before her, his own eyes clouding with emotion. "For a while. Until—until he began to court you."

He took a step toward her, and she backed up.

"I knew Elam was in love with you, and I knew he'd be a *gut* father to your children. I, on the other hand, had a court date to face, and I ended up being convicted of assault and spending six months in jail, so there was no coming back. I wanted you to have the life you deserved. I knew Elam could give you that."

"The life I deserved?" Lydia backed up farther until she bumped against the wall. She flattened her palms against the whitewash wall, steadied herself, and then brought one hand to her chest. "You and Elam got together and planned my future? Instead of telling me where you were and giving me a choice, you both just kept quiet, while my heart was breaking?"

All her wounds reopened. Her beloved Elam. How could he have lied to her? She'd been in such anguish, and he could have put an end to it. Instead he chose to pursue her for himself.

"I'm telling you all this, Lydia, for several reasons. First, it's the truth. Second, I want you to know that I never left because I didn't love you enough. And I knew Elam would treat you as you deserved to be treated. I, however, was a criminal."

"When did you write the note?" She choked out the words.

"Later that afternoon, when I realized I wouldn't be home for Christmas Eve supper or Christmas Day. I sent a note to you and one to my parents."

"Elam wouldn't do this," she said. "I don't believe any of it!"

But deep inside, she knew it was the truth. If there had ever been a chance of her forgiving Daniel, it was gone. Now she would struggle with how to forgive her husband for his role in this convenient lie.

"Why did you come back?" Lydia felt like she'd been hit in the stomach. "Not only did you leave me all those years ago, but now you tell me this news of my husband, that he lied to me so that I would be his. All the while, my heart was breaking for you. It is unforgivable. All of it."

Daniel reached for her, but she pulled away. "Lydia, I don't want mistruths hanging over us. I have confessed my sins before God, and now I declare them to you."

Lydia clamped her lips together in an attempt to squelch her sobs. She wished Elam was here to explain all of this to her…to say that he would never withhold information about Daniel just to win a place in her heart for himself. *Please, God…*

When Daniel wrapped his arms around her, she buried her head in his chest and sobbed. He could have been anyone—anyone willing to hold her up. But he was Daniel, and to stay in his arms would cause her nothing but heartache. No matter how much she had loved him, staying righteous in God's eyes was now compounded by her inability to forgive not only Daniel, but her husband as well.

She pulled away from him and pointed toward the door.

Chapter Eleven

Lydia placed a poinsettia plant on either side of the fireplace, and the flowery red blooms invoked bittersweet memories. Elam had loved Christmastime. She placed colorfully wrapped presents in various places throughout the den, adding an air of celebration to the room. But inwardly she was having trouble finding the spirit of the season. She'd been praying for a reprieve from the grief that festered inside her, but it continued to gnaw away at her from the inside out. Amid all her troubles, she knew that forgiveness was the only thing that would free her soul to find the peace she so desperately longed for.

"*Mamm,* when are we leaving for *Onkel* Daniel's baptism?"

Lydia arched a questioning brow at Anna Marie's casual acceptance of her uncle, whom she'd been less than fond of so recently. "Soon," she said.

She hadn't seen Daniel since Thanksgiving, and three days later, her stomach still rolled every time she thought about what Daniel and Elam had done. But there was no way out of attending the baptism, which would be at Daniel's new home at the old Kauffman place. Lena and Gideon told her that he'd moved in the day after Thanksgiving. She said Daniel had spent his time in the *Englisch* world doing odd jobs, mostly carpentry. And according to her sister Miriam, who'd stopped by Daniel's house to deliver eggs on behalf of their parents, he was doing an amazing job restoring the place.

Lydia rounded up Jacob and John, motioned to Anna Marie that it was time to go, and they loaded in the buggy to head to Daniel's baptism.

Lydia watched as the deacon ladled water from a bucket into the bishop's hand. Daniel sat with one hand over his face, to represent his submission and humility to the church. The bishop sprinkled Daniel's head three times, in the name of the Father, Son, and Holy Ghost, and then blessed him with a holy kiss.

It was such a sacred occasion, and despite the circumstances, Lydia was glad that Daniel received the sacrament of baptism after cleansing himself through prayer and confession, and that he had not accepted such a blessing without first being truthful with her, his parents, and the bishop.

But she couldn't seem to corral her emotions into one central part of her brain, where she might be able to process the information in a new way. Her thoughts were all over the place and filled with what-ifs. And it was that questioning of God's will that kept her up at night. If the events of that night had played out any differently, she wouldn't have Anna Marie, Jacob, or John, and she wouldn't have shared fifteen joy-filled years with Elam.

Every time she prayed for the strength of heart and mind to forgive both men, her heart wrapped itself in a self-preserving cocoon. She knew that for God to do his work, she would have to let down her barriers and allow herself to feel the pain, so his glory could help her move forward.

After Daniel's baptism, the women prepared chicken and wafers for dinner in the kitchen, while the men found seats at one of the many tables set up throughout Daniel's house. Lydia had brought a tomato pie to the event. Elam's favorite. As usual, there was a vast variety of offerings, more than enough to feed the one hundred in attendance: three ham loaves, four meat loaves, succotash, cabbage casserole, several types of potatoes, and at least two dozen desserts. Chow-chow, jams, jellies, and ten loaves of homemade bread lined the countertop.

Lydia glanced at the clock on the hutch in the kitchen. Straight up noon, and she could feel her stomach growling.

She had to admit, Daniel had already done wonders with the old Kauffman place. After four generations raised families in the home, the house was retired two years ago, after the last generation was unable to have children and passed on. A niece, who already owned a home in the community, inherited the place, and the farmhouse had been in need of much repair.

Lydia breathed in the smell of freshly painted white-washed walls and noticed new cabinets throughout the kitchen. Crisp green blinds were drawn halfway up on the windows, and festive garlands were draped across the windowsills, with tiny red bows attached. She poured brewed tea into a pitcher and handed it to Anna Marie, instructing her daughter to add sugar and begin serving the men.

Lydia picked up a bowl of pickled red beets and carried it into the den. Daniel was sitting with his father, the bishop, and two elders on the left side of the room. She veered to her right, where her own father was sitting, and put the bowl on the table.

Daniel's den was warm and cozy with a blazing fire in the hearth, and Lydia noticed the beautiful mantel above the fireplace—simple, with no ornate carvings, but bold and eye-catching. She wondered if Daniel was responsible for the fine carpentry. He'd always had a knack for building things. She thought of the cedar chest and wondered, not for the first time, what had become of the forsaken gift.

She took her time walking back to the kitchen, wanting to soak in every detail of Daniel's home as the what-ifs stirred in her thoughts. What might their home have looked like if she had married Daniel? Did they have similar tastes? While most Old Order homes were simply decorated, each one still possessed character and individuality. She saw Christmas presents placed around the house and bright poinsettias on either side of the fireplace, just as they were in her own home. A green, leafy garland spiraled around the railing of the banister that led upstairs, trimmed with holly and with a large bow at the foot of the railing. Her stairway was also decorated with garland and bows, but she couldn't put her finger on why Daniel's trimmings looked better than hers.

She lingered in the den for a moment and pretended to be checking tea glasses for refills, but her eyes kept involuntarily shifting to the flight of stairs that ascended to Daniel's bedroom.

Does he keep a box of tissues by the bed? A pitcher of water? A flashlight? Does he read at night before he goes to sleep? What color is the quilt on his bed? Which side of the bed does he sleep on?

The questions pounded obsessively in her head. She glanced in his direction, and his blue eyes rose and clung to hers. She jumped when someone touched her arm.

"Are you all right, dear?" Lena asked.

"Ya." Lydia faced Lena, but she could feel Daniel's eyes still on her.

"Daniel said that he told you of his trouble on Christmas Eve. I reckon that must have been difficult to hear." Lena's kind eyes shone with tenderness and sympathy.

"Ya," she said again. "But it didn't make me feel differently about things, Lena, like you said it might. I feel worse. I feel like Elam betrayed me too, and he isn't even here to defend himself."

Lena nodded. "I understand. Both boys behaved badly. Daniel should have come to us instead of running away. We would have felt shame, but we would have gotten through it and had our son in the community." Lena's brows drew together in an agonized expression. "Elam did not act in a *gut* way either. He also should have told the truth. But my dear, sweet Lydia"—Lena's voiced sharpened—"it is not our place to question God's will, nor to pass judgment on others." She paused. "I remind myself of this when *mei* own hurt rises to the surface."

Lena was a wise woman, and Lydia had always been close to her. "I know you're right, Lena." She glanced back toward Daniel, who was busy stuffing a spoonful of food into his mouth and listening intently to something his father was saying. "I'm just trying to find my way through all of this."

Women scurried around them as they stood off to one corner, whispering.

Lena smiled. "You already know the way, my child. Now you must travel the path of least resistance and welcome forgiveness into your heart. Let God heal what pains you."

"*Mamm,* we need more butter bread," Anna Marie said as she brushed by Lydia and Lena.

Lena gave Lydia a quick pat on the arm. "I have bread warming in the oven. I'll go get it." She started to leave, then stopped. "Lydia, I am chilled to the bone, and I'm not about to shuffle around here in my long cape. Upstairs is a closet at the end of the hallway. I saw a sweater in there while I was helping Daniel clean the place up last week. Must have been left behind by one of the Kauffmans. Would you be a dear and get it for me?" She winked at Lydia and headed to the kitchen.

Daniel watched Lydia going up the stairs. The thought of her that close to his bedroom sent tidal waves of longing and desire pulsing through his very being. He grew restless as he searched for an excuse to go upstairs. As Lydia disappeared out of sight, he pulled his eyes from the stairway and met his father's speculative gaze. Gideon's brows furrowed in Daniel's direction, and he feared a reprimand from his father for ogling Lydia in such a way.

But then Gideon's left brow edged upward mischievously. "Daniel, I reckon I've eaten more of this *gut* food than I should have, and it's left me with a bit of a bellyache. Could you fetch me something from your medicine cabinet?"

"Right away, Pop." Daniel's fork clanged against his

plate as he hurriedly pushed back his chair. He saw the hint of a smile on his father's face, which Gideon quickly masked as he reached for a piece of butter bread.

Daniel tried to keep his anticipation in check as he walked up the stairs. He hadn't been alone with Lydia since Thanksgiving, the night she cried in his arms. Her hurt had speared through his own heart, leaving him with regret and despair.

He wondered why she had gone upstairs and where she might be. There was a bathroom downstairs for guests. He glanced through the open door on his left, and then a few steps farther, through another open door on his right. Lydia wasn't in either of the extra bedrooms, which meant she was either in the bathroom farther down the hall or in his bedroom at the end of the corridor. His pulse quickened when he passed by the bathroom and she wasn't in there.

He slowly stepped around the corner to his bedroom, and there she was—sitting on his bed, running her hand gracefully across the dark-blue quilt atop his bed. Rays of sunshine shone through the window and danced on the wooden floor. She didn't look up, but the old stairs and wooden slats down the hallway had crackled beneath his feet, announcing his coming.

"Which side of the bed do you sleep on?" she asked. Her hand continued to stroke the counterpane in a way that tantalized Daniel's senses.

"The side you're sitting on," he said with a shaky voice.

"Hmm—" She raised her eyes to his. "It would have never worked. I sleep on this side too." She patted a spot beside her on the bed.

Daniel nervously ran his hand through his freshly

bobbed haircut. His sister had given him a proper trim yesterday in preparation for his baptism. "I would have gladly changed sides."

Hope was alive in his heart, and he feared she'd snatch it from him at any second. So he watched her, savored her, sitting on his bed in such a way. He expected her to get up and walk out of the room at any second. But instead, she slowly rose off the bed and began to wander around his room.

"Do you read before you go to sleep?" She turned to face him, and her expression was that of a woman basking in the knowledge of her power over him.

"Ya," he answered, his feet rooted to the floor. Her movements were intoxicating to him.

"Hmm—" she said again as she continued walking lightly around his room. She scanned every single item in the small room as if her life depended on it.

Daniel felt utterly scrutinized.

She picked up the small battery-operated alarm clock that he kept on his bedside table. "I have this same alarm clock in my bedroom," she said. Then she gently put it back in its place and continued around the room.

He hoped her scent would linger in his bedroom long after she was gone.

"Lydia—" He was finally able to push his feet into the room and draw near her, expecting her to back away. "I'm so very sorry about everything."

She didn't move, and her lips curled slightly. "I know you are."

Did he hear her correctly? Was she coming around? His heart danced a jig of victory, and he moved closer to her. "Can we please spend some time together, get to know each other again?"

She allowed herself a long gaze around his room, and then turned back and faced him with deep longing in her eyes, which her words defied. "No," she said, her voice uncompromising, yet with a degree of warmth Daniel found confusing.

Daniel heard footsteps coming up the stairs and down the hallway. He knew that his and Lydia's presence in his bedroom was inappropriate and would be frowned upon by anyone who found them here, but neither of them made a move to leave. They stood facing each other, longing in both their eyes, and neither moved until they heard Anna Marie's voice at the doorway.

Chapter Twelve

Lydia's delusional state of calm left her when she saw Anna Marie in the doorway. She'd assumed it would be Lena or Gideon, and she could have handled either of their reactions. But Anna Marie was another story. She braced herself for a harsh lashing from her daughter as she and Daniel stood side by side in the middle of his bedroom, looking like they'd been caught doing something they surely hadn't.

"Sarah and Miriam are looking for you," Anna Marie said with an air of unexpected composure, and even amusement. "I reckon they need your help serving dessert."

Lydia recalled the way Anna Marie had referred to Daniel as her uncle this morning, with a fondness in her voice. And now she seemed tolerant of Daniel and Lydia being alone in Daniel's bedroom together.

Lydia walked to where her daughter was standing in the doorway, and they both started down the hallway. Daniel followed.

When all three reached the bottom of the stairs, Lena gave Lydia a puzzled look. Lydia widened her eyes, mirroring her mother-in-law's expression.

"The sweater?" Lena asked.

"*Ach!* I forgot." Lydia twirled around to head back up the stairs, but Daniel gently touched her arm.

"I forgot to get something for Pop. I'll grab the sweater for *Mamm* while I'm up there." He stepped past her and took the stairs two at a time. Lena merely shook her head and walked back to the kitchen.

Anna Marie stood before her. Lydia was having trouble reading her daughter's expression.

"Daniel and I went upstairs together—I mean not together," Lydia stumbled. "We went upstairs because we needed to— No, *ach*. What I mean is, we—well, I reckon I was coming for a sweater for *Mammi,* and Daniel was, uh…"

"And *Mammi*'s sweater was in Daniel's room, no?" Anna Marie smiled sagely at Lydia.

This was role reversal at its worst. And Lydia had done nothing wrong. Frustration swept over her in a blanket of confused thoughts, and she shrugged and said, "I have to go help Miriam and Sarah." She shook her head and stormed away, embarrassed that she was behaving like someone Anna Marie's age.

When she entered the kitchen, the cleanup process was underway. Several women were lined up at the sink, one washing dishes, another drying, and a third putting the dishes where they belonged in the cabinets. The young girls were hauling the dirty plates in from the other rooms and stacking them in a pile by the sink. It was almost too crowded for Lydia to maneuver through the room, and she wasn't sure where she was needed. Then she spotted Miriam and Sarah in the corner.

"What do you need help with?" Lydia glanced back and forth between her sister and her friend. Miriam wasn't much older than her own daughter. And Sarah was also considerably younger than Lydia. All of a sudden Lydia felt old and even more ridiculous about her behavior in Daniel's bedroom.

"We just wanted to make sure you were all right," Miriam said. She looked toward her shoes for a moment, her glasses slipping down her nose. She gave them a push upward, then raised her eyes back to face Lydia. "We saw Daniel go upstairs behind you."

Lydia hadn't said anything to Miriam about Daniel, but of course her sister knew. Everyone knew. But Lydia was touched by her concern. "I'm fine," Lydia assured her.

Sarah leaned her face closer to Lydia's. "You were up there for quite a while." Sarah arched her brows and grinned.

Lydia opened her mouth to tell Sarah that her presumptions were out of line, but then she recalled her behavior in the bedroom. Even though she hadn't done anything wrong, she knew her conduct was improper. But then she noticed something. *Sarah is grinning.*

It was so nice to see her friend smiling. Each time she'd been around Sarah recently, the sadness was evident in her eyes. The closer it came to the anniversary of her miscarriage, the more she seemed to revert inside herself. Perhaps Lydia's affairs of the heart were a distraction for her friend. Although she didn't feel comfortable discussing it in front of her sister.

"Miriam." They all turned to see Miram and Lydia's mother holding two brown bags. "Can you carry these to the buggy for me? This one is a mite too heavy for your old mother." She lifted the bag on her left hip up and pushed it toward Miriam.

"You're not old, *Mamm*," Miriam said. She took both bags and walked out the door.

Lydia was glad when her mother went back to the other side of the room.

Sarah's eyes were wide with anticipation, and although Lydia wasn't proud of the way she'd acted upstairs, if a few details would brighten Sarah's day, then so be it.

Daniel retrieved the sweater for *Mamm* from the hall closet and then grabbed a bottle of Tums from the medicine cabinet in the bathroom for *Daed*. He slipped into his bedroom and breathed in, but all he could smell was the aroma of food permeating up the stairs. He glanced around for any trace that Lydia had been there and saw the indent in his blue comforter where she'd sat. Why had she come to his room? And what might have happened if Anna Marie hadn't interrupted them?

Lydia had said she was not interested in getting reacquainted with him, but Daniel didn't care what she said—her eyes had brimmed with unspoken passion. There was still something between them. After seeing the expression on her face, the thought of reestablishing a relationship with her didn't seem so far-fetched as when he'd first arrived. He just hoped and prayed that she would give him an opportunity to make up for what he'd done and give him a chance to love her forever.

He edged down the stairs, and the last person he wanted to face was standing near the bottom step with her hands on her hips. The crowd was dispersing, and Daniel slid past Anna Marie, but not without her calling him back. "*Onkel* Daniel?"

It was strange to hear her call him uncle. He cringed and turned cautiously around. *"Ya?"*

"Can I talk to you for a minute?" Her voice didn't have the sharp edge to it that he'd gotten used to from Anna Marie.

"I need to tell everyone good-bye. Can you wait a few minutes?" he asked, halfway hoping she couldn't. He wasn't in the mood for whatever she had to say about catching him and Lydia upstairs together. They weren't children and didn't need a reprimand from a sixteen-year-old.

"Ya. I'll wait." Her voice was smooth and unbothered.

He nodded in her direction and then headed into the den to say his good-byes. It was about fifteen minutes later when he found Anna Marie sitting at the bottom of the stairs, apparently having not moved from that spot. The women, including Lydia, were gathered in the kitchen, chatting about the upcoming holidays, and he imagined his father and the few remaining men were in the barn, telling jokes. He walked over to where Anna Marie was sitting, and she stood up.

"What did you want to talk about?" He prepared for the worst.

"I just wanted to say *danki,*" she said as she cast her eyes to her feet, which were twisting beneath her. Then she looked back up at him with glassy eyes. "Amos said you convinced him to stay and face his troubles. Otherwise, he might have left, and I would have died of heartbreak." Her voice rose as she spoke, and then she covered her face with her hands.

Daniel stifled a grin. Anna Marie was as dramatic as her mother at that age. "You're welcome," he said.

Anna Marie dropped her arms to her side and

sighed. "The story you told him…" she began. "I know you changed the names and all, but I reckon I figured it all out." She cast her eyes downward again. "I'm sorry all that happened to you, but I can't be sorry *mei daed* is *mei daed*."

"Of course not," Daniel said quickly. "Everything that happens is God's will. I made my choices that night, and I have to live with them. Your *daed* was a *gut* man and very deserving of your *mamm*'s affections."

"But she loved you first," Anna Marie said. She seemed to be trying to accept the concept that her mother could love someone else before her father.

"I'd like to think so," he said. "We were courting before everything—before everything happened."

Anna Marie tapped her finger to her chin. "You know…" Her eyes twinkled with mischief. "Amos is coming over this evening, and we are all going to play games, make cookies, and welcome in the Christmas season properly." She paused with a grin. "You should come."

Daniel thought he might fall over. "Really?"

"*Ya*. Amos will be arriving at five o'clock. And *Mamm* is making a ham with honey drizzled on top." She smiled, and he knew it was a genuine invitation.

Daniel was starting to feel optimistic about the days ahead. If Anna Marie was coming around, it gave him hope that Lydia could too. "I'd love to," he said, then paused. "But we should probably ask your *mamm* about it."

Anna Marie wrinkled her nose. "She'd just say no. Do you really wanna risk it?" She folded her arms across her chest.

Daniel grinned at his new ally. "I guess you're right. I'll see you at five."

Lydia had chastised herself enough about her behavior in Daniel's bedroom, flirting with him in a way unsuitable for any woman, especially an Amish woman. She was ashamed to face him, and glad that tonight would be a quiet family night filled with baking cookies and playing games. Amos would be spending the evening and having supper with the family, and Lydia planned to put any thoughts about Daniel to rest for the night.

After devotions with her children in the early afternoon, Lydia spent the rest of the day with Jacob and John in the kitchen. At twelve, Jacob liked to pretend that he was too old to lick the beaters when Lydia made desserts. But when he heard the fun that his *mamm* and brother were having in the kitchen, he joined them. John's sweet little face was covered with cookie dough and icing when Jacob entered the kitchen, and her elder son couldn't resist. They laughed, sang songs, and acted silly all afternoon. Anna Marie had spent most of her afternoon in the sewing area upstairs, finishing a new burgundy dress to wear that evening.

By early evening Lydia's heart was as warm as her toasty kitchen, heated by a small woodstove in the corner. She didn't use the old appliance to cook, but it provided a cozy atmosphere on these chilly nights, and she was able to keep her supper casseroles warm on top of it while her potatoes and celery finished cooking on top of the range. She took a peek at her ham in the oven and was pleased to see a golden glaze forming on top. *Perfect.*

"Anna Marie, Amos is at the door," she hollered

from the kitchen when she heard a knock on the door. She twisted her neck to see John in the den. "John, could you please put another log on the fire?"

Lydia checked her potatoes, dried her hands on her apron, then turned around to welcome Amos.

"Daniel!" she gasped. "What are you doing here?" She could feel a flush rising in her cheeks.

"I invited him." Anna Marie bounced into the room. "It's all right, no?"

Lydia's eyebrows rose at the same time her jaw dropped. She stood speechless, her eyes jetting back and forth between the two of them. Then someone else knocked at the door.

"Now, that would be Amos," Anna Marie said. She skipped to the door, leaving Lydia alone in the kitchen with Daniel.

"Lydia, I can go if—" Daniel hesitated. "If you really don't want me here."

I really don't want you here. She bit down hard on her lower lip but didn't say anything. As badly as she didn't want him in her home or in her heart, she was torn by conflicting emotions. But then he smiled, and Lydia reconsidered. "You might as well stay." She shrugged. "There's enough for everyone."

"Anna Marie seems to have softened toward me, and when she asked me to come for supper, I hated to say no." He said the words tentatively. "But if I make you uncomfortable, I'll go."

Ach. His arrogance! She was not going to let him get the best of her. "I'm not uncomfortable at all." She forced her lips into a curved, stiff smile.

"Hello, Daniel," Amos said. "It's *gut* to see you again."

Amos extended his hand to Daniel, and after they'd

exchanged pleasantries, Anna Marie suggested the men go into the den and warm themselves by the fire while she helped her mother finish supper. She sounded very grown-up.

Lydia waited until she could hear Amos and Daniel chatting, and then she put her hands on her hips and faced off with her daughter. "What are you doing, inviting Daniel here?" she asked in a whisper.

The bell on the timer rang. Lydia blew out a breath and swirled around to remove the ham from the oven. She placed it on top of the range by the potatoes and celery, then turned back around and waited for Anna Marie to answer.

"He's in love with you," her daughter said smugly.

Lydia felt weak in the knees. "That's ridiculous. He doesn't even know me anymore." She rolled her eyes. "Why would you say such a thing?"

Anna Marie let out a heavy sigh as a smile filled her young face. "I know about these things."

Oh, my dear daughter, you have so much to learn. "I thought you didn't like him. What made you change your mind?"

"It's wrong for me to harbor such ill will. Such thoughts are not proper in God's eyes," Anna Marie said with conviction.

Lydia sat down at the kitchen table and motioned for Anna Marie to take a seat across from her. She leaned her head back to check on the men in the den and saw that Amos, Daniel, John, and Jacob had busied themselves with a board game in the middle of the floor. Lydia kept her voice low so as not to be heard above their chatter.

"I'm glad to hear you say that, Anna Marie. But I have told you before, there is no courtship between

Daniel and me." She paused and narrowed her eyes. "Besides, you made it perfectly clear that you didn't want me to have anything to do with Daniel, outside of his being your *onkel*."

Anna Marie rose from the table, leaned down, and kissed her mother on the cheek. "I've changed my mind."

Lydia sat dumbfounded.

Anna Marie stood tall, touched Lydia on the shoulder, and gazed lovingly into her mother's eyes. She smiled. "Don't worry, *Mamm*. I will tell you everything you need to know about courtship and love." She left to join the others in the den.

Lydia was amused by her daughter's overstated display of maturity, but for some reason Anna Marie's words lingered in her mind. Maybe she did have much to learn about love, since the only two men she had ever loved had betrayed her.

Chapter Thirteen

Lydia couldn't sleep. Two hours had passed since Daniel and Amos left, and the children were already in bed. She kept replaying the evening in her mind. So much laughter and talking. The sounds of family.

Jacob and John clearly adored their *onkel* Daniel, and now that Anna Marie had opened her heart to him, Lydia struggled for a reason not to see Daniel when he asked her to join him for supper on Saturday.

Now, lying in her bed—the bed she'd shared with Elam for fifteen years—she wondered if she'd made a mistake by accepting Daniel's invitation. It would seem like a date, although she made it clear to Daniel that it would be two friends catching up on the past eighteen years, and nothing more.

"Elam, how could you have not told me about what Daniel did?" Lydia whispered. She pulled the covers taut around her chin and fought the shiver in the room and in her heart. "You let me cry on your shoulder, and all the while you knew where he was." A tear trickled down her cheek, and she dabbed it with her quilt. For the first time in months, Lydia allowed herself a good, hard cry. She stifled her pitiful moans with her bedcovers and let it all out, in some sort of effort to release all the pain she felt.

When she was done, she felt drained, and the torment was still there—a future with Daniel that tempted her, and a past with Elam that had been built on lies. She closed her eyes, too exhausted to fight sleep.

It was around two o'clock in the morning when she rolled over in the bed to see Elam sleeping beside her. It was completely dark, but somehow Lydia could see his face, illuminated in a way that allowed her to see every feature, every laugh line, and the tiny scar above his eyebrow that he'd had since childhood. She was lucid enough to know she was dreaming, but the sight of him gazing back into her eyes was a moment she wanted to hold on to forever.

Hello, my love, he whispered tenderly. He cupped her cheek in his hand, the way he'd done a thousand times during their marriage. Lydia closed her eyes and basked in the feel of his touch. *I've missed you.*

She was afraid to move, scared to breathe, for fear she'd wake up and he'd be gone.

I know you have questions, Lydia.

She could hear the regret in his tone, but she didn't care about the past right now. His lie suddenly seemed tiny in comparison to the fifteen years they'd shared as husband and wife. She closed her eyes and placed her hand on top of his as he continued to cradle her cheek.

"Elam," she whispered. "I've missed you so much."

I'm sorry, Lydia. I'm sorry I didn't tell you about the night in the alley. Daniel begged me not to, but I should have told you anyway, given you a choice. It's just that—

"It doesn't matter, Elam. It just doesn't matter." She

squeezed his hand, again fearing she'd wake up any second.

He smiled at her—so familiar, so real, so perfect—and filled with memories only a husband and wife could appreciate. Her wedding day flashed before her, and then the births of all three of her children.

It might not matter to you at this very moment, Elam said soothingly, *but in the morning, the decision I made so long ago will creep into your thoughts again.*

"Are you really here?" she asked. Lydia didn't care about anything else. "Stay with me, Elam. Don't leave me again. Please," she begged. Tears began to well in eyes already swollen from the night before.

There, there. Elam swept a thumb gently across her face and wiped away a tear that had spilled over. *You know I can't stay.*

"Then I don't want to wake up." Her body began to tremble as she cried in desperation.

Elam pulled her into his arms and held her close. *Of course you do, Lydia. What about our children? Our daughter needs you now more than ever. She is at a difficult age, and will need much* lieb *and support from you.* He paused and pulled her closer. *And then there is Daniel.*

Lydia tensed. "I don't want to talk about him."

Elam leaned back and tilted Lydia's chin upward. He fused his eyes with hers. *God blessed me so by allowing me to be in the first half of your life. Consider letting Daniel into your heart for the second half.*

"No." She pulled her eyes from his and buried her head in the nook of his shoulder. "Stay with me, Elam."

You must forgive him, Lydia. Only then will you find the peace you need to move forward. He paused. *I car-*

ried a heavy weight on my shoulders, Lydia, by not telling you the truth while I could. My love for you was all-consuming, and I was afraid that if I told you Daniel was living nearby, that you'd go to him. She felt his chest rise and fall beneath her. *And you would have. But I'm sorry I didn't give you that choice. Please forgive me.*

Lydia knew that she forgave him the minute she saw him lying next to her. They'd shared a wonderful life, and what she had learned seemed less important now. "I do forgive you, Elam."

Forgive Daniel too, Lydia. He's hurting.

"No." She could feel him slipping away. "No, Elam," she cried. "Please don't go."

I love you, Lydia. I'll always love you.

And then she woke up.

Daniel was completely out of practice with dating. He'd done very little of it over the course of his life. He'd found out early on that there wasn't going to be anyone to replace the love he felt for Lydia, so he'd more or less given up trying, especially after Jenny died. Jenny was very special, and he'd loved her, but it was never the kind of love he felt for Lydia.

From the little bit he knew about courting, flowers were always a nice gesture. Lydia had made it quite clear that this was no date, but both of them knew otherwise. He chose a traditional bouquet of red roses, sprinkled with baby's breath and greenery.

He knocked on the door with the nervousness of a teenaged boy.

Anna Marie swung the door wide. "Flowers are always a *gut* idea," she whispered. "*Mamm* is in the kitchen."

Daniel walked into the den. He'd worn his best blue shirt and black pants, along with a black felt hat and long black coat. Lydia entered the room in a dark green dress and black apron, looking as beautiful as always, but something was different. The glow of her smile warmed him from across the room, and her eyes glistened with a peacefulness she didn't seem to have before. It had been almost a week since Daniel had last seen her.

"Hello." She sounded nervous as well, but there was a hint of excitement in her voice.

Daniel handed her the roses. "I hope you like roses. I remember that you like orchids, but the boutique in Paradise didn't have any, and—anyway, I—I hope you like these." He was having trouble keeping his voice steady, and it was bordering on embarrassing. "Not that this is a date or anything," he added.

"The flowers are lovely."

Lydia's entire demeanor had changed since he saw her on Sunday after his baptism. Perhaps she'd found true forgiveness in her heart after all.

"Let me go put these in some water." She walked to the kitchen while Anna Marie kept him company.

"Where will you be taking *Mamm?*" Anna Marie asked. She had a concerned expression on her face.

"I thought I'd take her to Paradiso. Does she like Italian food?" He honestly couldn't remember.

Anna Marie smiled with approval. "It's a quaint place, and *Mamm* will be pleased."

"I'm ready," Lydia said. She grabbed her cape and bonnet from the rack by the door.

"Make sure your brothers handle their chores this evening, Anna Marie. And remember to put price tags on the jellies to take to market." She finished tying the strings of her bonnet. "And Sarah will be by to pick up some cookbooks to deliver for me when she goes to Bird-in-Hand this week."

"It'll be fine, *Mamm*." Anna Marie folded her hands together in front of her. Her eyes gleamed. "You two just go and have a *gut* time."

Daniel and Lydia's eyes met in mutual amusement at Anna Marie's grown-up comment. Lydia nodded at her daughter. Daniel didn't feel like Anna Marie was too far off base. He did feel like a kid out on his very first date.

Once they were in Daniel's buggy, he pulled the thick, brown blanket from the backseat and draped it around Lydia. He'd love for her to be sharing the blanket with him, but maybe on the way home.

"Danki." She turned to face him. Her eyes were filled with childlike enthusiasm that shone bright in the pale light of the moon. Yes. Something had definitely changed, and Daniel couldn't have been more pleased. He'd been praying hard that Lydia would give him another chance.

When they got to the restaurant, Daniel offered Lydia his hand to step down from the buggy. They fended off stares from the *Englisch* tourists when they walked in. It was easy to differentiate the locals from the visitors. The *Englisch* from this area didn't give the Amish a second glance. Daniel recalled how much the stares bothered him when he was growing up. But now he was with Lydia, and he wanted to scream to the world that he was home where he belonged. *So stare all you want.*

They'd barely finished their chicken parmesan when the waitress asked if they would be ordering dessert.

"Just *kaffi* for me," Lydia said.

Daniel nodded. "Two, please."

For the first time since he'd been back, his conversations with Lydia flowed effortlessly. He wasn't proud of the life he'd lived some of the time, but as he filled Lydia in about his past, she never judged him. Several times, when he felt particularly ashamed, her eyes had shone with more kindness and tenderness than he could remember from their youth, or deserved now. Lydia had always been kindhearted and loving, but this was different, and Daniel wondered if it was due to motherhood or if she had just matured into someone far grander than he could have imagined.

"Now you," Daniel said as they sipped their coffee. "I know you married Elam. And of course, you have three children. Tell me everything."

Daniel would be lying if he didn't admit that it stung a little to see her smile when she spoke about her life with Elam.

"It was a *gut* life with Elam," she said.

Her eyes drifted from his for a moment, and she shifted her weight in the chair. When her gaze returned to his, she seemed hesitant to continue. But Daniel nodded for her to go on.

"Elam was fortunate enough to be able to make a *gut* living working the fields. We always had a fine harvest. Since you left," she went on, "even more farmers are supplementing their income by holding jobs outside of our community. Many work in construction or building furniture. I don't know anyone who wouldn't prefer not to do this, but growing families, lack of land, the economy—well, it's just forced us out into the *Englisch* world more than we would like."

"What about you? I know you have your cookbooks

and that you sell jams and jellies at market. But what else occupies your time?"

"*Ach!* You know the answer to that." A gentle laugh rippled through the air, and right before his eyes, she transformed into the bubbly nineteen-year-old love he'd left behind. "Up at four thirty. Breakfast at five. Then there are the cows to be milked, which Jacob and John take care of, and Anna Marie and I tend to laundry, sewing, baking...."

She was still talking, but Daniel was only halfway listening. He was lost in the moment—her smile, the sound of her voice, her laughter, and sheer joy about the life she'd lived so far.

After Daniel paid the bill, they left. Once on the road, it seemed much colder in the buggy, so Daniel turned on a small battery-operated heater he'd brought from home and turned the fan in Lydia's direction. She bundled herself in the blanket and thanked him. Daniel's teeth were chattering wildly, and his body shook from the cold. He recalled the way they used to sit close together and share the warmth of the blanket and each other. But she didn't offer to share, and he didn't ask.

It was nearing seven o'clock, but there was still time for one more trip down memory lane, if Lydia would agree.

The old oak tree.

Chapter Fourteen

Lydia was tempted by Daniel's offer. Stars twinkled in thick clusters overhead, and she knew it would be a magical night under the old tree, but she wasn't ready for that yet. She was still working on being friends with him, getting to know him again, and truly forgiving him. She was praying hard about it, and it was all coming together nicely, but friendship was all she had to offer him at this point, and the old oak tree would spark things within herself that she wasn't ready to face.

"It's been a *gut* night, Daniel, but I think you best take me home."

Lydia could see the disappointment in his eyes, but he nodded.

She tried to imagine what it must have been like for him eighteen years ago. A conviction that carried jail time, and then the start of a new and unfamiliar life. If he'd only trusted their love more, he'd have known that there was nothing they couldn't have endured together.

She recalled the way Daniel spoke of his past, with remorse over the choices he'd made. But she'd also watched his face light up when he spoke about the old woman, Margaret, who showed him the way back to the Lord. And he'd spoken fondly of a woman named Jenny, and Lydia could tell how much her death pained him. It was strange to hear him talk about caring for another woman in that way. But even with all the years gone by, she could still see her Daniel in every word he spoke, his movements, and even the way he scrunched his nose when he was trying not to laugh.

Elam's words in her dream echoed in her head. *God blessed me so by allowing me to be in the first half of your life. Consider letting Daniel into your heart for the second half. Forgive Daniel too, Lydia. He's hurting.*

Daniel turned his head her way and caught her eyes on him. "Are you all right?" he asked with such tenderness it caused her heart to flutter.

"Ya," she whispered. She pulled her eyes away from his and sat quietly, lost in the moment. She couldn't help but wonder. *What if...*

Daniel pulled the buggy to a stop in front of Lydia's house. "Whoa, boy."

His pulse quickened as he helped her from the buggy, unsure what the proper protocol was. In his previous world, a simple kiss good night would solidify that the night went well and suggest that another date might be in order. But he was home, and this was Lydia. Doing things right had never been more important to him, and he felt his future hanging on this moment. He didn't want to scare her, but he'd never longed to take another woman into his arms the way he did right now.

At the door, she turned to face him. "*Danki* for supper, Daniel."

He searched her face and tried to read her expression. For a long moment, she gazed back. His heart pounded viciously against his chest, and he knew that he was going to kiss Lydia good night, the way he'd dreamed of for many years. He took a deep breath and leaned forward toward her.

In less time than it took for him to uproot his feet from their position, Lydia turned, opened the door, stepped through the threshold, and turned to face him. "Good night," she said abruptly. And the door slammed shut.

Daniel smiled. She might have closed the door on his intent to kiss her good night, but just the fact that she considered kissing him was enough to ensure he'd get a good night's sleep.

For a moment, Lydia stared at the wooden door. He'd almost kissed her good night, and she'd almost allowed it. She drew in a deep breath, then turned to see Anna Marie standing behind her like a mother hen waiting for her little chick to return.

"Well?" Her daughter raised questioning brows. "How did it go?"

Lydia untied the strings on her bonnet and refused to make eye contact with Anna Marie. She was fearful her daughter might see into her heart, into the secret chamber where a woman stores her most intimate thoughts. But the corner of her mouth tweaked upward unconsciously.

"*Ach,* it must have been *gut,*" Anna Marie said smugly.

Lydia hung her bonnet on the rack by the door and

untied the strings on her cape. "I am not discussing this with you, Anna Marie," she said firmly. Although she couldn't seem to control the grin that kept threatening to form on her face.

"Did he kiss you good night?" Her daughter's eyes widened with anticipation.

"Anna Marie!" She hung up her cape, then turned to face her daughter with her hands on her hips. "It's not appropriate for you to ask me such a question." She pulled off her gloves and walked to the fireplace.

Anna Marie was on her heels.

"He did, didn't he?" Anna Marie stood beside her in front of the hearth as Lydia warmed her palms. "He kissed you good night."

"As a matter of fact, no, he did not." Lydia narrowed her eyes in Anna Marie's direction. "Anna Marie, I'm glad that you are not harboring dislike toward your *onkel* anymore, but you need not be getting any silly notions in your head."

Much to Lydia's surprise, Anna Marie turned to face her, and her eyes were serious, her voice steady. "I just want you to be happy, *Mamm*."

Lydia sighed and grabbed Anna Marie's hands. "I know, Anna Marie."

"Pop is gone. And I know that you have a history, a past with Daniel." Anna Marie's forehead crinkled. "I didn't care for him much in the beginning because I feared he would try to take *Daed*'s place, and I wasn't sure if I was ready for that. But I will be marrying Amos next year, and Jacob and John need a father." Anna Marie looked hesitant to go on. "Daniel told Amos what happened the night he left you on Christmas Eve."

"What?" *That wasn't Daniel's place to do that,* Lydia thought as she waited for Anna Marie to go on.

"Oh, he changed the names, and he probably didn't tell him everything, but it wasn't hard for Amos to figure out that Daniel was talking about himself in the story. And he told Amos enough to keep Amos from making the same mistake he did."

Now Lydia understood why Anna Marie had changed her mind about Daniel.

"Mamm?"

"Ya?"

Anna Marie gazed lovingly into Lydia's eyes. "I'd really like to hear—to hear about you and Daniel, when you were young." Anna Marie looked toward her shoes.

Lydia thought hard for a moment. Wonderful memories floated to the surface of her mind. She lifted her daughter's chin and smiled. "You go brew us some *kaffi*. I want to go check on Jacob and John." She paused and studied Anna Marie for a moment, trying to really see her daughter as the woman she was becoming. "Then I will tell you about Daniel and me."

Anna Marie's expression lifted, and she bit her lip, then headed to the kitchen. Lydia went to check on her sons.

For the next two hours, Lydia and Anna Marie cuddled under a quilt on the couch in front of a toasty fire on the cold December night, and Lydia told her daughter all about her first true love. After all these years, she could still vividly recall every detail of the times she'd spent with Daniel—times that, until now, she'd kept secretly stored away in her heart, refusing to unlock her memories for fear of the pain that loomed there.

But as she shared these precious reflections with Anna Marie, Lydia realized that instead of fear and pain—something else was forming in its place and was growing with every word she spoke.

Hope.

Chapter Fifteen

Following a quiet day of rest and devotion on Sunday, Lydia awoke on Monday with a burst of energy she didn't remember having for a long time. She ran the broom along the wooden floor in the kitchen and recalled the conversation she'd had with her daughter on Saturday night, her spirit invigorated as she drew on memories from her past. And Anna Marie, a true romantic at heart, had hung on Lydia's every word with a sparkle in her eyes, often comparing her relationship with Amos to Lydia and Daniel's.

After the boys left for school, Miriam picked up Anna Marie for sisters day, a monthly affair that all the women in the community looked forward to. It was a time for sewing, quilting, baking, and any other project of the women's choosing. Mostly, it was a time for chatter—who was courting whom, upcoming baptisms, weddings being planned, etc.

Lydia declined the invitation this morning, but encouraged Anna Marie to attend. Lydia told her daughter she would take care of the Monday laundry chore. She preferred to be alone with her thoughts, which inevitably drifted to Daniel. She could still recall the way his eyes clung to hers Saturday night, familiar and full of desire. He would have kissed her if she hadn't forced herself to turn away. She'd wanted nothing more than to press her lips to his and recapture a tiny bit of their youth, if only for a moment.

Lydia knew her walls of defense against Daniel were crumbling, leaving her heart exposed. She couldn't help but wonder if there was enough love in her heart to forgive Daniel. Again, she heard Elam's voice in her head. *You must forgive him, Lydia. Only then will you find the peace you need to move forward.*

During her morning devotions, she'd prayed extra hard for guidance. Perhaps the quiet voice in her head wasn't Elam.

Lydia cleared the last of the breakfast dishes. She was drying her hands on a kitchen towel when she heard a knock at the door.

"I'm looking for Mr. Smucker," a woman said when Lydia opened the door.

The *Englischer,* in a fancy brown coat and matching knee-length boots, towered over Lydia. "I'm—I'm sorry," Lydia stuttered, "but Mr. Smucker passed away about two years ago."

"Oh no." The woman hung her head. "I didn't know that. I was told I could find him here."

The woman's teeth were chattering, and Lydia wondered if she should invite her in. She didn't look like an *Englischer* from Lancaster County. Her sophisticated attire distinguished her somewhat from folks in the area; she looked like she was from a big city. Golden blonde hair fell loosely on top of her head, and loose tendrils blew against high cheekbones. Her eyes were heavily painted, but not in an unbecoming way. Diamond rings adorned both her hands, and her nails were long and manicured.

Lydia wasn't sure if it was the kindness in the woman's sapphire-colored eyes or blatant curiosity that compelled her to invite the *Englischer* in, but she eased to one side of the door. "Please come in out of the cold," she offered.

The woman bit down on her trembling lip and narrowed her eyes in deliberation. Then she slowly walked inside.

"Is there something I can help you with?" Lydia asked as she pushed the front door closed. "I am Mr. Smucker's wife." She sighed. "I mean, widow."

"I'm so sorry for your loss," the woman said. "He was a good man." Her eyes clouded with tears, and Lydia couldn't imagine how her husband knew this woman.

"But no, you can't help me," she went on. "I wanted to resolve some issues with Daniel, and now that's not possible."

"Daniel?" Lydia's eyes widened in surprise. "Daniel Smucker isn't dead."

"What?"

"I was married to *Elam* Smucker, who passed two years ago." Lydia wasn't sure if she felt relief or alarm at this new information. "You are looking for Elam's brother, Daniel, who lives down the way." She pointed to her north. "At the old Kauffman place."

"Thank you so much!" The *Englisch* woman wasted no time heading toward the door. "I'm so glad Daniel Smucker is alive. I've come a long way to find him, and—" With her hand on the doorknob, she turned around.

Again Lydia saw kindness in her eyes.

"I'm sorry about your husband, Elam." Her bright red lips formed into a tender smile. "But I am very thankful to have found Daniel. I just hope that he'll see me after all this time. I pray that he will."

She gave a quick wave and was gone.

Lydia's mind spun with bewilderment, and the zest in her spirit plummeted. How naive she'd been. Daniel had lived among the *Englisch* for nearly two decades. It stood to reason that he would have ties from his past—beautiful ties. If that was the type of woman Daniel associated with in his former life, why in the world would he want anything to do with her?

She walked briskly to the bathroom and studied her plain face in the mirror. Tiny lines feathered from the corners of tired eyes, and her light brown lashes were sparse. The circles under her eyes were a shade darker this morning from staying up too late the night before. She leaned in closer to inspect lips that had lost their pinkish pucker and skin that no longer glowed with the benefit of youth.

She stood straight again and ran her hands along hips that had aided in the delivery of three children, and then she held her hands in front of her and spread her fingers wide. Short fingernails rounded out long fingers, which wrinkled slightly beneath her knuckles as she stretched them to capacity, giving way to more creases across the top of her hand.

What am I doing? She lowered her chin. Vanity was wrong in the eyes of God. Lydia knew in her heart that such pride was a sin and that her appearance in no way represented the person beneath her plain look. And yet she couldn't help but compare herself to the beautiful woman who'd resurfaced from Daniel's past. Lydia felt her stomach sink. *Why would he choose me?*

* * *

Daniel slowed his horse as he eased under the covered bridge in Ronks and enjoyed a brief reprieve from the flurry of snowflakes that had started earlier this morning. But even the bitter cold couldn't dampen his spirit. His heart was warm and his mind filled with thoughts of Lydia. Beautiful Lydia.

But for all her outer beauty, it was the woman inside with whom Daniel was in love. His Lydia. He was so happy knowing she hadn't changed a bit.

He headed up the Old Philadelphia Pike and made his way to the farmers' market in Bird-in-Hand. It was a shopping stop mostly for tourists, but Daniel wanted to pick up something special for Lydia. When they were kids, she'd said the bakery inside the market made the best molasses crinkle cookies. She had joked that she could never get her cookies to taste like the ones from the market.

Daniel suspected she had perfected the recipe after all these years, but he was going to buy her some of the cookies just the same.

Carol Stewart carried her red suitcase up to the second floor at Beiler's Bed and Breakfast—to the Rose Room, which lived up to its name with four walls painted a dusty pink color. She plopped her suitcase, coat, and purse onto the queen-sized bed, which was topped with a lovely white bedspread. Then she eased into one of the floral high-back chairs in the sitting area and pulled off her boots. She stretched her toes, leaned back, and blew out a sigh.

She'd stopped by Daniel Smucker's farm, but he wasn't home. She even waited for almost an hour to see if he would return. Her desperateness to see him was all consuming, and she was determined to somehow make things right. Perhaps after a short catnap, she'd try again. She was sleepy from her three-hour drive from New York City.

She thought back to the last time she saw Daniel, and the expression on his face when she left. He'd probably thought he would see her again. But she had run, the way she always ran when she couldn't face her troubles. She was through running now—from the memories of Daniel that haunted her, and mostly from herself. Her father was dead now, so nothing would prevent her from finding Daniel. She prayed that he could somehow forgive her.

Chapter Sixteen

Daniel passed by Lydia's house on his way home and was surprised to see her in the front yard, toting firewood. He stopped his buggy. Snow was falling and starting to accumulate. It was colder than cold outside. He jumped from the seat to give her a hand.

"Why aren't you at sisters day?" he asked as he crossed the front yard.

She shrugged and kept walking, bundled up in her heavy coat and gloves.

"Here, let me." Daniel caught up with her and scooped the two logs from her arms. She allowed it, but she looked more irritated than appreciative. He followed her into the house and set the wood on the rack near the fireplace.

"Danki," she said. She hung up her coat and took off her gloves, never once looking in his direction. This wasn't the same woman he'd said good-bye to on Saturday night.

"Lydia?"

"Ya?" She walked to the fireplace where Daniel was standing and suspended her gloves from two nails

sticking out of the mantel. She placed her palms in front of the fire.

"Is everything all right? Why aren't you at sisters day?" he repeated.

"I just didn't feel like going," she said, then shrugged.

Daniel remembered the cookies he bought for her at the market. "I'll be right back. I have something for you."

He returned a few moments later with a brown bag. "These are for you."

She opened the brown sack and pulled out one of the individually wrapped cookies, studied it, and put it back in the bag. The hint of a smile flickered across her face, but faded when she briefly glanced up at him. "*Danki.* I'll just go put these in the kitchen."

Maybe she didn't care for the cookies anymore. Daniel followed her.

"I remember how much you used to like these when we were kids. You said the best ones came from the farmers' market in Bird-in-Hand, so I picked you up some this morning."

She stowed the bag on the counter, not acknowledging what he'd just said. "There was a woman here looking for you this morning."

"Who was she?"

Lydia briskly moved past him, grabbed the broom, and began to sweep her kitchen floor. "I have no idea," she said sharply.

"An Amish woman?"

"No. *Englisch.* A very beautiful *Englisch* woman. She looked very big-city." She raked the broom harder across the floor.

Daniel crinkled his forehead and thought for a moment. "I can't imagine any *Englisch* woman looking for me here. What did she look like?"

"I told you. Very pretty."

Her voice was edgy, and it took him a moment to catch on.

"Hmm—" He rubbed his chin and watched the broom whipping across the wooden slats. "I know so many pretty women. I wonder which one it was."

"I'm sure I wouldn't know." Her face reddened.

Daniel stifled a grin. "Lydia, I'm playing with you. I don't know any pretty women who'd be looking for me. The only beautiful woman I'm interested in is standing in this kitchen."

She stopped sweeping and rattled off something in Pennsylvania *Deitsch,* so fast he couldn't understand what she said.

"Whoa, slow down."

"Daniel, it isn't proper for you to be here right now. I have chores to tend to." She started to run the broom over the floor again.

"Lydia, can you stop for a minute, please?" He cautiously moved toward her, and she propped the broom in the corner. She faced him, folded her arms across her chest, and bit her bottom lip.

"Are you mad at me because this woman showed up here, looking for me? I can't imagine who it is. Really."

"No, of course I'm not mad," she said. "I'm just very busy right now."

Daniel knew they'd taken a step backward. He didn't want to worsen things, but this hot and cold she played was irritating. He tipped his straw hat in her direction. "Then I'll let you get back to work." He didn't try to hide the cynicism in his voice.

Lydia walked him to the door. "*Danki* again for the cookies."

"You're welcome."

She closed the door, embarrassed by her childish behavior. But in addition to her struggle to forgive Daniel and move forward in their relationship, she needed to trust him. She'd done that once, and it hadn't served her well. She walked to the window and watched him walk to his buggy, feeling silly that she'd overreacted. He'd just opened the door to climb inside when a sleek, tan car pulled up behind his buggy.

Daniel closed the door and walked to the driver's window and leaned down. Lydia couldn't see who was in the car, since Daniel's body was blocking her view. She edged to her left, then to her right. Then she remembered seeing that same car earlier. Her recollection came about the time Daniel walked to the passenger side and climbed inside—with the elegant blonde-haired woman in the driver seat.

"Thank you for agreeing to have coffee with me," Carol said as Daniel fastened his seat belt.

He pushed back his straw hat, glanced briefly in her direction, and offered her the best half smile he could muster up. So many times he'd thought about what he might say to her if he had the chance.

"I'm going to Europe in a few days. When I heard you were back in Lancaster County, I felt compelled to find you before I leave."

Daniel could see why Lydia would think this woman was beautiful. Carol had delicate features and full lips. Her hair was golden, like a field of grain, and her blue eyes shone with a warmth Daniel hadn't expected.

But in his mind she didn't compare to Lydia, whose beauty ran from the inside out.

Lydia's reaction flattered him, but it was worrisome. He knew she was already struggling to find a place for him in her life, and he didn't want this to cause a permanent setback. His attitude when he left probably didn't help things, but she didn't need to be so snippy. The fact that Carol was in Lancaster County shocked Daniel as much as it had Lydia. He had never expected to lay eyes on the woman again.

"Is this place okay?" Carol pointed to the Dutch bakery on the right.

"*Ya.* That's fine."

Daniel fought the resentment that he felt toward Carol and told himself that he would listen to her with an open mind and heart. He'd prayed for her, despite the pain she'd caused.

Although, looking at her now, she didn't seem to be the monster he'd made her out to be. Maybe she'd changed. As she pulled her car into the parking lot of the bakery, Daniel reckoned he was about to find out.

It was later in the afternoon when Lydia took the buggy to Lena and Gideon's to pick up Anna Marie. Her daughter told her this morning that, after sisters day, she was going to go back to her grandparents' house for a while to work on a special quilt that she and Lena were making as a Christmas present for Sarah. It wasn't a full-sized quilt, but more of a lap cover. Lydia had seen the work in progress, and it was beautiful.

Everyone in the community adored Sarah and her husband, David, and the women also knew that Sarah was having a difficult time as the anniversary of her miscarriage approached. Lydia thought it was a lovely gesture for Anna Marie to want to make her something so special for Christmas.

"You've come a long way on this, Anna Marie." Lydia inspected the finely quilted squares bursting with every color in the rainbow. "And you've done a fine job."

"*Mammi* helped a lot, too," Anna Marie said as she tucked her chin.

Lena waved her off. "No, I reckon I just supervised." She pulled a pan from the oven. "Plain ol' sugar cookies, if anyone is interested." She placed the tray on her cooling rack.

"Your cookies are always *wunderbaar,* Lena." Lydia sat down at the kitchen table while Anna Marie stored the quilt back in Lena's sewing room upstairs. "How was sisters day?"

"It was a *gut* day." Lena put the last cookie on the rack and then joined Lydia at the table. "Why didn't you go?"

Lydia shrugged. "*Ach,* I don't know. I just had a lot to do around the house." She recalled her zesty spirit and how wonderful she'd felt this morning—before the *Englischer* showed up.

"You should have gone," Lena said. She winked at Lydia. "You know how chatty everyone gets. Maybe they wouldn't have talked so much about you if you'd have been there."

Lydia's eyes widened. "What? Why would the ladies be talking about me?"

"There was much speculation about you and Daniel." Lena's voice was hopeful, and Lydia hated to disappoint her.

"We went to supper. There's nothing to speculate

about. Was my daughter listening to everyone chat about me?"

Lena folded her hands on the table and sat up a little taller. "Actually, it was Anna Marie who started the conversation. She's glad you and Daniel seemed to be getting along so well, and I think she's hoping—"

"It was just supper, Lena." Lydia knew who was doing most of the hoping. But she regretted her own snappy tone. "Sorry," she said, then bit her bottom lip.

A few awkward moments of silence ensued until Anna Marie came bouncing back into the kitchen, about the same time Lydia heard a buggy pulling up in the driveway.

"Gideon will want some hot cocoa," Lena said. She stood up, walked to the stove, and lit the stove. "He's comin' back from Leroy Blank's place. Leroy wanted him to see a woodworking project he has going on." Lena shook her head. "It's too cold to be goin' anywhere."

"Yum. Sugar cookies." Anna Marie snatched a cookie and leaned against the counter.

Lydia heard the front door close and footsteps nearing from the den. But it was Daniel who rounded the corner, not Gideon.

"Hi," he said. He took off his hat and coat, hung them on the rack. "This is a nice surprise."

Daniel and Lydia's eyes met, but she quickly looked away. There was an edge to Daniel's voice, and she wasn't sure he found her presence a nice surprise at all.

Lydia bolted up from the table. "Anna Marie, we must go home and start supper. Jacob and John will be getting hungry soon." She retrieved her heavy coat, gloves, and bonnet from the rack where she'd hung them when she first arrived.

"Hi, *Onkel* Daniel." Anna Marie smiled at Daniel.

"Come along, Anna Marie. Get your coat on." Lydia tied her bonnet. She kissed Lena quickly on the cheek. "See you soon."

"Lydia, can I talk with you for a minute before you go?" Daniel asked.

"Anna Marie, come with me." Lena practically dragged Anna Marie by the arm through the kitchen. "I have something upstairs to show you while your *mamm* and *Onkel* Daniel talk."

"No, Anna Marie, we have to go," Lydia said firmly.

Anna Marie frowned playfully, and then mouthed the word *Sorry* to her *mamm* as her *mammi* pulled her toward the stairs.

"What is it, Daniel?" Lydia asked. She was all bundled up and ready to go, and he was just standing there staring at her. "Hmm?"

"I wanted to explain about that woman. You seemed upset about her coming here. She came to talk to me about something that happened a long—"

"Stop." Lydia held her palm up. "Please, Daniel. There is no need for you to explain. I'm sure there are many women from your past."

"And apparently that bothers you a great deal." He looped his thumbs through his suspenders.

"*Ach!* It most certainly does not." *How dare he?* "You and I agreed to be friends, nothing more. I don't care about your romantic past, nor should you feel the need to tell me about it. It's most inappropriate."

Daniel was quickly on her heels. "You know that I want to be more than your friend, Lydia, but I'm willing to accept your terms. But you have the wrong idea about Carol. My relationship with her—"

"I don't want to hear." Lydia covered her ears with her hands and shook her head.

"Can you please quit interrupting me?" Daniel thrust his hands on his hips. "That's an irritating habit you have when you don't want to hear something."

Lydia wanted to be mad at him and show anger, but instead her eyes began to instantly fill with tears. "If I'm so *irritating,* then why don't you just leave me alone?"

Daniel sighed, then reached for her arm. She jerked away from him.

"I didn't mean to hurt your feelings, Lydia. That's the last thing I'd want to do."

She stormed across the den and yelled upstairs. "Anna Marie. Let's go!"

When Anna Marie hit the bottom stair, Lydia grabbed her daughter's hand and pulled her toward the front door.

"Why does everyone keep dragging me around?" Anna Marie asked. She glanced back and forth between Lydia and Lena.

Lydia didn't answer. As the door closed behind them, one thing was for sure. Lydia had used bad judgment when she'd decided to let her guard down with Daniel, and now she needed to force some distance between them and patch the tiny cracks in her heart.

Chapter Seventeen

Daniel knew that by forgiving Carol, he'd made peace with some of his past as well. She'd wept openly and said she couldn't move forward without knowing that Daniel forgave her. He knew the agony of seeking exoneration from someone. He didn't want to leave Carol in that lonely place where past regrets gnaw away at your soul, where peace is within your grasp but yanked away by your own guilt. Daniel was familiar with that place.

He'd like to think that he'd forgiven himself for the decision he'd made Christmas Eve, but occasionally he revisited that dark place where Carol had been. Maybe now she could find the kind of happiness that had evidently eluded them both.

Perhaps Lydia would find a way to open her heart to him. He'd settle for just her friendship, if that's all she could give him, but after their last conversation, he realized that even being friends was a challenge.

It was quiet in his house. Too quiet. Too much time to think. He carried the lantern upstairs and got into bed knowing sleep wouldn't be coming for a while. He knew of something he could do in the meantime. He tried to clear his thoughts so he could truly commune with God.

God's will is not to be questioned. It was a belief he'd carried with him into the *Englisch* world. Even though he'd lost his way for a while, in his heart he'd always known that to be true. If he hadn't made the decision to leave, there'd be no Anna Marie, Jacob, or John. Elam might not have shared his life with someone as wonderful as Lydia.

He recalled the way Lydia's eyes iced over at the sight of him this afternoon. She'd just started to warm up to him when Carol showed up and put a glitch in things. If Lydia only knew. His heart had always belonged to her, even when she wasn't there to accept his love. He couldn't help but wonder if she'd thought about him over the years. Guilt washed over him for having such thoughts about another man's wife, particularly when that man was his own brother.

"I'm sorry, Elam," he whispered. "She was your wife."

He turned off the lantern, closed his eyes, and prayed for God to lead his thoughts in the right direction.

Over a week went by without Daniel and Lydia resolving their troubles, and Lena knew her son was suffering. She didn't know how to ease his pain, or Lydia's, for that matter. She served Daniel dippy eggs, buttermilk pancakes, bacon, and scrapple for breakfast on this cold December morning. His favorites, and it was worth her small effort to brighten his day.

"It will take time, Daniel," she said after Gideon went to tend to the animals. "Lydia needs time to adjust to you being here."

"I know, *Mamm*." Daniel moved his eggs around on

the plate. "But it's been over a week now. Did you see how she avoided me at church service on Sunday?"

Lena sat down at the table across from her son. "Daniel." She chose her words carefully. "You know how much your *daed* and me love you, no?"

He nodded.

"But your coming home after all these years took some time for us to get used to. I reckon we'd buried you, so to speak. Eighteen years is a mighty long time, Daniel. And it took many years for us to heal after you left." She paused as her forehead creased with concern. "I tell you this, son, not to hurt you, but to make you realize that Lydia is dealing with things the best way she can. These are strange circumstances.

"Nothing would please your pop and me more than for you and Lydia to court. The children need a father, and I think it is what Elam would want. But such issues can't be forced. God has his own time frame, and he will guide your way. Just be patient."

Lydia spread out the children's Christmas gifts on the floor in the den. With the boys at school and Anna Marie at the market with Miriam, she wanted to take advantage of this time alone to wrap some gifts. She set Lena and Gideon's gifts to her right, in a pile next to the presents for her side of the family. None of the items she'd made or purchased were extravagant, but she had a little something for everyone—everyone except Daniel.

She picked up the battery-operated hand mixer she'd purchased for Lena and wondered if her mother-in-law would use it. It would make things so much easier on her, particularly since the natural doctor in town said she'd developed some arthritis in her hands. The herbs the doctor suggested weren't helping, and Lydia thought the ease of the portable food mixer might help her. For Gideon, she'd purchased a special blend of herbal tea that he enjoyed, and she planned to make him a batch of raisin puffs.

Lydia picked up the pink diary she'd purchased for Miriam, since she felt like her younger sister tended to keep her feelings inside. Inside the diary, she'd written Miriam a special inscription.

For her other two sisters, Hannah and Rachel, she'd selected simple black sweaters. Each of her brothers, John Jr. and Melvin, was receiving a fine pair of leather work gloves. And for her parents she'd bought a battery-operated weather warning system, like the one she kept in her kitchen. She thumbed through the rest of the presents and made sure she had small tokens for all of her nieces and nephews.

For her son John, Lydia had purchased a new winter coat and warm gloves. Her bookworm, Jacob, was getting a collection of books from an author he enjoyed. She'd struggled with what to get Anna Marie, but in the end she'd chosen the set of china she'd received from Lena and Gideon when she and Elam were married. It would mean more to Anna Marie than anything Lydia could have bought her, especially now that she was planning to start her life with Amos.

Yes. There was something for everyone but Daniel. What could she possibly get for Elam's brother, the children's *onkel,* the man for whom she harbored such mixed feelings? She recalled his interaction with the *Englisch* woman, the way he'd hopped into her car and left. *Where did they go? What did they talk about?* She couldn't help but wonder if Daniel regretted his decision to get rebaptized. Maybe the woman hoped to reunite with him.

She tried to push Daniel from her mind, but she could still see the glow in his eyes when he handed her the molasses crinkle cookies. She'd shown little appreciation.

Lydia spread a roll of shiny red paper in front of her. She could feel the warmth of the fire behind her and wished some of that warmth would spill over into her heart and cast out the cold spots that lingered there.

Only ten days until Christmas. Lydia placed Miriam's boxed diary on the wrapping paper and folded it inward as she thought about what she could give Daniel for Christmas.

Daniel knew that Christmastime would be difficult for Lydia, so he'd stayed away from her for over a week. But tomorrow was Christmas Eve, and the entire family would be together. He took special care on this day to wrap Lydia's present. After he attached the bright red bow, he moved the gift to the far wall in his den. He glanced around the room at all the wrapped packages, and he knew he'd gone overboard. It just seemed there was so much to make up for.

Lydia's parents were hosting the worship service on Christmas Eve, and the community would have lots of time for visiting on Christmas Day and on Second Christmas, which was celebrated on the day following Christmas. Daniel knew that he and Lydia would be thrown together a lot over the holidays. He planned to give her all the space she needed, but he would continue to hope and pray that she would give him a chance. And hopefully he would find an opportunity to explain why Carol was here. It wasn't a subject he cared to talk about, with Lydia or anyone else, but Lydia had clearly gotten the wrong idea about her.

The weather forecast in the newspaper was calling for a foot of snow and blizzardlike conditions, starting the day after tomorrow, on Christmas Day. He pulled on his heavy black boots and prepared to ready his house for a storm. He worried how that would affect the community celebrations. Sarah and David Fisher were hosting a First Christmas celebration, along with several others in the district.

Surely Lydia would make sure any loose objects outside her house were secured, that shutters were fastened, and that food was in full supply in case they were shut in for a few days. How awful it would be if the weather kept everyone from enjoying the holidays with friends and family. He longed to go to her house to make sure she was prepared, but he knew she had the three children to help her.

Daniel pulled himself from his chair at the head of his kitchen table and headed outside to secure his belongings and tend to his animals. Tomorrow was Christmas Eve, and it would be a busy day.

Anna Marie snuggled into the brown blanket Amos gave her before they left on this buggy ride through the winding back roads of Paradise. A light snow was falling, and it was much too cold to be joyriding, but Anna Marie feared she might not see Amos over the holidays. He and his family would be spending Christmas Eve with relatives in another district, and she would be with her family at her grandparents' house. Then on Christmas Day, no one was sure how bad the weather would be and if it would be fit for travel. She and her family were planning to attend Sarah and David's gathering.

"I heard *mei daed* talkin' with *mei mamm,* and he said no one knows for sure when the storm is coming," Amos said.

"I hope it's not too bad to get out on Christmas Day," Anna Marie said as her house came into view. "It would be *baremlich* not to see you on Christmas." She smiled at her future husband. "Just think, we'll be married by this time next year. I'll be your *fraa,* Anna Marie Zook." A warm glow flowed through her, despite the chatter of her teeth.

"We best get you inside and warm," Amos said. He turned the buggy into her driveway.

"*Ach,* wait. Can you stop a minute? I want to grab the mail from the mailbox."

Amos pulled the buggy to a stop at the end of the long driveway, close enough to the mailbox that Anna Marie didn't even have to get out.

"I love being the first one to read the Christmas cards," she said. She thumbed through the stack of cards. "*Ach,* here's one from my cousin in Ohio!"

Three other cards were postmarked in Lancaster County, and she recognized all the names. But one piece of mail had unusual postage markings Lydia had never seen before. She held the letter-sized envelope up to show Amos. "What's this?"

Amos leaned toward her to get a better look. "That's a letter from overseas." He pointed to the postmark. "All the way from Europe. From France."

"It's addressed to *Mamm.*" Anna Marie eyed the return address curiously. "I wonder who Carol Stewart is?"

Chapter Eighteen

Lydia kissed her boys good night and forced a smile. "I love you both very much." She closed the bedroom door and headed down the hallway. She could hear Anna Marie bathing.

During the short buggy ride home from worship service at her parents' house, Lydia and the children had sung songs, but she was having a terrible time getting into the spirit of the season. A permanent sorrow seemed to be weighing her down. Twice she'd caught Daniel staring at her from across the room during worship, his expression forlorn and pleading for some sort of response. She'd merely looked away.

She hadn't seen him in over a week, and she'd felt a hodgepodge of emotion when she saw him this evening. Glorious visions of past Christmases with Elam and the children danced in her mind. But those good memories were invaded by recollections of a Christmas Eve eighteen years ago.

Grief, despair, and an unquenchable longing mixed with hopelessness. She plopped herself down on the couch in front of the fireplace and hoped the warmth in the flames would thaw the ice surrounding her heart. She closed her eyes.

Please, God, help me release the bitterness in my heart and truly forgive Daniel. Help me to welcome this prodigal son back into my heart with forgiveness and love—the same way you so unconditionally welcome back your children. I pray that Daniel and I will find a good place to dwell, a peaceful place, in friendship or whatever it is that you see fit for us. Help me to listen to the inner voice that is you.

Lydia rested her head against the back of the couch, kept her eyes closed, and tried to push aside all her other thoughts to make room for the one voice she needed to hear. But when no revelation came, she sighed, opened her eyes, and decided to thumb through the Christmas cards Anna Marie brought in yesterday.

She smiled when she saw that her daughter had already opened the cards. Anna Marie loved to be the first one to read good tidings from friends and family. Her cousin Mary had written a lovely note inside her card, and Lydia tried to stay focused on the blessed time of year as she read two more cards from friends in the area. At the bottom of the pile was an unopened envelope. Lydia's mouth dropped in dismay when she saw the return address.

Why would Daniel's old girlfriend be writing a letter to me all the way from France?

She twisted the envelope nervously in her hand. *This is the last thing I need right now.* But she slid her finger along the seam and unfolded the crisp white sheets of paper.

Dear Lydia,
    My name is Carol Stewart. I am the woman who showed up at your house looking for

Daniel. I'm so glad to have found him and feel particularly blessed that he spent several hours talking with me.

Lydia took a deep breath and considered not reading any further, but curiosity pushed her to continue.

We weren't far into the conversation before I realized that my actions many years ago greatly affected you. If I had done things differently, it certainly would have altered the course of your life.

Daniel tells me that you were married to his brother for many years and that you have three beautiful children. I am so sorry about the death of your husband. That must have been incredibly hard. I can't imagine.

Daniel and I talked a lot about God's will, in regard to everything that has happened, and it is through prayer and guidance that I decided to write you this letter. I suspect that Daniel has told you by now who I am, but on the off-chance he hasn't, I am a woman who has grown up with a lot of regret in her heart—regret that I ran from a crime scene eighteen years ago and allowed an innocent man to be convicted. Daniel went against all his beliefs to keep that horrible boy from hurting me more than he already had. But instead of going to court and explaining that to the judge, I disappeared and left Daniel to be prosecuted for a crime that Chad Witherspoon lied about. Chad's father hired a powerful attorney with a grudge against the Amish, and

Daniel didn't stand a chance. And because of all this, I understand that Daniel felt like he could never return to his community—or to you.

I am so very sorry for my part in all of this. I have carried around the guilt over what I did for so long, and I prayed hard that Daniel would forgive me. It wasn't until Daniel and I talked that I realized my cowardly actions affected your life as well. It basically came down to Daniel's word against Chad's, without me there to tell the police what really happened.

You see, I knew Chad well. We had been dating, and I was trying to break up with him when he savagely attacked me. He told me he'd kill me before he let me leave him. I was afraid of him, his family, and their power. And the one thing Chad didn't know, and still doesn't know: I was pregnant. So I too ran from everything I knew to protect myself and my child.

When Daniel told me that he has spent his entire life loving you and unable to be with you, I knew I had to write you this letter. He said that you are struggling to forgive him for leaving on that Christmas Eve. I can understand that. But I hope that in some way this letter will inspire you to forgive Daniel the way he so unselfishly forgave me. His forgiveness freed my soul in a way that I couldn't comprehend. I was finally released from the guilt I'd felt for my entire adult life.

It is clear to me that Daniel loves you,

*has always loved you, and longs for a place
in your heart. I think that he may be the best
man that I have ever known, and any woman
would be lucky to have him in her life.*

*May you have peace and be blessed this
Christmas season.*

In His name,
Carol Stewart

Lydia tried to control the tears streaming down her face, but through blurred eyes she watched the blue ink on the paper beginning to smudge. She swiped at her cheeks, dabbed the wet spots on Carol's letter, and placed the note back in the envelope. She could hear Anna Marie coming downstairs following her bath. Lydia quickly sat up taller and took a deep, cleansing breath.

Anna Marie strolled to the kitchen in her robe and slippers, then came back through the den carrying a glass of water. As she headed back to the stairs, she said, "Good night, *Mamm.*"

She looked at Lydia and smiled—a smile that quickly faded. "*Mamm!* What's wrong? What happened?"

"I'm fine, I'm fine." Lydia sniffled, held her head high, and lifted herself off the couch. "I have to go somewhere. I won't be long."

"*Mamm,* it's late, dark, and cold. Can't it wait till morning?"

"*Ach!* I'll be right back." Lydia ran past her daughter, up the stairs to her bedroom. Suddenly, the package of socks she'd gotten Daniel for Christmas seemed incredibly wrong. She reached into her dresser and grabbed something she thought he might like much more. Clasping it within her palm, she ran back downstairs, found a small gift bag, and shoved the item inside before Anna Marie could see.

"I'm not going far." Lydia took her bonnet and heavy coat from the rack by the front door. "Daniel's house is right down the road." She smiled at her daughter, kissed her on the cheek, and walked out the door.

Daniel couldn't imagine who would be venturing out this time of night in the cold, but he was certain he heard a buggy turning into his driveway. He closed the book he was reading, placed it on the table by his couch, and picked up the lantern. He walked to the front window and watched the buggy come to a stop and a woman run toward the door. *Lydia?*

He flung the door wide, grabbed her by the arm, and pulled her into the house. "Are you crazy? What are you doing out this late by yourself? It's freezing outside."

He gently pulled her toward the fireplace. Her teeth were clicking together as she pulled off her gloves and warmed her hands in front of the hearth. She was holding a small, red gift bag in one hand. Her clothing was dusted with snow.

"Let me take your coat and bonnet." Daniel held out a hand and waited for her to shed the coat. With one hand she clung to the bag. With the other hand, shaky fingers fumbled with the strings on her bonnet. Daniel hung her wraps on a hook by the door, then turned to face her. "What is it, Lydia? Is it one of the children? Is something wrong?"

"Everything is fine. I just needed—" Her lids slipped down over big, brown eyes for a moment. Then she slowly looked back up and blinked her eyes into focus, eyes glassy with tears. She sniffled. "I just needed to give you your Christmas present." She pushed the bag toward him.

"What?" Daniel accepted the gift with one hand and rubbed his forehead with his other hand. "You came over this late to give me my Christmas present?"

She shrugged, but a smile lit up her face, and Daniel realized—something had changed again. This time, for the better.

"I hope you like it."

Daniel opened the bag, looked inside, and then worked to control his emotions. He pulled out the red heart he'd given her the day he asked her to marry him. The small token fit in the palm of his hand, and Daniel gazed at the inscription. *My heart belongs to you.*

"Lydia...does this mean—"

She stepped forward, stared into his eyes, and said, "It means I love you. I've always loved you." She paused. "And I forgive you."

Daniel's legs threatened to give way beneath him. But as Lydia wrapped her arms around his waist and burrowed her head into his chest, he steadied himself and embraced her. "Oh, Lydia. My love. I've missed you."

"I've missed you too, Daniel."

He held her, and it took a lot to gently push her away, but he had a gift for her as well. "Lydia, I have a present for you too." He pointed to the large, oddly wrapped present to his right.

"Daniel—" she breathed. "Is that what I think it is?"

He was delighted when she walked to the present, squatted down, and pressed her hands against the massive structure. She twisted her head around and looked at him with eyes wide with excitement. "It is, isn't it?"

"Open it and see." Daniel walked to her side and squatted down beside her.

Lydia ripped the paper from the sides of the cedar chest and then stroked the wood gingerly. "Is it the same one?"

"I refinished the stain, but *ya*, it is."

She opened the chest. And there was the inscription.

To Lydia, from Daniel… I will love you forever.

* * * * *

ONE CHILD

By Barbara Cameron

Chapter One

Sarah heard the thin, reedy cry of a newborn. *Wake up!* she told herself. *Wake up! The baby needs you.*

But something was holding her down, binding her arms. She fought against it. *I have to get to my baby!* she moaned.

"Sarah! Wake up, it's just a bad dream!"

Jerking awake, Sarah stared into her husband's face. His eyebrows were drawn together in a frown.

"You were dreaming again."

She closed her eyes, opened them again, and sighed. No, the bad dream was waking and finding that she didn't have a child. *One child,* she thought. *If I had just one child, I could be happy, God. Is one child too much to ask?*

Then, just as quickly, she chided herself. It was wrong to talk to God that way.

David let go of her arms. "You haven't had one in a long time." He narrowed his eyes. "Have you?"

Sarah nearly squirmed under his inquisitive stare. She shook her head. Sitting up, she tried to swing her legs off the bed, but David's large frame blocked her way. "I can't believe I fell asleep. I was going to rest for just a minute after I came home from school."

He touched her arm. "You've exhausted yourself with *redding up* the house and doing so much at school with the Christmas program."

"I need to get up."

"Sarah…"

"David, please. People will be coming at four. I don't want our guests to think anything's wrong."

"Even if it is?" His voice was quiet, but the words felt like a slap.

David stood, and Sarah moved from the bed, avoiding his eyes. She smoothed her dress, grateful that she hadn't wrinkled it lying down. Going to the mirror, she stared at her face, seeing a conflicting message written on its oval shape: there were lavender shadows beneath her gray eyes, evidence she couldn't hide that she wasn't sleeping enough lately. But a sleep crease in her cheek showed she'd just gotten up from bed.

She rubbed a finger over the crease and hoped it would be gone before anyone arrived. Putting on the *kapp* she'd laid out earlier over her nut-brown hair, she started to turn. Then she caught a flash of movement in the mirror.

David stood behind her, the expression on his handsome face full of regret and dismay. But she wasn't ready to forgive his comment. "You need to get cleaned up." The words came out a little sharper than she'd intended.

"Look at me, Sarah," he said softly.

She did as he asked. It was a long look up, as David was a foot taller than her five-foot-two stature; it was even harder to meet his concerned gaze. "I'm fine, David. Really."

"I'm your husband, Sarah," he said. "There's no need to pretend with me."

She nodded and sighed again. "I know. But I want everything to go well tonight. I couldn't bear it if anyone was sad for me. Or felt sorry for me." She felt tears threatening, and blinked them back and took a deep breath. "Not tonight. It's too special a night for anyone to feel sad, whether it is my friends and my family—or you and me."

Tenderly, he cupped her cheek in his hand. "Your friends and your family care about you. They don't feel sorry for you."

"Everyone knows it's near the anniversary of my miscarriage," she said. "They've been watching me. I felt it today at the school program. And sad or sorry—it's one and the same thing, isn't it?" She looked away from the pain she saw flash into his eyes.

He stood there, seeming not to know what to say.

"David, you need to get ready."

"But, Sarah—"

"I have to check on things," she said, and before he could speak, she rushed from the room.

Downstairs, Sarah went from room to room, checking one last time to be sure all was as it should be. Her home shone. She'd cleaned for days, and when she was assured there was not a speck of dust hiding anywhere, she'd turned to decorating for Christmas. Work took her mind off what had happened this time last year. It kept her busy, gave her a sense of control she hadn't had then.

As she glanced around the living room, she should have felt satisfaction. The house had never looked better. A fire crackled merrily in the fireplace, and the drape of greenery that decorated the mantel David had built scented the room with fresh pine. Pots of bright-red poinsettias had been set around the room for a festive holiday touch. Candles flickered in glass votives and cast a warm glow.

Once, Christmas had been her favorite time of the year. Everyone gathered together to celebrate the birth of Jesus, and she would sit at the feet of her favorite uncle and listen to him read from the Bible the story of baby Jesus born in a stable to Mary and Joseph. The next day was more social, with visits and gift exchanges.

She paused at the window to look out at the barn where David had been spending most of his waking hours building the beautiful furniture that was his livelihood. As Christmas approached, the loss had lain between them when they sat at the table for a meal or spent the hours together before bed. Some losses were too huge for words. Sarah could only pray that somehow they would get through this.

She heard David entering the room and turned to offer him a tentative smile. She didn't want to have tension between them. She loved this tall, handsome man who worked so hard to build their home and provide for them, who had continued to show her that he loved and cherished her during some of the worst months of her life.

When she was sixteen, she had developed quite a crush on the quiet blond man with eyes the color of the summer sky. When she was twenty, she had married him. Three years later she loved him even more.

And miracle of miracles, he loved her, even though she felt that she had failed him.

"I'm sorry," he said simply, walking toward her. He

stopped before her and studied her face. "You look so tired."

She playfully slapped his arm. "Not what a woman wants to hear."

"Maybe tonight you can get some sleep."

She'd been having trouble sleeping for the past two weeks. Sometimes she slipped from bed and went downstairs to sit by herself. More than once she woke to find herself being carried back to bed in her husband's strong arms.

She went into his arms now, and they stood there, holding each other. "I'm sorry too."

There was a knock on the front door, and Sarah jumped back. "They're here already."

"I'll go check the fire," David called after her as she rushed to answer the door.

Miriam stood on the doorstep. "I hope Seth and I aren't too early?"

Sarah smiled and shook her head. "Of course not. Merry Christmas."

Peering around her, Miriam laughed. "We are the first, are we not?"

"Come in, come in," Sarah said, gesturing. "It's freezing out there! The temperature must have dropped ten degrees just in the last hour."

Stepping inside, Miriam handed over the casserole she carried. "It's *gut* that we moved up the time, *ya?* Our first storm of the season is going to be a bad one." She hung her outer things on a hook by the door, revealing her too-slender figure clad in her Sunday-best dress and *kapp*.

The heat from the kitchen steamed her round, wire-rimmed glasses, and she took them off and wiped their lenses. "Seth is putting the horse in the barn."

"Would you like some peppermint tea?"

"*Ya,* I would love some." Miriam left Sarah to wander into the next room. Returning to the kitchen, she accepted the cup of tea Sarah handed her and sat at the kitchen table. "Everything looks so nice. It must have taken you days."

"I'm glad you like it."

"Thank you for inviting us. Are you sure it wasn't too much work?" Miriam tentatively touched her friend's hand resting on the table. "I know—well, this must be a difficult time for you."

Squaring her shoulders, Sarah forced a smile. "I'm fine. And you—I'm so happy that you and Seth are seeing each other."

Miriam's smile transformed her features. "I just can't describe what it feels like to be with him. I never thought Seth would notice me. He's always had girls swarming around him like bees to honey." She stopped, shook her head. "But he makes me feel..." She lifted her shoulders, let them fall. "He makes me feel pretty."

"You *are* pretty," Sarah told her. "I don't know why you've always felt you weren't." Relieved that the focus of the conversation had switched from her sadness, Sarah studied Miriam. "Do you think you might be in love?"

They weren't rushing things, Miriam said, but Sarah had a feeling that theirs would be one of the first marriages next fall, after the harvest, after the banns were read. She listened to her friend talk about Seth. Was this the way she had sounded when she was first falling in love with David?

Her thoughts were interrupted by a knock on the door, and she hurried to open it.

Nine-year-old John Smucker stood on the doorstep. He grinned at her. "Merry Christmas, Sarah!" He held out a casserole. "I helped make the filling."

"It smells wonderful. Could you set it on the stove?"

He nodded and hurried to do as she'd asked. His sister, Anna Marie, followed him inside. Lydia, the children's mother, was still climbing the steps to the house and didn't see the exchange.

"Are those your biscuits?" Sarah asked Anna Marie.

Anna Marie nodded and smiled. "I know you like them." She pulled up a corner of the cloth that covered the basket and let Sarah take a sniff.

"Mmm, I can't wait. Would you put them on the counter with the other baked goods?"

Sarah turned back to the door to greet Lydia, Miriam's sister. Lydia was much older than Miriam, a widowed mother with three children, but she moved with a grace that made her seem much younger.

"Where is Jacob?" Sarah asked as she shut the door.

"Helping Daniel and Seth with the horses. He wanted to 'be with the men.'" Lydia sighed as she watched her eldest child leave the room with her *aenti* Miriam. "My *kinner* are growing up so fast. Especially Anna Marie."

Then Lydia turned her attention to Sarah. "And you, Sarah. How are you?"

"Looking forward to our sharing this special time," Sarah said firmly, looking away from the sympathy in Lydia's eyes. "I plan to enjoy this Christmas. Especially with all the happy news you and Miriam have shared with me."

Lydia hugged Sarah, and though the cheek she pressed against Sarah's was chilled, her hug was warm and loving. She leaned back and studied Sarah's face as David had done. "*Gut* for you."

"I want to focus on what I have, not what I don't have. I have a wonderful husband and a beautiful home he and his brothers built for us." Sarah lifted her chin and grinned. "And friends who have shared such *gut* news. Imagine, you and Miriam might *both* be getting married come harvest. Wouldn't that be wonderful?"

"Second chances," Lydia said, and a dreamy look came into her eyes. Then she caught herself and shook her head. "I sound like Anna Marie. But I'm not young."

"You are too," Sarah insisted. "Young and in love again."

Lydia laughed and hung up her outer things.

Sarah tilted her head and studied her friend. "You glow," she said quietly. "It's so *gut* to see that God gave you and Daniel that second chance. He's so *gut*."

"God or Daniel?" Lydia teased. But then she smiled. "And if you believe that God has been *gut* to me, and to Daniel, you must believe that he'll see that you get the gift of a second chance too. And don't pretend to not know what I mean. God wants us to have the gift of happiness, Sarah. In his infinite wisdom, he knows that a child for you and David would be his greatest gift to you both."

Sarah bit her lip and blinked at the sudden rush of tears. "You're such a *gut* friend to remind me that I must have faith. That's what David keeps saying."

"You've been a good friend to me too," Lydia told her, and she moved to hug Sarah again. "You listened to me when I needed it."

Sarah smiled. "That's what friends are for."

The two women moved toward the kitchen.

"You and Miriam are more than friends," Sarah told her. "I've always felt that you were like sisters to me—and especially since Linda and her husband moved to Ohio. I miss her." Sarah sighed. "I was hoping they'd be here this Christmas, but John is having surgery and can't travel."

"Perhaps they can come for Easter."

"We hope so."

"Goodness," Lydia said, her eyes widening as she looked at the plates set out on one counter. "Just how many kinds of cookies did you bake?"

Sarah laughed. "I lost count. But Seth is here. None will go to waste."

The house filled quickly as more friends and family crowded in, bearing covered dishes and platters that wafted delicious aromas.

Her favorite uncle and aunt were the last to arrive. "We stopped to check on your parents," *Aenti* Mary said, as Sarah helped her hang her bonnet, coat, and shawl on pegs in the mudroom. "They're feeling better, but they aren't going to join us."

"The flu really laid them low," Sarah said. "It won't be the same without them tonight, but it's best they stay in with this weather."

"It was *gut* you asked everyone to come earlier," *Onkel* Sam said, hanging up his own things. "Bad storm coming in tonight."

"Everyone's here," Sarah told him, rising on her tip-toes to kiss his cheek. His graying beard was bristly and cold.

He held up his Bible. "I remember how when you

were a little girl you would sit at my knee and listen to me read the story of Jesus' birth."

"It's still my favorite," she told him.

"Well, then, let's get started."

After greeting everyone, Samuel took a seat in the place of honor, the most comfortable chair by the fire. The *kinner* raced to sit at his feet, just as Sarah had once done. She took a seat on a nearby bench and watched as, with great ceremony, her uncle fixed his reading glasses on his long, narrow nose and opened the Bible.

"'This is how the birth of Jesus Christ came about,'" he began.

There was singing, much singing, of the old hymns in German after the Scripture and the readings. Sarah loved hearing the voices of her friends and family rise in songs of the season. There was no accompaniment; their voices were all that were needed to lift the songs to heaven. If she faltered a little on a song about the birth, no one noticed. David looked over at her, as if knowing that her thoughts had drifted to the baby they wished for. She smiled to reassure him.

The *kinner* were well behaved as usual, but Sarah saw them looking in the direction of the kitchen. Many of them had helped prepare the food, or made home-made candy or sweets for gifts. But it wasn't just eagerness to eat. All of them knew that when this day was over, Second Christmas, the gift-giving day, would be that much closer. Although the gifts, often homemade, would be modest compared to *Englisch* standards, they were still a treat to be anticipated and enjoyed.

Finally it was time for the food: roast chicken, filling, mashed potatoes with browned butter on top, a bounty of vegetables that had been canned after the summer harvest. And the desserts! Oh, my, there were so many desserts...pumpkin and apple and custard pies, several strudels, a shoestring apple pie made by Seth's mom, and every kind of cookie from molasses to ginger to raisin puff. Several of Sarah's cousins took over the task of making and serving *kaffi*.

Sarah felt David's eyes on her as she moved around the room, offering a plate of cookies.

"Everything looks wonderful," one of her aunts paused to say as she looked over the plate of cookies. "You've outdone yourself, Sarah."

"Danki."

David watched his wife as she moved about, seeing to the needs of their guests. After two hours, the strain was showing. Others might not notice, but he knew the signs. He walked over to join her as she offered cookies to Miriam.

Seth appeared at her elbow and chose a lemon snowflake cookie from the plate. Popping it into his mouth, he chewed appreciatively. "Mmm, I think this is my favorite."

"You said that about the last one," Miriam reminded him, but her tone was fond. "If you don't stop eating so many cookies, your stomach will burst."

He patted it and grinned. "It will be worth it."

When he reached for another, Sarah smiled and drew the plate back. "I'll wrap some up for you to eat later. Tomorrow, perhaps?"

"Your wife is cutting off my cookie supply," Seth complained to David.

Sarah held out the plate to her husband. "Cookie?"

Instead of taking one, David took the plate and

handed it to Seth, then grasped Sarah's hand and led her from the room.

"Thanks!" Seth called after them.

"David, we have guests," Sarah protested, but she kept the smile on her face.

"They can do without us for a time," he said quietly, refusing to let go of her hand. When they reached the kitchen, he took her other hand. "Look at me, Sarah."

Slowly she did as he asked. "I'm fine, David. Really."

"I told you before, Sarah," he said, looking deep into her eyes. "There is no need to pretend with me."

"David, please. We talked about this earlier and ended up saying things we regretted."

He dropped her hands and stepped back. "Fine."

She threw up her hands. "See what I mean?"

"Well, how am I supposed to feel? I thought we were doing better the last several months, that we were getting over the miscarriage."

"Getting over it?" Sarah whispered. "How do you 'get over' losing a baby?"

He ran a hand through his hair. "I don't know." He gave a quick glance at the doorway. "But we were doing better," he repeated. "Then the past two weeks… I've felt like I can't say the right thing, do the right thing."

She nodded. "It's the anniversary. Naomi told me it was hard for them." She took his hand and squeezed it. "But things feel different tonight. I'm enjoying myself, I really am. I'm glad everyone came." Rising up on her toes, she gave him a quick kiss. "We should be getting back to our guests."

There was a joyful shriek, and two-year-old Rebecca ran into the kitchen and threw her arms around

Sarah's knees. Laughing, Sarah bent to pick up the child. "Where are you going, *glay hotsli?*"

"Sorry, she got away from me!" Ruth, one of Sarah's cousins, tried but failed to give her daughter a stern look. She bent down. "Come to your *mamm.*"

Giggling, Rebecca just held on tighter to Sarah. "Farah," she cried, using her version of Sarah's name.

It cut at David to see the way Sarah closed her eyes as she held the little girl. Then she opened them and handed Rebecca to her mother with an overly bright smile.

"I'm enjoying teaching your *kinner* again this year. I can't wait until this little one joins us."

"Me either," her mother said dryly. "She can be a handful."

Ruth's husband appeared in the doorway behind her. "Ruth? We should be leaving now."

She turned to look at him. "So early?"

"You remember we talked about the weather. Everyone's getting ready to go."

"And I am sure they are no happier than I am," replied Ruth. "Oh well. At least the storm didn't come in time to keep us from visiting today." She bounced Rebecca on her hip. "Come, let us get your coat on."

Their guests found their wraps and said their good-byes.

"We had such a wonderful time," *Aenti* Mary told Sarah as the women cleaned up the kitchen. "I thought I would take some food by to your parents' house on our way home."

Sarah hugged her. "Thank you. Tell them that I love them and hope to see them tomorrow. If they can't come here, I'll visit them."

Aenti Mary patted her cheek. "I will. They would

have enjoyed seeing how you carried on their tradition tonight in your home."

One by one their guests left, bundled up against the rapidly lowering temperature. Snow swirled in the door each time it opened. Finally, the door stopped opening and shutting.

And David was alone with his wife.

"I'm glad that they don't have far to travel with a storm coming. But God will watch over them."

Sarah nodded and turned to start straightening the kitchen, but David reached out and caught her hand, pulling her into his arms. She laid her head on his shoulder, and he held her. And finally she let go, as she hadn't let herself do all the time they had entertained, all the hours leading up to it, all the days before.

"I'm sorry," she cried, wetting the shoulder of his jacket with her tears. "Sorry, sorry, sorry."

David stroked her back. "What are you sorry for?"

"For being so sad sometimes. For thinking of myself too often. For…for…" She paused, then plunged on. "For failing you."

He pulled back then and frowned at her. "You have not failed me."

"But—"

"I've told you time and again that you didn't fail us. God has a plan for us, Sarah. You must believe that."

"I'm trying."

"I know," he said, gathering her to him again. "I know. It's hard, but we must be patient. The doctor said there's no reason why we can't have *kinner*. We must trust God to send them."

The storm started two hours later, with a fierceness they only saw several times a year. Sarah was grateful that all their friends and family would be safely tucked in their homes. The wind howled, and snow splashed against the windows.

"Ready for bed?" David asked.

"Be right there." She walked over to the table by the front window and turned off the battery-operated candle she'd put there for the holidays.

Hand in hand, they walked to the stairs and were halfway up when they heard someone pounding on the front door.

Chapter Two

Sarah looked at David. "Who would be out on a night like this?"

David started back down the stairs, but she clutched his arm. "Wait! It could be someone bad—"

"Or it could be a neighbor needing help," he reminded her.

"Look out the window first!" she cried, following him. Reaching into a drawer, she pulled out a packet of matches and lit the lamp that stood on a table near the door.

The pounding got louder as David approached the door.

"Help! We need help!"

"Who is it?" David called out.

"My name's Jason. Our car went off the road!"

"David, no! Don't open the door!" Looking at him fearfully, Sarah touched her fingers to her lips and shook her head.

David gave her a level look. "Sarah, let me handle this," he said.

"Please, I couldn't find any other houses in the

storm," the man shouted. "I left my wife in the car, and it's freezing out here."

David opened the door immediately.

"I was about to give up hope!" the man said hoarsely, stumbling inside.

Sarah was relieved to see a tall, thin man who wore wire-rimmed glasses and an expensive-looking *Englisch*-style dress jacket. She guessed he was in his thirties. As Miriam had done earlier, he took off the glasses and wiped at the fog on them.

"I'm David Fisher, and this is my wife, Sarah."

"Jason Stevens. We've been driving around for hours," he said. "I have no idea where we are."

"Paradise." David shut the door.

"Paradise, *Pennsylvania*," Sarah added with a smile when Jason looked disbelieving.

"Oh. Wow. We really did get lost. Kate's always teasing me about not wanting to ask for directions." He held out his cell phone. "I can't get reception. The storm must've knocked out the towers. Can I use your phone?"

David and Sarah exchanged a look.

"We don't have a telephone," David told him.

"You mean it's dead."

"No, we don't have a telephone in the house—" He broke off as the man stared at him, then his glance swept around the mudroom. His eyes widened as he saw David's black felt hat and Sarah's bonnet hanging on pegs on the wall.

"You're Amish."

"Yes. We have a cell phone I use for my business, but if yours isn't working, I doubt mine is either," David said. "You're welcome to shelter here until the storm is over."

Jason cast a worried look behind him. "I left Kate in the car. I have to go back and get her right away."

"How far away is it?" David asked him, reaching for his coat. He pulled on boots, a wool scarf, and his hat. "I'll go with you. Maybe I can get it started."

"It doesn't matter if we get it started. I slid off the road."

"Then you'll stay here tonight."

"Thank you." Jason looked at the door. "Can we go now? I'm so worried about Kate."

"David, stop at the telephone shanty on your way," Sarah suggested. "Maybe the regular phone lines haven't been knocked down in the storm."

"*Gut* idea."

She watched him leave, her heart in her throat. He was walking off with a stranger into a bad storm. Quickly she sent up a prayer for her husband's safety.

Hurrying into the living room, she knelt at the hearth and got the fire going, then lit the lamps before going to the kitchen to make *kaffi*. The clock ticked, the sound echoing in the quiet room.

What was taking so long? She'd never thought of herself as having much imagination, but now her mind whirled with fears and stories of bad things that happened to people caught outside in such conditions, even in familiar territory.

When she heard the front door open, she ran to it.

A woman entered, followed by Jason. Then David stepped inside, and Sarah felt her tension drain. He shut the door behind him and shook the snow from the brim of his hat.

"You were gone so long I got worried!"

"The car was much farther away than I thought," David told her.

"I knew I'd walked quite a distance," Jason admitted. "I couldn't see anything in the dark for so long. I was about to give up when I saw the light burning in your window. Sarah, this is my wife, Kate."

"Nice to meet you," Sarah said. "Welcome to our home."

"I checked the telephone shanty, and the lines must be down," David told Sarah as he took Jason's coat and hung it up. "We need to get them warmed up quickly."

As if to confirm his words, Jason shivered. Sarah registered for the first time that he wore a dress shirt and pants with just a medium-weight jacket, hardly the kind of clothes to be wearing when tramping through the snow. His pants were soaked from the knees down, and when he moved, his shoes squished.

The woman pulled off her knit cap, revealing a small, heart-shaped face and chin-length black hair. Her face was white from cold and strain.

"Here, let me help you." Sarah rushed to assist the woman as she fumbled with the buttons of her heavy coat, damp with melting snow.

"Thanks. My fingers are so cold."

Sarah tsked-tsked. "You should have had gloves on."

Like her husband, Kate wasn't dressed for such frigid cold. And although she had on ankle boots, they were dressy footwear, not practical for the elements.

"We were in the car. I didn't think we'd have to get out in the weather. It was supposed to just be a quick trip, but we got lost in the snowstorm."

She was shaking so hard with cold that Sarah could almost hear her teeth chatter. The last button undone, Sarah looked on, startled, as the woman shed her coat.

She caught Sarah's expression and grinned. "Yup. Pregnant." She laughed as she rubbed her huge abdomen. "I feel like Shamu the whale."

Sarah glanced at David and saw that he'd gone still. As she took the coat from Kate, the other woman's hand brushed her arm.

"Your hand is like ice." Sarah pulled her shawl from a nearby peg and wrapped it around the woman's shoulders. "Go on into the bathroom, and I'll get you some dry clothes to wear." She turned to Jason. "David will find you something to wear too."

"Let's take care of Kate first," he said. "I don't want to chance her getting sick."

Sarah went upstairs and chose a flannel nightgown. After debating for a moment, she took one of David's robes, reasoning that it would be roomier for Kate's protruding stomach than her own garments.

Returning downstairs, she knocked on the bathroom door and when Kate opened it, she handed in the clothing. "I think you'll be comfortable in these."

"Thanks," Kate told her, shivering.

"Just leave your wet clothes in the sink and come get in front of the fire. Or if you want, you can take a bath."

"I think I'll be fine just getting into dry clothes, thanks. The fire sounds great."

When Kate came out, she was hugging herself. "This feels so cozy. But I don't think it's yours, is it?" She held out her arms to show how she'd had to fold up the sleeves of the robe. Her bare toes peeked out from the hem that nearly touched the floor.

Sarah laughed. "I thought David's might fit you better. Let's get some socks on you."

Kate handed them to Jason, and he stared at them blankly, then at her. She raised her eyebrows at him.

"Oh, right," he said. He knelt down to put the socks on her feet. "There you go, babe."

Kate grinned at Sarah and David. "He keeps forgetting I haven't seen my feet in a month."

Sarah settled Kate on the sofa with a woven throw and brought out a quilt as well and tucked it around her. "How's that?"

"I feel warmer already." She sniffed. "The coffee smells so good," she said wistfully. "I miss it. But I'll do whatever it takes so the baby will be healthy."

"I'll fix you some tea. Do you like chamomile?"

Kate wrinkled her nose. "Not as much as coffee. But hot tea will taste good right now."

"Christmas cookies," Sarah heard herself saying, as if she were standing outside her body. "Maybe some Christmas cookies will make it taste better."

"Thanks." Kate pulled the quilt up around her. "It's really incredibly kind of both of you to take us in."

Jason stroked his wife's hair. "I shouldn't have let you talk me into driving to your mother's."

"I wanted to see my family," she said simply. "Families are supposed to be together for Christmas. We didn't know the weather would turn so ugly."

Jason sighed. "That's just it. We know how the weather can be this time of the year. We shouldn't have chanced it."

"It'll be over soon, and we'll be on our way," Kate said optimistically.

But they could hear the wind picking up, howling around the house, hurling snow against the windows. Jason shivered again.

"Sit by the fire while I get you some dry clothes," David told him, frowning.

"I'll be okay—" Jason broke off at the stern look David gave him, and seated himself in a chair near the fire.

David looked at Sarah. "Make him stay there until I get him some dry clothes."

She nodded. It was worrying her, too, to see that Jason wasn't warming up.

David returned with a pile of clothing for Jason, then turned to Sarah. "Do you think the *kaffi* is ready?"

Sarah excused herself and followed him to the kitchen. "What is it?" she asked.

"I'm concerned about Jason. He's not warming up, and he's limping."

"Do you think he has frostbite?"

"I don't know. Let's watch him for a while." He leaned against the counter and watched her open a box of chamomile tea bags and place one in a cup for Kate. "Are you all right with this, Sarah?"

"With their staying the night? Of course."

"You're not upset?"

She poured hot water over the tea bag. "I was surprised when she took off her coat, but no, I'm not upset. After all, I'm surrounded by children every day at school." She opened a big plastic container of cookies and arranged some on a plate. "Could you have ever imagined two such people appearing on our doorstep on this night of nights?" Pausing, she looked at her husband. "God put them here tonight for a reason," she said slowly, as if to herself. She tried to smile. "I don't know the reason. But I don't have to for now."

David touched her cheek, and his eyes were warm on her.

"Let's go meet our guests, shall we?" she said.

He picked up the tray and followed her into the other room.

"I can't imagine living without electricity, can you?" Jason asked his wife. "It feels so strange. Even campgrounds have electricity these days."

"Honey, you'll survive without your computer and cell phone for one night. Promise." She looked around as she ran her hand over the arm of the sofa. "It's so cozy here. Jason, look. I think someone made this sofa. And I don't mean Rooms To Go."

But Jason was examining the clothes David had loaned him. "The pants don't have zippers. They've got buttons on them, and there are hooks and eyes on the vest. That's…different."

"Keep your voice down," Kate told him. "They're lovely people who probably saved our lives."

"I know. I wasn't making fun."

He saw David entering the room, followed by Sarah. "I'm sorry. I didn't mean to offend you."

David set the tray on a nearby table. "You didn't. I'm sure it's not what you're used to."

"It was kind of you to offer us dry clothes," Kate said.

"Fortunately, we're near to the same size," David said.

Jason smiled and stuck out his feet to show the rolled-up hems. "Well, close…"

"I don't mind being without electricity or a phone," Kate said. "I'd forgotten how nice it was to have an uninterrupted conversation."

Jason accepted his *kaffi* and cupped his hands

around one of the thick pottery mugs David favored. Sarah carried the cookies to Kate.

"Oh, the cookies look wonderful," Kate said, sniffing the gingerbread man she chose before taking a bite. "Mmm, look out. I could eat the whole plate. I'm starved."

"I didn't think," Sarah said, distressed. "I should have asked if you were hungry. When did you last eat?"

"Since she's been pregnant, she's been nothing but hungry," Jason said, winking at Kate as he reached for a cookie.

"Thanks a lot." But she grinned. "He's right, though."

"Eat as many cookies as you want," Sarah told them. "But I'm going to make you something more substantial."

"Jason's joking," Kate said, but Sarah was already moving swiftly out of the room. "Really, I'm fine. The two of you have already gone to so much trouble!"

"It's no trouble," David told her. "Sarah loves taking care of people."

"Man, what could be better than these?" Jason asked, stuffing another cookie into his mouth.

"You're not going to talk with your mouth full when the baby comes, are you?"

"No, Mom," he teased as he handed her the plate. "Oops, maybe I should be offering you some, David?"

"I ate too many already tonight. Sarah's been doing quite a bit of baking." He poked at the fire and then straightened. "How are you both doing?"

"I'm nice and toasty now," Kate said.

Jason nodded. "I'm fine, thanks."

David came out to the kitchen, where Sarah was making sandwiches and heating up some soup.

"Jason is still limping," he said. "He walked twice as far as I did, and in those dress shoes *Englisch* men wear. I'm going to ask him if I can look at his feet."

He watched her as she put the finishing touches on the two trays of food. "Why don't you take one of the trays to Kate and send Jason in here to get the other one?"

"Great idea." She rose on tiptoes to kiss his cheek. "You're so smart."

Sarah settled beside Kate on the sofa and handed her a mug of soup.

"Mmm. This smells so good. What is it?"

"It's not fancy, just vegetable soup I made for supper yesterday."

"Mmm," Kate said again after trying a spoonful. "This is even better than my mom's. Maybe I could have your recipe?"

"It's just a little of this and that. Whatever's left of vegetables from the week."

"That's how my mom cooks. I don't have her knack. Then again, I didn't really start cooking until Jason and I got married," Kate admitted. "I've never been that interested. But we can't eat out every night, you know? So I've been trying to cook more."

She picked up the sandwich and took a bite.

"How is it?" Sarah asked.

Kate swallowed. "Wonderful. Did you make the bread?"

Sarah smiled. "It's not that hard, really."

"Don't tell Jason. He'll want me to try it. And where am I going to find the time to do that around my work?"

Kate stretched and winced, then glanced furtively toward the doorway to the kitchen.

"Is something wrong?"

"My back's been hurting all day. I didn't dare tell Jason, or he wouldn't have driven us to see my mom." Frowning, she shifted and rubbed at it.

Sarah felt a chill race up her spine. "Kate, when's your baby due?" she asked quietly.

"In two weeks." She looked over at the lone cookie on the plate. "I guess I'd be terrible if I ate the last cookie? I mean, Jason had to walk so far tonight to get us help."

"Eat it. I have plenty more. But, Kate?"

"Yeah?"

"Is it…" Sarah hesitated, afraid to put her worry into words. "Is it possible you're in labor?"

Chapter Three

Kate shook her head and bit into the cookie. "Still two weeks to go, like I said." She finished the cookie and sighed, then realized that Sarah was looking at her. "What? Have I got sugar all over my mouth?" She wiped at it with a napkin.

"Kate, babies don't always come when they're supposed to," Sarah told her, choosing her words carefully. "Matter of fact, they don't *usually* come when they're supposed to." She smoothed her dress over her knees. "We have big families here, and I can tell you that for certain."

"I just saw the doctor last week, and she seemed to think I was right on schedule." But Kate was rubbing her lower back again. "Besides, the baby can't come early. We could never get me to the hospital in this storm."

Sarah bit her lip to keep from laughing at this *Englischer's* misguided "logic."

Kate looked at the doorway again. "Anyway, even if I were going into labor, our Lamaze coach says first labors usually take a long time. The storm'll be over soon, right?"

Sarah hesitated.

"Listen," Kate said, "promise me that you won't tell Jason what I said. I mean, it's probably just a backache from riding in the car so many hours today."

It was the first reasonable thing Kate had said in the last few minutes, thought Sarah. Her own friends complained about feeling uncomfortable when they were traveling in buggies and cars when their time grew near.

But asking her to not say anything to Jason...to keep a secret? Sarah had never done that.

Well, maybe *never* wasn't entirely truthful. After all, hadn't she been keeping her feelings a secret from her own husband? She was ashamed at how often she had been angry at God about the miscarriage. Although she and David shared all their concerns, she'd been too ashamed to tell him this. And wasn't that a form of keeping a secret?

"I won't say anything unless your husband asks me directly."

"He won't do that," Kate said confidently. "Jason's kind of introverted, you know? A little self-absorbed. And absentminded, because he's always thinking about some problem he has to solve. He's in IT. Information technology," she added when Sarah looked blank. "You know, computers. And talk about being impatient. I tease him that he wants patience, and he wants it *now!* I guess he's like that because computers move so fast."

She shifted to get comfortable again. "He's a really great guy, and I love him to death, but we have to work on communication, you know?" Kate gazed at the fire and didn't seem to expect an answer.

* * *

"I appreciate your concern, but I'm fine. I'm warming up."

Jason and David sat at the kitchen table, Jason finishing the soup and sandwich Sarah had prepared.

"You walked quite a distance in the snow," David said. "I just want to make sure you don't have frostbite."

"People don't get that sort of thing around here, do they? That's for—I don't know—mountain climbers in Nepal."

"Anyone can get hypothermia as well as frostbite when they're out in bad weather like this long enough. If you've finished eating, let's get those socks off and take a look."

Shrugging, Jason pulled off the socks and stared at his feet. "They look okay to me." He shivered again and started to put the socks back on, but David stopped him.

"You were limping earlier. We need to soak your feet."

Jason glanced at the doorway, then lowered his voice. "Well, I was practically carrying three people. I mean, Kate's a small woman, but she's gained some weight with this pregnancy."

David wasn't sure how to respond to the other man's humor. "You weren't carrying your wife when you came into the kitchen a few minutes ago." He frowned as he pressed a finger to the skin on Jason's foot.

"I feel like you're about to put a new horseshoe on me."

David smiled. "I'm not a farrier."

"A what?"

"A farrier. He's the man who shoes horses." He found a pan and filled it with warm water.

"Oh. But you have horses?"

"Yes. For our buggy. And for plowing."

"So you're a farmer?"

"It's a small farm compared to most around here, but yes. And I'm a carpenter. I think you're okay, but let's try soaking your feet, okay?"

Jason pulled out his cell phone and checked the display again. "Nothing," he muttered. "Cars, computers, cell phones. They get you dependent on them, then what do you do when they don't work?"

David lifted his shoulders. "Afraid I don't know."

"Oh yeah. Right. Sorry." He stared down at his feet in the water. "So I've stuck my foot in my mouth again."

"No, it's in the water."

"Uh—it's an expression—" He stopped when he saw David grinning. "Oh, you're joking."

"Feet feeling any better?"

"Yeah, I think so. Thanks."

"You're sure?" David saw the man's Adam's apple bob, and there was a suspicious gleam in his eyes as he stared at his feet. "If you're in pain…"

"I've never been so scared," Jason blurted out. "I tell you, that was the worst time I've ever had in my life, walking and walking and looking for help, and my wife's sitting back in the car, and who knew how long she could stay warm? And my baby. I'm supposed to be responsible for my family, and I almost let them down." He stopped, choked up.

David laid his hand on Jason's shoulder. "Everything's fine now. You're all safe. God is with you."

Jason struggled for composure. "Well, I...yeah..."

"I don't mean to make you uncomfortable."

"No, I know that. I'm sure it's...it's what you believe."

"You don't?" David added more hot water from the kettle to the pan.

Jason shrugged. "I don't know. I went to Sunday school and all that when I was a kid, but my family stopped going to church." He paused. "Kate's mother was asking what religion we're going to be raising our son in. I didn't know what to tell her. I mean, it's just not been something I've spent time thinking about a lot, you know?"

David thought about how much his faith was a part of his life, his being.

"Thing is, my family is Protestant, and Kate's is Catholic. I guess we'll be talking about that."

There wasn't any such discussion in David's community. And since most of the young men and women stayed and became attracted to each other, there wasn't any chance of a marriage between people of two different religions.

"Do you and Sarah have children?"

"Not yet."

"The Amish usually have big families, don't they?"

David shrugged. "Compared to *Englisch* families, I suppose so. We have the size family that God gives us. There were ten in my family, but Sarah has just one sister."

"Our boy might be the only one for a long time," Jason said. "It's pretty expensive to raise a kid these days."

Children were a priceless gift from God, thought

David. So what was this talk of what it cost to raise them? Before he could say anything, a yawn overtook him.

"Man, I'm sorry we're keeping you up. You probably go to bed early, right?"

"Most of the time. But we were up tonight."

"Were you going to put up your tree? I know some people do that on Christmas Eve or Christmas Day."

"We don't have Christmas trees."

"I guess I don't know much about the way you live."

"Let's take a look at those feet again."

Jason lifted one from the water. "Looks much better. Sure feels a lot better."

"Let's get your socks back on, and we'll show you where you and Kate can sleep tonight."

But when they went to their wives, they found that Kate had fallen asleep on the sofa with the quilt tucked under her chin. Sarah sat in a nearby chair, staring into the fire.

She looked up and smiled at them. "She was so tired, she dropped off right after she ate."

"She hasn't been sleeping much lately. Says she can't get comfortable."

His own wife wasn't sleeping well either, thought David, but for the opposite reason.

"Sure looks comfortable now." Jason walked over and stroked her hair. "I hate to move her."

Sarah exchanged a look with David. "We could fix you a pallet on the floor."

"That'd be like camping, wouldn't it?" David asked.

Jason looked stricken, and then he saw the corners

of David's mouth lift. "Okay, you're teasing me, aren't you?"

David just grinned.

"I thought the Amish were kind of stern, didn't have much of a sense of humor. Shows me not to make assumptions."

"We're just people like you," David told him, shrugging.

"Not like me," Jason said slowly. "If someone had knocked on my door like I did yours, I'm not sure I would have opened it. Oh, I'd have called for help for them if I could. But I'm not sure I could have extended the hospitality—the *caring*—that you two have."

"I don't believe that," Sarah told him. "I think you'd have done the right thing."

Jason shoved his hands in his pockets and looked thoughtful. "I don't know, I think there's so much crime out there in my world, people sometimes won't help out strangers."

David and Sarah exchanged another look. He could tell she was remembering how she'd been afraid for him to open the door.

Jason pulled out his cell phone and checked it. Shaking his head, he went to look out the window. "How much longer can this last?"

"A friend who was here earlier said it's expected to last through the night, maybe longer."

Jason sighed. "Well, maybe when we wake up in the morning it'll be over with."

Sarah glanced surreptitiously at the clock. It was already one in the morning, and the storm showed no sign of letting up.

Jason turned around to see Kate standing in the doorway.

"My stomach is cramping," she said.

He led her to a kitchen chair. "Maybe it's just upset. We've eaten a lot today, between dinner at your mom's and here."

Kate pressed her hands to each side of her abdomen. Her face took on an inward look that Sarah had seen before—at the bedside of two friends giving birth.

Crossing the room, Sarah knelt beside Kate. "Tell me what it feels like."

"Hmm?" Kate focused on Sarah's face. "Sort of a bunching feeling."

"Jason might be right. Add in the stress of the storm, and you might just be having stomach upset. Heartburn, you know, that kind of thing."

Jason paced the room, checking his cell phone. "This is making me nuts!" he muttered. "We need to get her to a hospital."

Sarah looked at David, then at Jason, then at David again.

David touched Jason's arm and motioned him toward the other room.

"I don't know much about having a baby," David began. "But I think the calmer we keep your wife, the better, don't you? If she gets herself worked up, well, it just seems to me she'll make herself feel worse."

"You're right." Jason raked his hands through his hair. "I know you're right. But you're asking me to calm her down when I'm freaking out myself. The baby's not due for another couple weeks."

David nodded thoughtfully. "Well then, let's just

hope that it's like Sarah said. Stomach upset or heartburn. But in any case, Sarah will know what to do."

"She's a nurse?" Jason asked, looking hopeful.

"No. But she's been with two friends who had babies, and she was raised on a farm. She'll know what to do," David repeated.

"C'mon, man, women and cows aren't the same."

"But the birthing process is much the same. Right?"

Jason looked over his shoulder. "You're probably right. But I don't think Kate should hear us saying so!"

"I'm feeling a little anxious," Kate admitted to Sarah.

"There's nothing to be anxious about."

"How can you say that? Have *you* had a baby?"

Pain stabbed Sarah in the heart. "No."

"Then don't tell me I shouldn't feel that way," Kate muttered. Biting her lip, she shook her head. "I'm sorry, I'm sorry. I don't mean to be short. I'm just worried. What if I go into labor and we can't get help?"

"Then I'll help you."

Kate's face cleared. "You're a nurse?"

Sarah shook her head. "But I know a lot about birth. I grew up on a farm. I helped my father with a lot of births."

"I'm not a cow!"

"Oh, I didn't mean it that way," Sarah rushed to say. "But birth is a natural process."

"Epidural," muttered Kate. "No one should have to do without an epidural. Jason and I have been doing Lamaze classes. Natural childbirth is one thing, but

I want an epidural on hand if I need it. The instructor says I can ask for it, no problem." She shifted to get comfortable. "Do the Amish have their babies at home?"

Sarah smiled. "Sometimes. I was with one friend when she had her baby at home. But many Plain women have their babies in the hospital just like *Englischers*. I was a birth coach for a cousin at a hospital when her husband was badly hurt in a buggy accident and couldn't be with her."

"Oh."

Kate had stopped rubbing at one side of her abdomen.

"How's the cramping?"

"It stopped." She blinked in surprise and then grinned at Sarah. "Cool."

Sarah smiled and sent up a silent prayer of thanks. *"Gut."* Glancing at the window, she made a decision. "This storm isn't stopping anytime soon, and you're tired. Why don't we get you and your husband settled in the guest bedroom? I think some rest will do you both good."

"I hate that we're putting you to so much trouble."

"It's no trouble at all."

That way David could get some rest too, thought Sarah, as she showed Kate and Jason to their room. Kate was already in nightclothes, so David went to get pajamas and a robe for Jason.

"Just call if you need anything," Sarah told them, and was surprised when Kate suddenly hugged her.

"We appreciate this so much, we can't tell you," Jason said, slipping his arm around his wife.

Sarah smiled. *"Gern schöna."*

Jason raised his eyebrows in question.

"So willingly done," she translated. "We are happy to have you here."

Chapter Four

When David walked into the kitchen, Sarah was at the sink, washing the coffee mugs and humming one of the Christmas hymns they had sung earlier that night.

The kitchen was her favorite room. He often found her humming as she did chores or bent over her lesson plans spread out on the kitchen table.

"So, our guests are all settled for the night. Maybe now we can get some sleep."

"I'll be up in a minute."

"Can't you do that in the morning?" When she merely glanced at him, he laughed. "Of course you can't."

Smiling, she finished drying the last mug and put it in the cupboard. "You can't walk away from your work area without putting away your tools either."

"True." He yawned. "I hope you can get some rest."

"I should be tired, but I'm not."

Moving to her side, he rubbed her shoulders as she wiped out the sink. "I know. I feel the same."

The shoulder rub felt wonderful, but Sarah frowned. "I was a little worried there when Kate said she was feeling cramping. You and I are used to witnessing birth, but Jason and Kate are used to city life. Birth only happens in a hospital." She paused. "What'll we do if Kate does go into labor?"

"We'll cope," David told her with a confidence he didn't feel inside. This was "woman stuff," and what man knew what to do about it? "She'll need our help, and we can't let her down. I'm afraid Jason won't be much help."

They were silent for a long time, staring out the kitchen window at the snow pounding against the glass.

"What are you thinking?" he asked after a long moment.

"I'm not proud of what I'm thinking." She tried to turn away, but he wouldn't let her. "Oh, David, I envy Kate. She's having a baby, and I want one. I want us to have a baby."

He gathered her into his arms, comforting her. "Shh, it's all right."

"No, it's not," she insisted, once again getting tears all over his shoulder. "It's a sin to envy."

"We're human, Sarah. We're not perfect."

She leaned back in his arms and reached into her apron pocket for her handkerchief. Shaking her head, she wiped her eyes. "I am most definitely not perfect."

"You are to me." When she started to pull away, he held on. "Except when you try to push me away. I grieve too, Sarah, and I need you."

She went still. "You've never said that before."

"It's not always easy for me to talk about such things." He took a deep breath. "But I do need you, Sarah. I need you, and I love you, and I want you to be happy again. We need to have faith," he told her seriously. "I believe we will have another child because I believe God wants us to have that gift. He isn't giving it to us this Christmas as he didn't last Christmas. But one day."

"I wish I had your faith."

He took her hand and placed it on his chest, holding it there. "Borrow some from my heart, dear Sarah."

She threw her arms around him and held him. "I love you. And I need you, too."

This time when she drew back, it wasn't to pull away. It was to raise herself up on tiptoes to kiss him.

"Oh, uh, I'm sorry," Jason stammered. He rapped an elbow on the doorjamb as he tried to back out of the room.

"It's all right," Sarah said.

"I—I didn't mean to intrude on a private moment."

"It's all right," Sarah repeated.

"I didn't think that—well, I thought…" He stopped and turned beet red.

David laughed. "Do you think we find our children under a cabbage?"

Jason turned even redder. "I—uh, I never thought about it. I—"

Laughing, Sarah moved away from David. "Don't let my husband tease you. Did you need something?"

"No, I was just going into the bathroom and I heard voices. I thought you had gone to bed."

"We're about to. Sarah was washing the coffee mugs."

"Kate can't go to bed if there's a glass in the sink either," Jason told them. "Well then, I'll say good night. Thanks again for everything."

David turned to Sarah. "Ready to go upstairs?"

"Just another minute or two."

* * *

Sarah was hanging up the dish towel to dry when Kate walked into the kitchen. "Notice how the men are always missing when it comes to kitchen work?" she asked wryly.

"Actually, David sometimes helps, although kitchen work isn't his favorite," Sarah told her.

"You should see the way Jason loads the dishwasher. I always have to do it again. Of course, I tend to be a little Type A."

"Type A?"

"Perfectionist." She wandered to look out the window, then turned and looked back at Sarah. "I'm sorry. I don't want to keep you up."

"Is there something else I can get for you?" Tilting her head to one side, Sarah studied Kate. "Another pillow or quilt? Some warm milk?"

"I just couldn't get comfortable," Kate admitted. "Not like I was on your sofa."

"Then would you like to sleep there?"

"Would you mind?"

Sarah laughed. "No, when I'm having trouble sleeping, it's my favorite place too."

Jason appeared as Kate was heading back to the living room. "I thought we were going to bed."

"Sarah says I can sleep on the sofa since I'm more comfortable there."

"Whatever the pregnant woman wants," he murmured, casting his eyes heavenward. "You never know what makes them happy. Or when. Ice cream just when I've settled down to watch sports on ESPN. Back rubs at 3:00 a.m."

"Oh, you have it so rough," Kate retorted, winking at Sarah. "How'd you like to carry The Belly for a while?"

"Kate, you don't mind if I sleep in the other room?" Jason asked.

She smiled at the hope in his voice. "No. I'll be fine."

"See you in the morning." He kissed her and left.

Kate snuggled up beneath the quilt. "Oh, this is lovely. We haven't had a fire in our new fireplace yet. Jason keeps saying he doesn't want to mess it up, and if I'm cold I should turn up the heat. But there's just something so soothing about a real, burning fire, isn't there?"

Sarah had never experienced electric heating, but she knew what Kate meant. "I'll just turn down the lamp."

"It looks so pretty in here, smells like Christmas. I love this room." She gestured at the book beside the lamp. "What were you reading?"

"The Bible. My uncle always reads us the Christmas story from the book of Matthew." Sarah waited. "Can I do anything else for you?"

"I know it's selfish of me, but would you mind sitting with me for a few minutes?"

"Of course not." Sarah sank down into the chair by the fire.

"Tell me about how you celebrate Christmas. You said you had friends and family over this afternoon?"

"We have two days of Christmas. The first one is about the spiritual side, about the birth of Jesus. Second Christmas, the second day, is when we exchange presents."

"Here, I thought you might like this," Jason said, coming back with an extra pillow for his wife. "So where does Santa leave the presents, if you don't have a Christmas tree?"

"We don't have Santa."

"Good call," Kate muttered.

Jason stared at her. "What are you saying? You think having Santa is wrong?"

Kate tucked the pillow he'd brought her under her tummy, then drew the quilt up over her. "I think it can set up a whole set of expectations, Jason. We've both seen our nephews watching all those commercials pushing toys, and then they do nothing but harangue their parents to get them."

"But they're kids—"

"Who grow up to want more and more *things*."

"This is about the TV again."

"We didn't need another one. We just bought one two years ago." She glanced at Sarah, then back at her husband. "We'll talk about it later."

"Right. See you both in the morning."

"Sorry," Kate told Sarah as Jason left the room quickly. "We've been having a—discussion lately."

"We have those."

"Really? You and David seem to get along so well."

Sarah didn't reply, and Kate continued.

"The two of us were already kind of stressed lately," Kate was saying. "We just moved into a new house we had built. I couldn't help much, being pregnant and trying to catch up on work before I go on maternity leave. Then there was all the getting ready for the holidays, the shopping and plans and everything." She cast a fearful glance at the window. "And now this snowstorm's just got me nervous. I didn't expect to be stranded somewhere and have Mr. Baby start acting like he wanted to come out."

"Try to stay calm," Sarah told her. "Everything will be fine."

Kate sighed. "You're amazing, Sarah. I really believe that when you say it."

Sarah smiled. "Most of the things we worry about don't happen."

"True," Kate agreed. She relaxed against her pillow. "I tend to be a worrywart."

Sarah tilted her head to one side and studied Kate. "I always wondered what one looked like. Now I know."

It took a minute for her words to sink in, and then Kate laughed. "No, I look more like a beached whale." She shifted again. "I know it sounds like a negative quality—the worrying, I mean—but it helps me think of the worst-case scenario, you see, and then I prepare for it."

"How does that help you?"

"Well, a lot of people think an attorney needs to know how to argue, and Jason would tell you I certainly know how to do that." She regarded Sarah. "I can see you're trying not to smile."

"Well, um, it was interesting the way the two of you, um, *discussed* a television set a moment ago."

"I read that husbands and wives spend just twelve minutes a day talking to each other, and I can believe it. Jason makes me nuts with his watching television. Absolutely nuts. You should be glad you don't have a TV, Sarah. Husbands can't tear themselves away from it. Especially during sports. I swear, Jason actually told me that if I go into labor during a football game, I'll have to wait for halftime before he drives me to the hospital!"

"I guess we're protected from that," Sarah agreed. "But surely he was joking."

"He'd better be."

Sarah thought about how much she and David used to talk and longed for the day when the ease they used to have would be there again.

"Televisions may be one negative by-product of electricity, that's for sure." Kate thought for a moment. "But there are some really wonderful things that use it that save me a lot of time. Like a washer and dryer. And a dishwasher."

Sarah pulled the throw she kept on the chair around her shoulders. "What do you do with the time you save?"

Kate opened her mouth and then shut it. "Well, more work, actually. Like paperwork for my job." She frowned. "Don't you mind that you have to work so hard to take care of your home when it could be easier?"

"This is the way I've always known," Sarah said simply, holding up her hands and then letting them fall into her lap. "And there's a joy in doing a job, isn't there? In staying in the moment while you're doing it, and doing it well, for the sake of the work?" She leaned back in her chair. "I enjoy thinking about my day as I do dishes."

"I never thought about it. I rush around so much." Kate fell silent. Absently she rubbed at her abdomen. "Even with the baby," she murmured.

The room was so quiet Sarah could hear the flames

licking at the wood, the ticking of the grandfather clock.

"Do you know there are women in my firm who have scheduled Cesareans so that they don't miss an important meeting at the office?" Kate said suddenly.

"You mean, they plan when they have their babies?"

Kate nodded. "I have a friend who's a college professor. When she was hired, her department chair told her they encouraged their female professors to have their babies in the summer when they didn't have to teach class."

"But you can't plan babies." *And I know that so well.*

"Exactly!" Kate frowned. "That's why I was getting so upset with this one," she said. "I mean, I've been so careful about everything, eating right, going to my check-ups, staying in town. The one time, the absolute one time I go a couple of hours away to see my mother, the baby decides to make me nervous he's going to come."

A little shiver of fear crept up Sarah's spine. "But you're not having contractions?"

"No. Tell me something."

"Sure, what?"

"You're not at all what I expected. I mean, I expected the way you dress, all that. But…" She held up her hands, obviously searching for words.

"But you've been wondering when I'm going to start spouting verses from the Bible and trying to convert you?"

Kate reddened. "Oh, Sarah, I—"

Sarah smiled. "We're very private people. We don't

believe in converting others. All we want is to live our lives the way we've done for hundreds of years."

"I'm surprised you and David let us in."

"We would never turn away someone who needed help," Sarah said simply. "I admit I was a little afraid when your husband first knocked on the door. We've never had someone do that at night." She stopped and, laughing, shook her head.

"What?"

"I'm sorry, I just had a Bible verse come to mind."

Kate grinned. "Lay it on me." When Sarah's brows rose, she rephrased it. "Tell me."

"'Be not forgetful to entertain strangers: for thereby some have entertained angels unawares.' It's from Hebrews."

"Nice," Kate said. "But Jason and I definitely aren't angels. We've put you to a lot of trouble."

"It's no trouble at all. *Gern schöna.*"

"So willingly done," Kate said softly. She watched the flames in the fireplace for a long moment. "Jason said he saw a light burning when he was walking down the road in front of your house."

Sarah nodded. "We were straightening up after our friends and family left."

Kate motioned again toward the Bible on the table. "Will you read me the story you mentioned?"

"Are you sure?"

"Yes. You know, church was important to me when I was a kid. I'm Catholic," Kate told her. "I always loved midnight mass. Then somehow I stopped going. Jason and I didn't even get married in a church, Protestant or Catholic." She glanced at the window and watched the snow beat against the glass. Shivering, she pulled the quilt up around her shoulders.

"Are you cold, Kate? Do you want me to get another quilt?"

"No, I was just thinking about what it's like out there right now. So, will you read it to me?"

Sarah picked up the Bible and opened it and began. "'This is how the birth of Jesus Christ came about....'"

Chapter Five

Sarah shut the Bible and smiled as she glanced over at Kate and saw that she'd fallen asleep.

Everything was so quiet. Snow fell in white drifts at the window, soft as cotton. The wind that had worried Kate had evidently died down, although that didn't mean that damage to power lines would be instantly fixed, or that cell phone towers would be working for her *Englisch* guests and their people.

If she went to bed now, Sarah felt she'd probably sleep. But she lingered, watching motherlike over a woman who was so anxious about the baby she carried, and sent up a silent prayer for her. Reading her favorite part of the Bible had soothed her and relaxed them both.

Who could have predicted such a strange end to such a busy day?

Content, Sarah sat and slipped into sleep.

She woke and blinked, finding herself in the chair by a dying fire. Shivering, she got up and poked at the embers, then put another log on.

But as quiet as she was trying to be, Kate stirred and sat up.

"Sorry, I didn't mean to wake you."

Kate rubbed at her eyes. "Oh no. Did I fall asleep while you were reading?"

"It's okay. You were tired."

"I need to get up. Baby's pressing on my bladder."

Sarah remembered that symptom, but said nothing as Kate padded off to the bathroom.

"Jason's snoring away," Kate said when she returned. "Did David go to bed?"

"He gets up early."

"Then that means you do too. I shouldn't have kept you up."

Sarah smiled. "I don't mind. We don't get visitors often."

"How long have you and David been married?"

"A little over three years."

"I didn't think you were at first. You don't have rings." She blushed. "Sorry, I notice everything."

"We don't wear them."

Kate rubbed her abdomen in slow, reflexive motions. "Jason and I have been married for four and a half years. We dated all through college, so it feels like I've known him forever."

It had been the same with her and David, Sarah thought.

"I never asked you what you do," Kate said. "You know, for work? Do you work outside the home?"

"I teach."

"My mom was an elementary school teacher. What grade do you teach?"

"All grades."

"Oh, like a one-room schoolhouse?"

"That's right."

"It isn't hard to teach all those grades at once?"

Sarah shook her head. "You just have to be organized. The older ones help the younger ones for part of the day. Sometimes they're working with their own brothers and sisters. It's *gut* for everyone, because the older children are reviewing what they learned, and the younger ones get to have sort of a look ahead to lessons they'll have one day."

"Have you always known you wanted to be a teacher?"

Sarah shook her head. "No, I didn't know that I wanted to be one. In our community, you don't choose to be a teacher—you're chosen by the school board members. I wasn't sure if it was something I'd like or be good at. But it's such an honor to be asked, I thought I'd try it. Now I love it. I teach reading and writing and arithmetic and our Amish history and religious principles. But every day is different because the children are growing and learning, and they surprise me every day."

She'd nearly resigned last year because of the baby coming. Usually teachers were young and unmarried, so the school board members had been generous in allowing her to stay after she and David married. Then, just before Christmas, when she was afraid her pregnancy would show and she knew she should tell the board, she'd miscarried.

"We had such a wonderful Christmas program yesterday."

"So now you get a break, huh?"

"No, we go back right after Christmas. Our school lets out earlier than public school because we're a farming community."

"I always loved going to my uncle's farm in the summer. What a change from the city," Kate mused.

She was quiet for a long time. "Sarah, is it too personal to ask if you and David plan to have children?"

The question caught her off guard, even though they'd been talking so personally. But then again, the *Englisch* were known for their directness and their curiosity about Amish life.

"We hope to," she said slowly. "We consider children to be gifts from God. Our families are usually big by your standards. David has nine brothers and sisters."

"Nine! Wow. I'm not sure we'll be able to afford to have more than two. I mean, what with what day care costs and all."

Day care. Sarah couldn't imagine it. The parents she knew worked on the farm or in home-based businesses, so day care wasn't something that was needed.

"That's why Jason and I were 'discussing' a new television earlier," Kate said. "We're like most couples, I guess; we have different spending habits. I'd like to take a longer maternity break, and how are we going to do that if we haven't got enough saved?"

Sarah didn't know how to comment on something that was another couple's business, but Kate didn't seem to expect her to. She stared pensively into the fire for a long moment, then turned to Sarah.

"I'm sorry, I shouldn't be keeping you up, telling you all my problems. But it's so easy to talk to you."

"I'm afraid I haven't got any *gut* advice. Our worlds are so different."

"You listen to me," Kate said slowly. "Really listen. Sometimes people act like they're listening, but you can tell they're already formulating what they're going to say. You seem to know that people don't always need advice. Sometimes they just need someone to listen. It's a gift, Sarah."

Sarah rose and went to sit on the sofa beside Kate. "I know you're feeling anxious. But truly, Kate, God is watching over you and your baby. And Jason." She smiled. "You know that, don't you?"

Impulsively, Kate reached over to hug Sarah. "I know this much. We were surely guided to where we needed to be at a time like this."

Sarah woke, sensing that something was different. The lamp had gone out, but she could see that Jason had come into the room and was sitting on the floor, wrapped in the quilt from his bed, his back leaning against the sofa. He held Kate's hand and was watching her sleep.

He turned his head and smiled at her. "Thanks for sitting up with her," he whispered. "Wouldn't you like to go up to bed? You must be stiff from sitting in that chair."

She was a little sore, she discovered when she stood and folded the throw. Bending, she stirred up the embers and added another log, trying to be quiet and not wake Kate.

But just as she went to tiptoe from the room, Kate sat up and cried out, "Mom!"

"No, sweetheart, we're not at your mom's," Jason said quietly, stroking her hand.

"I know. I'm not asleep," she said. "I just realized— we promised to call her when we got home. If she's heard about the storm, she must be worried sick. Even if she didn't, she'll be wondering why we haven't called."

Jason pulled out his ever-present cell phone. "There's

still no signal. I'm sure she knows that we'll call as soon as we can." He stood and helped his wife to her feet. After he watched her walk to the bathroom, he went to the window. "Looks like it's letting up."

"For the time being, anyway. It'll take a while before things are back to normal," Sarah cautioned. "The electric company won't send their workers out until daylight. Snowplows won't come until then, either."

Kate returned, looking worried. She sat on the sofa and pulled the quilt around her and yawned. "I fell asleep on her," she told Jason. "Sarah was reading me the Bible story about Jesus being born. She said her favorite uncle has been reading it on the first day of Christmas since she was a little girl. Such a nice tradition. We need to think about making some traditions for the baby, Jason. Decide what religion to raise him in."

Jason nodded and sat down on the sofa next to her.

"I was telling Sarah how much I used to love going to midnight mass. I loved the singing." She hummed under her breath as her eyes took on a faraway look.

"You'd have loved the singing today," Sarah told her. "Although the words are German."

Jason turned to Sarah. "So last night was kind of like church, and tomorrow's for giving gifts, huh?"

He had a childlike enthusiasm in his voice, Sarah thought. "We exchange them on Second Christmas— the second day of Christmas. Although our presents are usually practical and not as elaborate as you *Englischers* exchange."

"Like a huge television," Kate said, wrinkling her nose.

Jason ignored her. "What are you hoping David will give you for Christmas?"

Kate bopped him on the head with her pillow. "That's kind of personal, Jason."

"I don't mind," Sarah told Kate. She thought about it. "I can't think of anything I want."

That wasn't true, of course. What she wanted was too personal to share with strangers. And it wasn't a gift David could give anyway. Children were a gift from God.

"Jason told me your husband built this house."

Sarah smiled. "He's a *gut* carpenter."

Kate looked at the fireplace. "I wish we had something that nice over our fireplace," she said. "Our mantel is just this fake piece of wood the builder tacked on. If you actually put anything on it, who knows what might happen."

"Tell David. I'm sure he would build one for you."

"Really? You think he would?"

"He's a carpenter. He can even ship it to you."

"Wow. That'd be great," Jason said. "Or maybe we could come back and pick it up."

"You mean if you can find this place on purpose next time?" Kate teased.

Jason shrugged and looked a little abashed. "Hey, it's not my fault I got lost. You said yourself we could hardly see in the snowstorm."

"Men," Kate said, clucking her tongue. "They'd rather drive in circles for an hour than ask for directions. Is David like that?"

"We don't go very far, really. So directions aren't much of a problem."

Sarah looked at the window and wondered, hadn't God guided them to safety? Kate and Jason were so different from the couples she knew. Were they typical of *Englisch* couples?

Of course Jason *looked* very different from the married men she knew. For one thing, Amish men grew beards when they married. No mustaches, of course. Those weren't viewed as clean and reminded the early Amish of soldiers back in their native country. Sarah had thought David the handsomest man she'd ever known, and when he grew his beard, she had thought he became even better looking. And she loved the way his beard tickled when he kissed her.

David. She should go upstairs and join him.

"Speaking of travel, you have a horse and buggy, right?"

Sarah nodded.

"Do you think once the storm has died down and things look okay that David would drive us into town?"

"Of course."

Jason checked his cell phone once more and sighed. "I'm going back to bed, hon. You want to stay here or sleep in there?"

"I really like being here by the fire," Kate told him. "If you don't mind."

"Nope. See you later." He bent and kissed her head. "And you," he said, turning to Sarah. "Don't let her talk your ear off. You need to get some sleep."

David woke when Sarah came to bed.

"Everything okay?"

"Yes. Kate seems a little bit restless."

"How's the weather looking?"

"It's stopped snowing, for the time being anyway."

"Aren't you coming to bed?" he asked when she didn't make a move to undress or lie down. "You must be exhausted."

"I'm tired," she agreed, taking off her shoes and lining them up neatly beside the bed. She pulled off her *kapp* and loosed her long hair. "But I enjoyed sitting and talking with Kate."

He tugged gently on her shoulder, and she sank down on the bed next to him. "I'm sure it was a comfort to have another woman to talk to at such a time."

"She said the nicest thing. She told me I listened to her, really listened to her, and didn't try to figure out what to say next or offer advice the way some people did. She said it was a gift."

"She's right. You do have a gift for listening, for showing care by letting people talk. I've seen it. I've felt it myself when I'm troubled."

"How can you say that? I haven't always been what you needed," she said, turning to look at him. Her eyes gleamed in the dim light coming in through the window. "I've been so wrapped up in my own pain."

David brought her closer and kissed her temple. "Stop that. I won't have you say such a thing."

"I'm glad you insisted on letting Jason in when he knocked on our door. I don't want to think about what might have happened to those two if he hadn't found our house."

"God lit a path for him," David said quietly.

"Mmm-hmm," she murmured. She rested her cheek against his shoulder. "Imagine visitors on this night. And her pregnant. It struck me as I was reading Kate the story of the birth of Jesus."

"This isn't an inn," he told her. "And they're not Mary and Joseph."

She laughed. "I know. But it just seems so strange. Like I'm dreaming. But I'm awake."

"I don't know how. All the work *redding-up* the

house, working with your scholars so excited about the coming holiday, and losing sleep so much lately. Try to sleep now."

When he finally felt her relax, and her breathing evened out, he knew she slept. Carefully reaching down, he drew the sheet and quilt up around her shoulders.

He thought about Jason's confession that he'd been frightened he wouldn't find help for his wife and child. How upset he'd been that he hadn't kept them safe as a husband should.

But David had found that a man couldn't always protect those he loved. He stroked Sarah's hair. He didn't know why they had lost their baby, but God's ways were a mystery that man wasn't supposed to figure out, weren't they? In the face of things he didn't understand, David was trying to understand what he had so often heard from others in his community: the true answer to any question about God was faith. Sometimes his reason would be revealed. Sometimes it wouldn't. But faith was all.

He was nearly asleep again when he heard Kate shout his name.

Chapter Six

Sarah woke. She'd heard something—a cry? But this wasn't a nightmare—Kate was shouting for David.

Jumping up, Sarah ran for the stairs. David pulled on his robe and followed her.

Kate was standing by the open front door, tugging on Jason's arm. He was wearing his jacket.

"Please stop him!" Kate cried when she saw them. "He wants to go for help." She looked at Jason. "It isn't safe. You have to stay here!"

Stepping past them, David looked out. "The snow's starting to let up, but it's best if we wait until daylight."

"We can't wait!"

"Why do you suddenly want to leave?"

"Kate's in labor."

Sarah looked at her. "Are you?"

"No!"

"She's trying to hide it," Jason insisted. "I woke up and saw her acting like she's in pain."

Kate turned to Sarah. "It's just those funny bunching feelings I told you about."

"You knew about it?" Jason burst out, staring at Sarah. "Why didn't you tell me?"

"I asked Sarah not to say anything," Kate told him, sniffing. "I knew you'd overreact."

David glanced at Sarah and raised his eyebrows.

"I said I wouldn't lie, but I wouldn't say anything unless I thought she was really in labor." Turning to Kate, Sarah touched her shoulder. "What's happening?"

"The same thing as before, just a kind of bunching."

"Jason, I don't think you need to panic," Sarah told him. "I've been concerned about how uncomfortable Kate is, and of course I wondered if she could go into labor early. But we need to stay calm." She turned back to Kate. "Come on, let's go sit in the living room and talk, okay?"

Jason watched them leave the room, then he turned to David. "I can't take a chance that she's in labor. You can't argue with that."

David laid his hand on Jason's shoulder. "Like Sarah says, let's not panic until we have to. Sarah has been with women who have given birth. She'll know what we should do."

Jason ran his hands through his hair till it stood up on end. "I'm a nervous wreck."

"No need to be. Here, let's get that coat off, okay?"

"But…"

David calmly began unbuttoning the coat, and Jason let him, as if he were a child.

"I just don't want anything bad to happen."

"I know."

After hanging up the coat, David followed the other

man into the living room. Kate and Sarah were sitting on the sofa, talking quietly.

Jason immediately went over and hovered over Kate. There was no other word for what he did, David thought—he hovered.

"How about we fix some *kaffi*, Jason?" he suggested.

"Huh?"

"*Kaffi*. Let's make some *kaffi*."

Jason looked at Kate, and she nodded.

Jason followed David to the kitchen. "I'm telling you, I felt her stomach, and it was definitely doing something."

David opened one cabinet, then another, then another.

"You don't know where the coffee is?" Jason said.

"Sarah always insists on making it."

"Boy, no equal time in the kitchen here, huh?" Going to the cupboard above the stove, Jason found the canister of coffee.

"How did you know where it was?"

"Kate keeps it right by the stove too." Jason paced as David dealt with making the *kaffi*. "So what do we do if she's in labor? The cell's still not working. And the electricity's still knocked out. There's not a single streetlight on."

"There are no electric streetlights in this area."

"Oh. I thought they were just out because of the power outage." Jason jingled the change in his pockets and kept looking toward the doorway.

David wasn't sure that adding more caffeine to the situation was a *gut* idea, but he figured letting the two women talk without Jason hovering was a *gut* idea.

He measured *kaffi* into the stovetop percolator. "Sarah made chamomile tea for Kate earlier. See if you can find the tea bags."

"Oh, good idea." Jason went back to the same cupboard and found them. "Kate's been missing coffee, but she seemed to like this earlier." He opened the box, chose a tea bag, and placed it in a cup. "The pregnancy's been hard on her, what with her job and all."

"What work does she do?"

"She's an attorney."

David nodded. "She must be very busy. I hear the *Englisch* like to sue each other."

Jason gave a bark of laughter. "Oh, I'll have to tell Kate that one. She'll love it."

"Isn't it true?"

"Well, certainly people sue each other a lot. But isn't that true everywhere?"

David shook his head. "We don't believe in it."

"How do you resolve conflict?"

"We seldom have disagreements, but when we do, we talk them out. Ours is a small community, and we see each other a lot. We go to church in each other's homes, socialize, do business together. Marry within the community. So people learn to get along with each other."

"What about getting justice?" Jason leaned against the counter.

"Justice is God's work, not man's."

"You seem pretty laid-back, but everyone can't be like you."

David shrugged. "Most are."

"That's hard to imagine. Most of the people I know are pretty stressed." Jason looked toward the doorway. "Sarah seems so calm. Is she always like that?"

David smiled. "I call her Serene Sarah."

"What does she do? For work, I mean. Or is she a full-time homemaker?"

"Sarah is a teacher, and she also helps me with the business side of my work. Bookkeeping, invoices, that sort of thing. And she takes care of our home."

When the *kaffi* was ready and the water had boiled for tea, David found sugar and cream and set everything on a tray the way he'd seen Sarah do when they had guests.

When the men entered the room, Sarah said, "I think Kate might be having Braxton Hicks, Jason."

"I think we heard that term in Lamaze class, but I don't remember what it is."

"Sort of like practice contractions. Sometimes women have them for weeks before the baby comes. They help her get ready for the birth."

"So I didn't need to panic?"

"I told you," Kate told him.

Jason looked at David, then Sarah. "I'm sorry for getting you guys up."

"It's all right," Sarah told them. "We understand that it's an anxious time for you."

Jason checked his cell phone again.

"Jason, give that thing to me," Kate said. "It's just making you nervous."

When she continued to hold out her hand, Jason finally put the cell phone into it. "I'm just thinking about you," he told her.

"I know, sweetie," she said, patting the sofa beside her. "You're my hero."

David and Sarah exchanged a glance, and Sarah

tried not to smile as David lifted his brows. Interesting how *Englisch* couples—at least *this* couple—seemed to get along.

"Pregnant women have power," Kate said with satisfaction, watching as Sarah gathered up the coffee mugs and put them on a tray. She glanced at Jason and David sitting and talking at a small table in the corner of the room. "He actually gave me his cell phone. He never lets go of that thing."

Sarah left the room without replying. She set the tray on the counter in the kitchen and turned to see that Kate had followed her.

"Is something wrong?"

"No. Why?"

"You left the room kind of abruptly."

"I—just wanted to get these washed up."

Kate took a seat at the table. "I think I upset you by saying 'pregnant women have power.' I was just joking, Sarah. I don't push my husband around."

"I know." Sarah scrubbed at a mug.

"It was just my way of saying that Jason's been doing extra things for me because it hasn't been easy, this pregnancy."

Drawn in, in spite of herself, Sarah turned. "You've had problems?"

Kate nodded. "When I had trouble getting pregnant, we went in for testing, everything you can think of." She stopped. "Well, maybe you haven't heard of it all. The infertility runaround, I mean. It doesn't sound as though there's as much trouble with infertility in your world as there is in mine." She was silent for a moment, pondering that.

"Well, anyway, I know some people wait years and

years before they figure they need to do more than try," Kate continued. "But I'd had some trouble with endometriosis, and I'm thirty-five. I took hormone shots and everything. Didn't do any good. Finally we went for in vitro."

When Sarah looked blank, Kate explained that it was a surgical procedure to implant fertilized eggs.

"Then the fun really began," Kate told her. "I got pregnant, but I was so sick. Months of exhaustion, nausea, moodiness, you name it. I barely made it into the office. Jason ran himself ragged for me. Anything I wanted—you know, the cravings for ice cream in the middle of the night and all that. That's what I meant by pregnant women have power. He did whatever would make me happy. The last couple months, things have settled down. I've been tired, but I've been feeling good. That's why even though my due date isn't that far away, we went to see my mom for Christmas."

Infertility treatments, thought Sarah. She wanted to ask more about them, but she didn't want Kate to guess why. It seemed easy for the other woman to share personal information, but that wasn't Sarah's way... especially with someone who was *Englisch.*

Anyway, it didn't matter. These treatments were likely expensive, as *Englisch* medicine tended to be. And David would probably say that it was interfering with God's will. But medicine was of God, so wouldn't these treatments be too?

"So tell me, how did you and David meet?"

Sarah blinked at the change in topic. "I'd known him a long time. We went to school together." She sat down at the table. "He invited me for a ride after a singing."

"A singing?"

"That's where teenagers get together. They sing hymns and gospel songs, talk, have something to eat together, that sort of thing. Then sometimes a boy will ask to take a girl home in his courting buggy."

"Courting buggy. Sounds nicer than cruising— that's where guys drive around in their cars, hoping to persuade a girl to get in for a ride. But I guess whether it's a courting buggy or a car, guys get the girls to go for a ride, huh?"

Sarah smiled. "I suppose you're right."

"David isn't the way I pictured an Amish man."

"Well, they're not all the same any more than *Englisch* men are."

"I think you're the calmest person I ever met. There's something very soothing about you."

Sarah smiled. David called her Serene Sarah, but he was calm and quiet himself. Well, they both had been, until the night she miscarried.

Yawning, Kate stood. "May I dry those mugs for you?"

"No, thanks. Why don't you go back and sit by the fire?"

Kate glanced at the clock. "I can't believe we're all up at two-thirty in the morning. We've been very selfish with you and David since we got here tonight."

"You don't need to apologize." Sarah watched Kate rub her stomach. "Everything okay?"

Kate nodded. "I think I'll see how the guys are doing." Waddling just a little bit, she went into the other room.

David threw another log on the fire and frowned. Firewood was getting low. "I'm going to go get some more wood."

"Can I come?" asked Jason. "I'd like to help."

"Let's see if your jacket's dry yet. What size shoes do you wear?"

"Eleven."

"I have a spare pair of boots you can borrow. They're a little big, but that shouldn't be a problem."

"Where are you going?" Kate asked as they walked through the kitchen.

"We manly men are getting firewood," Jason told her with a grin.

"Okay," she said slowly. "Have fun."

The moon was so bright they nearly didn't need the big flashlight David carried. He handed Jason one of the canvas slings he'd brought, then bent to brush the snow from the wood.

"There's nothing on these, is there? Like spiders?"

"I think they're probably in a much warmer place right now."

Carefully, Jason picked up a piece of wood and examined it. Looking relieved, he began putting pieces in a sling. "I know you think I'm a wimp."

David straightened. "What? Why would I think that?"

"Because I gave in to Kate and handed over my cell phone and my watch. I mean, men control their women here, don't they?"

"Control?" David stared at him.

"Well, I mean, men are the heads of their homes here, aren't they? Isn't there something in the Bible about that?"

"Being the head of the home isn't the same as controlling," David said. "It means being the spiritual leader. The Scripture you may have heard is from Ephesians:

'Wives, submit to your husbands as to the Lord. For the husband is the head of the wife as Christ is the head of the church.' But for whatever reason, most people don't read the verse before it that says, 'Submit to one another out of reverence for Christ,' and the one after it, 'Husbands, love your wives just as Christ loved the church and gave himself up for her.'"

He bent to pick up more firewood and place it in the sling. "So you see, it's not about control, but sacrificial love and respect. But you're not saying that *Englisch* men are never guilty of trying to be the boss, are you?" He glanced over at Jason's sling and nodded. "I think we have enough. Let's go inside."

They put the firewood in the basket by the fireplace, discarded their coats and boots, and got themselves some *kaffi*. Seeing that the two women were still talking, David turned to Jason. "How're you at checkers?"

"Not too good."

"Let's play a game." He got out the board and set it on a small table in the living room. "Red or black?"

"Red."

As they played, Jason continued the discussion. "You tend to have pretty traditional roles here, don't you? The men work, and the women stay home."

David studied the checkerboard; he knew he was tired, but he'd have sworn something had changed. Rubbing at his eyes, he pondered his next move. "Stay home and work very, very hard, especially if there are many children and especially if it's a family that farms. I'm a carpenter and just do a little farming. But Sarah works outside the home as a teacher. I suppose we do have traditional roles at home, since she still takes care of the house more than I do and I handle the outside."

He was thoroughly boxed in on the checkerboard. With a sigh, he made a move and lost another two checkers to Jason. "What about you?"

"Me?"

"The two of you work. Do both of you take care of the house and the outside?"

"Yeah, Jason, do you?"

Jason jumped and turned to face his wife. "You sure sneak up on a man."

"Answer the question or be held in contempt," she said, her lips quirking in a grin.

"Yes, ma'am," he said, looking at her warily. "No, I don't do enough around the house."

"And isn't it true that we have a lawn service, so you don't do anything outside?"

"You're right."

"I rest my case."

Laughing, Jason held up his hands. "I throw myself on the mercy of the court." As he lowered his hands, a red checker fell from his sleeve. "Oops."

"Jason!"

Sarah finished the dishes, drying them with a cloth before putting them into the cabinet. Shutting it, she stood there for a long moment, thinking about all that had happened that night.

When she turned, David was standing there.

"I thought you were playing checkers with Jason."

"He won three games."

"Kate said he's competitive."

David laughed. "He cheats."

"Really?"

"Yeah." David grinned and told her what had happened. "I was wise to his tricks before that. After all, my brother is a master cheater at checkers."

"That's what he says about you."

"Only when he loses." David yawned and checked the clock. "I think I'll go play another game, see if I can beat him."

He smiled and kissed her, then walked back into the living room. "How about another game?" she heard him call.

Sarah was sitting at the kitchen table, wrapping a present, when Kate wandered in a little while later. She sat at the table and watched as Sarah wrapped a plastic container of chocolate-dipped peanut butter balls.

"Who's that for?"

"One of my cousins." She smiled at Kate. "I made a lot of peanut butter balls. I have a lot of cousins. Do you want some? I have plenty."

"No, I'm full, thanks. I think I'm going to lie down on the sofa if you don't mind. Aren't you going back to bed?"

Sarah glanced at the kitchen clock. "I might stay up. I just thought of one more present I need to wrap."

"Isn't that always the way? 'Night."

Sarah paused, then she got up and went to the pantry to retrieve a white pottery canister. She wrapped it, found a name tag, and wrote Kate's name on it. Then she put it back into the pantry to give to Kate when she and Jason left.

When she looked in on Kate and Jason after she finished putting away the wrapping paper, scissors, and tape, Sarah found them holding hands and talking quietly as Jason sat on the floor next to the sofa.

Did they realize how lucky they were? she wondered. Oh, not in material things. Sarah didn't care about that. But this Christmas, Kate and Jason were looking forward to being parents.

Sarah shook her head. She was determined not to be envious of them. Not tonight, of all nights. To be envious was wrong. But oh, how she longed for a child. Just one child. That would be enough.

Chapter Seven

Sarah woke and found herself sitting at the kitchen table. It took her a moment to remember that she had put her head down on it. She glanced at the kitchen clock and saw that it was 5:00 a.m.

There was a stillness...almost a hush to the air. Snow swept in gentle drifts against the window instead of gusts. But it was more than that. It was as if the air itself held something expectant.

Before she could move, Kate came into the room and stopped, staring at her wide-eyed.

"Well, it's déjà vu all over again," Kate said. "Have you been sitting here since I went in the other room?"

"Yes. I remember telling David I'd be up in a minute, and then I put my head down for a moment. It's been a busy week. Yesterday, I lay down on the bed for just a little while...and woke up an hour later." She got up. "How about some hot chocolate?"

"Great." Kate pulled out a chair and sank down into it. "Jason is asleep on the sofa. Men never seem to have trouble sleeping. Have you noticed?"

"David does a lot of physical labor, so he doesn't usually have any trouble."

"Jason works hard, but there's no physical labor involved. He mostly sits at a computer." She sat down and put her feet up on the seat of the chair next to her. "A lot of women at work say they have trouble sleeping at night. If we all got together, we could rule the world."

"I don't think women want to rule the world, do you? We just want to be surrounded by people we love, our friends and family."

"So how many people are you expecting? Providing the weather gets better, I mean. How many people are in your family?"

"Well, let's see. David has seven brothers and two sisters, but they may not all come. I hope my parents will come, if they're feeling recovered from a really nasty bout of flu. And I have three aunts and four uncles, thirty-five cousins—"

Kate spluttered and set down her mug. "Thirty-five?"

"Some families have a lot more." Sarah handed her a napkin. "You have a marshmallow mustache."

Wiping it away, Kate shook her head. "Thirty-five?" she repeated.

"My mother came from a family of eight, and each of them had children, so..." She shrugged and sipped at her chocolate.

"Gee, and I thought I came from a big family. I have three brothers and half a dozen cousins, mostly male, so it was a rough-and-tumble kind of family. Maybe growing up the way I did made me stand up for myself and then later, stand up to defend my clients." She traced a circle on the tablecloth. "Jason was an only child, and his parents were into this whole thing about making him a super-smart kid. So he's really great about stuff like computer programming, but he doesn't cope so well with some things."

Sighing, she shook her head as she rubbed her abdomen. "He panics so easily. You saw the way he wanted to go looking for help because he thought I was going into labor. I mean, when he walked here to your house after the car went in a ditch, that was a good idea. But rushing out of here to go who knows where because he saw me having those cramping feelings, well, that's just plain overreacting. It could have been dangerous for him."

She pushed away her empty mug. "The Lamaze coach said she'd never seen such a nervous father-to-be. It makes me wonder how he's going to behave when the baby's here. Is he going to panic every time our kid scrapes his knee or gets a bloody nose?"

"Being raised in a large family, you get a lot of both," Sarah reflected. "I suppose if you're an only child and kept away from other children a lot, it could be a problem. But you can help him learn to calm down, can't you?"

Kate propped her elbows on the table and studied Sarah. "You know, this has been interesting, being here with you and David. I'll admit I had some misconceptions about the Amish."

Sarah lifted her shoulders. "I know the *Englisch* often think we're quaint or old-fashioned. We puzzle them because we avoid things like electricity and cars."

"I get it about electricity now. But why no cars?"

"That would promote pride. An owner would say, 'Look at my car. I have the nicest, the fastest, the most expensive.'"

"Keeping up with the Joneses," Kate mused, then had to explain what that meant.

"Not that there's not already a little of that with buggies being made a little bit different or better than others. But cars. Well, they make it easy to leave, perhaps avoid family and work and responsibility. But you know, no one should put us up on a pedestal. We just want to live our lives our way, simply, and according to our faith."

"Well, I know one thing. Jason and I have talked more tonight than I can remember since our honeymoon."

"Talking is *gut*," Sarah agreed. She and David, too, had talked tonight in a way that they had not been able to for a long time.

"You okay?"

"Hmm?" Sarah blinked. "I'm sorry. I was just thinking of something David said tonight." She waited for Kate to ask what she herself had called "too personal," but she didn't. Perhaps it was because once again Kate was rubbing her abdomen and looking like she was listening to some inner voice.

"*Guder mariye*," David said to Jason as he stumbled into the kitchen, rubbing at his eyes.

Sarah shook her head. "No, Merry Christmas, remember?" she corrected with a smile.

"That's right. Merry Christmas to you."

"Five-thirty in the morning," Jason said, shaking his head. "I haven't been up this early on Christmas morning—or any other morning—since I was a kid looking to see what Santa left under the tree."

"You didn't have to get up," Kate reminded him.

"I smelled bacon," he told her, grinning at Sarah. "And something wonderful baking."

Sarah turned from the stove and smiled at him. "It will be ready soon."

"It's stopped snowing," David announced as he looked out the window.

Jason and Kate cheered.

"I'll be in the barn," he told Sarah and went to put on his coat and hat.

"Can I come with you?"

Surprised, David turned to stare at Jason. "I'm just going to the barn." When Jason just stood here, waiting, he nodded. "It isn't heated," he warned, but Jason was already putting on his jacket and the boots he'd been loaned earlier.

The two men trudged through the snow to the barn. David pushed open the doors and stepped inside. He couldn't help grinning as Jason registered the smells of horse and hay and manure, and recoiled a little.

The *Englischman* looked around curiously. And then Ned neighed, and Jason jumped a foot.

"Ever been around horses?" David asked, smiling.

"Just a pony ride when I was a kid." He looked askance at Ned. "He's a lot bigger than a pony. Is it safe to pet him?"

"Sure."

Reaching out, Jason touched the horse. Ned snorted and drew back, baring his teeth. Jason jumped again.

"He's just showing off," David said calmly. "Here, you can feed him."

"I—uh, that's okay."

David thrust the bucket into the other man's hands. "It'll be fine. Really."

"I kind of need my hands for my work," Jason muttered, but he sidled up to the stall. "Here, nice horse, here you go. Nice whatever-it-is you get to eat. Not my hands."

Ned perked up his ears and watched with interest as Jason approached and poured the feed into his trough. As he started chomping on the oats, Jason reached out and tentatively patted the horse. Ned turned to rub his muzzle against Jason's hand.

"That's cool!"

"Ned loves whoever feeds him," David told him, handing him food for the other horse.

"You really *do* have horsepower, huh?"

"*Ya*. Maybe you'd like to shovel your way out of that joke, *Englischman*."

Laughing, Jason held up his hands. "Okay, okay." He walked away to prowl the section of the barn set up as David's work area.

"Hey, you do terrific work," Jason called as he looked over the furniture items in different stages of progress. He ran his hand over the chest of drawers David had been sanding. "Sarah told us you might make us a mantel for our home if we asked."

David nodded. "What kind of wood do you want?"

"I don't know much about it. Maybe the kind you used to make yours, but with a darker stain to match our furniture?"

"Just send me the measurements, and I'll quote you a price. I can arrange for it to be shipped to you, or you can come pick it up."

"That might be nice. Picking it up, I mean. Maybe stop by to see you and Sarah after the baby's born, show him off and take the mantel home with us." He walked around some more and stopped at a workbench where a piece of black plastic covered another object.

"What's this?" he asked, but he was already lifting a corner of the plastic to reveal a carved wooden cradle. "Wow, this is beautiful. Kate would dearly love something like this. Could I buy it?"

"It's not for sale." The words rushed out, sounding harsher than David intended.

"Oh, it's like a family heirloom or something. I thought you made it."

David took a deep breath. "I did. It was just sort of a special order. I can't sell it."

David had made it soon after Sarah had told him that she was carrying their child and kept it a secret from her. It had been his idea to present it to her shortly before she gave birth.

"I understand if you can't sell this one. But wow, this would be something Kate would love even more than the mantel. How long would it take for you to make one in the same kind of wood? Would you be able to do it before the baby's born?" He pushed the cradle and made it rock. "I want it no matter what it costs. It's a work of art. But I'd like to make it a surprise for her."

"It's just what I do," David said. *Hochmut*—pride— was to be avoided. "I'll start on it tomorrow."

"Great." Jason covered the cradle. "Must be cool, working with your hands, creating beautiful things like this. I really liked shop class when I was in high school. Made a small table once. 'Course it was nowhere near the quality of your work."

"Remember that I've done it for many years. But if you're really interested, you could set up a small area in your garage at your home and start with some simple projects as a hobby."

Jason considered that. "Yeah, maybe I could. Might

be good for me after sitting at a computer all day. Then when I go home, I spend too much time watching another tube—the TV."

"Well, we're done in here," David said. "Ready for some breakfast?"

"You bet." Jason followed him out of the barn and watched him fasten the door. "You know, maybe I could get some power tools and do what you said, set up a worktable. What's a simple project you think I should start with?"

David thought about that as they made their way back to the house. "Maybe a little rolling toy, like a wooden duck, for your baby? Or a rocking horse?"

Jason beamed. "Great ideas."

They went inside and washed up and then sat down at the table with their wives to eat breakfast. David and Sarah bent their heads in silent prayer. If their guests followed suit, he didn't know or care. He looked up and smiled at them.

"Let us enjoy this food God has provided for us on this special day."

Chapter Eight

❦

The men—especially Jason—were enthusiastically shoveling in the breakfast Sarah made, and she was busy jumping up to fetch more biscuits and jam and *kaffi*. Still, she couldn't help noticing that Kate was just pushing the eggs around on her plate and only nibbling at a biscuit.

She was also shifting uncomfortably on her chair.

But when Sarah looked at her, lifting her brows in question, Kate glanced at Jason, then back at Sarah, and shook her head.

So Sarah bided her time, ate her own breakfast, and fortified herself with two cups of *kaffi* to stave off the haze of tiredness that had caught up with her.

"Sarah, this is an amazing breakfast," Jason said as he accepted a second helping of bacon and eggs. "I haven't had a breakfast like this in—well, I can't remember."

"I cook breakfast for you sometimes," Kate protested.

"Yeah, you do," he admitted. But he didn't say any more, instead putting another bite of biscuit in his mouth.

Kate put down her fork, struggled to her feet, and

left the room. A few seconds later, they heard the spare bedroom door shut.

Jason paused, holding the biscuit halfway to his mouth. "What? What'd I say?"

Sarah bit her lip. "I don't think Kate's feeling very well. She was shifting around in her chair, and she wasn't eating."

Jason looked at his wife's plate and sighed. "And here I was, stuffing my face and not even noticing." He put the biscuit back on his plate.

Sarah patted his hand. "Why don't you take her a cup of tea and talk to her?"

He brightened. "Great idea. No, don't get up. I'll make it."

David finished his breakfast and rose to look out the window. When he turned back to her, Sarah saw that he was frowning. "It's started snowing again. Hard."

Jumping to her feet, Sarah joined him at the window. "David, I'm concerned about Kate."

He drew her to him and rubbed at the tension in her shoulders. "Let's not borrow trouble. It could just be that she's tired and a little irritable. None of us had much sleep last night."

She nodded. "I think I'll go see if there's anything I can do."

When she knocked at the door, Jason opened it. "Oh, good, I was about to come get you," he said.

Kate sat on the bed, rubbing her back. She looked up. "Sarah, I'm sorry. I was rude to leave the ta—"

Sarah waved a hand, halting her words. "There's no need to apologize, Kate. I can tell you're not feeling well."

Tears welled up in the other woman's eyes. "My back hurts worse, and I just feel miserable."

"Why don't you try lying on your side, with a pillow tucked between your knees?"

Sarah went to the closet for an extra pillow. She handed it to Jason and watched as he helped Kate tuck the pillow beneath her abdomen. "Does that help?"

"I think so. The sofa felt better for a while, but maybe this will be good now."

Sarah touched Kate's hand lying atop the quilt. She wished she could do more for this woman who was feeling such distress. She knew what it felt like to worry about a pregnancy, knew what could go wrong. "I know you're feeling tired and stressed. But there's no need. All you have to do right now is rest, *liebschen*."

"Liebschen," Kate repeated, already sounding drowsy. "That sounds nice. What's it mean?"

"Dearest," Sarah said.

Kate glanced at the window. "When do you think they'll send out snowplows?"

"It usually takes an hour or two after it gets light." It wasn't a lie, but it wasn't a direct answer either.

"Then they'll find our car and come looking for us?"

"I'm sure they will. They'll figure you went for help to the nearest house. Do you think you could sleep now?"

Kate nodded. "I think so."

"I'll be in the kitchen. Just call me if you need anything."

"Thanks, Sarah." The words were barely out of her mouth before Kate's eyes closed and she slept.

"Yes, thanks, Sarah," Jason whispered.

Smiling, she gestured for him to follow her from the room. She was concerned that Kate's back pain had not gone away, but seemed to be getting worse. But she hesitated, not wanting to send him into a panic again.

A silly story popped into her mind, one that Jacob Yoder had told more than once. Jacob never remembered how often he told a story—or maybe he pretended to forget and just liked the telling. In Jacob's story, an *Englisch* man had telephoned home to check on the family pet that his brother had agreed to care for while he was out of town. "The cat fell off the roof and died," he was told.

"Oh no!" the man exclaimed. But then he admonished his brother, "Couldn't you have eased me into what happened? Maybe the first time I called, told me the cat had gotten up on the roof and you were doing your best to get it down? Then the next day, you could have said the cat fell and you were having the vet take care of it. And then finally, you could have said, 'I'm so sorry. We did everything we could, but the cat passed on.'"

"You're right," the *Englisch* man's brother said. "I'm sorry."

"That's all right," the man told him with a sigh. "I guess the cat lived a good, long life and it was his time to go. So, how's Mom?"

"Uh, well, she's on the roof," his brother said.

It was not a *gut* joke, thought Sarah. But it gave her an idea about how to help Jason.

David had cleared the table and put the dishes in the sink. Now he sat at the table, drinking another cup of *kaffi* and looking at a book he kept of the furniture he'd made and sold. Sometimes he used it to show customers what he could do in terms of design and colors.

She poured *kaffi* for Jason and herself and then

joined him at the table as they sat to drink it. "You know, Jason, I'll be glad when the snowplow gets here," she said to him. "Kate's been so uncomfortable with her back. It might be a *gut* idea to take her to be checked out at the local hospital before you head home. Just as a precaution."

A flicker of fear raced over Jason's face, and he started to rise.

David laid a reassuring hand on his shoulder. "The roads will probably be cleared by the time she wakes. If not, and she's still not feeling well, we'll figure out something else."

Jason chewed on a fingernail. "Okay." He looked at his mug of coffee, then at Sarah. "Would you mind if I took this in to the bedroom? I think I'll sit in there and keep an eye on Kate."

"That's a *wunderbaar* idea," Sarah told him. "When she wakes up, I'm sure she'll feel like you were watching over her and the baby."

Jason beamed. "Thanks."

David watched as the other man left them, and after he heard the bedroom door shut, he turned to smile at Sarah. "That was very clever. You managed to tell him she wasn't feeling well in a way that didn't alarm him. And you gave him the idea to think of something he could do even if it's just to sit with her."

"It was nothing," she said with a shrug. "I hope the snow will stop soon."

David nodded and looked at the window again. "I was thinking that I could make a sign and put it up in the yard. Anyone going by—road crews or someone with county services—would see it and stop to see if we need help. There's probably some plywood in the basement."

"That's a wonderful idea."

"Just as soon as it lets up, I'll do it." He clasped her hand. "In the meantime, we only thanked God for our meal earlier. We didn't get to do our morning *gebet*. Let's do it now."

She nodded, and they prayed as they did each morning and evening. And then she was left alone at the table, listening to the clock tick off the minutes to the time when her guests would leave and family and friends would return to celebrate the day.

David walked into the bedroom a little later and saw that Sarah stood at the window in her bedroom. Her shoulders were slumped as she stared outside. He slipped his arms around her.

"It doesn't look like it's going to die down," she told him. "I think it might be picking up instead." Turning, she sank down in a chair at the table and put her head in her hands.

"Sarah, it'll be all right. You know these snowstorms don't last long. It'll be over soon."

She turned to him. "Promise?"

Smiling, he shook his head. "I can't promise that. God's in charge. If it's his will, it will stop soon."

She sighed. "You're right." Turning, she picked up the book lying open on the table beside the bed.

"What are you reading?"

She hesitated for a moment and then held it up. It was a book about what to expect during pregnancy. "I thought it might help me help Kate."

"And has it?" he asked. "What does it say about Kate's symptoms?"

Sarah glanced at the doorway. "At first I thought it might just be tension. Then I thought it was just the back pain women suffer at the end sometimes, or Braxton Hicks contractions. The bones in the pelvis soften a little, and the uterus starts contracting so it'll be easier for her when the time comes for the baby to be born."

"That makes sense."

"*Ya.* But I'm afraid I just *want* it to be that. You know. Practice contractions." Taking a deep breath, she voiced the fear she'd been holding inside. "David, I'm scared the storm won't let up, and she'll have her baby here."

David's breakfast threatened to come back up. He tried to block the memories that came rushing up, memories he'd managed to tamp down for a long time, of how helpless he'd felt when Sarah had miscarried. The doctor had said she was fine, that it was an early miscarriage and there was no reason she wouldn't get pregnant again. She'd healed quickly—at least her body had.

Deliberately, he forced away the memories. "We can't do this," he told her firmly. "Nothing's happened yet. Nothing might. And Kate's not going to lose her baby." He reached out for her other hand and clasped it.

"I know."

"Worrying won't help."

She nodded.

"If we worry, we insult God. He knows what he's doing."

She pulled back and smiled tremulously. "Then why didn't he have Kate get stranded at a hospital?"

"Because maybe she's not going to need one. Maybe she needed your calmness these past hours, and when she leaves, she's going to go home and not have the baby until her due date."

"I don't feel calm now, David. I'm scared."

David lifted her chin and made her look at him. "You need to be calm for her. Be Serene Sarah."

She laughed and shook her head.

"We should pray," he told her.

She drew in a shaky breath, then let it out. Nodding, she let him draw her over to sit on the side of their bed. They clasped both hands and bent their heads, and David led them in a prayer for Kate and her baby.

When they finished, he looked up and saw Jason standing in the doorway.

Jason blushed. "Er—I'm sorry, I don't mean to interrupt."

"It's all right. We were just finishing."

Their guest seemed to be at a loss for words for a moment. "I—you were praying, weren't you?"

David nodded.

"For Kate?"

David looked at Sarah and then back at Jason. "Yes."

Jason visibly struggled for words. "Thank you," he said at last.

David walked over to lay a hand on Jason's shoulder. "Your wife and your child are safe in His hands, Jason. You must believe that. You need to stay strong and be there for her."

"Yeah, the Lamaze coach said something like that. The last part, I mean." He sighed. "Listen, I didn't mean to intrude, but Kate was asking for Sarah."

Sarah got up. "Is her back feeling any better?"

Jason shook his head. He looked helplessly at the window. "Do you think if we prayed, God would make it stop snowing?"

David and Sarah exchanged a look.

Sarah looked at him kindly. "Why don't the three of us pray to remember that He's here with us and all is well?"

"Okay. That'd work. Right?"

Kate looked up when Jason and Sarah entered her room. Her lips trembled. "You were gone a long time."

"Sorry, baby," he said and bent to kiss the top of her head.

Sarah moved to stand beside the bed. "Jason said your back is still troubling you."

She grimaced and moaned a little. "And these stupid contractions, or whatever they are. I wish we could make them stop until we can get to someone to check them out."

If they stopped, then how could anyone check them out? Sarah wondered. But she wasn't going to ask. Kate was feeling so miserable, it was no wonder she didn't make sense. "May I?" Sarah asked, holding out her hand.

"Sure."

Sarah bent down and touched Kate's abdomen. Beneath her fingers there was a tightening, a movement, a sort of rhythmic contraction.

She glanced at the window. The curtains were closed to keep the chill out, but she knew that it was still snowing hard outside. The only thing she could do was keep Kate calm until the weather changed.

Sarah showed Kate the book she held in her other hand. "This book is *gut* for telling women what they should expect at each stage of their pregnancy."

"I have that one, too!" Kate exclaimed.

"I was reading up on Braxton Hicks contractions,"

Sarah hurried on. "I think that's what you've been having."

"Then I sure have been getting a lot of practice," Kate muttered.

"Sometimes a woman's body needs it, I suppose," Sarah said. "I had a friend who had false labor. Twice her husband took her to the hospital, and twice they were sent back home. When she finally went into labor, the nurses at the hospital told her the third time was the charm."

Kate shifted and tried to smile. "You *want* to believe that this is Braxton Hicks or false labor or whatever. I do too."

Sarah took her hand and squeezed it. "I just want you to feel better and, when it's time to have your baby, to have it where you're most comfortable. And I don't think that's in my home."

Kate squeezed her hand back. "You do make me feel better." She lowered her voice. "Too bad you can't be my birth coach."

"Jason would be disappointed."

Sighing, Kate nodded. "He'll be there. I'm just not sure how much support I'll get from him."

"Expect the best from him, and he might just surprise you, Kate."

"He's trying. He brought me tea and rubbed my back for a long time. And he sat with me." She traced the pattern on the quilt with her finger and smiled. "We talked about what to name the baby. We're sort of getting down to the wire now, and we haven't agreed on a name."

"You said it's a boy?"

"Yeah." She reached over to the bedside table to retrieve a small book from her purse. "I've been looking through this book like crazy, trying to come up with a name."

"May I see that?"

"Sure." Kate handed it to her.

Sarah flipped through the pages. "We don't have that many names we use here. First names, I mean. So we have a lot of people with the same names." She handed the book back to Kate. "To avoid confusion in school, we say Anna B. and Anna S. and so on. There aren't that many different last names here, either, since we don't have a lot of people coming into our community from outside. I suppose if I had two children with the same first and last names, I'd ask if they had a nickname they wanted to use."

She leaned over Kate's shoulder and looked at the list of the most popular names for the previous year. "I'll bet there are children with the same first name in *Englisch* schools, too, since some names are always more popular in your world, too. See, Jason was one of the top names last year, so there will be a lot of little Jasons in school soon!"

"At least we don't have to come up with both a boy's name and a girl's name like they had to do before ultrasounds. I really like Aidan. Or maybe Jordan." She bit her lip and frowned. "Or Christopher."

Sarah smiled. "'Bearing Christ inside.'"

"Huh?"

"That's the meaning of Christopher."

Kate looked up the name. "You're right. How'd you know that?"

Now, why had she done that? Sarah asked herself. "I've seen the book. Kate, you didn't eat anything at breakfast. Are you feeling hungry at all?"

"A little bit," Kate admitted.

"I'll go fix you something. I'll bring you a tray."

"Thanks, but I think I might get up and come to the table. My back is feeling a little bit better, and maybe walking will help it."

That was *gut* news, thought Sarah.

When she walked into the kitchen, David and Jason were huddled over David's sample binder. Was it her imagination that they jumped apart guiltily?

"How's Kate?" Jason wanted to know.

"Better, I think. I'm fixing her something to eat."

The men exchanged a glance. "How about another game of checkers?" David asked Jason.

"Sure, that'd be great."

"No cheating," David warned him.

"No problem."

The men were both smiling as they left the room.

After she got Kate settled at the table with scrambled eggs and a biscuit, Sarah went to ask David and Jason if they wanted coffee.

Instead of playing checkers, they were once again huddled over David's sample book. And if Sarah wasn't mistaken, they were looking at baby furniture.

Jason looked up and started flipping the pages when he saw Sarah approach. "Oh, hi. David's showing me the stain colors for the mantel."

Sarah hesitated, not certain what to say. "That's *gut*."

"He does wonderful work."

She nodded and looked at her husband, but he didn't meet her eyes. Strange, she thought. It was as if the two men were being...secretive? David never acted that way.

"Kate okay?"

"She's having something to eat."

"I think I'll see how she's doing, get some coffee."

David opened his mouth and then shut it. Sarah sat down opposite him in the seat that Jason had vacated. "What's the big secret?"

"Jason wants to have me make something for Kate and have it be a surprise."

"She already knows about the mantel. She asked you to make one, remember?"

He nodded.

Sarah shook her head in disbelief as she stared at him. "Are you keeping secrets from me?"

"If I tell you, you'll tell Kate."

"No, I won't."

He folded his arms across his chest. "No?"

"No."

"You don't know how to keep a secret."

She wished that she didn't. But she couldn't tell him that. "I won't tell Kate."

"Won't tell Kate what?"

Sarah jumped and turned to see Kate standing there, munching on a biscuit.

"That Sarah got you a Christmas present," David said.

Sarah shot him a look, but he just lifted his shoulders. Sighing, she shook her head. He hadn't lied.

Kate grinned. "You didn't! You didn't need to do that!" Then she tilted her head as she studied Sarah. "How did you get me a present without leaving here?"

"I had something I thought you'd like."

"What is it?" Kate demanded, grinning like a kid. "Can I have it now? It's Christmas!"

Laughing, Sarah nodded. "Sure. It's in the kitchen."

"Ooh, a food gift! I love food gifts!" Kate followed her back into the kitchen and watched as Sarah went to the pantry and drew out the present she'd wrapped just hours ago.

"You can unwrap it, but it's not something you can eat now. You have to take it home and make it. But it's easy," she said quickly when Kate looked doubtful.

Kate popped the last of the biscuit into her mouth, chewed, and swallowed it. She ripped open the paper, revealing a pottery crock with a recipe card tied to it. "Friendship Bread" was written on a card attached. "Oh, it's a recipe!"

"There's a starter dough for you to make the bread," Sarah explained. "You don't use all of the starter, so you can give it to a friend with the recipe and they can make the bread, too. A friend gave it to me, and I'm giving it to you, and you can give it to one of your friends. So it gets passed on and on and on."

"That is *so* sweet!" Kate said, her eyes growing moist. "I'll remember you when I make it, Sarah!" She rose to hug Sarah, bending awkwardly. "I have to show it to Jason."

"We'll put it in your bedroom for when you leave later."

Kate glanced at the window, and her face crumpled. "Oh, Jason, no! Look!"

Jason looked at the window, then back at Kate. "Sweetheart, it'll be all right. I'm sure it's going to die down again real soon."

Tears ran down Kate's face. "I can't do this anymore, Jason. I can't do this anymore."

Gathering her into his arms, he looked at Sarah and David over her shoulder. "Shh, calm down. You need to stay calm."

"I know," she sniffled against his shoulder. "I know. But I've been trying, and I'm just so tired of worrying."

He kissed her temple. "Then don't worry. Everything is going to be just fine."

"You can't promise that."

"Yes, I can," he said firmly, setting her from him so that he could look into her eyes. "I'm not going to let anything happen to you."

She stared at him. "You can't promise that," she said again.

He touched his forehead to hers. "I would give my life for you and the baby. But it's not going to be necessary. Nothing bad has happened. And as soon as we can, I'm going to take you to the nearest emergency room to be checked out, okay?"

Kate's breath hitched. "Promise?"

"That's a promise I can keep." He kissed her again. "Now, would you like me to carry you back to bed?"

She shook her head. "I don't want you in traction when I deliver the baby."

He laughed and hugged her. "I can carry you. You're not as heavy as you think."

"Not as heavy as Shamu anyway." Kate turned to Sarah. "I know it sounds crazy, but do you know what I'm craving right now?"

"No, but if you tell me, I'll see if we have any on hand. Pickles? Ice cream?"

"Nope. Christmas cookies. I want Christmas cookies."

Laughing, Sarah brought a plate to the table and lifted the plastic wrap that covered it. "We just happen to have Christmas cookies. Lots of them. I couldn't seem to stop baking this past week."

"Got in the Christmas spirit, huh?" asked Kate, chomping the head off a gingerbread man.

"Yes," Sarah said, smiling at David. "I did."

Chapter Nine

David could feel the mood of the other three slipping over the next hour.

Jason had gone back to his pacing. Kate was sitting, looking moody as she stirred a cup of tea. Sarah cooked and cast concerned glances at the others when they weren't looking.

David stood looking out the window and wondered what he should do. What he *could* do. He couldn't make the weather better or the snowplow show up. He couldn't make Kate feel better.

Members of his church did not believe in proselytizing or witnessing their faith. It was not the way of the Plain people.

But he wondered if he had let Sarah down. Each time that Kate or Jason had needed to be assured that all was well, Sarah had, in her own quiet way, demonstrated that she truly believed it would be. She believed it but didn't just say it. She had found ways to reassure and comfort their guests.

At breakfast, when Kate had stormed from the kitchen, David had let Sarah be the one to speak to Jason. Women knew more about this kind of thing, he'd told himself. All through this past year he'd tried to step outside his grief and remember that he needed to be a strong man spiritually, not just physically, for both of them. He wasn't so sure he'd succeeded—or if the prayers he'd said for them both had finally worked. Now, in the last day and a half, Sarah seemed to be finally coming out of her grief and stepping toward healing.

She'd wondered aloud if there was a reason, a higher purpose, for the visit of this *Englisch* couple to their home. It showed so clearly that she was trying to rely on God. He'd had little to do with that, thought David. And what had he done since these strangers had arrived at their door? Had he helped Sarah enough, as a man who should be demonstrating spiritual leadership in the home?

He knew the answer. He'd tended to the mundane practicality of getting the couple to the home, and then Sarah had not just taken on the burden of their physical comfort but tried to provide emotional comfort as well.

As she glanced over and saw him watching her, she sent him that quiet, loving smile that always warmed his heart. He smiled at her, too, and hoped that she felt his love.

Turning from his reverie, he took a deep breath. "I know you're upset that the snow hasn't stopped, and plows aren't here yet," he told Kate and Jason. "But it's morning, and we've gotten through the worst of it, through a worrisome night."

Jason glanced at Kate, and she nodded.

"This could die down at any moment," David went on, looking at Sarah. "The snowplows could be on the way."

"He's right," Sarah said.

"So maybe we could just cheer up a little on a day like today?" he asked. "We're warm; we're safe. We have all the food that we could want to eat. We should be grateful, *ya?*"

Jason grinned at him. *"Ya,"* he echoed, rubbing his wife's shoulders with his hand.

"David had a wonderful idea, Jason. He thinks we should put a sign in the front yard so that the first road crews to come this way will stop at our house."

"That'd be super! Kate, isn't that a great idea?" Jason jumped up. "Where's the stuff to make the sign?"

"I have some plywood in the basement." David was nearly run over by Jason, heading toward the door to the basement.

"We'll be down there," David said a little unnecessarily. The sound of Kate laughing warmed his heart.

Once downstairs, David lit a battery-operated lantern and poked around in a pile of lumber. He lifted out a square of plywood that was about two feet by two feet. "We can nail a stake to it, paint a message on it, and put it out in the front yard." He rummaged among the scraps of lumber.

"I thought I remembered a stake down here," he said with satisfaction. He set it down on the workbench he'd built in the basement and found nails and a hammer. "Have you used a hammer much?"

Jason shook his head. "Kate puts up pictures and stuff."

David handed him the hammer.

"You want me to nail it?"

"You might as well get started, if you're going to try a simple project like we talked about earlier."

"Yeah." Jason took a nail and positioned it on the stake.

"Let me show you what I do to keep from hammering my fingers."

Jason watched him and grinned. "Cool. Thanks." Carefully he hammered the nail, then another.

David found some black paint and a brush. "What do you think it should say?"

"Hmm. Maybe "Need medical help"?

"Sounds *gut*. How are your painting skills?"

"About as good as my carpentry skills. But I'll give it a shot."

As Jason carefully lettered the sign, David couldn't help remembering how he'd felt so scared that night Sarah was cramping. The doctor told him to bring her right in. Fortunately, there hadn't been a snowstorm. But he'd been consumed with fear seeing Sarah's white face, felt so helpless as he held her while the doctor told them that she'd lost the baby.

"Looks good, if I do say so myself," Jason said, jerking David from his thoughts.

Some of the tension seemed to have left the other man's face. Maybe doing something useful like this had helped him cope.

"We'll put it out soon," he said.

"Good." Jason flexed his shoulders and sighed. "It was a long night, huh?"

"But you got through it, both of you. I know it's hard not being in control of things. You want to protect your wife—you still do. But staying calm for her when she needs it, doing little things to take care of her...well, that's what's really important, isn't it? Not trying to control what we can't control anyway?"

Jason leaned against the counter. "I could have done better."

"We all could, in most circumstances," David said slowly. "So we all try harder, work at living the way we should according to our beliefs. Our faith."

"Are you guys building an ark down there?" Kate called from the top of the stairs.

"It's a snowstorm, not a rainstorm, hon," Jason called back.

David smiled. "Let's show them what we've got."

When the men returned from the basement, Jason was carrying a crude sign. He showed it off with an air of satisfaction that reminded Sarah of her scholars at school.

"Good job, honey," Kate told him. She sank into a chair at the kitchen table and accepted a cup of chamomile tea from Sarah.

David went to look out the window. "We need to wait a little while before we take it outside. Wind's kicking up too much."

As if to confirm his words, something hit the side of the house with a loud *thump!*

"What was that?" Kate asked, pressing a hand to her heart.

"Could have been a tree limb; could have been something the wind tossed from the ground," David told them. "It's one reason it's not safe to go out right now. We'll see what it was when the wind dies down."

"I hope you can have your celebration later today," Kate said.

Sarah nodded. "First Christmas is my favorite. But it's nice to get presents, too!"

"My coworkers gave me a baby shower last week, so

the baby's already got presents waiting. Someone even gave me a Christmas tree ornament that says 'Baby's First Christmas' on it." She sighed. "I got so much stuff there's no way that the baby can wear all of it." She stopped, cocked her head. "Say, do Amish babies wear Pampers?"

Sarah laughed. "Yes, sometimes. Some mothers use cloth diapers, but disposable ones are very convenient when families are attending church or are away from home."

Jason shifted restlessly.

David looked at Sarah. "Do you want me to prepare the house for our guests?"

"Not yet, thank you," Sarah told him.

"What's to prepare?" asked Kate, looking around her. "I've never seen such a spotless house."

David showed them how much of the downstairs was actually one big room. The partitions that separated the living room and kitchen areas could be moved to accommodate the members of their church when it was their turn to host biweekly services. "We actually had about a hundred twenty-five people here for our wedding—some of our family who live in other parts of the country came," he told them.

"What a cool way to adapt your home," Jason said. "I've seen pocket doors, but nothing like this."

Sarah and Kate exchanged smiles as their husbands bent their heads together in a discussion of the merits of the partitions and what was involved in making them. Jason asked endless questions about tools. Before long, they'd gone downstairs to the basement again.

"Men and their toys," Kate said, laughing and shaking her head. "Jason saw the furniture David is making in the barn and remembered how much he used to like shop class in high school. He wants to get some power tools when we get home and try making something." She stirred her tea. "I think it'll be a good break for him away from the computer."

Sarah thought about how much David enjoyed working with wood. He'd always been like that, ever since she'd known him. He worked so hard and seemed to gain so much pleasure from his craft. It earned him a *gut* living, too, so that if the time came that she stopped teaching to stay home with their children, they would be fine.

David had been so supportive of her teaching. It was a calling, he said, one that she'd never thought would be offered to her. Both of them completed school at eighth grade and then pursued vocational training with adults, as was the way of their community. But they were both insatiable readers and liked nothing better than to talk about what they'd read.

"I think I'll go lie down again if you don't mind," Kate said.

"Of course I don't mind." Sarah stood and offered her hand to help Kate from the chair.

"Thanks." Instead of releasing Sarah's hand once she'd gotten to her feet, Kate looped Sarah's arm in hers, and they walked companionably down the hall. "You know, if we'd met sometime, someplace other than here, I think we might have been friends."

Sarah stared at her in surprise. "I think so too."

"I know Jason doesn't think I'm very domestic," Kate told her. "But I enjoy making a home for us."

She let go of Sarah's arm when they reached the bedroom. Kicking off her shoes, she sank down on the bed. "The thing is, I've wanted to be an attorney since I was a little girl, and you don't fool around if that's your career goal. You have to study every minute you can, take extra courses, cram for the bar exam. Then, when you get the job, you have to prove yourself over and over and hope you make partner."

She sighed. "And you can't ever let on that you want other things too, like time with your husband and to have a baby and take some time off, not just a few weeks and then hand the baby over to someone and pump breast milk during your lunch break for bottles at day care that someone else gets to give him."

Her breath hitched, and tears began rolling down her cheeks.

Sarah sank down into the chair beside the bed. "Kate?"

"I'm sorry. I'm just having a pity party." She wiped at her cheeks with her fingers. "Hormones, you know?"

When Sarah handed her a handkerchief, she stared at it. "I've only seen a real one once in my life, when my grandmother gave me hers." Kate mopped at her tears. "I just want to spend some time at home with my baby, and I don't know how I'm going to make that happen."

She looked at Sarah. "It's not just the money I'd lose if I stayed home. Maternity leave isn't encouraged in my law firm. I've heard other women there teased for having 'mommy brain.' You know, when a woman seems distracted, everyone assumes she can't keep her mind on her work, that she's thinking about her baby."

"Is the office the only place you can do your work as an attorney?"

When Kate didn't answer, when she just stared at her, Sarah wondered if she'd overstepped.

"No," Kate said finally, lifting her chin. "No. I need to remember that."

Patting the other woman's shoulder, Sarah rose. "Why don't you rest for a little while?"

Kate nodded, and Sarah drew the quilt over her.

"Do you want me to get Jason for you?"

"No. He'll get upset that I've been crying."

Sarah quietly shut the door. Kate's up-and-down moods reminded her of the roller coaster in a nearby amusement park for the *Englisch* tourists. She stood there for a moment, thinking, and then moved swiftly down the hallway and went upstairs to her room.

She heard David call her name.

"In here," she called over her shoulder. She didn't turn when she heard his footsteps behind her.

"What are you doing?"

"Just—getting some things."

"Sarah?" He touched her arm and made her turn. "What's wrong?"

"I'm getting things ready, just in case."

"Ready? For what?"

She dumped the pile of sheets and towels into his arms. "Kate's been acting like she's in labor. I just want to be prepared in case she starts having the baby and we can't get her to the hospital."

David bent so that she could place another set of sheets on top of the stack he held. "I hope you're wrong."

"Me too."

"But you seldom are," he murmured, and he leaned down to kiss the tip of her nose.

She smiled. "I'll remember that the next time we have a discussion."

They walked downstairs, and Sarah had David put the linens in the pantry closet, where Kate and Jason wouldn't see them.

"Look, is it my imagination, or does it seem like it's getting lighter outside?" she asked as she walked over to the window.

"It does look a little lighter," he conceded as he joined her.

Jason wandered in. "Kate's taking a nap. Thought I'd see what the two of you were up to."

"Just talking," David told him. "Join us."

Sitting down at the table, Jason stared off into the distance for a moment, and then he looked at them. "Kate and I have never talked so much. It seems to help both of us right now while she's so anxious about the baby and all."

He rubbed his finger on the grain of the wood on the table. "Not having all the stuff that takes our attention away from each other—you know, the phones, the computer, the television—well, I never realized that it makes such a difference. I mean, I always thought we were together at the house, so what was the harm in taking a call or texting someone or catching a game on the television? I think when we get home I'm going to be sending back that new television and keeping the old one—and the computer—off more."

"I think that will make Kate very happy," Sarah told him, and she smiled.

A few minutes later, Kate appeared in the doorway, looking pale and strained. She held her hands under her abdomen as though it was too heavy to walk without supporting it.

"Hi," she said, leaning against the doorjamb. She tried to smile, but it was obviously an effort.

The three of them rose like puppets on a string.

"I hope you won't think I'm crying wolf," she told them. "But I'm in labor."

Jason rushed to her and helped her to sit down. "It's just nerves, baby. False labor. Braxton Hicks, remember?"

She shook her head. "It's the real thing."

Sarah went to her side. "How close are the contractions?"

"Five minutes."

"Let's get you back to bed."

Kate cast a glance at the window, then at Jason. Her lips trembled, but she was obviously trying to stay calm. "I don't suppose—I don't suppose you've seen any snowplows?"

The three of them looked at each other. No one wanted to be the bearer of bad news.

"Not yet," Sarah spoke up. "But it can't be much longer."

Jason lifted Kate into his arms. "Hang in there. It's going to be okay."

She laid her head against his shoulder. "I'm so scared. I don't want to have the baby early. I don't want to have it without my doctor. I don't want to have it here." Her voice broke, and she started crying.

"Shh," he murmured. "It's going to be okay."

Sarah and David watched him carry Kate back into their room. Before they could move he was back.

"What are we going to do?" he asked them. "I'm scared to death. I don't think I can hold it together for her."

David placed his hands on the other man's shoulders and looked him in the eye. "You can, and you will. You did great just now. Right, Sarah?"

She nodded and smiled.

"This shouldn't be happening," Jason said. "Not in this day and age. What if something goes wrong?"

"Women have been having babies at home since time began," Sarah told him. "I've even read that it's become a trend in your *Englisch* world to have a midwife and have the baby at home. The three of us are going to help Kate, and everything is going to be all right."

Jason took a shaky breath. "The Lamaze instructor said first-time labors can be long."

Sarah nodded. "Contractions five minutes apart don't mean the baby's coming in five minutes. And labor can stop too."

"Okay. I'm going back in there with her. You're coming with me, right?"

"I'll be right there."

David dropped his hands, and Jason turned and left the room.

Grasping the back of a kitchen chair, Sarah took her own shaky breath and then looked at David. "Jason's not the only one worrying that something can go wrong," she said. "I'm scared. I couldn't bear it if they lost their baby. We know what kind of pain that is."

David took her hands in his and squeezed them. "You want to help Kate, don't you?"

She searched his face. "You know I do."

"If God has given you the desire to help, he's already given you the ability to do it."

"Oh, David, do you think so?"

When he nodded, she took a deep breath. "I hope you're right," she whispered.

"Let's say a quick prayer."

They bent their heads and prayed, and then he gathered her into his arms for a hug. "You go help Kate, and I'll get the supplies you brought downstairs."

She walked into the bedroom and found Kate

panting through a contraction. Jason was talking her through it, holding her hand as he sat on the chair beside the bed. Kate finally relaxed against the pillows and blew out a breath.

"Wow. They're getting stronger," she told them.

A few minutes passed, and David hadn't come into the room. It wasn't like him not to do exactly as he'd said he would do.

"I'll be right back," Sarah told them and slipped from the room.

When she walked into the kitchen, the sign that Jason and David had made was gone. So were David's coat and hat.

Chapter Ten

Sarah came back with the sheets and placed them on top of the dresser. Jason looked up, and he must have sensed her tension. He raised his brows, and after a quick glance at Kate, Sarah shook her head in silent warning.

Kate's forehead grew damp with perspiration as the contractions came closer and closer, harder and harder.

"I'm going to get a wet washcloth," Sarah told Jason.

She walked quickly into the kitchen and ran water over several cloths at the sink. Turning, she saw that Jason had followed her.

"Where's David?" he asked.

Sarah bit her lip. "He went for help," she said finally.

"But he said it wasn't safe. Why would he do that? He wouldn't let me."

"He wanted you to be with your wife."

"Instead of safe with his?"

She nodded. "He knew I was worried about Kate.

Neither of us wants anything to happen to your wife or your baby."

"But the two of you keep saying everything will be all right."

"We still believe that," she told him firmly. "You and I are going to do everything to help Kate get through this, whether it means she has the baby here or help comes and she has it at the local hospital. And David will be fine," she said, more for herself than for him. "He knows this area. You don't."

"Jason!"

He jumped at the sound of Kate's voice. "Coming!"

Then he surprised Sarah by turning back to her, and she saw him straighten, draw himself up.

"We're going to be fine," he told her. "We can do this if we have to."

He hurried back to Kate, and Sarah stared after him for a long moment. She'd told Kate to expect the best from him and she'd get it; now Jason was showing her that she was right.

"Don't leave me alone again!" Kate cried, grasping at his hand.

"I won't, baby. I was just seeing if Sarah needed any help."

"I don't think she needed help carrying a couple of washcloths!"

Jason winced at her tone, but kept the patient smile on his face. "You're right. I was just gone a minute, but it must have seemed longer."

"Don't patronize me!"

"No, baby, I wouldn't dream of doing that."

Sarah handed him a dampened washcloth, and he

wiped Kate's face gingerly, as if half-afraid she'd snap at his fingers.

Kate looked at Sarah. "I'm sorry. I sound like a shrew."

Sarah walked over to sit in the chair beside the bed. "From here on in, I don't want to hear any apologies. You say anything, yell anything you want. We'll understand."

"You bet," Jason told her.

"I wanted him to be more sensitive," Kate muttered to Sarah. "But this is a bit much."

"Be careful what you wish for," Sarah told her, chuckling.

"I know I've been complaining about not feeling well, but I didn't want the baby to come early." Tears welled up in Kate's eyes.

"Two weeks isn't that early," Sarah reassured her. "And complaining doesn't make a baby come sooner. But let's not get ahead of ourselves. You could be in labor for a while."

"Is that supposed to make me feel better?" Kate said in disbelief as another contraction rolled over her.

Sarah shook her head. "No, I just mean that first births aren't usually quick. Help could still come. You may have this baby in the hospital just like you want."

"Tell me about your friends," Kate said breathlessly after the contraction passed. "You said you were with two of your friends when they had their babies."

"Emma had her baby at home," Sarah said, remembering. "It was two years ago, winter, like now. We took turns, several of us, sitting with her, rubbing her back, doing some quilting, singing, reading to her."

"But she didn't have any drugs for the pain."

"She was fine," Sarah told her. "You will be too. I promise."

"Easy for you to say," Kate groused.

The words were like a blow. Kate must have seen their effect on Sarah, for she immediately looked appalled. "I'm sorry. That sounded so mean."

"No apologies, remember?" Sarah told her, trying to sound light. "Anyway, she was in labor for five hours, and we all had a wonderful time with her until a little visitor arrived. A girl."

"Where was her husband?" asked Kate.

"He'd gone to an auction. But she'd planned to have the baby at home, so that's what she did."

"She wanted it that way?" There was real disbelief in Kate's voice.

"I remember reading somewhere that 90 percent of the people walking around in the world right now were born at home."

Kate was shifting around, trying to get comfortable. Sarah rose and brought another pillow from the closet. "Let's have you roll onto your side and put this under your tummy," she suggested. "Then Jason can rub your back."

"Oh, that sounds good."

Grinning, Jason took the chair Sarah had vacated and started rubbing his wife's back. "You're doing good, baby."

Kate smiled. "What are you going to call me when the baby's here?"

"Sweetheart," he said. "How's that?"

"Nice," she said, smiling. She licked at her lips. "Can I have some water?"

"I'll get you some ice chips," Sarah said. "That's what they gave my friends when they got thirsty."

"Thanks. And, Sarah?"

She turned. "Yes?"

"I hope David's not feeling neglected."

Sarah could feel color rising up into her cheeks. "Uh, no, I don't think so."

Once in the kitchen, Sarah made a beeline for the window. It was still a dismal gray outside, with snow smacking the windows as if someone were scooping up one big handful after another and throwing them at the panes.

"Where are you now, David?" she whispered. Her heart threatened to burst from her chest. "God, please keep him safe," she prayed. "Please guide his steps."

She had to keep busy or she'd make herself crazy with worry. Pulling out a plastic bag, she filled it with ice and slapped it on the kitchen table to break the cubes into small pieces to put into a bowl.

When she returned to the room, Jason was using his watch to time a contraction. "Four minutes," he mouthed to Sarah.

It was going faster than she expected, maybe because Kate had really been in labor for some time, she thought. Handing the bowl to Jason, she cautioned him to feed Kate a few pieces at a time so she wouldn't get uncomfortable and have to get up to use the bathroom.

A few minutes later, Kate cried out. "Oh no," she said, looking embarrassed. "I think my water just broke."

"No problem," Sarah assured her. "That's why I brought more sheets. It's all part of the process."

"But the mattress…"

"It has a plastic protector on it. Sometimes when we have church service, mothers bring their children in here to nap. Let's get you up and change the sheets, see if I need to get you a fresh nightgown."

But when Sarah gathered the soiled sheets up to carry them out of the room, she saw that they were not only wet but streaked with blood. Her stomach pitched. Being with Emma and her other friend who'd given birth had prepared her for the eventuality, but she hadn't been responsible for them as she was now. A midwife and other women, older ones who'd given birth themselves and were experienced with such things, had been present.

Then, too, one of them could have run to a telephone down the road or driven in a buggy for help. There hadn't been a snowstorm, cutting off contact with the outside world.

David, please find help quickly, she prayed. *Please.*

David used a rock to pound the sign into the frozen ground in his front yard. Then, hunching his shoulders against the cold wind, he slogged through the snowdrifts, relying on memory more than sight. He gave a moment's thought to getting Ned, but it might take too much time to go to the barn for him. That might give Sarah a chance to come out and try to stop him.

He wasn't happy about leaving without telling her first. They always talked over big decisions. But it hadn't been a decision at all when it came down to it. She would realize that after she stopped being upset.

Neither of them wanted Kate and Jason to lose their baby.

And he knew the area so well, he told himself. He

knew exactly how far away the closest houses were, where it was best to seek help. He'd be fine.

He was determined to be, for himself, for Sarah, and for that unborn baby.

Sarah had made him think about this situation in a way he hadn't, about the way they'd suddenly had these guests at this time of year…at this time in their lives. Perhaps she was right that there was something very meaningful about them appearing like this. Was it a message from God? He didn't know. He was simply supposed to trust.

David trudged on, staying in the middle of what he knew was the paved road. If he wasn't careful and strayed too close to the edge of it, he could trip over a rock or step in a hole covered by the deceptively benign-looking mounds of snow.

The telephone shanty that several families shared was down the road. Even though there was no reception for the cell phones, David hoped that regular phone service had been restored.

He fumbled with the lock on the door, finally pulling off his thick gloves and stuffing them in his pockets to try with his bare hands. But the cold made his fingers feel thick and awkward, and the lock was obviously frozen. Picking up a rock, he tried to bash it open, knowing his neighbors would forgive his destruction because of the emergency. Still, he couldn't gain entry.

Admitting defeat, he pulled his gloves from his pockets, but the wind whipped them away. He chased them across the road, skidding and nearly falling. They bounced merrily ahead of him like leaves on an autumn wind.

The effort of chasing them in the wind and snow

wasn't worth it, he decided. Shoving his hands in his pockets, he walked toward the nearest house. It wasn't a long walk, maybe a mile. But fighting the wind, it felt longer, like it must have for Jason when he was trying to find someone to help him on a dark, snowy night. Climbing the stairs, he knocked on the door of John Zook. After a few minutes of knocking, David remembered that John and his wife had gone to visit their daughter in the next town the week before. He'd wasted valuable time.

He trudged another half mile. The Lapps were home, but they, like Sarah's parents, were suffering from the flu that seemed to be going around. David refused Levi's offer to go with him to find help, insisting that he return to his bed.

David had made the walk down this road many times, but never in such bad weather. Walking against the wind was tiring him. How Jason had done it the night before he didn't know. And then he shook his head at the thought. Of course Jason had made it. He'd had the survival of his wife and his baby on his shoulders.

As David himself did now.

The phrase about being his brother's keeper came to mind. It wasn't too much to do what he could for Jason. In the brief time he'd known the *Englischman,* David had come to see him as basically a *gut* man who tried in his own way to do the right thing. If the situations were reversed, David felt that Jason would be looking for help for Sarah.

His feet felt like blocks of ice. Heavy blocks of ice. How was it possible to get so cold so fast, he wondered, then shook his head. Hadn't he chided Jason last night for not taking hypothermia and frostbite seriously?

The *gut* news was that the sky was lightening and it seemed the snow was stopping. Encouraged, he quickened his steps.

David climbed the stairs to the Stoltzfus house and banged on the door.

Mary Stoltzfus opened the door and stared at him. "David! What are you doing out in this weather? Come in, come in."

Brushing the worst of the snow from the shoulders of his coat, he stepped inside and shut the door. It was then that he noticed that Mary's foot was encased in a cast.

"What happened?"

"I slipped and broke my ankle last week. Now, tell me why you're out in such weather."

"We need help. An *Englisch* couple got stranded at our house, and the woman is in labor. I couldn't get into the telephone shanty."

Mary clucked her tongue and shook her head. "Might not have helped anyway," she said pragmatically. "The lines often go down at such times."

David reached for the door handle. "I need to get on my way, see if I can raise some help."

"Try the Hostetlers next door."

Nodding, David left the house and trudged toward the Hostetler house.

He brushed his hand over his face. He thought he could see lights coming at him in the gray day. He blinked against the falling snow. No, he wasn't imagining it. There were two headlights beaming through the snow, a big blade of a snowplow approaching.

He let out a shout of joy, of praise to God for answered prayer. "Here!" he shouted, running out into the middle of the road, slipping and sliding. "Here!" and waved his arms.

The snowplow slowed and then stopped. David ran up to the driver's side.

"We have a woman in labor at my house!" he called up to him. "Can you call for help?"

"Sure thing. Get in."

David ran around to the other side of the vehicle and climbed inside. Shivering, he gave directions to his house while the driver radioed for paramedics.

Home had never looked so *gut,* David thought as he climbed down a few minutes later and ran for his front door.

It felt like he'd been gone looking for help for hours, but he knew it hadn't been. Maybe Kate was still in labor and Sarah hadn't had to help her deliver. Maybe he was still in time.

He hoped and prayed that all was well. God's will, he repeated over and over. Surely he would help bring this child safely into the world on Christmas.

Chapter Eleven

"This baby's really coming!" Kate gasped.

Sarah grinned at her. "You're right."

Jason mopped his wife's perspiring brow. "She's always right."

"Sarah, you're my witness," Kate said, then gasped as another contraction swept over her like a tide.

"I'll put it in writing, counselor," her husband told her as he checked his watch. "Contractions are a minute apart."

The more it became a possibility that they might have to deliver the baby themselves, the calmer the three of them had seemed to become, as if they'd entered into a pact to do whatever was necessary, Sarah thought. Help wasn't coming yet, and they were going to have to rely on each other to bring this baby into the world safely.

Sarah watched Jason close his eyes, and his lips moved soundlessly.

Now that her contraction had passed, Kate focused on her husband. "Are you trying to take a nap?"

Jason opened his eyes. "Of course not." He leaned

down and kissed her forehead. "I was just saying a prayer for you and the baby."

Kate immediately burst into tears. "That is so sweet," she sobbed.

"Going into the last stage?" Jason asked Sarah quietly, and she nodded.

"Kate, how about I get behind you in bed and help support you like we learned in the class? I think it's time, don't you?"

"That—that'd be good."

He kicked off his shoes, helped her sit up a bit more, and slid behind her in the bed. "There, that better?"

"Yeah." Kate took the tissue Sarah handed her and clutched at her hand. "You said to expect the best."

Another contraction began, and the three of them watched its ripple across Kate's abdomen. Another followed, fast, and another and another.

"I think he's coming!" Kate cried. "I have to push!"

"Pant through it," Jason counseled.

"I need to push!" she cried. "I need to push! Sarah, can you see the head?"

Sarah's heart skipped a beat as she checked the progress of birth and saw the top of the baby's head. "Yes!" Awed, she looked up at them. "Yes, I can see the head!"

"Can you get him out?"

Sarah shook her head. "It's best to let him come naturally."

"It hurts!" Kate clutched at Jason's hand, and he winced at the pressure.

"Uh, Kate, I need that hand," he said with a grimace. "Don't break my fingers."

"I'm not doing this again without an epidural!"

"We're not ever doing this again," Jason promised fervently.

"It won't hurt for long, and you'll have your baby, Kate." Sarah checked again, and her heart started pounding.

The baby's head emerged. "Kate, he's coming! You can push now!"

Kate pushed, cried out, and then pushed again, and suddenly Sarah was holding a slippery, squirming baby in her hands.

"He's here!" Sarah exclaimed as the baby wailed and waved his arms in protest at leaving his mother's warm body. He scrunched his eyes shut at the bright light, then opened them and looked around.

Trying to stay calm, Sarah followed the steps the book had recommended, checking that the baby's airway was clear, that there was nothing in his mouth or nose to obstruct his breathing. He felt so tiny, but in reality, she thought he might weigh seven or eight pounds.

Grabbing one of the clean towels she'd placed on the bed, Sarah wrapped him in it quickly, before he could get chilled. And then she put him in Kate's outstretched arms.

"Oh, he's so beautiful!" Kate said, staring at him with wide eyes. "Jason, look at him! He's got your nose."

"And your dark hair," Jason told her. His hand shook as he reached out to stroke his son's cheek. His Adam's apple bobbed as he swallowed, and Sarah saw tears in his eyes. He leaned over and kissed Kate. "I love you. I'm so proud of you."

Tears slid down her cheeks. "I love you, and I'm proud of you, too." She lay back against him, looking exhausted but radiant. "I can't believe we did it," she said, shaking her head in disbelief. "I can't believe we did it."

As much as she wanted to watch the miracle before her, Sarah returned her attention to Kate. The book made it clear that the danger to the mother and the baby wasn't over yet.

Sure enough, a few minutes later, Kate grimaced and looked at Sarah. "Oh, I'm having another pain! I'm not having another baby, am I?"

Smiling, Sarah shook her head. "It's not another baby. It's the placenta, remember? The afterbirth."

Just as she'd done with delivering the baby, she let nature take its course and watched it slide out without pulling on it. Another worry she could let go of, Sarah thought.

Jason looked at her, concerned. "Is she all right? She's not bleeding too much or anything?"

So he knew the risks just as she did. "She's doing fine." She paused and met his eyes. "You both are."

"Should we cut the cord?"

Sarah hesitated and glanced back at the doorway. It didn't appear that help was coming. She nodded and reached for the scissors she'd disinfected earlier. "Here, the new daddy gets to do the honors."

She told him what the book had said, and he accomplished the task with surprisingly steady hands. Afterward, Jason held the baby while Sarah helped Kate into a clean nightgown and tried with a minimum of moving her to remove soiled sheets and place new ones beneath her. And then, when she saw that there was nothing else she could do for them, Sarah left the room so the new parents could have some private moments with their son.

Now that she was alone, the tears could come. Sinking down into a kitchen chair, Sarah cried. The tears she shed were tears of relief, tears of joy, tears of awe at being present at a miracle, the wonder of a new life coming into the world. She had never felt so close to God as at that moment, helping to bring one of His children into the world. There was no pride, only gratitude that He had helped her at every step. David had said that He would, that if God had given her the desire to help, that He'd give her the ability as well.

Surely this was a time she would not forget for the rest of her life. She whispered a prayer of gratitude for the precious gift of being witness to the birth, a request for Kate and the baby's health and safety. All was right and *gut* here in her home, here in God's kingdom on earth. She wiped her eyes and blew her nose.

Calm now, she went to the sink and washed her hands. And then she went upstairs and knelt before the hope chest she kept at the foot of her bed.

From it she drew the quilt she'd lovingly sewn those first months when she'd carried her baby under her heart. She stroked the tiny squares of fabric and hesitated for only a moment. Then she reached in and took out a tiny cotton nightgown, an undershirt that wasn't much bigger than her hand, a package of newborn disposable diapers, and a box of cleansing wipes. Carrying them downstairs, she knocked on the bedroom door.

"Come in," Kate called.

Jason sat beside the bed holding the baby, staring at him as if he couldn't quite believe he was here.

"I thought you might like to dress your baby," Sarah told her as she held out the things she'd brought.

Kate stared at them, then her eyes lifted to Sarah.

"I—Sarah, the quilt is gorgeous. You made it, didn't you?"

"Yes."

Kate's eyes filled with tears as she took the quilt from Sarah and stroked it. "It's a work of art. But I can't take it…you need to save it."

"I can make another," Sarah told her. "I *will* make another."

For a long moment their eyes held, and then Kate nodded slowly. "Yes, Sarah, you will. I know you will."

Sarah watched as Kate placed the baby on the bed. Using the wipes, she cleaned the baby and laughed when he protested, wiggling and making faces. Kate held up one of the diapers and remarked on how small it looked, but when she fastened it on the baby, it still looked big on him, his little scrawny legs sticking out. The undershirt was next, and then the nightgown. Finally, she wrapped him up in the quilt, tucking it lovingly around him.

And then she held him out to Sarah. "Would you like to hold him?"

Sarah smiled. "Oh yes!" Carefully she accepted the baby from Kate and took the chair Jason offered. She sat down and cradled the baby in her arms, watching as he sighed and closed his eyes for his first nap. What a wonder, she thought, studying his features, his tiny hands that looked like starfish lying atop the quilt.

She looked up at Kate. "Remember the Scripture verse I told you about? 'Be not forgetful to entertain strangers: for thereby some have entertained angels unawares.' It looks like we've entertained the tiniest angel too. He is so beautiful."

The front door crashed open, and the noise startled the baby so that he threw up his hands and grimaced before settling back to sleep.

"Sarah? Sarah?"

David approached the guest room with caution, not sure what he'd find.

"It's okay, come on in!" Sarah called.

His eyes went immediately to the baby his wife held in her arms, wrapped in a quilt he recognized, then he looked at Kate sitting up in bed.

Jason threw his arms around David and hugged him. "Thank God you're safe."

"Yes," David managed to say. "But I see you didn't need help after all."

"Safe?" Kate looked from David to Sarah to Jason. "You've got snow all over you," she said, frowning. "Have you been outside?"

Jason turned. "You could say that. Sweetheart, David went for help."

"You did? But it was still snowing."

He shrugged. "It stopped while I was out. Anyway, I'm sorry I didn't get you help in time for you to have your baby at the hospital."

She held out her arms. "Come here."

"No, I don't want to get you cold and wet," he protested.

But when she continued to hold out her arms, and he looked at Sarah and saw her nod, he took off his hat and did as commanded.

"Thank you," Kate said, holding him tight. "Thank you."

Pulling back, uncomfortable with thanks for doing so little, he looked down at the baby. "What a fine *boppli* you have." He grinned at Jason. "He has your nose."

Jason laughed and clapped a hand on his shoulder. "Yeah, I know. Good thing he's a boy, huh? Wish I had a cigar to offer, but Kate thinks that's a terrible way to celebrate a birth. Let's go get you warmed up. You look frozen." He gave David a sly glance. "Should we get a footbath out too?"

David shook his head. "The feet are fine. My boots are warmer and sturdier than those shoes you had on when you tromped through the snow, *Englischer*."

"What's that?" Sarah asked when she heard a commotion outside the window. "Is someone out front?"

David walked over to pull the curtains aside and look out, then he turned and gave them a big grin. "Yes. Help is here. The snowplow driver called emergency services. Kate, one day you can tell your son that he went for a ride in an ambulance on his birthday."

David and Sarah sat at the kitchen table, staying out of the way as the paramedics took over, coming in to check on Kate and the baby, then going out to fetch a gurney.

She reached across the table and took his hands in hers. "I wanted to be angry at you when I saw that you left. I was so scared of you being out in the storm. But Kate isn't the only one who should be thanking you for going for help. You knew I was frightened of having to deliver the baby. I was so afraid something could go wrong."

"I was, too. I didn't want Kate and Jason to go through what we did." He swallowed and fought for control for a moment, then he smiled at her. "Everything worked out. Maybe we both could have had a little more faith?"

She nodded and smiled. "I love you."

"I love you too."

Jason came into the room and pulled on his jacket. "I guess this is it," he said, shifting from one foot to the other as he looked at them. "I know you two are probably sick of us by now."

"Don't you say such a thing," Sarah admonished. "We enjoyed having you here."

"Well, uh, thanks." He shifted some more. "Listen, do you think—I mean, would you come see us later at the hospital? I mean, if you can?"

"We would love to," David said immediately.

Kate was wheeled out just then, cradling the baby in her arms, both of them tucked up into a quilt against the cold weather. "Did you ask them to come see us later?" When Jason nodded, she grinned. "Okay then, here we go!" She waved one of the baby's hands at them before tucking it inside his quilt.

Sarah grabbed her shawl, wrapped it around her shoulders, and walked outside to watch Kate being put into the ambulance. To her surprise, a buggy pulled up in front, to the side of the ambulance.

"We came as soon as we heard you needed help," called Lydia as she stepped down.

Miriam alighted from the passenger side and came rushing up. She pressed her hands together as she gazed at the baby. "Oh my," she cried, and her eyes shone with excitement. "What's this? I can't wait to hear what happened!"

"The Amish grapevine at work," David told Jason with a smile.

Two of David and Sarah's neighbors and their children walked over and stood with Miriam and Lydia. Kate proudly showed the baby to them.

"It's a miracle," someone murmured, and others nodded.

"*Mamm?* Is that Baby Jesus?" six-year-old Eli asked.

Laughter rang out in the still, cold air, but the adults exchanged glances, thinking of another birth so long ago of one child who had changed the world so much.

With Kate and the baby safely loaded into the ambulance, one of the paramedics turned to Jason. "Ready to go, Daddy?"

He grinned. "You bet."

"Jason, wait a second." David touched his shoulder to stop him. "Leave me the keys to your car, and I'll see that it's fixed and brought to you at the hospital."

Leaning closer, so the others couldn't hear, he whispered, "And I'll put the cradle in it so you can give it to Kate when you take her and the baby home."

Jason handed him the keys, and then he hugged David again, hard. "You saved our lives," he said, blinking back tears. "And you," he said, turning to Sarah and hugging her. "You helped me help my wife the way I wanted to but was too afraid to try. We won't ever forget either of you."

"We won't ever forget you and Kate and the baby, either." She reached for David's hand and squeezed it.

Jason climbed inside the back of the ambulance and sat next to Kate. The paramedic shut the doors, then stamped through the snow to climb into the front passenger seat and shut the door.

With lights flashing and siren blaring, the ambulance drove off. David drew Sarah close to him, and they watched its progress down the road.

As friends and family piled into the house, David reflected on what Jason had said. Perhaps he and Sarah had saved the lives of this man and his family. But this family that a storm had brought on a holy night had affected him and Sarah, too, in very profound ways.... Although their marriage hadn't faltered, exactly, there had been a distance between them sometimes that he'd wondered if they could bridge. But from the time their guests had arrived, they had found ways, so many ways, to reach out to each other.

David felt Sarah shiver.

"Let's go inside," David told her. "It's cold, and besides, everyone is waiting to know what happened."

Inside, their guests had gathered in the living room and were chattering with each other.

He gathered Sarah into his arms and held her. When they finally stepped apart, she turned toward the stove. "I should put *kaffi* and tea on."

"I'll go in and tell the others what happened. Unless you want to?"

She smiled. "You go ahead."

Idly, she stood there at the stove. Her glance fell on the calendar nailed to the wall nearby. In the way of every woman who wanted a baby with every fiber of her being, she had become obsessed by the calendar, she realized. Month after month her hopes grew and then were dashed.

"Sarah?"

She jerked as he touched her arm. "What?"

"You're so tired you're just standing there. Maybe you should sit down before you fall down from exhaustion."

Shaking her head, she found her attention drawn back to the calendar. "I've been thinking," she said slowly. "Since I lost the baby, I've found myself disappointed each month I didn't get pregnant again. But I love you, David. We're a family whether we ever have children or not."

"We *will* have a baby one day," David said firmly.

"You said I could borrow some of your faith," she told him. "I do believe that God will send us *kinner* one day. But it's time for me to stop telling Him I'm impatient for them. Do you know, I actually told Him that if I had just one child, I could be happy?"

"I can't imagine you talking to God that way."

She smiled. "I did. But I'm not bargaining with Him anymore." She hugged her husband. "I'm happy and grateful for you and my wonderful life, my wonderful family and friends." Slipping her hand through his arm, she urged David toward the living room. "Let's go celebrate Christmas with them, shall we?"

* * * * *

An Amish Christmas
READING GROUP GUIDE

* Guide contains spoilers, so don't read before completing the novellas.

For reading groups with five or more members, the authors will participate in the discussion of this collection. If you're interested, go to www.Amishhearts.com.

A MIRACLE FOR MIRIAM

1. Miriam allowed Seth's youthful rejection to affect her self-confidence, even as an adult. Instead of seeing herself as a beautiful woman of God, she continued to see herself as unattractive and undesirable. What can we do to protect our hearts against the thoughtless and cruel words of others?

2. Proverbs 29:23 states, "A man's pride shall bring him low; but honor shall uphold the humble in spirit." How did Seth's accident "bring him low"? How did he vow to change?

3. List some reasons why Miriam didn't trust Seth. Think back to a time where you had difficulty trusting someone else. What allowed you to trust again?

4. The Amish value *demut* (humility) over *hochmut* (pride), and strive to be as humble as possible in all situations. Is humility difficult to achieve? How can we practice humility in our daily lives?

1. Throughout the book, Lydia struggles with forgiveness. First she must find it in her heart to forgive Daniel, and later she must forgive her deceased husband. Have you ever found yourself in a situation where you needed to forgive someone who has passed on? Did forgiveness give you a sense of peace or resolve, even though you were not able to voice your feelings directly to that person?

2. Anna Marie is experiencing her running-around period *(rumschpringe)*. Is her behavior different from that of *Englisch* teenagers at this age? If so, how? Is Lydia more trusting about her daughter's actions than *Englisch* parents might be, or is this simply reflective of a generational shift across both cultures? For example, Lydia states that her parents would have been much stricter with her if they'd caught her sneaking out of the house. Are you less strict with your children than your parents were with you?

3. The Amish believe that all things that happen are of God's will. Is Lydia being true to her faith by questioning the way things happened, harboring ill will, and struggling to forgive—or is she just human? Have you ever questioned God's will in a situation where a different outcome would have affected far more people than just you?

4. Daniel and Lydia were each other's first loves, yet they went on to live separate lives. Do you know anyone who has reunited with his or her first love? Did it work out?

1. As Christmas approaches, Sarah is still experiencing grief over the miscarriage of her first child. While the loss of a person dear to us may be the biggest, hardest loss we will experience, there are other forms of loss that are difficult to cope with in life. Some of these losses include the loss of a dream, a job, a house—even the loss of a body image when a person has an accident, stroke, or other trauma that changes the way we look and move. How have you coped, and possibly even grown, from a loss in your life?

2. The Amish rely heavily on the concept of "God's will" as a way of living spiritually. How do you interpret God's will, and how do you use it to sustain your faith?

3. Why do you suppose we have such a fascination with the Amish? Many people admire the Amish for separating themselves from the *Englisch* world and living life according to their terms. Have you ever wanted to live a simpler life? Since most of us can't—or don't want to—join an Amish community, how can we live a simpler, more faithful life where we are?

4. What are some of your favorite memories of the season? How do you make sure to remember that "Jesus is the reason for the season"?

Amish Recipes

Shoestring Apple Pie

This crustless "pie" is very simple and inexpensive to make. After baking, let it cool completely; then scoop out of the pie plate with a large spoon. Serve with whipped cream or ice cream. Enjoy!

4 cups peeled, finely chopped apples
1 cup white sugar
2 tablespoons flour
¼ cup water
2 eggs, beaten
½ teaspoon cinnamon
4 tablespoons butter, divided

1. Preheat oven to 450°.
2. Grease two 9-inch glass pie plates with cooking spray.
3. Combine all ingredients until sugar is dissolved and apples are moist. Divide mixture between the two pie plates.
4. Dot each pie with 2 tablespoons butter.
5. Bake in the oven for 15 minutes, then turn down the temperature to 350° and bake for 20 more minutes, or until apples are soft.

Source: *A Taste of Home* from the Schlabach family.

Molasses Crinkle Cookies

1. Mix together well:

   3 cups vegetable oil
   4 cups brown sugar
   1 cup molasses
   4 eggs, beaten

2. Add:

   8 teaspoons baking soda
   1 teaspoon salt
   2 teaspoons cinnamon
   1 teaspoon nutmeg
   1 teaspoon ground cloves

3. Stir well. Mix in the following with your hands:

   2 cups whole wheat flour
   6 cups all-purpose flour

4. Form into 1-inch balls and roll in white sugar. Bake at 350° for 10 minutes.

Makes approximately 10 dozen—plenty for sharing!

Source: Courtesy of an Old Order Amish friend.

FRIENDSHIP BREAD

Give this recipe to your friends to make their own Friendship Bread.

1 cup starter (see following page)
⅔ cup vegetable oil
2 cups all-purpose flour
1 cup sugar
3 eggs
1½ teaspoons baking powder
½ teaspoon baking soda
1 teaspoon cinnamon
½ teaspoon vanilla
½ teaspoon salt

Here comes the fun part: add chopped apples and raisins (one cup of raisins and one apple) or chocolate or butterscotch morsels or nuts (about a cup or so). Pour into a greased 9 x 5 x 3" loaf pan and bake in a preheated 350 degree oven for about 45 minutes. Allow to cool for 15 to 20 minutes before removing from pan.

There are as many recipes for Friendship Bread as there are friends! I've seen some use pudding for added richness and different flavors. For an extra-special gift, put the starter in little crockery pots you can buy at the store, and tie the handwritten recipe and a wooden spoon on with ribbon.

Be sure you keep a cup of the starter to keep it going for the next time you want to make a batch of Friendship Bread.

STARTER

Note: Do NOT use a metal spoon for stirring the starter.

1. Mix the following ingredients in a big, deep glass mixing bowl.

   1 cup sugar
   1 cup milk
   1 cup all-purpose flour

2. Partially cover with a lid or use a piece of cheese-cloth held with a rubber band or string. Store at room temperature—do NOT refrigerate.

3. Each day for 17 days, stir; skip stirring on day 18. Stir for the next three days, then, on day 22, stir and add the following:

   1 cup flour
   1 cup sugar
   1 cup milk

4. Stir and partially cover again. On days 23, 24, 25, and 26, stir the mixture and cover again. On day 27, stir and add the following ingredients:

   1 cup flour
   1 cup sugar
   1 cup milk

5. Stir. There should now be about 4 cups of starter. Divide into four portions and give 1 cup each in a container to two friends. Reserve 2 cups.

Source: Courtesy of an Old Order Amish friend.

Acknowledgments

KATHY FULLER:

This book wouldn't have been possible without the help of several spectacular people. Thank you to my terrific editor, Natalie Hanemann, for putting this project together, and for her amazing editing skills and encouragement. It's a privilege to work with her. I also express my gratitude to LB Norton, who told me to trust my writing. Those words really clicked with me. Another big thank-you to the team at Thomas Nelson, who are all fantastic. And a special thank-you to Barbie Beiler, who graciously read the manuscript for accuracy.

Most of all, I want to thank my fellow authors, Beth Wiseman and Barbara Cameron. From the moment we started brainstorming these stories, we became friends, and that friendship has blossomed into something very special. Thank you, ladies, for being on this journey with me!

BETH WISEMAN:

Thank you to my friends and family who continue to support me on this incredible journey. With each new book, I am learning to balance my time a little better, and your patience with my tight deadlines is much appreciated. My friendships and personal relationships are important to me, and I will always find the time to nourish them.

Patrick, thank you for providing me with an environment that affords me this grand opportunity to live my dreams—dreams of writing full-time and of living the rest of my life with you, my forever love.

Eric and Cory, dreams do come true. Work hard, strive to be the best you can be, and maintain a relationship with God. Talk to Him as you would a dear friend. He listens. He blessed me with the two of you.

To Natalie Hanemann—I'm so blessed to have you in my life, as both editor and friend. You push me to hit my writing potential, and I always end up with a better book after your input. Equally important is the friendship we share. God puts people in our life for a reason, and I feel sure He was smiling when He introduced the two of us. Thank you for everything.

My entire fiction family at Thomas Nelson is awesome. I am so honored to be a part of this group. I thank God for each and every one of you.

Thank you to LB Norton for your editorial assistance. It was a pleasure to work with you.

Kathy Fuller and Barbara Cameron, I'm honored to work with you on this project, and I treasure our friendship. You are both very special to me.

A sincere thanks to my dear friend, Barbie Beiler. As always, your Amish and Mennonite background helps me to keep the books authentic. You always make time amid your busy schedule to read the manuscripts prior to publication, and I am so grateful to you. You are a blessing in my life, my friend.

To Anna B. King, thank you so much for the time you spent on the phone with me, making sure that I understood the details of Christmas as celebrated in an Old Order Amish community. By the time this book goes to print, I will have met you in person in Pennsylvania, and I am really looking forward to that—to meeting Barbie's mom!

Thank you to my agent, Mary Sue Seymour. You are a special person, and I value our professional relationship as well as our friendship. Thank you for everything.

Special thanks to those "first responders" who read behind me as I write—Reneé Bissmeyer, Rene Simpson, and my wonderful mother, Pat Isley. You all keep me on my toes and push me forward to completion. Rene, thank you for reading behind me on this particular novella and for all your input.

To my friends and "sistas" who constantly promote the books, thank you so much. Just to name a few— Laurie, Dawn, Melody, Valarie, Pat, Carol, Amy, Bethany, and Gayle. You gals are great!

And always, my most heartfelt thanks goes to God for providing me with this wonderful opportunity to spread His Word through inspirational stories about faith, hope, and love.

BARBARA CAMERON:

Thank you to my family and friends who are so supportive of my writing. Writing is, by nature, a solitary activity, and all of you sustain me with your encouragement. I want to thank my daughter, Stephany, and my son, Justin, for being God's greatest gifts to me, and for letting me know early on that they understood how important writing is to me. And thank you to the real Sarah, best friend for so many years and such a joy to know.

Thanks to three special longtime friends who are fellow writers: Rita Shell, the first person to read my work; Donna Cianciulli, whom I met when we were teachers long ago; and Judy Rehm, a wonderful Bible scholar I consult often. Thanks to Linda and Rob Beziat, two warm and generous friends who have been so supportive. And to Beth Wiseman and Kathy Fuller, new writing friends and collaborators, thanks for the fun and friendship as we worked on this collection.

Thanks also go to Mary Sue Seymour, my agent, who encouraged my inspirational stories, and Natalie Hanemann, editor at Thomas Nelson, who invited me to be a part of this wonderful collection of Amish novellas. Thanks, too, to LB Norton, who along with Natalie helped make *One Child* a stronger story.

I also want to thank Linda Byler, who is Old Order Amish and took time from the stories she writes to answer my many questions and to read my manuscript for accuracy. Linda, it meant so much to me when you said such wonderful things about my story. I so appreciated it. Thanks, too, to Beth Graybill, director of the Lancaster Mennonite Historical Society, for answering my questions and asking Linda if she would be willing to talk to me. Your doing this was such a blessing to my work.

And most of all, thank you to God, who heard the desire in my heart to write when I was a teenager and provided opportunities for me to grow and learn with so many wonderful mentors and opportunities. You have truly given me a priceless gift.

HEARTWARMING INSPIRATIONAL ROMANCE

Contemporary,
inspirational romances
with Christian characters
facing the challenges
of life and love
in today's world.

**NOW AVAILABLE IN REGULAR
AND LARGER-PRINT FORMATS.**

Steeple
Hill®

For exciting stories that reflect traditional values,
visit:
www.SteepleHill.com

LIGEN07R

LARGER-PRINT BOOKS!

**GET 2 FREE
LARGER-PRINT NOVELS
PLUS 2 FREE
MYSTERY GIFTS**

Larger-print novels are now available...

YES! Please send me 2 FREE LARGER-PRINT Love Inspired® novels and my 2 FREE mystery gifts (gifts are worth about $10). After receiving them, if I don't wish to receive any more books, I can return the shipping statement marked "cancel". If I don't cancel, I will receive 6 brand-new novels every month and be billed just $4.74 per book in the U.S. or $5.24 per book in Canada. That's a saving of over 20% off the cover price. It's quite a bargain! Shipping and handling is just 50¢ per book.* I understand that accepting the 2 free books and gifts places me under no obligation to buy anything. I can always return a shipment and cancel at any time. Even if I never buy another book, the two free books and gifts are mine to keep forever.

122/322 IDN E7QP

Name _____ (PLEASE PRINT) _____

Address _____ Apt. # _____

City _____ State/Prov. _____ Zip/Postal Code _____

Signature (if under 18, a parent or guardian must sign)

Mail to **Steeple Hill Reader Service:**
IN U.S.A.: P.O. Box 1867, Buffalo, NY 14240-1867
IN CANADA: P.O. Box 609, Fort Erie, Ontario L2A 5X3

Not valid to current subscribers to Love Inspired Larger-Print books.

**Are you a current subscriber to Love Inspired books
and want to receive the larger-print edition?
Call 1-800-873-8635 or visit www.morefreebooks.com.**

* Terms and prices subject to change without notice. Prices do not include applicable taxes. Sales tax applicable in N.Y. Canadian residents will be charged applicable provincial taxes and GST. Offer not valid in Quebec. This offer is limited to one order per household. All orders subject to approval. Credit or debit balances in a customer's account(s) may be offset by any other outstanding balance owed by or to the customer. Please allow 4 to 6 weeks for delivery. Offer available while quantities last.

Your Privacy: Steeple Hill Books is committed to protecting your privacy. Our Privacy Policy is available online at www.SteepleHill.com or upon request from the Reader Service. From time to time we make our lists of customers available to reputable third parties who may have a product or service of interest to you. If you would prefer we not share your name and address, please check here. ☐

Help us get it right—We strive for accurate, respectful and relevant communications. To clarify or modify your communication preferences, visit us at www.ReaderService.com/consumerschoice.

LILP10R

REQUEST YOUR FREE BOOKS!

2 FREE INSPIRATIONAL NOVELS
PLUS 2
FREE
MYSTERY GIFTS

Love Inspired.
HISTORICAL
INSPIRATIONAL HISTORICAL ROMANCE